NONE DARE CALL IT TREASON

In *None Dare Call It Treason* Dr Gavin writes
with first-hand knowledge of the men, the time
and the place. As a British war correspondent
she met many leaders of the French
Resistance in liberated Paris, and followed
closely their reactions to the ambition of
Charles de Gaulle. A bestseller in hardback,
this excellent novel will enjoy as much success
in paperback as all of her previous ones have
done.

'An authentic, revealing story of the
Resistance as it really was.'
Evening News

Also by the same author,
and available in Coronet Books:

None Dare Call It Treason

Catherine Gavin

CORONET BOOKS
Hodder and Stoughton

First published in Great Britain
1978 by Hodder and Stoughton Limited

Coronet edition 1980

Set, printed and bound in Great Britain for
Hodder and Stoughton Paperbacks, a
division of Hodder and Stoughton Ltd,
Mill Road, Dunton Green, Sevenoaks,
Kent (Editorial Office: 47 Bedford
Square, London, WC1 3DP) by
Cox & Wyman Ltd, Reading

ISBN 0 340 24863 7

TO WIRT WILLIAMS

PART ONE

WE, General de Gaulle, Leader of All Free Frenchmen,
Realising that at all points of the globe, millions
of Frenchmen, or French subjects, and French territories
have called US to the task of leading them in the war:
Declare that the voice of these Frenchmen, the only one
which the enemy, or the organisation of Vichy which
depends on it, has not been able to silence, is the
voice of the Country and that WE have, in consequence,
the sacred duty to assume the charge imposed upon US.

Charles de Gaulle
Brazzaville 1940

1

That summer the American soldiers began to appear in Britain.

There had been distinguished visitors from Washington ever since the United States entered the war by way of Pearl Harbor : fact-finding delegations, inspection teams, military observers and advance echelons of all the Services, but they had hardly been noticed in the battered streets of London. Now, beginning on the July day when the U.S. First Division disembarked at Greenock, the Americans were everywhere.

They were a living assurance that after two years of fearful disasters by land and sea, help had come at last to the island fortress.

The great thing was that help had not come too late. The

will to survive, which had taken Britain through the first and worst year after the fall of France, the year of the blitz, the year alone, had been strong through all the reverses of the second. The new Russian allies, in their turn, were fighting for survival. The new Japanese enemies had reached the height of their success. Hong Kong lost, Rangoon and Singapore lost, India disaffected, Greece gone, Crete gone, and Rommel within a hundred miles of Alexandria : so stood the tale of defeat in the summer of 1942, when the Americans arrived.

They were deployed and housed wherever space could be found for them from Northern Ireland to southern England. They moved in to the new camps and airfields and the old barracks with a verve and confidence which distinguished them from the shattered foreign legions which had taken refuge in Britain in the summer of 1940. In London they ambled along Piccadilly from Soho to Hyde Park like a friendly army of occupation, wisecracking, free-spending, mysteriously bemedalled and apparently quite incurious about where the tide of war would take them next. Few of them realised that their destination and their fate were being decided less than a mile away, at the new headquarters of General Eisenhower.

Twenty, Grosvenor Square, was a requisitioned block of luxury flats, still in the process of being transformed into a military establishment. Not far away, at Claridge's Hotel, a transit headquarters had been set up on the fourth floor for General Marshall, the Army Chief of Staff. He had flown in with two other special representatives of President Roosevelt on what was called a secret mission – so secret that no mention of their visit would be made in the British press until the V.I.P.s were back in Washington. The bustle at Claridges, the labelled luggage in the lobby, the installation of communications links and a cipher centre, with the U.S. Marines on guard outside sixteen rooms, made the mission an open secret to every guest in the hotel, and to a good many outsiders as well. To how many, and to whom, Joe

Calvert had not fully realised until the twenty-third of July, when he lunched at the Savoy with Renaudon.

It was later than he intended when his taxi dropped him at the north-west corner of Grosvenor Square, and as he showed his pass to the Marine guard at the door of Number Twenty, he saw that the lobby was as crowded as usual. Americans in uniform were jostling English workmen in overalls, carrying planks, ladders and bags of tools, and eight or nine men were waiting for the one available lift. Calvert pushed his way to the foot of the stairs and ran up three at a time to his temporary office at the rear of the building.

His secretary was temporary too, young, English and anxious to please. She looked up nervously from her desk in a cubbyhole which might have been a built-in wardrobe in one of the former flats, when Calvert came in.

'Anything from Washington?' he said.

'One cable, sir, received half an hour ago. I put it in the folder on your desk with a telephone message from the embassy.'

'Right.'

'And Mr. Kemp rang down from upstairs, to ask if he could see you for a few minutes before your next meeting.'

'Let me have a look at the cable first.'

Calvert's own office was cramped and stuffy, with a single window which gave no view and very little fresh air, but he hadn't pulled rank or protested when they assigned it to him, because he didn't expect to be staying long in London. He opened the folder, laid in the exact centre of the big empty desk, with an eagerness which turned to a sharp sense of disappointment. The cable was in clear language, and dealt with a routine State Department matter; it was of no more importance than the embassy's telephoned reminder that Calvert was expected at a cocktail party in honour of an exiled monarch whose chances of regaining his throne after the war were slim. It made no mention of the mission to Moscow which had been the subject of top-level discussions before Calvert left Washington. That was two weeks

9

ago, and as the days went by he was beginning to think that he had been encouraged to set his sights too high; that Averell Harriman, and not Joseph Calvert would be appointed American Ambassador to the U.S.S.R. He shrugged, and looked up at the unsuitable sunburst clock, relic of some luxury bedroom, before speaking through the half open door to his secretary.

'Tell Mr. Kemp I'll be glad to see him now.'

Talking to Kemp would help him to concentrate on the business of the day. There was no sense in letting his mind dwell on a Russian future which might never materialise, or on the Russian past, when a young Vice-Consul Calvert had lived through years of war and revolution in what he still thought of as Petrograd. It was absurd, at his age, to feel such impatience at being detained in London, soothing the prima donnas at General de Gaulle's headquarters in Carlton Gardens, when the place where he could be most useful was the Kremlin.

'All right to come in, Joe?' said the familiar voice.

'Sure. Come on in and sit down.'

Bob Kemp, seconded from the State Department to the new Office of Strategic Services, was fifteen years younger and twenty-five pounds heavier than Calvert. He pushed aside the flimsy chair used by the secretary when she took dictation, and dragged up a blue brocade armchair left over from the former furnishings. He swung one leg over its carved and gilded arm.

'Did you get your movement orders for Moscow?' he asked.

'Not yet.'

'Tough luck, Joe. You're really sweating this one out.'

'That's what it feels like. Meanwhile I've had an interesting lunch with Renaudon.'

'First off,' said Kemp, 'tell me how he knew you were in London.'

'Plenty of snoopers round Claridge's these days. Probably somebody tipped him off, and he called me.'

'And how did he appear to you? Changed, since we knew him at Vichy?'

'Yes and no. He talks as well as ever. Very logical, very persuasive, and always ready with the smile. But when I walked into that little cocktail lounge at the Savoy Grill, I swear I didn't recognise him.'

'He can't have aged that much in two years. Less.'

'His hair's going grey. He joked about it, and said blond hair would have made him too conspicuous in the job he's doing now.'

'He really is in the Resistance, then?'

'Up to the neck.'

Calvert's head was lowered. His own hair was still brown, with a few threads of grey in it, and he sat with his elbows on the desk and his chin resting on his folded hands. It was a characteristic attitude, patient and noncommittal, and nothing revealed more clearly that Calvert's Foreign Service training dated from before the First World War than his capacity for sitting still. Kemp was one of the new restless breed. He had unslung his leg from the arm of the chair, and now his right foot was vainly groping, on the blank side of Calvert's desk, for an open drawer to use as a footstool.

'So our agents were right about Renaudon,' he said. 'Of course he had no real authority at Vichy, but we figured he wouldn't last long with that lot. And he didn't hang around after the Marshal's fraternal handshake with Hitler at Montoire. Remember he disappeared from circulation just before you and I went back to Washington in December?'

'He turned up again in Lyon at the end of January.'

'Did that cute little wife go with him?'

'He told me she went back to her parents in Paris, with a special German escort across the Line of Demarcation, when he threw in his hand at Vichy.'

'Faithful to the Marshal, eh?'

'Looks like it.'

'But he kept on going?'

'Kept on going, and got a job in an engineering firm at

St. Etienne. He was trained as a civil engineer, of course, I'd forgotten about that. A few months later – I suppose when they were sure of him – he was recruited into a Resistance group called "Combat".'

'We've heard of it.'

'Then he started moving about in the Unoccupied Zone, using his business calls to contact other groups and try to get new groups started. I fancy the pace got pretty hot after a while, because eventually the British took him off by submarine from some place west of Marseille, and brought him here via Gibraltar to join de Gaulle.'

'When was this exactly?'

'Early last month.'

'He's been in London ever since?'

'So he says.'

'Completely sold on de Gaulle?'

'Oh, absolutely! "One leader only : de Gaulle!" He said it several times, and he obviously meant it.'

'What did he want from you?'

Kemp had tilted back the heavy chair at a dangerous angle while he fired off his questions about Renaudon. On the word 'you', he brought the front legs to the floor with a clatter.

'He wanted me to use my influence with the President to get de Gaulle officially invited to the United States.'

Kemp whistled. 'That's a new angle!'

'Isn't it though? When he called up and asked me to lunch, I thought he would try to pump me about de Gaulle's meeting with the Chiefs this afternoon. But Renaudon's aiming higher than that. What he wants is for de Gaulle to be invited to Washington and New York, in that order, with a newsreel of the President's welcome to the White House, and a ticker-tape parade along Fifth Avenue for the Leader of *La France Libre*.'

'*Combattante*, since July the fourteenth.'

'Hell yes, *La France Combattante.* Like in combat with the Vichy French in Syria.'

12

'Skip Syria, Joe. That was a British bust, not ours. How did *you* react to Renaudon's proposal?'

'First,' said Calvert, and his thin sallow face was half amused and half serious, 'I told him he greatly over-estimated my influence with the President. Second, that not Churchill and Stalin combined could persuade Mr. Roosevelt to make any sort of gesture towards de Gaulle this summer – not while the Secretary of State is still rabid about his attempt to grab St. Pierre and Miquelon.'

Kemp groaned. 'Those two-bit islands! Nothing more than a bootleggers' drop between the U.S. and Canada in the prohibition days!'

'Exactly. Well, Renaudon made a slight mistake there. He started to lecture me about the strategic importance of the islands, and de Gaulle's right to take them out of Vichy custody, so as to deny the use of a powerful radio station to the Germans. I wasn't in a mood to be lectured to by a guy I used to know as part of the Vichy set-up. My God, I remember him gloating with the rest of the Vichy crowd when de Gaulle persuaded the British to attack Dakar and the whole thing was a fiasco. So I gave him the full treatment. I told him de Gaulle had gone back on his pledged word to leave St. Pierre and Miquelon alone when he ordered Admiral Muselier to seize the islands "without letting the foreigners know" – "Oh yes!" I told him, "we know what he said; d'you think we don't intercept his messages? A hell of an ally your boy turned out to be!"'

'He didn't like that, I'll bet.'

'He just smiled, and said we didn't understand de Gaulle. He said the Free French held a plebiscite on the islands on Christmas Day (think of it, Bob, just three weeks after Pearl Harbor!) and ninety-eight per cent of the population had rallied to de Gaulle. I said ninety-eight per cent of four thousand five hundred was hardly impressive, and the few score kids who joined the Free French forces could scarcely make up to de Gaulle for the beating he took later on. Prevented from signing the United Nations Declaration, kept out of the British occupation of Madagascar, losing face when the Canadians and ourselves took control of the radio station! I told him de Gaulle had violated the Monroe Doctrine, and driven a wedge between the U.S. and Britain at the very moment they needed each other most—'

'Sounds as if he got your goat, Joe.'

Calvert relaxed and laughed. 'I admit I was riled, but when you've had to listen to Cordell Hull raging about de Gaulle and blaming Churchill for giving him such a build-up—! But Renaudon wasn't riled. He smiled, and interrupted me to say there certainly had been an unfortunate misunderstanding at St. Pierre and Miquelon, a storm in a teacup, which really occurred because the American people had never had a chance to know and understand General de Gaulle.'

'It's not for want of hearing about him,' Bob Kemp grunted. 'All those committees pouring out propaganda across the hemisphere! He's got his men everywhere, in South America and Mexico and from Canada to the Caribbean—'

'But that's not the same as seeing and hearing the man himself, according to Renaudon. Hence the pitch for an official visit. I told him to forget it, until next year anyway. He nodded, and said the Americans would all admire de Gaulle as soon as they saw his movie.'

'Is *he* going to be in the movies?'

'Hardly, unless he makes it big in Movietone News. But according to Renaudon, Warner Brothers are going to film *The de Gaulle Story*, with the complete approval of the general's agent in New York.'

'Which agent would that be? He's got so many.'

'His literary agent, for all I know. Warners have hired William Faulkner to write the script. He's leaving for the Coast this week.'

'Faulkner must be hurting for money.'

'Could be.'

'A movie, eh?' said Kemp. 'I remember when General Spears swore he'd make de Gaulle's name known to every newspaper in the world in six months' time, *if* he got the right PR man for the job, but even Spears didn't think of a movie. Of course de Gaulle and Spears fell out over the Syria business, but anyway, de Gaulle got himself on the cover of *True Comics* last January . . . The trouble with that guy is, he believes his own publicity.'

'Renaudon believes it too. He's in quite a messianic mood about *mon général.*'

'That's bad,' said Kemp. 'There's only room for one messiah in *La France Combattante*, and Big Charlie grabbed the job off for himself when Spears brought him to England in 1940. Would you say Renaudon was very close to him?'

'He was pretty cagey about that. I don't think the general allows his followers to come too close to the throne. It might destroy the illusion.'

' "The psychology of the superman is solitary" – that sort of thing?'

'I thought that was Al Capone.'

'Same idea.'

'Bob, I think we've got to take Renaudon seriously. He's a clever politician, with a lot of drive, and he's sold on the idea of getting American recognition for the French National Committee and its Leader—'

'I suppose that's what de Gaulle's visit today is all about,' said Kemp. 'He'll find George Catlett Marshall as hard a nut to crack as F.D.R. But I'll have a word with our old pal from Vichy. Did you tell him I was in London?'

'He already knew you were here, *and* with the O.S.S. Colonel Passy runs a very comprehensive information service.'

'Which apparently we've got to work with, before and after the invasion. Is Renaudon one of Passy's bunch at Duke Street? Or do I reach him at the Carlton dream factory?'

'I suggest you call him at the Cumberland Hotel,' said Calvert. 'He's booked in there as Alain Renaudon.'

'What, no alias? No fancy moniker from the Paris subway system?'

'Not so far.' Calvert looked at his watch and rose. 'Bob, I've got to go. I don't want to be late for the Chiefs and their visitor.'

'You won't be.' In the little outer office Kemp said, 'Thank you, Mr. Minister,' for the benefit of the secretary, and held the door ceremoniously open. But in the corridor, before turning towards the back staircase, he asked in a lowered voice :

'If Warners do make his movie, who gets to play de Gaulle? Charles Boyer?'

Calvert was smiling as he made his way along the corridors to the front of the building. After his bleak little office the view across Grosvenor Square seemed bright, and he paused by a landing window to enjoy the summer sunshine on the façades of the American Embassy and the fine eighteenth-century buildings opposite Number Twenty. It was over a year since the last heavy air raid on the capital. On that May night Whitehall had become a raging torrent from burst water mains and the Horse Guards Parade was pitted with bomb craters, while among the floods and the fires, the palace, parliament and abbey took the brunt of the enemy's fury. Most of the traces of that night's work had been obliterated. Hoardings and boardings covered the damage done in Mayfair, and Calvert, watching a few nannies and their charges in the Grosvenor Square gardens, thought they gave the place a fleeting illusion of peace. In a few moments the illusion vanished as a limousine flying the Cross of Lorraine turned into the square from the direction of the Connaught Hotel. Although Joe Calvert wore spectacles for reading, his long-distance sight was excellent. He was sure enough of the car's occupant to say 'Your visitor will be here in a minute !' when he entered Admiral King's office, and found the U.S. Chief of Naval Operations talking to men whom Calvert had met for the first time only a few days before.

'Let General Marshall know!' the admiral rapped out to an aide who was arranging glasses on a side table on which champagne in a cooler had already been set. King's manner, habitually blunt and abrupt, was stiff to the point of intimidation. General Marshall, always serious, looked graver than usual when he came in and included all the company in a brief nod of greeting. He had steered clear of General de Gaulle on his earlier visits to London in April and in June, resisting all Ambassador Winant's efforts to make him meet the importunate Frenchman. The confrontation could be put off no longer, but Marshall came to it with the most positive commands, given to each of the officers present, that de Gaulle was to get no information whatever about the future Allied plans.

These orders from their President and Commander-in-Chief had not been inspired by de Gaulle's abortive coup at St. Pierre and Miquelon at the end of 1941. The embargo went back to the fiasco at Dakar in 1940, attributed to the lack of security at the Carlton Gardens headquarters. Notoriously careless talk, and even suspected enemy infiltration, had destroyed the Dakar operation, after which de Gaulle, not daring to show his face in London, had found a new refuge in Brazzaville. That dismal little river port far up the Congo had one thing to offer to the Adventurer: a radio station. Over Radio Brazzaville the voice of Charles de Gaulle was soon heard denouncing Vichy, proclaiming that his French National Committee was the legal government of France, and issuing manifestoes on his own status and the future government of the French Empire. These speeches were made during the blitz on London, when nobody had time to listen to them, and even Mr. Churchill tired of the de Gaulle albatross which his own romantic impulse had hung round Britain's neck. In Cairo and Beirut, after the short campaign against the Vichy French in Syria, the general's intrigues had made more enemies than he could well afford. Now, in search of friends, he had come képi in hand to the door of Twenty, Grosvenor Square.

'General de Gaulle, sir,' announced the naval aide, and stepped back thankfully into the hall. The group of Americans made a forward movement which might have been construed as a welcome to the Leader of All Free Frenchmen. De Gaulle's mask of hauteur, worn so long as to have become a second skin, slipped a little at the sight of them.

He had staked a good deal on this meeting. Furious at being kept in the dark at the time of the British expedition to Madagascar in May, he had taken it as fresh proof that the British intended to annex French territories for themselves, the suspicion which in Syria had turned into an obsession. He was now absolutely determined to be consulted, and to have his legion take part, when the American forces invaded the European mainland. As he had told his entourage, he intended 'to stop talking to underlings – it was like looking through the wrong end of a telescope', and he had invited General Marshall and Admiral King to wait upon him at Four, Carlton Gardens. Only when their seniority of rank was stressed did he consent to be driven to Grosvenor Square. Now he was in their presence and the telescope was adjusted : it revealed many more persons than he had wished to see.

He was immediately at a disadvantage on two counts. In France, since his cadet days, he had rejoiced in the flattering nickname which Bob Kemp translated as Big Charlie, and was accustomed to be the tallest person at any staff conference. But some of these Americans were so tall as not to be dominated by a man of six foot four, nor were they to be dominated by a display of temperament. As a French Army politician Colonel de Gaulle had been a failure. All that his persistent lobbying on his own behalf had achieved was the dropping of his name from the promotion list of 1936, but in London he had learned fast. He discovered that to the Englishmen of the age and class he met nothing was more horrible than the idea of a scene, and for two years, by an adroit mixture of bullying and emotional blackmail, he had outwitted them by the mere threat of scenes. But the

American officers, he knew by instinct, would not be impressed by his usual tactics, for they were men who had marched in their youth to a different drummer. He exchanged curt handshakes with them all.

'Is this your interpreter?' he said, looking at Joe Calvert, the only civilian in the room.

'This is Mr. Joseph Calvert, General,' he was told. 'One of our advisers from the State Department.'

With an ineffable switch of the nostril de Gaulle dismissed the State Department. He presented his own interpreter, a stiff-necked aide who imitated his master's manner, and, as they all sat down, Joe Calvert saw that his name had not registered at all. He was not offended. It was probable that de Gaulle had forgotten, or had never known, that for three months in 1940 Joseph Calvert had been the leader of a working party at Vichy which organised the American embassy to Marshal Pétain – that embassy whose mere existence had been considered as an insult by the Free French and their Leader. He composed himself, as at so many confrontations in so many capitals, to listen and observe.

'A glass of champagne, General?' said Admiral Kirk.

'*Merci*.'

It was the *merci* of refusal. The interpreter rapped out, 'General de Gaulle declines with thanks.'

There was a murmur of regret, a little half-hearted sipping, and then General Marshall had some polite things to say about the brave stand made by a Free French force at Bir Hakeim earlier in the year. De Gaulle bowed slightly, and remarked that after the heroic efforts of his troops, it was regrettable that Tobruk should have surrendered to the Germans after all.

Calvert sensed General Marshall's irritation : from being courteous to the visitor, in his old-fashioned way, he was becoming ultra-polite and stiff. De Gaulle, for his part, behaved as if he and the Army Chief of Staff were alone in the room. His last look at the admiral had been given when he refused the champagne. The three younger generals were totally ignored. If possible, he sat more ramrod straight in his chair, and, with his interpreter translating every sentence, he launched into a speech he had carefully prepared.

It was hardly an original speech, and Calvert had read press digests of it many times before. In the two years since his flight from France, Charles de Gaulle had drenched England with his oratory, in floods on the B.B.C., in torrents breaking over the Albert Hall, where he had recently been the star of a great show-business display modelled on Hitler's Nürnberg rallies. He had seven publications in England alone, with newsprint supplied by government allocations, to put over his propaganda. He had six military or paramilitary organisations under his command. With confidence, he launched into a powerful sales pitch, the expression of his delusion that he could force the Americans to include him in their plans for a cross-Channel invasion.

Calvert, who had moved his chair slightly to the rear of the embarrassed group, studied their reactions when de Gaulle made the grandiose proposal to offer General Marshall all the troops under his own command, whether in Britain, French West Africa, Syria or New Caledonia. General Marshall sat with his arms folded, saying nothing. Admiral King, who like millions of Americans thought Japan was the real enemy, and the Pacific the real centre of war, looked impatiently at his watch. General Clark, whose long-nosed, charmingly wry face was as grave as Marshall's, shifted uneasily in his chair. General Eisenhower, whose wide mouth was usually ready to break into a smile, compressed his lips at the offer of troops. One of his tasks was to plan the eventual absorption of two million American troops into Britain, and then to launch them towards the liberation of Europe. De Gaulle claimed to have seventy thousand men in arms, scattered across the world. It was not enough to give him the bargaining power he needed; and every man in the room remembered, at the mention of New Caledonia, that the area had been occupied in the spring by American troops under General Patch. The offer of French troops from Nouméa was an empty boast.

Joe Calvert's professional control kept him from sighing. He knew, better than almost any other civilian in Twenty, Grosvenor Square, that one of the crucial decisions of the Second World War was to be taken that week, and from the demeanour of the American Chiefs he believed it had been taken already. Over the weekend at Chequers, later in the Cabinet room at Downing Street, the Americans had pressed for an invasion of continental Europe. Mr. Churchill, with the ultimate approval of President Roosevelt, had argued for a landing in French North Africa, with American troops driving east to join the British in the desert. In such a crisis of decision General de Gaulle and his importunities were totally irrelevant.

The icy silence in the room seemed at last to chill de Gaulle. He had stated in his monologue that Soviet resistance to the Germans was such an inspiration that *La France Combattante* would rejoice in the opening of a second front in the west, and this had met with no more encouragement than a brief 'Quite so.' Now he decided to take the bull by the horns. Still addressing General Marshall, and him alone, he said,

'*Dites-moi, qu'est ce que vous pensez faire pour le deuxième front?*'

And the interpreter barked out, 'Tell me your plans for the second front!'

The only reply was a noncommittal murmur, a refusal by all the men present to carry the discussion further. De Gaulle lifted his arms and let them drop limply upon his knees, in the motion which with him meant complete discouragement. He rose majestically from his chair while the interpreter leaped to his feet behind him.

'Gentlemen,' said Charles de Gaulle, 'I shall not take up any more of your time.' The curt handshake was offered again, the képi and white gloves picked up; the naval aide, summoned by a bell, had just time to get the door open

21

before the two Frenchmen reached it. The whole scene had taken no longer than half an hour.

In the release from tension everybody spoke at once.

'So that's the hero of St. Pierre and Miquelon!'

'Churchill says he has an inferiority complex. I didn't see much sign of it.'

'Somebody should send him a copy of *How to Make Friends and Influence People.*'

'Extraordinary performance,' General Marshall said. 'What's your evaluation, Mr. Minister? Isn't this the first time you've met him?'

'Yes, it is,' said Calvert. 'I thought General de Gaulle certainly ran true to the form we've heard so much about. But it's only fair to say that he wasn't well served by his interpreter. "Tell me the second front plans", for instance, was a good deal rougher than what de Gaulle actually said.'

'The general's intention was clear enough,' snapped Marshall. 'What was your impression of the man himself?'

'He struck me as being a very limited individual, General.'

'In what way?'

'He has a one-track mind. He asked you to reveal top secret plans because he sees the whole war in terms of France. He's spent two years telling us all that he *is* France, and now he's mortally afraid that when we begin the liberation of French territory he'll be kept out of the operation, and lose face – not only in France but everywhere. It's fear that makes him impossible to work with, as the British know to their cost.'

'I didn't know you were a psychologist, Mr. Minister.' That was General Marshall, icily polite; it was General Eisenhower who said surprisingly:

'I didn't think he was as bad as all that. He's hypersensitive, and as stubborn as an army mule, but probably he's not a bad guy at heart. When it comes to the crunch he may be ready to play along with us.'

'When it comes to the crunch,' said Calvert, 'it may de-

22

pend on the support he can rally inside France. He never lets up on the radio propaganda, and if the French accept him as their new boss, then he'll have to be taken seriously. At present he knows nothing about diplomacy. He doesn't even know that it never pays to play little tricks on great Powers, as he did at St. Pierre and Miquelon. But the French won't care about that, and I had reliable information today that some of the Resistance groups are preparing to give him their support.'

'Thank you, Mr. Minister,' said General Marshall dryly. 'In the meantime, we shall carry out the President's order to withhold all military information from General de Gaulle.'

2

Jacques Brunel was beginning to suffer from cramp. He had been sitting among the limestone crags beside the sea for two hours, and although it was mild for November the night chill was starting to penetrate his heavy leather *canadienne*. He wanted to stretch his legs on the plateau of turf above the rocks where three paths met, but the place was too exposed. Although it was the dark of the moon, a moving figure might possibly be seen against the white of the railroad embankment behind the path which led to Monte Carlo beach. It met, by the greensward under the pine trees, the rocky path which led to Cap Martin and the Roman road to Menton, which had once been Brunel's home. The third path led up to the hut among the ilex and the ivy, where he had hoped by this time to be drinking hot rum with a man called Charles. It was known locally as the *douaniers*' path, often used by customs officers hoping to make an arrest, but as the war entered its fourth winter few officers and fewer smugglers in the commune of Roque-brune were likely to be actively employed. It was safe enough, Brunel assured himself. It was only the waiting that was tedious.

There had been a storm the day before, one of those November storms that periodically lashed the Côte d'Azur, splashing rain on Brunel's office windows as the mistral roared through the streets of Nice. If the furious seas had continued to pound the rocks of Cap Martin the British agent might have been unable to land; as it was, the *calan-que* beneath Brunel's post among the rocks was filled with the ebb and flow of waves that had dropped to normal. All that was left of the storm was the low cloud ceiling which had quenched the stars. In other years there would have been stars on the surface of the Mediterranean, the riding-lights of the fishermen's boats from Menton, but Menton was under Italian occupation now, and the fishing was strictly controlled. There was no sign of a Vichy patrol boat or police craft, watching for the arrival of a British submarine.

Brunel scanned the empty sea. To the east, the point of Cap Martin was obscured by a promontory, well protected by barbed wire, on which the owners of the villa up above had built a jetty for their pleasure boat. That villa was empty like many others. The Côte d'Azur was crowded with wealthy refugees from Paris, but at Cap Martin the Italians were too close for comfort, barely three kilometres away along the valley of the Gorbio. There would be no spying eyes in the luxurious villa tonight, and on the west Brunel could see only a reflection of the dimmed lights in Monte Carlo, and the outline of the great crag called the Dog's Head which hung above Monaco.

The hands of his wrist-watch, shining green in the darkness, had moved twenty minutes nearer to daybreak when he saw the shape rising slowly to the surface of the sea. From the shore it had the outline of a whale lolling and inactive in the deep. Brunel knew activity was there, ceaseless and quick, but he heard nothing, saw no light until the sea itself carried the sound of two paddles moving steadily towards the shore.

He got to his feet and went as near the verge of the *calanque* as he dared, straining to see and hear, and at last switched on his electric torch, sweeping the tiny pencil of light round the entrance to the miniature harbour, stabbing it down and down where the water surged beneath his feet. On the ninth wave something came into the cove, and a voice hardly audible above the surge of the sea said,

'Le capitaine Jack?'

'Présent!'

'Bonjour, mon capitaine, ici Charles.'

'Soyez le bienvenu, Charles.'

Brunel jumped down across the rocks. He seized the shabby satchel lifted up to him and held out his right hand to the newcomer, who scrambled ashore dragging a canvas canoe. As soon as they were on the turf both men set to work, smashing the oars and slashing the canvas into strips with their sheath knives, the man called Charles nodding approval as Brunel indicated the thickets of lentisk and rosemary which grew at the foot of the umbrella pines. The remnants of the canoe, which had weighed less than ten kilos, and the splinters of wood were easily hidden among the bushes.

'Ten minutes' walk uphill,' whispered Brunel. 'The footing's treacherous. Better let me go first.'

Behind him, Charles slipped on the wet leaves embedded through many seasons on a rough cement staircase which led upwards to darkness and a deep silence. He was startled to hear the whistle of a steam engine in the distance.

'Train. Keep back!'

There was plenty of cover among the pines and ivy. The only danger was the light from the oncoming engine which threw into bold relief the portal of a tunnel and spread yellow through the trees and undergrowth. Charles could see the driver leaning out of his cab and the fireman shovelling coal, and he gave a quick look at the tense, lean-featured face of the man beside him. Then the train lights were gone, while five carriages went past with blinded windows. They heard another whistle on the far side of the tunnel.

Brunel motioned the other man to come on. The stair became a cement path, the footing was better, and there was a scent of flowers in the air. They turned aside at a mossy wall, covered with briers which tugged at their sleeves, protecting a low stone building half hidden by the spreading ivy. The door was fastened by a padlock, rusty on the outside but opening with oiled precision to Brunel's key. 'Don't move,' he said as the door opened. 'I'll light the candles.'

Two candles set in tin holders on a wooden table under the shuttered window bloomed into yellow flame, and Brunel held out his hand. 'Welcome again,' he said. 'I'm Jacques Brunel. I was beginning to worry about you, but you're here with time to spare.'

'Charles Maxwell,' said the young man formally. 'I was worried sick on Wednesday. There was a flap on at Gibraltar, and I was afraid the sub. would be diverted to another mission. But her sailing orders came through all right, and now she's off to her destination.'

'While you made a first-rate landing. You must have come ashore dry-shod.'

'Almost.' In fact his feet and trouser bottoms were sopping but he wasn't going to admit it to the legendary Captain Jack.

'You'll be all the better for a good hot drink.' Brunel lit a primus stove set ready with a pan of spring water. 'Sit down while the water boils, it won't take long.'

'Thanks a lot.' Charles Maxwell took his place on a divan covered with a red and black woollen spread and unbuttoned his cheap raincoat slowly. 'What sort of place is this, anyway?' he said, looking around.

It could have been any sort of ramshackle place from a gardener's outhouse to a farm shed, except for the scanty furniture. There was a corner cupboard in which Brunel was rummaging. Two stools stood underneath the table, a high rack held fishing rods and tackle, while sea boots, espadrilles and dusty tennis shoes were arranged on a low shelf. Two tennis rackets in their wooden presses were slung between pegs fixed in the walls.

'This? You could call it a staging point for people like yourself,' said Brunel. 'A man called Pierre Lavisse and I bought it for a place to keep our sports gear in, before the war.'

'Does Lavisse use it for a staging point too?'

'He can't very well, he's a prisoner-of-war in Germany.' Brunel set a tray with a bottle of Rhum St. James on the table, and offered a blue packet of cigarettes.

'Gauloise?'

'Wonderful.' The water in the little pan began to bubble, and Brunel watched with amusement as the boy took his first drag of the strong tobacco. He was young for the job, but he looked the part all right : short and stocky, with curly dark hair and dark eyes, he might have been born anywhere in the Midi. The shabby raincoat, the cheap blue suit and the gaudy tie were what any badly paid clerk in Nice would wear. Brunel mixed the rum and boiling water and handed a full glass to his guest. Who said unexpectedly :

'That train we saw. Was it going to Menton or on into Italy?'

'I've no idea. The carriages were blacked out, so they were probably used for military personnel.'

'I thought we were in a demilitarised area here.'

'Tell that to the collaborators ! But something's up, they're getting nervous at Vichy now. Is your drink all right?'

'It's great, and so's the Gauloise. My first since the summer of '39.'

'Were you in France in '39?'

'Yes, on holiday at Le Lavandou. We went to a little hotel there every summer for years.'

'That accounts for the accent, then.'

'Will it pass?'

'Pass? It's sensational ! But you didn't pick up that Marseille twang in Le Lavandou.'

'We had a pretty good gang of beach kids there, and we explored the whole coast from Marseille to Nice. That's why I'm here – I was winkled out of my regiment for this caper.'

'Let me top that up for you. Do you know Nice well? It'll make today a lot easier if you do.'

'I can find my way around. Even in the Old Town if I have to.'

Brunel smiled. 'I'm taking you there for breakfast,' he said. 'You're my responsibility until I put you on the Cannes train this afternoon.' His voice sharpened. 'What's your home address?'

'Eleven, Rue des Phocéens, Marseille.'

'Your father's name? His occupation?'

'Marius Aletti, retired stevedore. My mother's dead.'

'All right,' said Brunel. 'Now let's work from the papers. I won't insult "F" section by asking to see the outfitters' names and the laundry marks on your clothes, but your papers I have to see, before we start for Nice. You're carrying them, of course?'

'The whole lot.' Maxwell's hand went instinctively to an inner pocket, and then he stopped. Two submarine journeys had left him tired and tense, as well as emotionally keyed-up by his first adventure as a secret agent, and this strange halt in the lonely hut was preying on his nerves. He had, except when the train went by, hardly seen Brunel's face, for the man had pulled out a stool almost beyond the yellow circle of candlelight and kept the fur collar of his *canadienne* well up to his chin. Maxwell, in the course of his training, had been warned of infiltrators in the French Resistance, some of them German, some native-born. Agents had been met on arrival by 'reception committees', sometimes only one man strong, who took them to just such 'staging points' as this, which led to prison or a firing squad. He said, 'Just a moment, please. I suppose you are – who you say you are?'

Brunel took an identity card from his own pocket and handed it to Charles Maxwell. 'This one's not a forgery,' he said. He lifted a candle and let the light shine on his face.

The face in the candlelight and the face in the photograph on the card were the same : thin, sharp-featured, older than the age attested by the 'Born at Menton, October 29th, 1911'. The name was Brunel, Jacques André, *avocat*, French citizen, living at 15, Rue Droite, Nice. Maxwell handed back the identification with an embarrassed smile. 'I'm sorry,' he said.

'You were quite right,' said Brunel. 'Don't trust anybody or anything, that's my own prescription for survival. Are you carrying a gun?'

'Nothing but the knife.'

'That's better if you're searched. But all we have to worry about between here and Nice is a spot check by the Vichy police. That's why I must be sure about your cover, if only for Dupont's sake, the man who's going to drive us into town. I came over on the late bus last night and slept for a while on the divan.'

The divan was hard and uncomfortable and had no pillow. Maxwell took out his wallet, and handed over the identity card of Charles Aletti, born June 3rd, 1919, insurance salesman, etc., with his work permit, ration cards, demobilisation papers dated at Marseille, July 10th, 1940, medical certificate (unfit for military service), driving licence and insurance certificate.

'Perfect,' said Brunel. 'Where are your working papers?'

'In my briefcase.' He lifted it on to his lap, unfastening the straps.

'I wonder why they issued you with a *b.e.v.*?'

'What's a *b.e.v.*?'

'*Baise en ville*. You don't know that expression? ... I must say you travel light!'

There were socks and underwear in one pocket of the bag, and a cardboard portfolio of documents in the other. They testified that Aletti, Charles, was the representative of a well-known insurance company in Marseille.

'I hope you know a lot about selling insurance.'

'I should do. It was my job in civvy street.'

'Really?'

'My father put me into it when I left school. He was the manager of the Lanarkshire and General Insurance Company, at their head office in Glasgow.'

'Lanarkshire?'

'Does that ring a bell?'

'I was hospitalised at Dykefaulds in Lanarkshire, after the campaign in Norway. They were very good to us there.'

'I'm glad to hear that,' said Maxwell. 'We lived about ten miles on the Glasgow side of Dykefaulds before my father retired. He and my mother live in Carrick now, at a place called Burns Bay.'

Brunel pushed the French insurance company's portfolio into the briefcase. 'We'd better be going,' he said. 'We've a bit more walking to do, through the carnation fields and then along the road. Between the post office and the intersection with the Route Nationale, there's a little grocery kept by a man called Jean Dupont, who served with me in Norway. He goes in to the Nice market every Friday morning. He'll give us a lift, and then I'll take you to my flat for breakfast.'

'That sounds great, but when do I meet Couteau?'

'Nestor arranged that for this afternoon, and Couteau knows where to meet us. How much cash are you carrying?'

It was a snap question, like the earlier question about the fictitious home in Marseille, and once again Charles did not hesitate. Saying nothing about the large sum in the money belt next his skin, he took a folding purse from his inside pocket, and displayed such crumpled French notes and small coins as a young insurance agent might be expected to carry. 'That all right?' he asked.

'Fine.' But Brunel picked up one of the new Vichy coins, bearing on the obverse the Fascist symbol of authority, stolen from ancient Rome : a bundle of rods with the beheading axe in the middle. He flicked it contemptuously with one finger. 'The latest in French currency. Great, isn't it?' he said. 'Let's go.'

The primus stove, the bottle and glasses, were replaced in the cupboard, the candles were snuffed out and the hut padlocked. Then Brunel led the way up the steps, across the path and over a wire fence beyond which lay the carnation nurseries which lent their sweetness to the cool damp air. There was another cement path, very narrow, between the rows, where buds were unfolding, petal by fringed petal, into the flowers whose colours were drowned in darkness, and at the end a wall over which they dropped to the country road leading past the silent post office.

There was a footpath with kerbstones and the road itself was metalled, but in spite of these signs of civilisation Charles found his surroundings nearly as lonely as the stairs leading upwards from the sea. He could see nothing but high walls on his right, containing the gardens of invisible villas, and iron railings, broken at intervals by handsome wrought-iron gates, on his left. He had the sensation of walking through a tunnel of darkness, and when a dog began barking he drew a startled breath.

'It's all right, he can't see us.' Brunel's low tones were reassuring. 'We're nearly at Dupont's place now.'

'Does he live at the grocery?' asked Charles, to prove that he had command of his voice.

'No, he and his family live on the far side of the carnation fields. He's always alone at the shop in the early morning.'

As he spoke, Charles saw a faint light ahead. It was just enough to show the outlines of a little shop, having the words 'Alimentation Générale' above the shuttered window, with a small garage adjoining. When Brunel knocked on the garage door they were both blinded, as it opened, by the light from a powerful torch.

'Bonjour, chef!' said a voice from behind the torch. 'Comment va?'

'Bien, Jean. This is Charles, he had a good trip.'

'Salut, Charles. Come in, both of you.'

There was not much room to enter, for the little garage

was almost filled by a grocery van with three long cast-iron cylinders on the roof, containing the compressed coal gas which Dupont used instead of petrol. They edged round the side of the vehicle by the light of a lamp dangling without a shade from the ceiling, and Charles saw that Jean Dupont was a man in his middle thirties, of the same short and sturdy build as himself. Dupont shook his hand enthusiastically.

'Charles is a Scotsman,' said Brunel, 'he knows Dykefaulds. You and I haven't forgotten our friends there, have we?'

More vigorous handshaking and exclamations about *gentillesse* were interrupted by Brunel's asking if the van was ready to start.

'Sure, *chef*, but can I have a word with you first?' They moved towards a door leading to the dimly lighted grocery, and spoke so quietly that Charles only heard an exasperated 'When was this?'

'Not fifteen minutes ago, *chef*. Just as soon as I opened up.'

'You didn't tell her you were expecting me?'

'I said, if I saw you in Nice I would pass on the message.'

'Good enough! D'you think it's really urgent?'

'Everything's urgent for Madame Fabienne.'

'We'd better stop, then, on the way in.'

'Anything wrong?' asked Maxwell.

'A ten-minute stopover, that's all, when we get to Monaco. Let's get cracking, Jean.' Dupont wound a woollen muffler round his chest and took his beret from the seat of the van. Brunel was reminded to say to Charles:

'Your kind of salesman would be wearing a hat. Didn't they issue you with a hat in London?'

'I got oil all over it in the submarine and chucked it away at Gibraltar. I'll buy another one this morning.'

'Okay. Jean, remember, if you're asked, he's your cousin from Marseille.'

'Marseille is right, with that accent,' said Dupont cheerfully. '*Mon cousin*, will you be all right in the back with the empty crates?'

'Right as rain.'

Brunel opened the garage door and closed it after the van pulled out, taking the passenger's seat beside the driver. All he could see of the British agent was the top of a curly dark head behind a pile of baskets. He checked his watch : they were running well up to time, and the grocery would open at eight o'clock, unless one of the *ersatz* tyres blew out on the way back. He hoped not on the way there, for the sooner he had the kid safely indoors and eating a decent breakfast the better he would be pleased. Everything had gone well until he heard about Fabienne's reckless telephone call.

'You all right back there?' he asked.

'I'm okay. I'm picking up the landmarks now.'

'We're through St. Roman and coming into the Principality. Neutral ground – officially.'

The steel-coloured band of the sea was outlined against the darker mass of the land, and a breeze was shaking the palm trees in the gardens in front of the Monte Carlo casino. Brunel turned squarely round to talk to Charles as the van ran down by the harbour.

'I'm getting out at the top of the Rue Grimaldi,' he said. 'You and Jean wait in the Place d'Armes, and don't leave the van till I come back. Jean, drop me off at the corner of the Rue de la Turbie. First right – there ! Look out !'

Charles saw Brunel run up the narrow street towards a flight of steps and disappear from view. In the thick darkness which had cloaked all their movement since he came ashore he saw nothing of a door opening to Brunel's knock, halfway up the steps, nor of a girl who held out her two hands to the man, and called him darling, and begged to know where he had been.

'I tried your flat three times between one o'clock and two,' she whispered. 'I thought something must have happened to you. I got so frightened—'

'S-sh! We can't talk here, Marie'll be down in a minute. Let's go up to your office. Quietly, though!'

His boots were louder than the slippers on the uncarpeted stair which led from the side door and the kitchen premises to the ground floor of an old-fashioned hotel, where the smell of last night's tobacco hung about a lounge filled with heavy sofas and small brass-topped tables. On one side of the locked front door was the porter's *loge*, with an empty chair in front of the telephone switchboard; on the other was the office, with an enamel plaque on the glass door which said 'Mdlle. Leroux – *Privé*'. The girl switched on the light in the office and Brunel followed her in.

'Why did you phone Dupont against my orders?'

'Because I had to find you, Jacques, and he was the only one I dared to call so early. I thought he just might know—'

She was a handsome girl, straight and tall in a plain black dress, with black hair cut in a fringe across her forehead and knotted high. She cupped both hands round his cold face.

'You're freezing, darling! Oh, why didn't I think of making a pot of coffee before Marie got out of bed? Shall I make some now? It won't take long.'

'I can't wait for coffee, Fabienne.' He took her hands in his.

'You've been on a job, haven't you? Up in the hills?'

'I'm on my way home, so for God's sake tell me what's the matter. You told Dupont you wanted to see me urgently—'

'César is back.'

'Oh!' said Brunel, and released her. 'Yes, I suppose that *is* news. Back where? In Nice? In Monaco?'

'He's asleep upstairs. In Room Twenty-four, where I thought he wouldn't be disturbed by the trains. And he wants to see you as soon as possible. Shall I go and tell him you're here now?'

'What's all that row outside?' Jacques had turned away, and was peering through a chink in the shutters.

'It's only the railwaymen, coming on duty at the station.'

'Is it that late?' He offered her a cigarette, lit one himself, and blew a whiff of smoke at the official portrait of the sovereign prince of Monaco and his grandson Prince Rainier. 'Listen, Fabienne. Let's not make more of a cloak-and-dagger nonsense out of all this than we have to. If César is sound asleep in Room Twenty-four he's a luckier man than I am, and you'd better let him have his sleep out. After all, he hasn't been parachuted in over the Dog's Head : we know he crossed the Line as long ago as the first week in September. He can wait a few more hours to talk to me.'

'But he called your number three times after he arrived last night, and asked me if *I* knew where you could be.'

'Then all you have to do is show him the cause list in the morning paper, and point out that the Palais de Justice is where I certainly can be found. He can reach me there or at my *étude* any time this forenoon.'

'But he wants to brief you before the meeting with Couteau.'

'He knows about that? He's been in touch with Couteau, then?'

'No, but he had dinner with Roger Malvy in Villefranche last night, and Roger drove him over here about ten o'clock.'

'Ah, I thought we should hear of Monsieur Malvy, sooner or later. You're still seeing him, Fabienne?'

'Yes, why not?'

'Are you going to go on seeing him after his wife comes home?'

'*If* she comes home! Everybody knows Chantal was in love with Marc Chabrol—'

'Years ago, maybe. I don't want you to get hurt, my dear. Remember, Pierre Lavisse is bound to come back again some day.'

'Will he be the same Pierre? Will he recognise me? Or will everything be changed and poisoned by the war?' She controlled her rising voice, and almost whispered, 'Jacques, you and I might have known happiness together when you first came back from England—'

'No,' he said sternly, 'there was no happiness for us. Only, for a while, there was a shared loneliness.'

The Place d'Armes was filling with grey light while Charles and Dupont sat in the truck, and they could see lights going on in the shops under the arcade and hear the sound of hoses and stiff brooms. A few stalls were already being dragged into place in the open, where friends called out to one another and dogs barked. There was the note of a trumpet from high on the Rock, as the carabiniers changed guard at the gates of the sovereign prince.

'Going to be a fine day,' said Dupont comfortably, and Charles agreed. He asked what road they would take once they were clear of Monaco and officially back in France.

'I stick to the Basse Corniche all the way, I never risk the Upper. The *flics* knew me and the van, see, and there's far less chance of being hauled up for a check if you're always driving the same pattern. But' – Dupont looked shrewdly round at his passenger – 'if we *are* stopped, remember not to say too much. Just show your papers and answer the routine questions, and whatever you do, don't try to outsmart them.'

'I'm hardly likely to do that,' said Charles feelingly.

'Good! It's the smart boys and the heroes who worry Captain Jack and me.'

'What did you mean about not risking the Upper Corniche?'

'Because that's where the Vichy cops have been patrolling in strength, there and on the new Moyenne too, since the breakout at Fort de la Revère.'

'Were you and Captain Jack in that?'

'It wasn't our operation to begin with, but we were up to the neck in it before the end. You know what happened? A whole bunch of R.A.F. boys were sprung together, and came out down a coal chute, through the moat and into the sewers. They fetched up in a tunnel near the station at Cap d'Ail, and then they had to wait nearly two weeks in Monaco before we could start them west to Marseilles. That was where the *patron* came in, he knows the Marseille run blindfold.'

'You were with him in Norway, weren't you?'

'He was my officer.'

'And you fought at Narvik?'

'Namsos. That bloody shambles!' Dupont spat over the side of the van. 'Nobody'd heard of Namsos, when we came home. It was all Narvik, Narvik – hell, you couldn't blame them, at least Narvik was a victory. '*Le Général Béthouart, le vainqueur de Narvik*' – to hear people talk, you'd have thought Béthouart was another Foch. He went off to Africa, to serve under Weygand, after the armistice. Well, at least he didn't join de Gaulle.'

Maxwell was silent. He had his own opinion of General de Gaulle, but he was under orders to avoid discussing politics.

'The *patron* hankered after following Béthouart to Casablanca,' continued Jean Dupont. 'I believe he'd of done it too, if he'd been fit. But he was badly knocked about at Namsos, he was in that Scottish hospital a lot longer than me. Kidney damage, they said it was; his wounds were infected by the time we got to Scotland. Oh well! He got into this racket instead, and turned out to be one of the best *passeurs* in the business. Ask any of the kids he fixed up after the Revère break-out.'

'The R.A.F. boys got clean away from Revère, didn't they?' said Maxwell. 'There was a lot of excitement about it in London.'

'Yes, it was a good job, except maybe for the hang-up here and at Monte Carlo. Hallo! Here come the railwaymen. Time's getting on.'

It was another squad of workers, carrying tools, following those whom Brunel saw passing the windows of the hotel.

'Are they going to work on the line?'

'They have to clock in at the station first.'

'Is that where Captain Jack went, to the station?'

'I wouldn't know, but here he comes.'

'Sorry about the delay,' said Brunel, swinging himself up to the passenger's seat. 'It was worthwhile, though. I learned something interesting, Charles; I'll give you the details later.'

'It was urgent, then?' Dupont enquired, as the van trundled up the hill to Cap d'Ail.

'I don't know about urgent, Jean, but César's back.'

Dupont whistled expressively, and Charles asked, 'Who's César?'

'Tell you at breakfast.' Brunel folded his arms, and hunched himself on the hard seat as if fatigue had suddenly caught up with him. Charles Maxwell said no more. A broad band of orange light had appeared on the horizon, vivid against the indigo surface of the sea. As the sun rose, all the night shadows, real and imagined, seemed to melt away. In the winter brilliance the little towns of the Riviera appeared one by one: Eze with its banana trees, called *la petite Afrique*, then Beaulieu and the pointing finger of Cap Ferrat; Villefranche, with an Italian cruiser in the bay; and then, in full sunlight, the ancient scourge of the Saracens, the chateau of Nice on its fortress rock.

3

'Here's where I live,' said Jacques, as they came down the Rue Droite. 'If you don't mind waiting a minute, I'd like to get some bread.'

'Sure.' They walked on to the corner of the Rue de la Loge, and Charles waited outside the bakery, looking about him. On the other side of the street the house indicated by his host stood four storeys high, one of them ornamented by marble balconies, pilasters and pediments in the monumental style of the grand past, and all displaying the dingy laundry, cheap curtains and birdcages of the impoverished present. Above a corner shop a cannon ball from the Turkish wars was embedded in the wall.

Jacques came out of the bakery carrying a paper bag and a *baguette* with a wisp of wrapping round the middle.

'That bread smells good!'

'He uses wood for firing.'

The wood-baked bread added one more aroma to the pungency of the narrow street, where all the little shops were open now and filling with customers. Garlic and coffee, new bread and spilt wine, which Charles had always thought of as the smell of France, were supplemented here by muskier flavours, for the Old Town of Nice had always had its North African population, and *les sidis* had their own coffee booths and stores as dark as the souks of Casablanca and Algiers. It was Friday, and many of the women surging in the narrow space between the tall old houses had already been at the fish market. Charles side-stepped to avoid a swipe from a slab of dried cod as they arrived at the doorstep of Fifteen, Rue Droite.

There was no need to alert the concierge with the timeless cry of *'Cordon, s'il vous plaît!'* for the heavy door was constantly opening and shutting as the inhabitants of Number Fifteen went off to work. They slipped in past a group of laughing girls, and Charles had only a moment to realise that he was in a huge shabby vestibule with a vaulted roof before he was hurried up a curving stair with a balcony above an inner patio open to the sky.

'It's like a ruined palace,' he said as they reached the third floor.

'It was a palace long ago, before the Revolution,' said Jacques, taking out his keys. 'They still call it the Palais Lascaris in the Old Town.'

He ushered Charles into a lobby half filled with a carved Provençal *armoire*, and opened a door on a twilit room where only a thin streak of sunshine came through the join in the shutters.

'It's stuffy in here. I'm sorry, but I fasten everything up when I go off for the night.' Jacques pulled aside a heavy net curtain and opened the wooden shutters. The house across the way appeared so close that Charles said two people with long arms could reach out and shake hands across the street.

'Well, hardly that, but we're a bit too near for good security, hence the curtain,' said Jacques, opening the window wide. Daylight revealed that the living-room was furnished with what Charles thought of as 'antiques', and in the room next door he saw a swan in flight from the top of a vast bed, holding brocade curtains in its beak, with two more swans supporting a swinging mirror above the marble-topped dressing-table. The only modern accessory was a radio set, flanked by old silver combs and brushes.

'Chuck your raincoat down anywhere,' said Jacques. 'You can shave and have a bath while I get the coffee going. There'll be enough hot water for the two of us.'

An unshaded light illuminated the bathroom, where the only ventilation was an airshaft leading into the chimney system of the old house. 'The old gas geyser does pretty well,' said Jacques, 'if you don't mind taking a chance on being blown up! You'll have to draw a jugful off for shaving, I'm afraid, there's no hot water in the basin. Those are clean towels on the rack.'

'Terrific.' The gas jets on a ring beneath the copper geyser sprang with a roar into a sinister blue flame, and the hot water spurted explosively into the freshly enamelled tub. As Charles bathed and put on clean underclothing he heard the sound of a coffee grinder in the kitchen, and smiled as he fastened the money belt above his shirt. When he returned to the living-room it was fresh and even warm, for a small electric fire was burning on the hearth of an empty pink marble fireplace closed by an iron screen, and the aroma of coffee was spreading through the flat.

'Can I give you a hand?' he called, over the clatter in the kitchen. Jacques was putting china cups and saucers on a big japanned tray.

'All set.' Jacques dumped the tray on a round mahogany table near the window, and set out the jug of coffee, the jug of boiled milk, a saucer with two small pats of butter and a pot of country honey. He had already brought in a delicate china plate which held the bread cut into slices, and the four brioches which had been in the paper bag.

'French bread and honey, and café au lait!' said Charles. 'It's a banquet, Captain Jack!'

Brunel laughed. 'Jack will do,' he said. 'The other was an old hospital nickname from the Dykefaulds days, it never seemed to sound right here.' In this domestic setting he was a far less intimidating figure than in the lonely hut at Cap Martin. With the bulky *canadienne* and the heavy boots removed, he was seen to be slightly built, though tall, with dark hair and eyes, and strong features blurred by a twenty-four hours' stubble.

'Coffee's where I begin and end as a chef,' he said. 'The rest of the time I eat out. The concierge comes up in the afternoons and cleans up the place, and that suits me well enough.'

'How long have you lived in the Palais Lascaris?'

'About – let me see – about eighteen months.' He refilled the coffee cups. 'When I was repatriated I didn't know that if I went to my parents' home in Menton I would be completely useless, because Menton was, and still is, in Italian hands. The Italian frontier isn't at the Pont St. Louis now. It lies along the valley of the Gorbio.'

'You hadn't realised that? I certainly didn't.'

'Of course you didn't, there was barely space in the English newspapers for the details of the armistice. All that mattered was what they called "the fall of France".' He shook his head. 'Where were you in the summer of 1940?'

'Me? I was at my O.C.T.U., not far from Salisbury Plain.'

'Then if you were in Britain, and I was there myself from May until September, you'll remember how we all lived one day at a time. The only thing that mattered was Britain's survival, and the things that had happened to France seemed like nothing but a – a filthy dream ... I came up against reality the day I landed at Marseille.'

'What did you do?'

'Obeyed my instructions and went straight to de Valbonne, the man you're going to meet at Cannes today. He wasn't called Nestor then, but he was a wise one all right. He advised me to go right back to Marseille and join Donald Caskie, the Scots pastor from Paris who was running a Seamen's Mission in the Rue de Forbin, with British servicemen hidden in the cellars. That's how I got involved with one of the best escape routes across the Pyrenees, and two of the best men in the whole Resistance.'

'And how you got the name of one of the great *passeurs* of 1940,' said Charles.

Jacques looked genuinely surprised. 'Oh no, not me,' he said. 'The pastor and a Scots officer called Ian Garrow were the top men in Marseille. I suppose I was useful as an interpreter for all the Tommies and airmen we got across the border into Spain, and I made a lot of trips north and east to pick up the men who'd been left behind after Dunkirk. But after the New Year the wound I got at Namsos started acting up again, and I landed in the military hospital at Limoges. That's how I'm still a free man today.'

'What happened?'

'The Seamen's Mission set-up was blown by an Englishman, and Caskie and Garrow stood their trial in Fort St. Nicholas. Caskie drew a two years' suspended sentence, with *résidence surveillée* in Grenoble. From all I hear, he doesn't confine himself to Grenoble, or his activities to preaching : the Gestapo's sure to pick him up again one of these days. Garrow got ten years' imprisonment, and he's in Meuzac prison now ... Have some more coffee?'

'Is there enough for both of us?' There was, and it was

scrupulously divided. 'Carry on,' said Charles. 'You were in the military hospital at Limoges—'

'—Complete with my medical discharge papers. Well, then my brother-in-law took over. He's a country doctor at a little place called Oradour sur Glâne, not far from Limoges. I went home with him, and my mother got a railway warrant from the Italians on compassionate grounds. She stayed with us until the end of March and I travelled back with her as far as Nice.'

'I bet you hated letting her go home alone.'

'Of course I did, but she approved of what I meant to do, and I get to see them both sometimes – there *are* ways and means, you may be sure! My father's a clever solicitor in Menton, more than a match for those Italian jackals, and he fixed it so they've no Italians quartered on them now ... One of the things maman had to tell me was that this apartment had been left to me by an old aunt of my father's. What *she* would say if she knew her precious flat was being used as a safe-house by British agents, I would rather not imagine.'

'Anti-British, was she?'

'Grand'tante Marthe never forgave the British after Kitchener kicked the French out of Fashoda, thirteen years before I was born. And talking about safe-houses, you'd better memorise my phone number before you go.'

'Sure,' said Charles, glancing at the telephone on the desk set cornerwise to get the best light from the window. There were some packets of documents near the old-fashioned handset, and he had seen law books in the shelves on each side of the chimney piece.

'Do you use this for your law chambers too?'

'No, I've an *étude* near the Palais de Justice, and I share a clerk with another man. I couldn't see clients here; the flats in the Palais Lascaris have been divided and subdivided since the seventeenth century, and now they're bursting at the seams with refugees ... I ought to be at my office now, I'm appearing in court today. Before I go and change, let me explain about Couteau. You'll meet him in a restaurant this afternoon. But first I think I'd better tell you what I found out in Monaco, while you and Dupont were waiting in the market square.'

'I've been wondering about that.'

'Dupont had a call for me to go to the Hotel Mimosa. It's quite a small place, belonging to a French couple called Leroux. They retired to Beausoleil last year, and left their daughter Fabienne to run the show. She used to be Pierre Lavisse's girl friend – you remember, the chap who shared the hut with me? – and she's helped us out from time to time. I wouldn't call the Mimosa a one hundred per cent safe-house, but César took a chance on it last night.'

' "César is back",' said Charles. 'That's what you told Dupont. Back from where?'

'From London.'

'And that's who you went to see?'

'Not exactly. Fabienne Leroux wanted me to know he'd been trying to get in touch with me last night. But I didn't want to see him until I'd had a word with you.'

'With me? I've never heard of any César, at least not in the Resistance.'

'Not even by his real name, which is Alain Renaudon?'

'Renaudon. It doesn't ring a bell. You say he came from London?'

'He went to London in June to join de Gaulle.'

'Oh! In that case he was probably sent back here by "R.F." section. They do liaise with our people in "F", but mostly with Colonel Passy and the B.C.R.A.'

'That's a new one on me.'

'The *Bureau Central de Renseignements et d'Action*. It was set up out of Passy's old *Service de Renseignements*, when they moved from St. James's Square to Duke Street last March.'

'What an active life the Free French live – in London,' said Jacques Brunel. 'Even before I left, Carlton Gardens wasn't big enough to hold the secret service, and they've had at least two moves since then. Where's Duke Street?'

'It's not far from our own place in Baker Street. Ten Duke Street, Manchester Square – d'you know where the Wallace Collection is?'

'Vaguely.' Jacques offered his cigarettes. 'When I was recruited by the Special Operations Executive in London, there wasn't any "F" or any "R.F." section. But I don't think Alain Renaudon, alias César, would have joined forces with the S.O.E. From what I know of the man and his ambition, he'd only take his orders from de Gaulle himself.'

'Oh, you know him already, do you?'

'He was head of the school when I was a new kid at the Ecole des Roches. He was top student, top athlete, top in leadership and initiative – the lot. Everybody predicted a great future for him.'

'And—?'

'He had a great future until 1940, now he has a rather messy past. He did brilliantly at the Ecole Polytechnique and was off to a fine start in engineering. He joined a firm which handled big public contracts, and used it as a stepping-stone into politics. Meantime he'd married into the Bonapartist aristocracy, and by the time war broke out he was too important to be called up with the reserve. So important that he ended up at Vichy.'

'You don't mean he was in the government?'

'Hardly that, he was too young. He can't be more than thirty-six or thirty-seven now. But he was – what's a *chef de cabinet* in English?'

'Principal private secretary. P.P.S.'

'P.P.S. to one of the less important Ministers. Bridges and Highways or Waters and Forests, I can't remember which. But a few months of Vichy were enough for Renaudon. Remember, a *chef de cabinet* is usually a career diplomat, and it's said Renaudon had his sights set on the Quai d'Orsay. He must have thought he had a better chance aboard the Gaullist band wagon, because now he wants to win the whole of the French Resistance for de Gaulle.'

'And this is what he wants to talk to you about?'

'I imagine so.'

'I don't see why you felt you had to discuss it with me. You surely know "F" section's not supposed to get involved in French internal politics.'

'No, but you'll be seeing Renaudon today. He intends to be present at your meeting with Couteau.'

Charles said angrily, 'How the hell does he even know about it?'

'From a very talkative member of the "Knife" circuit called Canif. Who heard about your visit from our equally chatty friend Couteau.'

'Damnation,' said Charles, 'I wasn't supposed to meet anybody in Nice but Couteau and yourself. Least of all a Gaullist agent. This Renaudon—' he began, and stopped. 'Don't you think you ought to tell me more about Couteau and Canif?'

'Couteau's real name is Pierre Orengo. He's a man in his forties, married with a family, one of the old Niçois stock from before the *rattachement*.'

'The what?'

'Italy gave Nice back to France during the Second Empire. Orengo's father made a sizeable fortune trading in olive oil, and Orengo hangs about the warehouse, but he doesn't do much himself except run amateur dramatic groups. The "Knife" network's one of them.'

'They think a lot of him in London.'

'I know they do. Canif's a much younger man, an architect, also from an old local family and married to a doctor's daughter. His name's Roger Malvy.'

'And they both live in Nice?'

'Orengo lives in a villa up at Cimiez, and the young Malvys have a flat in one of the modern "palaces" on the Promenade des Anglais. I don't recommend either place as a safe-house.'

'Why not?'

'Too much chatter.'

'Oh hell!' said Charles. 'Jack, you've got to fix it the way London wants. Get rid of Renaudon and whoever else turns up, and let me have at least ten minutes with Couteau alone.'

'Long enough for you to get a receipt for the money you brought him?'

Charles gave him a hard stare. In the last few minutes he had shed his diffidence and taken on a new authority.

'Right!' he said. 'I have got money for Couteau. Whatever you say about amateur theatricals, he's running a huge circuit and running it damned well, and he's got to be paid accordingly. I knew you were only trying to trap me with that question about the cash I was carrying, because of course I've got five thousand pounds, in francs, in the belt I'm wearing, and of that three thousand goes to "Knife". It's the largest payment London's sent them yet. That's why I don't want my meeting with Couteau to be mucked about.'

'Don't worry, it won't be.'

'Thanks. You still haven't told me the name of the restaurant where we're going to meet.'

'This is the plan,' said Jacques crisply. 'You're on your own for the rest of the morning. Stay here if you like. You could get a couple of hours' sleep on the sofa and have time to buy that hat before the shops shut at noon. Then, at one, I want you to meet me at a restaurant called "Le Faisan", just a few yards beyond the flower market.'

'Near the Opéra?'

'Yes, but on the other side of the street.'

'I'll find it.'

'The dining room's upstairs. After luncheon, you and Couteau will meet in another room on the premises. There's a private door at the back, and Couteau will come in that way.'

'That sounds good.' In his relief Charles took the risk of saying :

'London didn't say anything about your own network. If

47

you're short of cash, I could easily make you a down payment now. They're not particular to five hundred pounds or so.'

The silence lasted long enough to make him sure he had said the wrong thing, but Jacques' reply, when it came, was perfectly pleasant. 'That's very generous of you. My only real expense at present is black market petrol, and I can easily pay for that myself.'

'But—'

'My network, as you call it, is so small it hasn't even got a fancy name. I know Couteau claims to have five hundred men in "Knife". I've only got thirty, in five groups of six, between Nice and the old Italian border, but they're nearly all veterans of the campaign in Norway and they're all ready to fight again. They'll fight like the devil for the French Republic against its enemies when the right time comes and the Allies land in France. Tell them *that* in Baker Street when you go home.'

The change of tone was so complete, the passion so naked, that the younger man was taken aback. 'I don't have to wait till I get back to London,' he said prosaically. 'I'll send your message as soon as my wireless operator joins up with me.'

'You're expecting a "pianist"? Meeting you at Nestor's?'

'With a courier. The section wants us to use couriers to carry messages rather than risk using the phone.'

'Girl couriers on bicycles, playing at being Boy Scouts?'

'They're dedicated women,' said Charles stiffly. 'Weren't there women in the circuit when you were a *passeur* in Marseille?'

'They were operatives, not couriers, and some of them were brilliant. But personally I don't like the idea of women at war. Girls get hurt too easily.' Jacques got up and stretched, and then began to pile the breakfast things together on the tray. 'I've got to shave,' he said. 'Don't worry about this stuff. The concierge'll take care of it when she comes in.'

48

Charles heard the sounds of dishes being dumped in the sink, and then of water running in the bathroom. I hope I left enough hot for him, he thought uneasily, and went to retrieve his raincoat from the bedroom before his host came back to dress for the business day. Standing in the doorway between the two rooms he saw what Jacques had meant about the division of the apartments. Clearly the living-room and the bedroom had been one big salon in an earlier century, because he saw (looking up at the ceiling for the first time) that both rooms were covered by one vast fresco in blue, terracotta and earth colours, so faded that he could hardly disinguish the theme of plunging horses and chariots, flying clouds and classical figures with hands outflung in a crisis of woe and despair. I wouldn't care to live with that thing hanging over me, he thought. The Palais Lascaris is a pretty dismal place.

Under the painted ceiling the rugs on the beautiful wood floors were frayed and the pattern of the wallpapers, once a riot of flower bouquets, was blurred by time. A sofa which Madame Récamier might have adorned was set cornerwise to the fireplace, and was remarkable for its proportions and mahogany-scrolled head, but shreds of red brocade uphol- stery were visible beneath the threadbare violet velveteen. The few steel engravings had spots on their mountings, and there were no photographs of the young barrister's family or friends. It was all impersonal except for the books in the upper shelves of a magnificent secretary, unpolished for years, in the corner opposite the sofa. Charles was looking at them when Jacques came out of the bathroom in his dressing-gown.

'What do you think of Grand'tante Marthe's library?' he asked. 'Amazing what a lively taste the old girl had!'

'Varied, at least.' From the Feydeau farces through Ohnet (*Le Maître de Forges*, once thought very daring) through Gyp and *Le Mariage de Chiffon*, the collection led predic- tably to *La Garçonne* and *Aphrodite*, revealing the mildly salacious tastes of a solitary and aging woman. Charles was leafing through *L'Amant de Lady Chatterley* when Jacques returned.

He was wearing a dark suit and black shoes, with a white shirt and a noncommittal tie. Freshly shaved and with his dark hair brushed flat, he looked a different man from the rough who had helped the British agent to destroy his canoe on the wild shore at Cap Martin.

'Not sleepy?' he said. 'That stuff's liable to keep you awake if you are.'

'I don't feel like sleeping. I'd rather go out and have a good look at Nice before I meet you at "Le Faisan".'

'If you go along the Promenade, maybe as far as the Negresco, I'll be interested to hear your opinion of wartime Nice.' Charles nodded. He was watching Brunel, who seemed uncertain whether to go or to stay, propping up some of the books in the shelves, opening the *armoire* to get out a hat and a light overcoat, all with an ill-assurance which was new.

He cleared his throat. 'Look, Charles,' he said, 'the "Faisan" is a discreet restaurant, or we wouldn't be meeting Couteau there, and within certain limits we can talk freely at luncheon. But we obviously can't talk about Britain, and ... there's one thing ... I want to ask you now, while we're alone.'

'Go ahead.'

'You told me in the hut that your parents live at Burns Bay in Scotland. Do they know the Deputy – the M.P. for Carrick, Mr. Grant?'

'Neil Grant? Sure they do, and I do too. He and his wife used to come to our house a lot. Do *you* know him, Jack?'

'He – was very kind to me when I got out of hospital. And I was interested – he once told me Carrick's a marginal constituency – I wondered how his electors felt when he joined the army.'

'It might just turn the trick for him at the next election. There's a solid Labour vote in Carrick, in the mining district to the north, but even there nobody accused him of neglecting his constituents when he enlisted. If he'd wangled an admin. job in the Judge Advocate General's department there might have been complaints. But an officer on active service with the Eighth Army, that's different. How did you know he'd enlisted, anyway? Did you hear it on the B.B.C.?'

'He wrote to me. There was a pretty good mail service to the Unoccupied Zone until about a year ago, but I've heard nothing from Neil for a long time. I couldn't help wondering—'

'He came through El Alamein all right, if that's what you mean. There was a long spiel about it in the Burns Bay *Gazette*. But it's amazing, your knowing Neil Grant at all. I didn't know he had anything to do with Dykefaulds Hospital.'

'I didn't meet him there, it was in London. They had me down to Lime Tree Cottage a few times.'

'Oh yes. That place is let now, to some business firm that wanted to get out of London while the raids were on. Mrs. Grant took a flat in Burns Bay for herself and the kids, and she's done Neil a power of good in the constituency. My mother says she's a terrific worker, leads every war charity drive there is.'

'Lucy Grant!' said Jacques, 'I can't believe it. She was such a fragile, retiring creature when I knew her, I can't imagine her coping on her own, let alone bossing other people around.'

'She rose to the occasion, like all the rest of them. And everybody was sorry for the family when Neil's sister was killed in the London blitz. That was the reason he enlisted, as you probably know.'

'Alison wasn't killed in London,' said Jacques. 'It was before the blitz began, when a stray Boche dropped a bomb on Kingsmead-on-Thames.'

'Are you sure?'

'I was there.'

'Oh God, how awful for you!' said Charles. 'There in Kingsmead when it happened?'

'No, worse luck. I was at the cottage with her family.' He gave Charles a strained look. 'Well ... that's a long time ago. I'm glad to know the others are all right. Thanks for telling me, Charles. I'm off now.' He muttered something about locking the door, said more clearly, 'See you at one!' and was gone.

Twenty minutes later Charles Maxwell latched the windows, switched off the one-bar radiator, and made sure the door was securely locked behind him. On the landing he stood still for a moment, savouring the feeling of being on his own at last. Since leaving England he had been shepherded everywhere, first by the Royal Navy and then by Jacques Brunel; now he was at the beginning of an independent mission. Jacques had hurried him upstairs, so he walked down slowly, looking at the faded frescoes and the busts in their baroque niches, seeing how beautiful the floor tiles had once been, and coming to the understanding that three centuries ago this old house had really been a palace, the home of fashion and nobility. As he went – and he paused on one landing to look down the second staircase which, as Jacques had told him, led to a door opening on a street behind and parallel to the Rue Droite – he was aware that he was being watched by more than one pair of eyes. The walls of the Palais Lascaris were too thick, and the conversation had been too absorbing, for him to be aware until now that there were other tenants in the place, but the doors were opening stealthily, and the window curtains were moving slightly in the apartments which looked out on the rear patio and the back door. He could hear voices, and little children whimpering at his back.

He had learned in Brunel's apartment to study the ceilings of this strange house, and in the arched roof of the vestibule there was the same cloudy splendour as he had seen three flights above. Here the horses and chariots were faded almost beyond restoration, but the quarterings of a coat of arms were clear enough for him to distinguish a two-headed eagle, crowned, a Maltese cross, and the motto *Nec Me Fulgura.*

A woman was eyeing him from the concierge's *loge*, but rather to his surprise she did not challenge the stranger, and Charles wondered if she thought he had been spending the night with one of the girls. There were a lot of girls in the Rue Droite when he came out into that teeming canyon : some of them queuing up to buy the scanty ingredients of their midday meal, while others leaned out of their ground-floor windows to greet the passer-by. One of them pointed at Charles's briefcase as he went past, and said something with a shrill laugh to her companion. He gave them a wave of the hand and walked on grinning. He had realised what was meant by a *baise en ville.*

He only had to walk straight down the Rue Droite towards the sea; passing the alleys and cul de sacs which were part of the impenetrable warren of the Old Town, and then he was at the corner of the Cours Saleya. That was where Dupont had let them out of the van and wished them luck, and now Dupont and his friends were back behind the counters of their own stores, while the customers of the great market were Nice housewives, sniffing and prodding the merchandise on the stands. Charles Maxwell walked through the place in fascination. He had lived for two years on army rations, filling but not fine cooking, and he knew that the pinch of civilian rationing in Britain was increasingly felt. Now he saw crates of poultry and rabbits for the table, stands heaped with cuttlefish, squid, *rascasse* and *lotte*, sole, *dorade* and sardines fresh from the sea. Crossing the market to look, he saw that the butchers' shops along the pavements of the Cours Saleya were bare, and the dairy produce non-existent, but then, back in the market again, there were mouth-watering vegetables. Aubergines and the small artichokes called *violets* shone in all the shades of purple next to new potatoes, amber-frilled *cêpes*, young lettuces and the oranges, tangerines and lemons which were no longer to be found in Britain. The coloured piles were rivalled by the flower market, a riot of carnations, roses and sweet-scented violets.

There were enough bare-headed men in the market, the vendors and the porters clearing a way for themselves with crates and boxes piled into hand carts, for Charles not to be conspicuous without a hat, but he remembered that one had to be bought, and after walking round the stalls and the shops a second time, noting the prices, he started looking for a hatter. Because he was a very thorough young man he also looked for 'Le Faisan', so as to avoid any delays and asking directions at one o'clock, and took his bearings by Garnier's opera house with its rose-red marble columns, and playbills which showed him that Nice was enjoying a very fine opera season. The Opéra looked as if it should be surrounded by a vast square and busy boulevards, as in Paris, instead of by dubious hotels ('Rooms by the Day or the Hour'), cafés, and buildings trailing rags of history. Napoleon Bonaparte slept here, Pope Pius VII slept here, the plaques on their façades declared. The shops opposite bore dates going back to before the *rattachement* of 1861. One even claimed to have been handed down from father to son since 1820, and there, between the tea shops opened to cater to English visitors of Queen Victoria's reign and souvenir shops which were also out of date, Charles found the unobtrusive entrance of 'Le Faisan'. It had a small pink pediment, unornamented but upheld by two caryatides in the style of the Second Empire. The front door, which was already open, was more modern in appearance, being of frosted glass protected by an iron grille in the middle of which was a pheasant in wrought iron. Beyond it he could see a small lobby carpeted in green, with another glass door at the far end.

There was a hatter's shop at the next street corner, where a disapproving old gentleman sold Charles the only up-to-date hat in a collection of bowlers and summer straws. It was a real gangster's hat, a *borsalino* with a snap brim, and just what a chatty young insurance salesman might be expected to admire. Wearing it at a rakish tilt he felt more confident than ever.

Now he was equipped for the walk he had promised himself – and Captain Jack – across the Place Masséna and along the Promenade des Anglais. But Charles loitered outside the hatter's, drawn by an instinctive curiosity towards the law courts and the public *persona* of that rising young barrister and Resistance worker, Maître Jacques Brunel. He had not been chosen for a mission to France merely because of his appearance and French accent, or his knowledge of the Riviera towns : the men who recruited him into S.O.E. had seen in Lieutenant Maxwell, during the landings in French Madagascar, a capacity to understand and work well with the disgruntled Vichy officials with whom the British had to deal at Diego Suarez. But young Maxwell had not encountered any individual Frenchman as complex as Jacques Brunel. In the course of one morning Brunel had been the keen interrogator, who asked all the questions and knew all the answers; the host, who offered freshly ground coffee and under-the-counter brioches, the best he had to give; the resistant with a passion for security, and then the man who had recalled, with a look and tone of pain, the death of one girl in the holocaust of 1940. I want to hear him plead, thought Charles, and began walking back towards the market.

There he made his first mistake, for at the far end of a square filled with potted chrysanthemums for sale he saw a handsome white building with balconies which he took to be the Palais de Justice, but which was in fact the Préfecture, another of the old 'palaces' in which Nice abounded, and once the home of the Grimaldi princes of Monaco. He realised his mistake before the sentries began to take an interest in him, and turning down a narrow street to the left was soon in front of the Palais de Justice. It was an imposing building in the monumental style, with the words *Liberté Egalité Fraternité* spaced out over each of the three entrance doors beneath the flag of France.

Charles went up the steps in a crowd of other people, and entered the vestibule. The place was buzzing with policemen, any one of whom might ask to see his papers and trip him up with some question he couldn't answer, but there was a swarm of men and women to occupy their attention. Litigants, witnesses, friends of the accused, young women weeping and older women taking care of crying children were so numerous in the halls and corridors that Charles was unnoticed as he studied the bulletin board which told him that Maître Jacques Brunel was appearing for the plaintiff, Marie Angèle Thibaud, in a demand for eviction before the Tribunal de Grande Instance.

He took his seat near the back of the public benches. The case had not attracted many spectators, and he had a clear if bewildering view of the court. His only brush with the law had been an appearance in the Sheriff Court at Ayr, on a charge of speeding in a built-up area (Admonished and Dismissed) but he had seen innumerable courtroom movies, and was perplexed by the absence from this tribunal of the indispensable jury. The three judges in scarlet gowns were impressive, and so in an unexpected way was Maître Brunel. In the *avocat*'s toque and black robe, with a stole over one shoulder, his voice was fuller and far more flexible than it had sounded in his strange old palace of the not-so-sleeping beauties. It was a most persuasive instrument, and the defendant, a thick-set, coarse-featured man in an expensive suit, listened scowling as Jacques put the plaintiff's case to the court. Defendant had rented the villa from the plaintiff's mother, a widow since deceased, on a three-six-nine lease in 1929, and had failed to pay rent since the lease expired in 1938. Then there was a reference, which Charles found hard to follow, to the case of Marie Angèle Thibaud v. Argile and Tuile, in which judgment was given, with costs, for Mademoiselle Thibaud. She had claimed the return of her property from the defendant in June 1940 – 'at which moment,' the grave beautiful voice said, 'our country was in danger.'

56

En ce moment, la patrie était en danger. Even Charles Maxwell knew that it was almost a French cliché, but the emotional modulation of the appeal was such that all three judges nodded solemnly, as if they saw the analogy between defeated France and the orphan girl defrauded by a brutal and grasping man – 'who,' as Maître Brunel said, 'had carefully avoided serving his country in her hour of need.' The people in the public section of the court were obviously stirred. Among them Charles saw a man as cheaply dressed as he was himself, not unusually tall, and only distinguished in that Mediterranean ambience by fair hair streaked with grey, who smiled brilliantly and nodded approval as Jacques resumed his seat. The defending counsel made the best of a bad job, but the judges had made up their minds already, and his argument that Mademoiselle Thibaud, while still a minor, had failed to carry out needed repairs to the villa in dispute, did not convince them. 'If this lady received no rent, why should she be expected to pay for repairs?' asked one, and in short order the court unanimously found for the plaintiff, Mademoiselle Marie Angèle Thibaud.

An argument about costs followed, but Charles left the court-room before it was over. He had been increasingly worried by the interest of a policeman, who changed his position several times until he was actually standing behind the young man, with his hands on the back of the bench. He slipped out along with two women who were bored by the proceedings, and got out of the building without feeling a hand on his shoulder. He was only a short distance from the New Town and the Promenade des Anglais. As he settled the new hat on his head and walked rapidly away, he was still thinking of Jacques Brunel and his special pleading. He thought it was like using a sledgehammer to crack a walnut.

4

The promise of the caryatides at the front door was carried
out by the upstairs dining-room of the 'Faisan' restaurant,
which was almost as much a museum piece as the old apartment in the Palais Lascaris. This room was pure Second Empire : long and low, with small lace-curtained windows looking down on the Rue St. François de Paule, over which the
sacred silence of the luncheon hour had fallen. 'Le Faisan'
had been opened in the early days of the *rattachement,* when
Bonapartism was high fashion in Nice. Within its walls the
Battle of Sedan had never been fought, the Republic never
proclaimed, and the official portrait of Marshal Pétain, the
Chief of State, had replaced the fine engravings of Napoleon III and the Empress Eugénie which hung above the
high, mirrored buffet against the back wall. A later hand
had added a few of the bright murals popular on the Côte
d'Azur at the turn of the century, depicting scenes from the
Odyssey in a Riviera setting. Ulysses returned to Penelope
at her loom beneath the pines of Cap Martin, the Sirens
sang their songs from the red rocks of St. Raphaël, and
under a picture of Nausicaa at play under the lemon trees
of Menton sat Jacques Brunel, reading the *Eclaireur de
Nice.*

'Glad to see you, monsieur,' he said formally, rising to
shake hands when Charles came up to his table. 'I was
afraid you might have trouble finding the place.'

'I hope you haven't been waiting long, monsieur,' said
Charles with equal formality. 'I didn't mean to be late.'

'You weren't late, I was a little early. You bought a paper
too, I see.'

'There wasn't much news in it.'

'Nothing but the handouts from Vichy. *Bonjour*, Marie, what's the best thing on the menu today?'

'Fish, of course, Maître Brunel. A good bouillabaisse, perhaps?' The stout, middle-aged waitress, encased rather than dressed in black with a white cap and apron, hardly glanced at the barrister's guest. Maître Brunel, that quiet, regular patron, had so many different acquaintances, some of them far shabbier than this one, that a new little commercial traveller was of no interest to the 'Faisan's' staff. She laid two menu cards on the table and stood waiting.

'We'll have an apéritif and think it over,' Jacques told her. 'Monsieur Aletti, what would you like to drink?'

'Oh, I don't know. A white Cinzano?'

'Two white Cinzanos, please.'

Charles looked around him with interest. The tables were not crowded together, so that it was hardly possible to overhear any conversation. The white tablecloths were stiffly starched. The white china was marked with a Bonaparte laurel wreath in gilt, the heavy silver engraved with a pheasant. Although the market cafés and bistros had been crowded from the hour of noon, the 'Faisan's' guests seemed to arrive late rather than early, several groups of men coming in after Charles was seated. They all appeared to know Jacques, and exchanged nods or quiet *bonjours* with him.

'My guess is that this is a barristers' hangout,' said Charles.

'Yes, a lot of the bachelors come here every day. But I can see some businessmen here too, and the three ladies at the table nearest the door are the best fish merchants in the market.'

Jacques picked up the menu. It was a very short one, and no doubt familiar, but Charles saw with amusement that his host was giving it the utmost concentration. The *passeur*, the lawyer, the complex human being had all been absorbed into the quintessential Frenchman, thinking of nothing but *un bon déjeuner*.

'Would you really like a bouillabaisse?'

'They only make good bouillabaisse in Marseille, monsieur.'

'And where do you think they serve it best? I've never been able to make up my mind.'

'At Basso's on the Quai des Belges,' said Charles promptly.

'That's a thoroughly conventional choice. Well, if bouillabaisse is out, how about a *soupe de poissons*? Or is that too fishy if we're going to have fish later? It's Friday, they'll have a good selection. I don't recommend the other soup, it's only hot water flavoured with celery.'

It was obviously not a black market restaurant, for no meat, cheese or cream ices appeared on the menu. They decided on a ratatouille of aubergines and tomatoes to begin with, and for fish, the *mostèle* of that day's catch with a few boiled potatoes. The wine list was examined, and after serious discussion a bottle of white Estandon was chosen.

'*A votre santé, monsieur*,' said Jacques, for the Cinzanos had been brought, 'I hope you've had a profitable morning.'

'Some of it was very interesting,' Charles smiled. 'Congratulations on your victory.'

'Thanks. I saw you in court, as soon as I got up to plead.'

'Did I put you off?'

'*You* didn't.'

'You mean something did? You looked quite unruffled to me.'

'That's part of the act. But I was surprised to see the man you and I were discussing earlier, sitting not very far away from you.'

'The man who lives here, or the man who's been travelling?'

'The traveller.'

'Chap in a brown coat, with blond hair turning grey?'

'You noticed him too, did you? I thought he might try to reach me in my office, but he turned up in court instead.'

'Did he speak to you after the court rose? I left before the end.'

'I saw you going out. What happened?'

'I lost my nerve when that cop came and stood right behind me,' Charles muttered.

'Yes, well, you didn't have to worry about that fellow, he's one of ours.' Jacques broke off while the ratatouille was served, and tasted the wine. 'That's fine, Marie, thanks.' There was no wine waiter, three competent waitresses were serving the whole room.

'Did you win on the costs?' Charles asked, as the woman filled his glass.

'Yes, costs were given against the defendant, he'll find this an expensive morning's work. My client's troubles aren't over, unfortunately. It's one thing to get an eviction order from the tribunal and quite another to get it executed. The papers have to go to a *huissier de justice*, and the legal calendar allows him to take his time ordering the *commissaire de police* to turn the fellow out. I'll probably get another call for help from that poor girl in about six week's time.'

'She wasn't in court herself, was she?'

'No, she lives in Toulouse. I sent her a telegram with the result when I was on my way to meet you. She's a helpless creature, what the novelists call *'l'éternelle victime'*. So I was glad to nail that rascal who was swindling her.'

'Do you really find such cases interesting?' said Charles diffidently.

'*Intéressant* in the money sense?'

'N-no, just interesting to work on.'

'Of course I do, but it shouldn't have been heard in that tribunal at all,' said Jacques, deliberately misunderstanding him. 'My father has won scores of eviction cases in the *Petite Instance* court. Mademoiselle Thibaud insisted on briefing me; she says she's had confidence in me ever since I won another case for her six months ago. You heard Messieurs Argile and Tuile named in court? They were the embezzling trustees who thought they could defraud a minor orphan who happened to be a girl. Girls haven't much luck,' said

Jacques, crumbling a morsel of the coarse restaurant bread, and Charles thought, as the plates were changed, that here was the theme underlying all they had already said. Girls haven't much luck ... Girls get hurt too easily ... She was killed by a German bomb, and I was there.

But Brunel continued, prosaically enough, and for the benefit of the waitress, 'I've got a case coming up in the Fifth Chambre Correctionnelle on Monday that looks as if it might be more exciting. I'm defending the young son of a man "well known in sporting circles", as they say in England. Larceny and "verbal menaces",' he added in explanation. 'What do you think of the fish?'

'Very good indeed,' said Charles, with exactly the shade of reserve proper to a Marseillais. Jacques laughed, and said it was as good as anything to be had in the Vieux Port, and they exchanged Marseille small talk until the *mostèle meunière* was enjoyed to the last mouthful. 'Let's have a slice of apple tart,' said Jacques. 'One thing we aren't short of nowadays is apples.'

'There don't seem to be many shortages in the Nice market.'

'Ah, you had a look around, did you? Was this before or after your flight from the halls of justice?'

'The market before, the Promenade des Anglais after.' And when the apple tart was served Charles quietly described his walk along the promenade to the Negresco, where he had bought the newspaper and sat for half an hour at a sidewalk café, sipping a *pastis* and reading the astonishing list of theatre and cinema shows, concerts and ballet performances to be enjoyed all along the Riviera. He had watched the endless procession, to him equally astonishing, of people who seemed to be on a perpetual holiday : handsome men and beautifully-dressed women, nursemaids bringing attractive children down to the beach, the whole scene like the stage set of a musical comedy under the blue skies of the Côte d'Azur. 'How is it done, Jack?' he whispered under the clatter of plates as the waitresses cleared away. 'Have people here been living like that ever since 1940? Wearing Paris clothes and costume jewellery, and staying at those smart hotels? Except that you don't see as many motor cars, it's exactly the same as it was before the war.'

'Well, not quite,' said Jacques. 'Before the war it was going to go on for ever, now it could blow up in their faces any day. They're living on borrowed time, and some of them may even know it. I wanted you to see them before the time runs out.'

'I'm damned glad I saw the Old Town first.' Jacques nodded approval, and sat back to let the waitress put two coffee filters, with the liquid dripping into glasses, on the table between them. 'You'll see plenty of sights like this morning's before you get as far as the Canebière,' he said. 'The Croisette at Cannes is the Promenade des Anglais over again : a fool's paradise for wealthy refugees. It'll go up in smoke the moment the Germans get tired of Laval and the Marshal and make up their minds to cross the Line.'

'D'you think that's likely to be soon?'

'I thought it might happen after that disaster of a raid at Dieppe last August. Now they'll probably wait until the Americans show their hands. Then goodbye to the *dolce vita* on the Riviera, and this time there won't be any Spain to run to. Would you like a liqueur?'

'No thanks. I want to keep my head clear for whatever comes next.'

'Not a brandy? No more coffee? Then let's go downstairs.' He asked the waitress for the bill.

'I thought the glass door led to a conservatory,' said Charles, as they came down one side of the graceful double staircase.

'It leads to the *cabinets particuliers*, which probably haven't been used as such since 1914. You can use one for your talk with Couteau. He'll be coming in by the back entrance – there's a passage leading into the lobby of an office building on the Rue Alexandre Mari. It's an insurance office, now I come to think of it – just the thing for you.' He was talking for the sake of talking, for the boy was visibly nervous, and the garden they had to cross was an ominously dreary place. It was paved in cement, with no greenery except a few laurustinus bushes, but there was a trickle of water in the little centre pool where two goldfish swam miserably round and round under the blind eyes of a leaden lute-player. Charles unconsciously touched the money belt beneath his waistcoat as they entered another lobby, uncarpeted this time, and Jacques jerked his thumb at the door on the right hand side. 'For later,' he murmured, and pushed upon the door ahead. '*Bonjour*,' he said. '*Bonjour, messieurs.*'

There was a scraping sound as seven chairs were pushed back from a long bare table, and a stout man came forward with outstretched hand. '*Bonjour, Jack! Et soyez le bienvenu, Charles!*'

Charles Maxwell mechanically returned the greeting. All he could think of was that seven men, instead of the expected one, were about to become familiar with the voice, appearance and possibly the mannerisms of a supposedly secret agent in Unoccupied France.

'All the leaders of the "Knife" circuit are here to greet you,' said Couteau cheerfully. 'Let me present Canif – Coupoir – Epée – Fleuret – Poignard – and Sabre.'

Charles shook all the extended hands. '*Enchanté*,' he said. 'I didn't expect to meet so many new friends all at once.' He looked them over : Canif, or Penknife, the young architect whose name he had been told was Roger Malvy, seemed to have a cutting edge, and so did Sabre, a small man with a long nose and a sarcastically twisted mouth. The other five looked like prosperous businessmen, and as soon as the greetings were over they resumed what was obviously a continued complaint about the cold. The restaurant had been warmed by a big wood-burning stove and by the midday sun shining on the closed windows, but this downstairs den was glacial. It was made even more depressing by a pile of up-ended chairs and tables near a door at the far side of the room.

'We're all delighted to meet an English comrade who's come direct to us at Nice,' said Couteau. 'Antibes has been the favoured port for your people much too long! Shall we sit down, messieurs, and hear what Charles has to tell us about his trip?' Jacques Brunel took a chair next to the non-plussed young man. Go ahead, he silently and savagely addressed Couteau, shout it out, we'll be at proper names and addresses in five minute, all ready for somebody to sing to the Vichy police. And you might tell this kid from Baker Street that the reason why Antibes is no longer what you pompously call the favoured port, with that easy landing at the public gardens, why in fact Antibes is blown for ever-more, is because the last London agent who risked it there was met by a reception committee like this one, only making as much noise as if the town brass band and the fire brigade had come along too. With the result that five useful French-men are now in prison, and one British agent is God knows where.

Jacques Brunel was not a member of the 'Knife' circuit. He knew that Couteau, or Orengo, claimed a following numerically strong on paper, but – like Maxwell in his snap judgment – he believed that the only two effective mem-bers of the top echelon were Canif, otherwise Roger Malvy, and the man they knew as Sabre.

Malvy had served at the front in an artillery regiment, and had done as well as any man could in the rout of 1940. He was strikingly good-looking, with the general reputation of being a fool about women, which could be dangerous in the Resistance. Jacques, who knew him well, was aware of the particular problems in Malvy's life, from his well-founded jealously of his wife's involvement with her cousin, Marc Chabrol, to his own current affair with Fabienne Le-roux. Sabre, who taught French history at a boys' high school, had served in the Army of the Alps and fought in the defence of Menton. He was intelligent and patriotic; Sabre's weakness was that as a schoolmaster of passionately radical views he was too fond of addressing his pupils in terms which had already earned him a reprimand from the Vichy Minister of Education.

'What are your plans, then, Charles?' That was Sabre, in the tone of one encouraging a backward student. Tell us your plans, tell us your contacts, tell us about your safe-houses, Jacques continued his silent comments : those babblers have the same idea as the Gestapo. He looked at the one empty chair at the long bare table, which must have overflowed with good things at the business lunches of the past, and wondered if at the last minute César had funked offering his throat to be cut by the 'Knife' circuit. But before Charles could reply the door beside the piled furniture opened, and César himself came in.

Alain Renaudon, alias César, was a handsome man of a type more admired in England than in France : blond and blue-eyed, with the fresh complexion of his Breton ancestors. He was thinner and less self-assured than when he gave Joe Calvert luncheon at the Savoy in July, and he had often regretted the invitation. No official request for General de Gaulle to visit America had been received at Carlton Gardens, and for the rest of his stay in London Renaudon had been subjected to a relaxed but constant American surveillance. Even after Joe Calvert had gone to Moscow with Mr. Churchill, the number two man in a delegation headed by Averell Harriman, Bob Kemp or one of his O.S.S. henchmen had been at every social occasion where Renaudon might be; always friendly enough, but prone to ask embarrassing questions about the progress of the movie to be called *The de Gaulle Story.* It was still a long way from going before the cameras. William Faulkner had handed Warner Brothers a thirty-nine page script on August 13th, on the familiar theme of de Gaulle's identification with Joan of Arc, which was turned down. Even with the help of Frederick Forrest, 'the king of the pulps', and with the title changed to 'Free France', Faulkner had only finished sixty-six pages by October 13th, and there were rumours that he would be given another assignment. Alain Renaudon wished he had never mentioned Warner Brothers' project to the Americans in London.

Fortunately nobody in France knew anything about it. César had landed in Brittany, and was on the run north of the Line of Demarcation for over a month, with nerve-racking changes of papers and identity. Even in the south he felt far from safe, and he was exhausted by weeks of argument with the highly individual, touchy, quarrelsome and patriotic leaders of the Resistance networks he was trying to weld into one. He was braced for more arguments in Nice, and probably in Cannes as well. Anywhere that the resisters were controlled by one of de Gaulle's pet hates – 'F' section of the S.O.E.

The 'Knife' men greeted him warmly, however, and he shook hands all round, leaning across the table to pat Couteau's shoulder. "Br-r! You're cold in here,' he said. He tossed his hat on to the pile of furniture and sat down without unbuttoning his brown overcoat. 'Go on with your meeting, please. Don't let me interrupt you.'

'Charles was going to tell us about his trip,' said Couteau.

'I'm sure César's travels are more interesting than mine,' said the British agent hastily.

'Did you come back by parachute, César?' asked Fleuret, with a malicious smirk.

'Not me, I'm far too big a coward,' said César easily, 'No, I came by sea. That's what delayed me in London – waiting for a flight. I hoped the British would fly me back, but they aren't very cooperative about laying on flights for any of de Gaulle's personal representatives.'

'Is that what you are now?' said Jacques.

'Yes, I am ' – with a bold stare.

'Do you like that better than your job at Vichy?'

'The R.A.F. can only spare about thirty aircraft for all the Resistance work in Europe,' Charles interposed. 'They've got some pretty heavy commitments elsewhere.'

'Yes, of course,' said César with quick sympathy. 'That's why I took a chance on a sea crossing, at General de

Gaulle's request. He was very witty about my arrival in England in a British submarine. "How did you enjoy being kidnapped by those British?" was what he said.'

'Doesn't he realise that without the British you and he would never have reached London?' said Jacques.

'Of course he does. But then nobody at Carlton Gardens, from the general down, is exactly happy about our new recruits having to be processed through the Patriotic School.'

'What the devil's that?' asked Coupoir.

'It's a place in South London, where all the new arrivals have to go for interrogation. Oh, a perfectly courteous interrogation, with innumerable cups of tea, but very searching – about who you are, where you've come from, why you're there: I wasn't released for thirty-six hours.'

'And then what happens? Are you turned loose in London?'

'No, our people go to a central depot for a welcome and debriefing by our own officers. They undergo physical checks, naturally. And some of them,' he added unwillingly, 'are interviewed by psychiatrists as well.'

'To test their sanity?' said Jacques.

'To test their reliability, I suppose. But I was very fortunate: as soon as the British released me I was joined by Colonel Passy in person, and was soon in a comfortable room in the Cumberland Hotel.'

'General de Gaulle received you at once, didn't he?' said Canif, and Jacques, remembering that they had dined together at Villefranche, guessed that the young architect was feeding César the lines of a dialogue decided upon the evening before.

'He received me at Carlton Gardens the very next day,' said César, 'just after he met his Cabinet.'

'His *what*?'

'Well, his Commissioners then. The members of the French National Committee charged with special areas of interest.'

68

'Tell me one thing,' said Jacques. 'Does the "Cabinet" have the right to vote?'

'They express their opinions when the general invites them to do so, but they don't vote.'

'Jack, this isn't a debate,' said Couteau, very much the chairman. 'Just let César tell his story.'

'I was going to say,' César continued, 'that at our first meeting General de Gaulle did me the honour to propose that I should undertake a lecture tour in the United States, describing France under German occupation, and the aspirations of *La France Combattante*.'

'I'd have jumped at it,' muttered somebody, and there was a suppressed laugh.

'Would you?' said César radiantly. 'I didn't! I told the general, with the greatest respect, that I thought I could do him a greater service by making those aspirations better known to the various elements of the Resistance inside France.'

'If he even knows the Resistance exists,' said Sabre.

'I don't think that's fair comment. We all know that last June the general sent a goodwill message to the whole Resistance. It was published in three of our clandestine newspapers, including *Combat*. We know he promised a better future for France after the war, with new men as her leaders, beginning with the election by *universal* suffrage of a new national assembly to take the place of the old Chambre des Députés.'

'Thanks to men like Pineau and Brossolette,' growled Sabre. 'They dragged those concessions out of him. It still doesn't mean de Gaulle understands the moral force of the Resistance, nor its military potential. Can you tell us if he's putting any pressure on the British to send us arms?'

'Sabre has a point there,' said Jacques. 'So far they've only sent us propaganda. Five hours' prime time on the B.B.C. for the Free French every day, and a huge allocation for Colonel Passy's secret service!'

Charles Maxwell listened fascinated to the wordy argument which followed. He now knew exactly why he had been warned never to become involved in French political discussions. His orders had been to pay Couteau and get out of Nice, but at the same time he was getting a lesson from an expert in how to command an unexpected storm. César did not raise his voice. He made no emotional appeal to *la patrie en danger*, such as Jacques had used in the law courts, in easy conversational tones he simply asked to be allowed to finish what he had to say.

'We mustn't underestimate the value of propaganda, either at home or abroad,' he said. 'A lecture tour in the United States, undertaken by the right man, would be of great value to our cause, and when I heard his eloquent pleading in the Palais de Justice today, it struck me that our friend Captain Jack would be just the man for the job. And as for the secret service, we must remember that Colonel Passy has the complete support and confidence of the general. Passy's a genius in his own right! At his new offices in Duke Street, he's set up a remarkable filing system, with thousands of cards in a series of metal cabinets. Each card is the key to a separate dossier for each recruit, each sympathiser, or each enemy of Fighting France. Passy uses squares of colour to indicate the degree of each person's resistance or collaboration, so that every dossier is a study in depth of the subject's political affiliations, religion and sexual proclivities. Colonel Passy—'

'Has this man Passy got *our* names in his files?'

César smiled. 'I should think it's highly probable. But let's go back to what Sabre was saying about arms. Believe me, the general is fully aware of the need to arm the Resistance. For some time past he's been planning the organisation of a secret army, a guerilla army if you like, but placed under military discipline, which will rise when he gives the signal in support of an Allied landing. Of course that will only be possible if *all* the Resistance groups, without reference to political distinctions, are prepared to recognise General de

Gaulle as their only leader. That's what I've been working on since I came back to France.'

'César's energy has been fantastic,' Canif came in on cue, 'Tell them what you told me last night – about the Communists.'

'I'm glad to say the Communist *"Front National"* came into line,' said César modestly. 'They're willing to accept de Gaulle. So will *"Combat"*, the group I joined myself after I left Vichy, which I'm sure Captain Jack is about to mention. So will *"Libération"*, both north and south. When I was in Paris recently I contacted groups in the civil service and among the intellectuals who realise that de Gaulle is the leader our unhappy country needs. So, gentlemen, I hope you'll decide to add the "Knife" group to the growing majority.'

There was some tepid applause. César looked round the table and knew he hadn't carried them yet, by any means. Canif and Epée were on his side, Sabre and Fleuret against, Couteau wavering, and two uncommitted. He guessed that the mention of the Communists had scared them, as it usually did. And then there was Brunel—

Who said, 'I agree with Canif that César has been extremely energetic. I'm sure the story of his adventures will give a great boost to the myth-making machine at Carlton Gardens. But what he's really asked us to do – I mean asking you, because I'm not one of the "Knife" circuit myself – is to prepare the way for de Gaulle's return to France as the head of the government, if not the head of state – which will come later.'

A chorus of protests drowned César's expostulations. De Gaulle, he said, wanted nothing but the liberation of France and the defeat of the Axis Powers. He had no personal ambitions – he was a patriot and a soldier above all else.

'All right then, let him do some fighting,' said Jacques. 'And against the Axis Powers, for a change. All he's done so far is attack his fellow-countrymen.'

'That's a gross exaggeration!'

'What about Dakar? What about Syria? De Gaulle signed an agreement with Churchill that the Free French would never be required to take up arms against France. He broke it before two months were out. He'd have attacked in Madagascar too, like a shot, if the British had given him a chance. He'll attack us across the Channel tomorrow, if the Allies risk taking him along when they open the second front. Or is he planning to fight at the head of the secret army?'

'Jack!' César's patience was beginning to wear thin. 'You've been a soldier, you held a commission, you must know something about the chain of command. Why do you harp on Dakar and Syria? Why don't you acknowledge how bravely the Free French fought the Italians at Koufra, and covered themselves with glory at Bir Hakeim?'

'Koufra was only a skirmish round an oasis, and at Bir Hakeim Koenig's men held Rommel up for a few days, no more, on the perimeter of his march to Tobruk. You can't pretend Bir Hakeim was another Austerlitz, and what else is there? Look at Sabre!' said Jacques, moved to make a sudden gesture across the table. 'He was in the defence of Menton, the battle that lasted fourteen days and was still going on when Pétain had surrendered and de Gaulle was broadcasting from London. Sabre! You knew my friend Lieutenant Gros, who held the outwork of the Pont St. Louis with eight men, and never gave in until it was all over at Bordeaux. We both knew the men who held the blockhouse at Cap Martin, and stopped the Italians on the road to Nice. There were as many heroes in the Armée des Alpes as there were at Bir Hakeim, but nobody ever heard of *them* on the B.B.C.'

'He's right,' said Fleuret, and César saw that the emotional Sabre was very close to tears. He searched for words to break the spell of silence. But it was Jacques Brunel himself who rose and said, 'Charles wants to have a private word with you, Couteau. And after that I'm going to see him to the station. If you take my advice you won't hang around here much longer. Ten of us in one room, and known to be here by about a dozen more! Do you realise that if the Gestapo were to raid us now, they'd have the biggest haul of resisters since the Germans shot the fifty hostages at Nantes?'

5

When the train left for Cannes, Jacques Brunel walked back to his office down the broad, tree-lined avenue which was one of the main arteries of Nice. In the blue November twilight, with a wind blowing off the sea like the forerunner of another mistral, the city had lost some of its noontime animation, although the cafés were as full as usual; some of them had coke braziers burning behind the glass fronts stretching halfway across the pavement. Brunel and the young British agent had found time for a long talk in the warmth of a similar brazier on the terrace of the Café Terminus.

There were larger iron braziers at some of the street corners, where the chestnut vendors were twisting hot chestnuts into three-cornered paper packets for the boys and girls coming out of school. The smell of the chestnuts and the sound of lively young voices gave the avenue a feeling of cheerfulness which evaporated in the Place Masséna, where the male figure of the Statue to the Sun, with horses on its head and at its feet, glimmered white in the last light of the day. Jacques went down the Rue de l'Opéra and back through the empty market, where the street cleaners had already cleared away cabbage leaves and flower stalks, to the beginning of the familiar warren of the Old Town.

The Rue Barillerie, behind the parallel to the Cours Saleya, had none of the colour and vivacity of his own Rue Droite. It was little more than an alley, filled with the garbage cans of the market restaurants on one side, and boasting some shabby shops of a utilitarian sort on the other. Here was a locksmith's with keys in its grimy windows which might have fitted the locks of the Bastille, a paint shop, and, open to the street, a *tôlerie*, or sheet-iron shed, with a few rusty stoves on the pavement. Here was also a small garage, or more correctly a motor workshop, where Jacques Brunel kept his 1938 Peugeot.

Henri Froment, who owned the workshop and did a far bigger trade than its unpromising exterior suggested, was one of the six-man Resistance group which Jacques led in Nice. The others were Paul, the policeman who had alarmed Charles Maxwell in the Palais de Justice; Louis, a ticket agent at the main railway station; a clerk in the Préfecture de Police; and Daniel Profetti, who kept a bar of doubtful reputation on the Rue Paradis, and whose son Dany was to appear before the Fifth Chambre Correctionnelle on Monday. Jacques considered that Henri, the *garagiste*, and Profetti, an amateur forger, were the two most useful members of his Nice detachment.

'*Bonsoir, mon capitaine,*' said Henri, coming out of the dimly-lit back premises and touching Jacques' elbow with his own in token of a shake from his grimy hand, 'ready for the road tomorrow?'

'Yes, if the car's all right.'

'I got a new set of spark-plugs from a pal of mine in the Place Garibaldi, they should do a bit of good.'

'New tyres are what she really needs,' said the Peugeot's owner. 'How about petrol? I was down to five litres.'

'The tank's full, and I put two extra bidons in the back.'

'Good work, Henri. I'll pay for that now.' He counted out the notes. Buying illicit petrol was Brunel's only transaction on the black market, and he was not ashamed of it. The car was his best means of keeping in touch with his groups outside the city.

Henri put the money in the pocket of his blue boiler suit and asked when the car was wanted in the morning.

'Not before eleven, Henri. I've got a lot of work to do first.'

'It's your day for seeing *madame vot' mère*, isn't it? Give her my best respects.'

'Thanks, I will. She often asks for you.'

'She's a real lady.' Henri moved a little closer to Jacques, just as the street light came on from the wall above the garage. The dingy lamplight fell across his balding head and square, reliable face, the face Jacques remembered from the harbour at Namsos on the last day of the evacuation, with blood upon it where there was only a streak of black grease now.

'Are you going straight home, *mon capitaine*?'

'I'm going back to the office for an hour first. Why? What's up?'

'Paul came by when he was going back on duty. He says they're going to do a real round-up tonight, house to house, spot check for papers, the lot.'

'In the Old Town?'

'No, Carabacel.'

'That's all right, then.'

'You'll walk slap into them if you go across the square.'

'I'll go round the other way. Thanks, Henri. See you to-morrow.'

He went away as quietly as the market cats lurking near the garbage cans of the desolate street, moved right at the little square where the potted chrysanthemums had been on sale in the morning, and turned into the Rue de la Préfecture. He saw at once that Paul's warning had been timely, for the street itself was lined with police vans as far along as the Bureau des Etrangers, and with a sideways glance he counted eight or ten more in the Place du Palais de Justice. As he walked circumspectly westward he saw the policemen getting aboard, and what was ominous, a score of men in a different uniform waiting to get aboard with them. Black berets, gaiters, gauntlets, worn by the militiamen as yet not often seen in the streets of Nice : if the

Milice was on the job it was one more of the day's indications, which began with the blacked-out train entering the tunnel under the 'excisemen's path' at Cap Martin, that the authorities of the Unoccupied Zones were beginning to be nervous. One or two of the policemen boarding the nearest van looked in his direction, and saluted as they recognised the well-known and respectable figure of Maître Jacques Brunel. He reached the door on the north side of the Place where his name, followed by the words '*Avocat au Barreau de Nice*', was displayed on a brass plate. There was a glimmer of light behind the blind of his own office, which was on the second floor.

'What, are you still here, Monsieur Bosio?' The old clerk, half asleep in a chair beside the little anthracite stove, got unsteadily to his feet.

'I didn't know when to expect you back,' he said in the accusing tone he often used to Jacques. 'Someone has to stay in the office, even if it's seven o'clock at night—'

'It's barely half past six,' said Jacques. 'Maître Pastorelli's gone home, has he?'

'Certainly, and I locked up his office. He told me to go home too, you'd better go on home, Bosio, he said, but then all that racket began outside, and I said to myself, I'm better off inside than out if there's a *razzia* on—'

'It's only a routine check,' said Jacques, lifting a corner of the blind, 'and they're on the way to wherever it is now—'

'It's Carabacel,' said the old man, who was quite as well informed as Paul or Henri. 'Bothering honest folk at their supper, it hadn't ought to be allowed. Monsieur Profetti's solicitor was here at five,' he continued with a change of tone, 'he asked to see you tomorrow afternoon about the character witnesses. I told him he'd better come at nine, was that right?'

'Quite right, Bosio, thanks. Is that the only message?'

'There's a telegram from the young lady in Toulouse. And the letters in your basket.'

76

'I'll have a look at them, and then I'm going to go over the papers in the Profetti case. Don't you hang around any longer, Bosio. I'm just as capable of locking up as you are.'

When the old clerk grumbled himself away Jacques opened the window from the top as he watched his safe progress across the now empty square. He let the wind from the sea freshen the room before he lowered the blind again. Bosio's devotion to the anthracite stoves made the rooms abominably stuffy in the afternoons; both Jacques and Maître Pastorelli complained about it. He removed his overcoat and switched on the desk lamp. He read Marie Angèle Thibaud's ecstatic telegram of thanks with a smile, went through the business letters, and drew the Profetti dossier resolutely towards him.

He wondered how the police were doing in their house-to-house search through the humble Carabacel district, and how many suspects they would hunt down in the workers' tenements. He was glad young Maxwell had got safely away before the *razzia* began. Jacques pictured the boy arriving at Cannes, marching off with his wonderful sense of direction towards the route de Fréjus, just as he, Jacques, had walked in despair on a September night two years before. Alison Grant had been killed in England only a few weeks earlier, and her ghost walked with him through the streets of Cannes as if she had risen from the common grave where he had seen her laid with the other victims of the German bomb. He had only spoken of Alison once since he came back to France, when in a moment of weakness he had told Fabienne Leroux about the Scots girl with whom he had been happy. Today, for the first time, he had heard Alison's name on the lips of a man who knew her brother and his wife, the Neil and Lucy of that lost summer, and the memories already growing fainter had all come back to him.

Jacques had nothing tangible to remind him of Alison. Not a photograph, not a present, not a letter : she had gone out of his life as quickly as she entered it on the day she came into the French wards at Dykefaulds with comforts for the wounded men from Norway. Now he remembered walking with her in a flowery English lane, taking her to lunch at a French restaurant in London, picking fruit in her brother's garden only an hour before she went to her death – all the tender images growing blurred in a life increasingly harsh and dry, unsoftened by bought sex or simple affection, and vanishing at once when the office telephone rang.

The sound jarred unmercifully on his overwrought nerves. Jacques let it go on for a minute while he forced himself back from the past to actuality, and then picked up the old-fashioned handset with a mechanical *'Allô! J'écoute!'* There was nothing to be heard but a slight thrumming of the wire. He gave his number, and waited again. He heard a soft click at the other end. The caller had the wrong number, or thought better of the call, and either way it didn't matter. The spell was broken, the memories of the past receded, and Jacques wearily went back to work.

To get a suspended sentence for Dany Profetti, eighteen years old, juvenile delinquent and potential criminal, would demand not only an eloquent barrister, but as many character witnesses as the defence could call. The young hooligan had run amok in the Madeleine quarter, breaking windows and terrorising peaceable citizens, robbing a grocer's till with threats of violence and finally resisting the police in the execution of their duty. Jacques intended to present Dany as the victim of society, overcome by his country's surrender and in need of the army discipline which in normal days would have been his lot at this time of his life – and he was sure that his argument was not entirely mendacious. There was good stuff in Dany Profetti. Two and a half years earlier he would have fought as well at Namsos as Jean Dupont or Henri : two years from now, when the Resistance had stopped arguing about de Gaulle and passed to the attack, he might be as good a soldier as the men Jacques had recruited in the mountain villages, waiting with the old guns hidden in the thatch or beneath the tiles for the order to rise and strike. Dany had to be brought safely off on Monday, if only because his father was an expert at forging the papers needed in a hurry for men at the end of their tether, on the run.

He heard two of the police vans come back to the Place du Palais de Justice – which surely meant a short *razzia* in the quarter called Carabacel – and the sound of heavy footsteps and heavy grumbling voices, before he heard the front door bell. It jarred him as the telephone had done, and he remembered too late that he had fastened neither the bolt nor the chain after Bosio went home. But it was not a police ring, it was too soft, and not followed by a hammering on the panels. He went quietly into the lobby and said, 'Who's there?'

'César.'

Jacques pulled the door open. 'Come in,' he said, 'I was half expecting you.'

'You were?' They were in the office now, and César was warming his hands at the chilling stove.

'That was you on the telephone, wasn't it, about twenty minutes ago?'

'I wanted to make sure you were in, Brunel.'

'You must be crazy to come here at all. Couldn't you see the police in the Place du Palais? Or the vans in the Rue de la Préfecture?'

'I'm sorry if I've broken through your precious rules of security. I felt I had to see you before leaving Nice.'

Jacques leaned wearily against the door. 'Oh God!' he said. 'What is it now? What have we possibly got to say to one another?'

'May I sit down?'

Jacques motioned him into the client's chair. César sat down, still with the brown overcoat buttoned to the neck, and looked up at him with an attempt at a smile.

'I want to say I made a bad mistake today,' he said. 'I should have come to see you earlier. I tried to reach you last night – of course you were meeting Charles – and when

Fabienne Leroux showed me the court list in this morning's paper, I thought it would be interesting to hear you plead. I never dreamed you had such power.'

Jacques shrugged. 'It was an open and shut case,' he said.

'You're thrown away on a courtroom in the provinces, you must know that. After the war you could have a great future in Paris.'

'You're the second person to tell me that today. Not about Paris, but about the limitations of provincial justice.'

'Who was the other? Not Couteau?'

'The man who just arrived from London.'

'That kid? I wouldn't have thought he had that much discrimination.'

'Then you under-estimated him. I thought he handled himself well this afternoon, in rather difficult circumstances.'

'But he looked very uneasy. I suppose he's telling his troubles to de Valbonne now. You hustled him out fast enough, but you were right, of course. There *were* too many of us in one room, and I don't suppose "Le Faisan" is a hundred per cent safe.'

'The British are always warning us about the need to de-centralise the groups.'

'We don't have to take all our orders from the British, do we?'

'Only all our money.'

The bitter words stirred Renaudon to exasperation at last. 'Can't we talk for five minutes without a quarrel?' he exclaimed. 'All I'm trying to say is that if I'd seen you alone, before the "Knife" group met, I might have been able to explain a few things you seem to have misunderstood. Then probably the meeting would have gone better than it did. As it was you excited Sabre. He raved on after you left about the sacrifice of Menton and the heroism of the Armée des Alpes, till in the end we left with nothing settled. No promise of allegiance to the general – nothing.'

'So what will you do now?'

César smiled again. 'Couteau has invited me to dine and

sleep at Cimiez tonight,' he said. 'I think I'll manage to talk him round.'

'You're going to spend the night at the Villa des Oliviers? How are you going to get up there?'

'He'll have a car waiting at the Orengo warehouse. Why? What's the matter?'

'Those villas above the old arenas are too conspicuous to be safe. And the street where Couteau lives ends in a cul-de-sac.'

'I'm touched, Brunel.' César laughed softly. 'After so much hostility this afternoon, I didn't think you'd care a damn for what became of me.'

'I'm not hostile to you, Renaudon. Only to the man you say you represent.'

'Only to General de Gaulle. It's his point of view I want to put before you – if you care to listen.'

'Carry on.' Jacques pulled out his own chair from behind the desk and mechanically offered cigarettes. He was aware that Alain Renaudon, alias César, had manoeuvred him into a position where he had to listen, short of throwing the man out. Short of throwing him into the hands of the police, now coming back from the Carabacel quarter in a mood to interrogate any solitary person crossing the Place du Palais. He was being seduced, as others had been before him, by Renaudon's sheer animal vitality and extraordinary charm of manner. In his twenties Jacques had been very susceptible to charm in a woman : charm in a man he viewed with real disgust. No allowance had been made for charm in the statutes of the Code Napoléon, which it was his duty to interpret and apply.

'I must admit,' the charmer began, 'that General de Gaulle has made some serious mistakes in the past two years. He's been churlish to the British and gone out of his way to annoy the Americans, and some of the men closest to him are not the best of advisers. Not that he cares to take advice from anyone. But' – he hurried on, seeing that Jacques was about to speak – 'what seems to worry you most

81

is the interpretation of that clause in the 1940 Agreement which says that his forces will never be required to take up arms against France. You spoke this afternoon of his actions at Dakar and in Syria—'

'His making war *on Frenchmen*, Renaudon.'

'Does it ever occur to you, my dear Brunel, that for de Gaulle the men of Vichy, and their armed forces, are *not* Frenchmen?'

'What are they then? Subhumans?'

'In his mind, rightly or wrongly, there's only one France, the France which follows him. That clause in the Agreement means that since Vichy is not France his followers are free to take up arms against Vichy anywhere.'

'*La France, c'est Moi!*' said Jacques, and the other man flicked off his cigarette ash with a little disclaiming gesture. 'The Agreement was made personally, between Mr. Churchill and the general,' he said. 'I've heard it whispered around Carlton Gardens that a secret treaty was made at the same time, accepting General de Gaulle's definition of the word *France*.'

'Nothing Mr. Churchill does where that man is concerned would surprise me now,' said Jacques. 'But if it happens to be true, it doesn't make matters any better. My job is to interpret the very letter of the law; a secret understanding is inadmissable evidence, and an understanding which defines two races of Frenchmen, the master race in London and the outcasts here in France, is so like Hitler's *Herrenvolk* that it makes a nonsense of our fight for freedom.'

'But at present you're not fighting, Brunel, you're only temporising.'

'I didn't temporise at Namsos, when you were on the road to Vichy. If what you say about a secret understanding with Churchill is correct, then de Gaulle must believe himself to be above the law, and that he isn't. He stands condemned to death for desertion by a military court – *in absentia*, that goes without saying. How d'you think he would fare in a civil court if he were tried for treason?'

'By God!' said Renaudon, 'I believe you *want* to see him tried for treason – with yourself as prosecuting counsel!'

'I wouldn't qualify,' said Jacques. 'He would be tried by the High Court in Paris, and the *procureur de la République* would prosecute. However, I don't imagine it's come to that. If and when the Allies bring de Gaulle back to France, nobody will dare accuse him of treason. They'll be too busy incriminating the collaborators.'

Renaudon lifted the lid in the top of the anthracite stove and dropped the butt of his cigarette into the embers. 'You're a hard nut to crack,' he said. 'I'm sorry we're not to have you with us. Dare I hope that at least you won't come out against us?'

'I'll come out against de Gaulle's candidates in the Alpes Maritimes whenever we hold the free democratic elections that he's promised. All that his programme amounts to so far is Fascism without a doctrine : a corporate state, a mono-lithic leadership, a vendetta against the old parliamentary parties of the Third Republic. It doesn't sound like a posi-tive policy for the renewal of France.'

'Ah yes,' said Renaudon, getting to his feet. 'You had political ambitions of your own, not so very long ago, hadn't you?'

'I'm sure that's included in Colonel Passy's filing system.'

'It may be; I didn't look to see. Passy's only doing his duty, according to his lights . . . It seems to be quiet enough outside now.'

Jacques drew the blind aside again. A few street lamps cast a faint glow over the empty vans. 'If you mean to risk it, now's the time. But tell me this before you go. You've hinted more than once – oh! very discreetly, but I can take a hint as well as the next man – that my political ambitions, and whatever I may be as a barrister, would all be rewarded under de Gaulle's régime. What sort of reward have you in mind for yourself?'

Renaudon spoke without hesitation. 'I'd like to be his prime minister.'

'The prime minister of a Gaullist France. You don't think your wings might drop off if you fly too near the sun? You're a faithful servant of the general now : isn't it possible he might find you a dangerous rival?'

'What the devil do you mean?'

'I mean that you seem to have been received with open arms at Carlton Gardens and that new place, what's its name, in Duke Street. Put on the payroll, told all the secrets, sent back to France on a special, top level mission—'

'What then?'

'Could it be that you're not expected to return from your mission? Isn't a man who took the oath of allegiance to the Marshal a slight embarrassment at Carlton Gardens?'

Renaudon smiled, and laid his hand on the door knob. 'You don't understand,' he said. 'Remember what we learned in our sacred studies class at the Ecole des Roches? I assure you that there is more joy at Carlton Gardens over one sinner that repenteth, than over ninety and nine just men.'

6

Madame Theophile Brunel, born Marguerite Verbier, stopped her little Simca on the mountain road and looked down the Val de Gorbio to the sea. She had always loved the valleys more than the seashore : ever since she came to the Côte d'Azur as a bride of twenty, happy but sometimes homesick for Paris, her great pleasure had been to take the long rambling walks and rides on donkeyback which people enjoyed in those days, to gather a bouquet from the profusion of wild flowers and the carpet of violets which lay on each side of the mountain tracks. Now it was November, not the violet season, but the peasants' cottages with the red tiles were there just as they used to be, and their gardens were rich with winter roses and convolvulus. There were lemon trees planted in terraces, with here and there an orange tree laden with bright fruit, and she could see old men and women working between new rows of lettuce and tomato. The Val de Gorbio was perhaps the most fertile of the four valleys which ran from Menton into the foothills of the Maritime Alps and up to the little old fortress villages which had once defended the land against the Saracens. Now the land had been conquered by a different enemy, but the fruits of the soil came forth after their season, and the inhabitants, so stubborn and patient under their exuberance, waited in silence for their deliverance.

Madame Brunel was not often alone. When her busy life offered her a breathing space like this, she was content to sit in her little car with the windows rolled down, basking in the winter sunshine, and quite deliberately counting her blessings. It became more of an effort with every month the world war lasted, as the gulf widened between the woman she was and the girl she had been. It was growing hard to remember the Marguerite Verbier who had been young in the Paris of the *belle époque*, inseparable from her pretty cousin Rose, without a care in the world beyond the problems of their first flirtations and the filling up of dance programmes. Rose had been dead for years, heartbroken by the death of her husband in the great battle of Douaumont. Marguerite had been the lucky one. Her husband came home safe from the Other War, her son came back alive from Norway, and her daughter Marcelle, with her husband and their little girl, was living happily in the tranquil village of Oradour-sur-Glâne. It was wrong to repine because Menton was under Italian occupation. She and Théo were not molested in their own home in the charming suburb of Garavan. They were in good health and had enough to eat. Even the Italian occupants were less aggressive since over one hundred thousand of their comrades in arms had surrendered to the British in the African desert.

The patrols on the Occupation frontier, towards which her Simca was headed, were increasingly lenient towards the French people who gathered on each side of the barbed wire to talk to their relatives and friends.

It was even more wrong, or so Madame Brunel often told herself, to worry about her son Jacques, at a time when two million young Frenchmen were prisoners of war in Germany. Her boy had recovered from his wounds and was following his chosen profession; his mother was proud to know – from what little he had told her at Oradour – that he had also chosen to work for the Resistance. He was living in his own home, quite comfortably she believed, although Madame Brunel had never liked the Palais Lascaris or the gloomy flat on the third floor where she had paid so many duty visits to cantankerous old Grand'tante Marthe. Delighted that the visits had paid off, leaving his son with what any French bourgeois would think *une belle propriété*, Maître Brunel called his wife ridiculous for wishing that Jacques had a more cheerful place to live in, and a nice young wife to share it with him. How could a satisfactory marriage contract be drawn up in these times, said the solicitor, but Madame Brunel felt that young people were still marrying in occupied Menton, where the narrow streets of the Old Town were jammed with baby carriages. Dear Jacques – something had gone wrong somewhere, some spring of feeling had been broken at the moment of France's defeat and surrender, and she could only grieve silently as her good-natured, clever boy turned into a harsh embittered man.

She switched on the car engine, and drove slowly down towards the Gorbio highway. It was a good road now, for the Italians had been working on it, whereas the road by which she had come was no better than one of the old cart tracks leading up to the ancient villages of Peille and Ste. Agnès, and also to the sanatorium where Madame Brunel did four days' voluntary work each week. She had always been actively interested in the children's colonies and fresh-air homes in the hills above Menton, though only as a lady patroness and organiser of charity fairs. Since the Occupation, and the shortage of staff, she had given her services as a nurses' aide, glad of the hard work which tired her out and made her sleep without dreaming of Paris in German hands and obscure dangers waiting for her children. The Italians gave her a special petrol allowance for this work, which helped her to make an occasional trip to the Occupation frontier. At fifty-three, she didn't think she had the energy to cycle all the way to the Gorbio road from Garavan.

Madame Brunel backed the little car carefully into a yard where five hens were pecking at a mess of boiled potato peelings and bread crusts, behind a cottage almost at the junction of the roads. She had struck up an acquaintance-ship with the owner, whom she always heard addressed as *monsieur le fontanier* and believed to be a retired employé of the municipal waterworks, the days being long past when the women of Menton drew their water from the public fountains. There was a group of people on the other side of the wire whom she often saw there : three from the Menton side and two with a baby from the free side, so far as any place in the Unoccupied Zone of France was free. She had never worked out their relationships, for they were always agitated, laughing and crying and talking at the pitch of their voices, but she waved to them all, her companions in misfortune, after she locked the car and went as close as she could to the barbed wire.

Marguerite Brunel was a tall woman, with fair hair tucked under a plain felt hat, and though she was growing broad in the beam her pre-war coat and skirt, tailormade in Paris, still clipped her neatly at the waist. The Italian patrols approved of her. They were sentimental about motherhood, and one of them actually shouted down the valley path to let her son know *la mamma* had arrived. Jacques quickened his pace. He had come scrambling up the line of the Gorbio, sometimes through undergrowth, and sometimes skirting the peasants' gardens, until he emerged on the road at the junction of the way to Peille. There the slovenly sentries were always ready to accept a few coins to spend at the country wineshop higher up the hill, where they spent most of their time.

Jacques came running up to greet his mother, slim and quick in a thin tweed suit, and hatless, so that she smiled at the lock of dark hair which sometimes fell across his brow, but as he came up to the wire she saw by his sunken dark eyes that he had been going short of sleep.

'*Maman chérie!*' It was impossible to kiss, and unwise to try to shake hands between the strands of barbed wire, because the one thing the Italians dreaded was the passing of some contraband object from one person to another. They could only smile their assurance of a deep and shared affection, and each said immediately how well the other was looking. Jacques passed on Henri Froment's respectful message.

'And how's my father?'

'Fit and busy, and eager to know how the Thibaud case came out.'

'The eviction order was granted, of course. There was no problem, once Mademoiselle Thibaud made up her mind to go to law.'

'Poor girl. Your father says she should be grateful to you.'

What the solicitor had actually said was, 'If Jacques has any sense he'll keep in touch with that young lady, and pay his addresses to her as soon as the war's over. In spite of her embezzling trustees she must be the best-endowed *partie* between Menton and Toulose.'

She looked forward to telling him Jacques was so little interested in courting an heiress that he started to give her some details of the Profetti case, because he was aware that his father was greedy for news from the Palais de Justice. But Madame Brunel had news of her own to give, and interrupted him :

'That's marvellous, darling, I'm sure you'll get the poor boy off,' she said. 'But Jacques, do listen, something quite

88

out of the ordinary has happened.' She looked quickly at the Italian guard, who had lost interest in them, and was marching up the road with a great show of authority to chivvy the group at *le fontanier's* door.

'What is it, maman?'

'You remember I told you about the contingent of Italian children who were coming to the sanatorium at the end of October?'

'The bombed-out kids? Of course I remember.'

'Three *monitrices*, or nurses' aides I suppose you could call them, brought the children up from Naples. Naturally I thought they'd all be Italians. But one of them turned out to be American.'

'What's an American girl doing in Naples? Is she married to an Italian?'

'Oh no, she's not married. Her stepfather, who died a few months ago, was an Italian, quite a rich man, I believe. This girl's been doing welfare work among the children, and she was sent along with the sanatorium party to be with them for a few weeks until they settled down. Now she's decided that she wants to stay in France.'

'Much good that'll do her,' said Jacques. 'Why didn't her mother ship her back to the States while the going was good?'

'The mother died about a year ago, before America came into the war.'

'Was *she* an American?'

'No, her first husband was an American. She was Russian, and a widow when he married again.'

'That's quite a three-ring circus,' said Jacques. 'But the girl claims to be an American?'

'She *is* American, and the poor little thing feels she's living in an enemy country.' Madame Brunel looked wistfully at her son. 'I thought you might help her to get out.'

'Out of the sanatorium?'

'She's left there already. She's staying with Madame Belinska now.'

'How does Madame Belinska come into it?' said Jacques patiently.

'She was a friend of Pauline's mother, before the Other War, in St. Petersburg.'

Pauline, a pretty name. 'D'you mean this girl just walked out of the sanatorium and went to the Baroness Belinska at Carnolès? That sounds more like a White Russian than an American to me.'

'They gave her a travel warrant for Naples via Genoa, and I drove her down myself to Carnolès.'

'*You* drove her down, while they thought you were taking her to the station? Mother, I wish you hadn't got yourself mixed up in it! When was this, exactly?'

'Thursday afternoon.'

'So your girl's been with the baroness for two whole days. Does my father know?'

'Good heavens no, of course not. What could he do to help? But you could help, darling, I'm sure you could. And Madame Belinska's very anxious to consult you about it. Couldn't you cross over tonight and give poor little Pauline your advice?'

'I'll advise her to go home to her Italian friends and stay there,' said Jacques. 'How much better off does she think she'll be in France?'

Madame Brunel sighed. 'Please, Jacques,' she said. 'It's the first time I've ever asked you to do anything for me since we were at Oradour. You've helped so many people on their way to freedom; won't you try to do something for a girl nobody wants to help at all?'

The Italians were clearing the road in front of the *fontanier's* cottage, and one of them shouted to Jacques to come away from the barbed wire. He could hear their angry words to the French people with the baby. They were restless and edgy, like the Nice police the night before, and Jacques felt a sudden fury at the helplessness of his countrymen. It tilted the balance of his caution to an oblique desire for revenge.

'All right,' he said. 'I'll cross tonight and have a word

with your young friend. On your way home this afternoon, you might go round by the Alexandra and tell the baroness I'll try to be with her before seven, and then you drive home to Garavan and stay there. I don't want you to be out on the roads after dark.'

'But I hoped you and I could meet at Madame Belinska's and have some time together. It's months since we had a proper talk!'

Her son's heart smote him as he saw her disappointed look. 'I wish we could,' he said, 'but it really isn't wise. Stay at home with father and try not to worry. Leave it to old lady Belinska and me to sort out. Damnation, they're going to move us on already' – as the Italian soldiers came threateningly towards them – 'all right, *signori*, we're going now. *Au revoir, p'tite maman*, give my love to my father. And drive carefully!' he called as she turned away.

Madame Brunel did not look round or wave. Jacques knew she had tears in her eyes when their brief meetings ended, and for him too there was something pathetic in the sight of that figure, no longer elegant, and the knob of faded fair beneath the felt hat, as his mother walked back to the Peille road and her car. He watched her drive away before he started back through the lemon terraces to the valley floor and made for Carnolès, where his own car was parked. He was quite oblivious of the sunshine and the crystal air, or of the beauty of the Val de Gorbio, where the autumn leaves of the cherry trees stained with red the long hill on the Roquebrune side. His over-riding mood was one of exasperation. For a man who disapproved of women in war he was in a three-cornered trap of femininity, caught between his mother, the Baroness Belinska – an old White Russian who was one of his father's most demanding clients – and a total stranger on the run from Italy. Jacques swore aloud as he reached his car and started picking burrs and trails of bramble from his clothes.

For an active young man, crossing the armistice frontier was not a serious problem. The Italians were unable to guard it all, even with barbed wire and barriers, and they were bound by the agreement to keep out of the demilitarised zone which ran west for fifty kilometres and included the city of Nice. Jacques, with his car keys in his hand, looked back appraisingly at the guards lounging round the big red and white pole which hung on hinges across the road. They were Bersaglieri in theatrically feathered hats, looking to the Frenchman like spear-carriers in a comic opera. He knew better than to underestimate them, however, because they knew that the punishment for lack of vigilance would be a posting to the Russian front, where Italians under German command were dying in the snow outside Kiev.

Jacques drove west through Carnolès. It had once been an independent lordship, fought over by the Lascaris and the Grimaldi : there was now a cluster of shops round the square where the Tree of Justice had stood and the princes met their people at its foot. If the war ever ended, the city of Menton might stretch its suburbs out to include Carnolès, but at present there were only a few villas and orchards surrounded by tall canes along the road down to the shore of the Mediterranean. The sea was calm and blue, for the wind had fallen overnight, and the sun was high. Ahead of him, at the entrance to Cap Martin, there was a desolation of fallen masonry, a memorial to the twenty-third of June in 1940, after France had surrendered, when the French defenders of the blockhouse further up the hill were resisting still. Several of the pretty villas had been destroyed as the Italians bracketed to find the range, but the blockhouse was impregnable : there, at that very point, the Italians had been halted on their victorious march to Nice by the sacrifice of Menton and by the soldiers of the Armée des Alpes.

He followed the road along which a tramcar had once meandered between Menton and Nice, and came to crossroads, just beyond the white-walled Mairie, where since time immemorial a little settlement had existed round an ancient Roman tomb. There Jacques entered an old-fashioned café behind a tall hedge, nodded to the woodcutter and two of the men who worked in the carnation fields through which he had led Charles Maxwell, and asked the landlord for a glass of red wine and something to eat. He kept his own hens, like the *fontanier* on the Gorbio road, and Jacques had the great treat of two new-laid eggs, boiled, and served with a slice of rough country paté on the coarse bread. While he ate, he reviewed all he had to do in the afternoon, and the extreme probability that he would do as his mother asked after darkness fell.

The Resistance group he ran in Cap Martin was not as compact as the group in Nice, for the members were strung out all along the shore of the long commune of Roquebrune. He had left Nice early enough to see two brothers called Carpani, who kept a bicycle shop at St. Roman just outside the Principality of Monaco, before the shop closed at twelve and Jacques went on to meet his mother. He still had three men to see in the immediate neighbourhood, and one of them was a doctor, with whom he intended to spend some time. The sixth member of the group was employed by the gas company at Carsolès, and the best time to see him was when he left the gasworks at the end of his day's work. That would bring Jacques back to Carnolès after dark, not a mile from where Baroness Belinska and an unknown girl would be waiting for him to appear.

A week earlier he would have flatly refused to have anything to do with the escapade of some silly girl, half Russian and half American of all unlikely things, who wanted to get out of the frying-pan of Naples and into the fire of Unoccupied France. He would have scolded his mother for having been the accomplice of her departure from the sanatorium, and told her to make the chit either go back to the sick children or home (if she had a home) to Naples. But now he had been softened by the memories of Alison, evoked by his conversation with the boy who knew her family : here was another girl in the clutch of war, who needed the help he would have died to bring to Alison, if Alison in her happy confidence had ever asked for help. He could certainly listen to her story before condemning her to return to Italy.

And if he could help her further that would at least be positive action. Renaudon's taunt had got beneath his skin. 'You're not fighting, you're only temporising' – it was a half truth, and a wounding one. 'Activists' and 'temporisers' were well-known distinctions inside the Resistance, and he liked to think that Jacques Brunel had been as active as the circumstances would allow. It was the long tedium of waiting which in the past months had sapped some of his initiative, only tested by the unexpected emergency after the prison break at Fort de la Revère.

When lunch was over Jacques drove the short distance to Jean Dupont's grocery, where his former corporal beamed at the news of a telephone call from Nestor, saying in guarded terms that their visitor was now safe at the Villa Rivabella. 'Charles was a good guy,' said Dupont. 'When's the next arrival due?'

It was not much further on to the side road leading to Cabbé, where a plumber whose workshop was near the railway station had been keeping an eye on the movements of the trains. A blacked-out train had gone in the direction of Menton every morning before dawn for a week, and he didn't think it was carrying either looted food or military personnel. There were men aboard, and some other watchers who had glimpsed their uniforms thought detachments of the Militia were being brought into the demilitarised area. It was a bad sign. The enemy was on the move, and pray when (said the plumber, who had left-wing views) did the Resistance mean to open a second front to help the Russians?

'We'll have to wait until the Americans give us a lead, it can't be much longer now,' said Jacques, and the plumber retorted sulkily that the Americans were taking their time about it. He was growing impatient, like all the rest of them, and it was no wonder; they had spent two years in doing little more than talk. Jacques said what he could by way of encouragement and went back to the car. The sun was dropping westward over the Dog's Head, and he decided unwillingly that he had no time to visit the mountain villages. The men he trusted there, old soldiers every one of them, were strung out in the peasant cottages between the ancient strongholds of Roquebrune and Gorbio, and could only be reached by tracks where he had to go on foot; that expedition would have to wait until next weekend. Jacques Brunel did everything possible to keep in touch with the hill dwellers, for he believed that when the Allies at last appeared in the South of France the fortress villages would be the natural centres of local uprisings : Eze, Roquebrune, Gorbio, Ste. Agnès, Castillon and Castellar were all strong points in his own plan of attack. His experience of combat had always been in mountain terrain, first in manoeuvres during his basic army training in the Haute Savoie, and then in deadly earnest in the Norwegian campaign, and it was his instinctive belief that one day he would fight again in his own mountains, where the setting sun was now gilding a light powdering of snow on Mont Ste. Agnès and Le Berçeau.

He drove back past the Roman tomb and the Mairie, past the little police station where a faded Tricolore hung limply above the door, to Dr. Alfred Lecampion's villa at the edge of an olive grove. The doctor, a native of Normandy, had spent all his professional life in Indochina, returning from Saigon in 1938 to enjoy his retirement in the sunshine of the Riviera. After the disaster of 1940 he was urged to go back into harness, and now had a thriving practice extending all the way to the armistice frontier. His importance to the Resistance, for the time being, was that as a doctor he was sometimes allowed to cross the frontier and attend an emergency case in Menton. This enabled him to contact the butcher in the Rue Trenca who led the most inaccessible of all the groups recruited by Captain Jack. He was also the only person to whom Jacques could talk freely on the subject of Alain Renaudon, alias César.

Although he was careful, as usual, to be the last person to consult the doctor at his afternoon surgery, a private conversation was not possible at once. Madame Lecampion, who still hankered after the colonial society of Saigon, was flattered that a rising young barrister should come all the way to Cap Martin to consult her husband when there were so many good doctors in Nice, and insisted on his being brought into her little drawing room, stuffed with Indochinese artifacts, for *le five o'clock*. She and Jacques had a standing joke that his time in Britain had given him a taste for afternoon tea, and there was a good deal of play with a silver teapot and a silver cake basket before the lady said she would leave them to their cigars, and carried her tea tray through the door which Jacques held open. Then he was able to tell her husband the story of Renaudon's visit.

'What exactly is it that worries you about him?' said the doctor when the tale came to an end. Dr. Lecampion was a small man, trim and alert like a terrier, and prepared to tackle the problem of Renaudon like a terrier worrying a bone. 'The old tie-up with Vichy? Or the new tie-up with de Gaulle? I shouldn't fret too much about his enthusiasm for *Le Grand Moi* if I were you. The converts are always the greatest zealots – we've seen that in the Church.'

'No, it's not César's conversion to Gaullism I'm worried about. If he'd gone straight to London after he chucked Vichy, I wouldn't have been surprised. If we'd heard of him defying Rommel in person at Bir Hakeim it's just what I'd have expected from the star turn of the Ecole des Roches. It's not even his return to France as de Gaulle's evangelist that scares me, Freddy. It's the way he came!'

'He came through the Occupied Zone, didn't he? I remember the word was passed on when he crossed the Line.'

'Yes, but how did he land?' insisted Jacques. 'Couteau told me when we got him out of the meeting that he came in by Brittany, in order to see his parents. I never heard of any drop in Brittany since the Boches set up the Maritime

Area, twenty-five kilometres deep round the coast. Then César said himself he'd been to Paris. It's reasonable to suppose he saw his wife.'

'I thought they were separated.'

'She certainly went back to her parents when César broke with Vichy. The newspapers made a big thing out of her loyalty to the Marshal, and it seems her father's well known as a collaborationist.'

'I'm afraid that's true enough. My wife's a great reader of the women's magazines, and she says the gossip columns are full of the Marquis de la Rochejacquerie and his lovely daughter Madame Alain Renaudon. They dine at Maxim's with Otto Abetz, the German ambassador, and they sup with General Stülpnagel at the Doge – you know the sort of thing?'

'Well enough,' said Jacques. 'I don't suppose they took César along to Maxim's, but madame hardly seems the right wife for a dedicated Gaullist. Freddy, I'm worried. Who brought him over to France? Who took him to see his *collabo* wife, the toast of the German High Command? Who allowed him to roam freely around the Occupied Zone, at a time when every suspect's rounded up and clapped in prison? Has he been turned round again, and is the great César a V-man?'

'*Vertrauensmann.*' Dr. Lecampion spoke the word softly: it was dreaded throughout the Resistance. A confidential agent of the Germans, infiltrated into any Resistance network, was an agent of death and destruction to its members. And Renaudon knew all the networks now. 'That's a terrible accusation to make,' he said. 'Are you sure you haven't let your prejudice against General de Gaulle affect your judgment of his representative?'

'God knows,' said Jarques. 'That may be so. It's just a feeling I have, that César's brought trouble with him, and that boy from London felt it too. He means to tell Nestor about it – has told him already for all I know.'

'I'd be glad to hear Monsieur de Valbonne's opinion. I'm

going to a medical meeting in Cannes next week; I think I'll call at the Villa Rivabella while I'm there.'

'Would you, Freddy? Then that's a load off my mind . . . You know, I'm beginning to think I'm not cut out for a conspirator. All the aliases and cloak-and-dagger stuff may very well be necessary, but what I want to do is fight in the open. I never told you this, but when General de Lattre came back from North Africa last February and took command of the Sixteenth Military Division at Montpellier, I'd more than half a mind to join him.'

'If the M.O. had passed you *bon pour le service*,' said the doctor shrewdly.

'Wouldn't you?'

'On the strength of the last check-up I gave you, yes.'

'Well, then! But the thought of garrison duty at Montpellier, serving in the Armistice Army, put me off the idea. We'll see what happens when the Americans attack.'

They were back at the perennial theme : when would the Americans attack, and where. At last Jacques stubbed out his cigar and said he must get to Carnolès before Jean-Pierre came off the shift. He had spoken his mind about Alain Renaudon, but he had said nothing to the doctor about the stranger girl who was at Carnolès too.

The gasworks at Carnolès was on a back road running parallel to the promenade, and Jean-Pierre, intercepted near the gate, climbed into the front seat of the Peugeot and sat quietly talking to Jacques in the shadow of the overhanging trees. Along the promenade, which ran from the old Roman road around Cap Martin to the harbour of Menton, there were only a few villas, decorated with plaster flowers and medallions in the Genoese style still popular along the Ligurian shore, but the hinterland was dotted with little cottages each surrounded by a garden or orchard, and in one of those Jean-Pierre, a single man, lived with his mother. He was an equable fellow, less insistent than the others in his group about the need for action, but very proud of having recruited three of his mates to the Resistance side in the past few weeks. Jacques had not the heart to counsel caution, and indeed the idea of a whole Resistance cell inside a key point like the gasworks had a strong appeal.

He was tempted to ask Jean-Pierre to go back with him to the false frontier and wait in the car while he took the risk of going to call on the Baroness Belinska. If he brought that girl back with him it might be a priceless help to have somebody in the driver's seat, ready to get the car away at a second's notice. But he had never asked for help before, and his constant desire not to involve others in any danger kept him silent now. When he started the car Jacques drove through the narrow lanes of landward Carnolès and put Jean-Pierre down at his own garden gate before he went on to the Alexandra Hotel.

This was the name of the residence, now more an apartment building than an hotel, where the Baroness Belinska and a score of other White Russians lived. On the west façade there could be seen by daylight a shield with the three crowns of Sweden and the date 1925, but any association with Sweden had been long forgotten, and the shabby building was known in Carnolès as *la Maison Russe*. Most of the inhabitants were middle-aged when they began their exile on the Côte d'Azur : the young and strong, the remnants of General Wrangel's army, had gone from Constantinople to Paris and a poverty-stricken but active life. Those who huddled in the Maison Russe or shared ramshackle villas in the neighbourhood had grown old, like the Baroness Belinska, living on memories and some vague pensions, with a little white-painted Russian Orthodox church as the centre of their lives. The Italians allowed the church services to continue : they had nothing to fear from a congregation of ghosts.

Jacques heard the sound of chanting from the church when he stopped his car, and remembered that the Saturday evening vesper service would be in progress. He pulled the car round again to face towards Nice, and parked it close to the brick wall of a large garden, under the sweeping branches of a row of neglected evergreens. Watching from the shadows, he saw the red and white barrier balanced across the road, near a nursing home where a blue revolving lamp revealed an ambulance against the kerb. Beyond the church the lamps at the barrier were bright enough to show him the outline of a black Citroën with a Paris licence plate. There was nothing except the make of the car to indicate that it was the property of the Militia, who were accomplices of the Vichy police rather than of the Italian troops, but the many signs that the *miliciens* were infiltrating the area made Jacques proceed with especial caution. He went round the corner into a side road, climbed the brick wall, and dropped down into the garden of the evergreens.

It was large enough to be a small park, and he had never seen lights, nor any sign of life, in the big house it surrounded. He went soft-footed across the grass to the far wall, and there his problems began, for behind the nursing home and the Russian church there was a network of lanes and paths, some of them ending in compost piles belonging to the nursery gardens which supplied the public parks of Menton. Jacques was making for the back entrance to the nurseries, divided by a low wall from a little orange grove guarded, as he knew, by an Alsatian dog which would start barking at the slightest sound. There were three rows of barbed wire on the top of the wall, but he had put the wire cutters he carried in the Peugeot's tool bag into his pocket when he stopped at Cabbé, and it was the work of a moment to snip and roll aside the obstacle. A few metres down a little lane, and he was back on the Gorbio road again.

From where he stood he could see the lights of an Italian army truck, pulled across the intersection, and much too near the service entrance to the Alexandra Hotel. Jacques could see and hear men standing round the truck, but there was no move towards him; he took a deep breath and ran for it, across the road into the narrow lane which led upwards along a muddy path into the grounds of the hotel. A broad terrace, on which the Russian exiles liked to sun themselves, ran round the front and the west side of the building. He saw lights under the blinds of some windows, but no one looked out to challenge his soundless steps along the turf edging of the dilapidated flower beds, and at the far end, up some ornamental steps, there was a door which opened to his touch. The passage beyond was feebly lit and damp, and he halted to get his breath back and smooth down his hair. Madame Belinska's flat was on the ground floor, at the back. He walked towards it through the main hall, which was covered with a threadbare carpet, and where on four previous visits to meet his mother or his father at the Alexandra Hotel he had never seen a living soul. The inhabitants of the Maison Russe were old hands at concealment, and opened their doors for nobody after darkness fell.

This door opened to his gentle knock. Not immediately, for the Baroness Belinska was a heavy, slow-moving old woman who walked with a stick, but he could hear her shuffling into the tiny entrance hall, and presently the door was eased back on the safety chain. Jacques said 'Good evening!' quietly, and heard the chain snapped off. 'Good evening to you, Monsieur Jacques,' said the familiar voice. 'Come in and let me see if you're still all in one piece. You hadn't any trouble getting over?'

'None whatever.' She preceded him into what she called her salon, an overheated parlour stuffed with ikons, ornaments, sepia photographs signed by long-dead Romanovs ('to dear Natalie, Livadia 1912 – Alexandra'), vases of carnations from the Menton market, and a repoussé silver tea service on a brass-topped table from Samarkand. It hadn't changed since the days when Jacques Brunel, a law student at the Sorbonne, went there in the vacations with his father, who helped the baroness with her tiny funds. In the strong light from a central chandelier he could see that she hadn't changed either. She wore, as always, a black velvet caftan under an Oriental shawl. Her thick white hair, greasy with brilliantine, was bound with a filet of the same black velvet. On closer inspection Jacques saw that the caftan was covered with the white hairs shed by an aged Pomeranian bitch, which left her cushion by the log fire to snuffle blindly at his shoes.

'Sit down, Monsieur Jacques,' said Madame Belinska, pointing at the sofa with her amber-handled cane. 'Your mother said you'd forbidden her to come back tonight.'

She was at her old trick of aggression, cutting him down to size with her 'Monsieur Jacques' as if he were still the student of ten years ago, but he was determined not to let her over-ride him. 'I understand you have a visitor, madame,' he said. 'My business is with you and her, not with my mother.'

The curt tone worked, as it always worked with Madame Belinska, and she turned to her little sideboard with a laugh. 'Sit down, monsieur,' she said again. 'You shall see Marie Pavlovna in a minute. Have a little glass with me, and don't let's begin by quarrelling.'

Jacques knew her little glasses, which invariably contained some sticky, sweet concoction. He helped her to her armchair before sitting down on the sofa, put the glass to his lips and detected maraschino.

The Pomeranian bitch, dribbling slightly, climbed on to Madame Belinska's lap. She patted the animal absent-mindedly, and said in a more conciliatory tone, 'I must admit I was irritated when your dear mother arrived without any warning a couple of days ago, bringing me a girl I believed safe with her stepfather's family in Naples for the duration of the war.'

'How long do you give it, baroness?'

'Apparently too long for the patience of Marie Pavlovna.'

'Is that her name? I thought my mother called her Pauline. I've never even heard her surname.'

'Preston. Her father was an American from Baltimore. I like to call her by her mother's name, because I was very fond of her mother, Monsieur Jacques. I knew all her family in St. Petersburg, before the Revolution.'

'And Mr. Preston, was he in Russia too?'

'No, they met and were married in Paris. Paul Preston died only a few years later, and Marie remarried and went to live in Italy. The child says her stepfather was always kind to her.'

'But he died too. She doesn't seem to have much luck, your girl. Couldn't you keep her with you for a while, until she gets her bearings?'

The old lady reared up in her chair. 'Impossible, monsieur! Absolutely impossible! Don't you understand, she has no right to *be* here! If the Occupation authorities knew I was sheltering an American citizen, there would be the most serious consequences! She would be sent to an internment camp immediately, and *I* might be ordered to leave the Alexandra Hotel!'

'Oh come,' he said, 'it can't be as bad as all that. The place has been your home for twenty years, and your neighbours turn a blind eye when I come here to meet my parents—'

'For how long? Only an hour at a time and only a few times in all! My neighbours are in the same boat as me; we have an occasional visitor from across that foolish border, and the manager winks at it, he hates the Italians too. But a permanent guest, whose papers aren't even in order – he would never permit it. Even for these two days, it's been difficult to get food for her. I daren't take her into the dining-room, where we all have luncheon together, and I've had to bribe one of the maids to buy little extras at the shops in Carnolès.'

Jacques knew that food was the real problem. For the old White Russians who lived from hand to mouth, rationing and food cards were mysteries in the present and carried awful memories of the past, and he saw that Madame Belinska was genuinely afraid for her own wrinkled skin. He said, more gently than he had spoken so far, 'I'm sure my mother's sorry she brought you an unwelcome guest.'

'Dear Marguerite – always so impulsive, but that child talked her into it, I know. Marie Hendrikova's daughter!

She would have been *most* welcome here in other circumstances, but – this awful war – I can't be uprooted a second time, Monsieur Jacques! I'm too old and too tired! That girl has got to go away and leave me in peace! You're young ... maybe she'll listen to you! Persuade her to go back to Naples and let me alone!'

'It might be the best solution, madame. But Miss Preston seems to have taken some very determined steps to get away from Naples, don't you think?'

'Ridiculous! She talks of the Pradellis as if they kept her in a dungeon and fed her on bread and water. I know them slightly, they're wealthy people, cultivated, cosmopolitan; they behaved very generously to her mother.'

'But if she won't go back and you won't keep her, what am I supposed to do?'

She said coaxingly, 'I'd like you to take her to some good friends of mine at Nice.'

'Who are they,'

'Dr. and Madame Moreau. You must have heard of him, the famous children's doctor. I'll ask them to take her in for a few days.'

'And then?'

'She wants to get to Lisbon. And from there, back to her family home in Baltimore.' At the look of consternation on Jacques' face the old lady put down her empty glass and fumbled in a silver box for a piece of the marshmallow, *pâte de guimauve*, which was one of her self-protective indulgences. Jacques watched the fat hand select the sweetmeat, and reflected that whoever was fed on bread and water Natalie Yurievna Belinska was not likely to go short of candy and liqueurs. 'I can't guarantee to take her any further than Nice,' he said.

'She has plenty of money, if that's a consideration.'

'It wouldn't be a consideration for the Moreaus, they don't take paying guests.'

'Do *you* know the Moreaus?'

'I play bridge with them occasionally. I know their

daughter and son-in-law better – the Roger Malvys.'

'How very interesting,' said Madame Belinska. 'Is it true that Chantal Malvy has left her husband?' She licked her lips over a second piece of marshmallow.

'No, of course she hasn't left him. She suffers from asthma, and it got worse after the baby was born, so Dr. Moreau sent them up to the Mont Dore for the summer. They're coming home soon.'

'I wouldn't trust that handsome young Malvy as a grass widower if *I* were his wife!'

Jacques got up. 'I really ought to see Miss Preston now. Where are you hiding her?'

'She's in the guest room. Do you want me to call her?' Madame Belinska fumbled for her stick.

'Don't get up, madame, I can find her.' Jacques turned back at the door. 'I'll have to think about taking her to the Moreaus,' he said. 'They're not the sort of people you can dump a strange girl on without any warning. Why don't you write a letter of introduction for your visitor? Don't use her own name, Preston sounds far too English; just write a few lines saying she's an old friend's daughter, and you'd appreciate any kindness Madame Moreau can show her while she's in Nice. That doesn't commit you or them, but it does give the girl some sort of status in their eyes.'

That would take care of the baroness for the next ten minutes. Jacques had never been in Madame Belinska's guest room, nor supposed that it existed, but in that tiny flat it had to be the room where furniture was being pulled about and someone seemed to be struggling with a heavy weight. He tapped at the door and heard the word '*Entrez!*' The girl who turned to face him was trying to hoist a leather suitcase to the top of a scarred walnut highboy, two feet taller than herself.

She put the suitcase down and offered him her grimy hand.

'You must be Jacques Brunel,' she said. 'I'm Polly Preston.'

7

'What on earth are you doing – shifting the furniture?'

'There isn't much of it *to* shift,' said Polly Preston. There was in fact nothing but the highboy and a single bed with a thin counterpane, now covered with two big satin envelopes which might have contained underwear, a collection of toilet articles and a leather rucksack. They both involuntarily smiled at the shortcomings of the Baroness Belinska's guest room, which was only a boxroom with a bed in it and a barred, uncurtained window set high up in the wall. The smile became a laugh as they surveyed the old portmanteaux, the dusty cardboard boxes, the débris of photographs demoted from the parlour, and the ikon of the Virgin of Kazan. It was as easy as that : with scarcely a word spoken, Jacques and Polly laughed together.

'Does Aunt Natasha want me in the salon?'

'I told her you and I must have a talk first.'

'Oh, fine, but let's sit down.'

Jacques seated himself cautiously on a narrow shelf which ran beneath the window, while Polly perched on the edge of the bed. She was a small girl, pale and square jawed, with dark hair falling to her shoulders, and that was as much as Jacques could see by the light of a dim electric bulb covered with a shade of orange crêpe. She was wearing a black coat and skirt, and her blouse was white with a pattern which might have been dark red or dark brown. He couldn't tell if she was pretty, but Polly's face was all animation when Jacques said, 'I gather you were expecting me.'

'Oh yes ! When your mother came to tell us you'd be here this evening, I knew it would be all right. You *will* take me back to Nice tonight, won't you?'

'And if I do, what then?'

'I'm supposed to stay with a doctor's family, friends of Aunt Natasha. And after that I want to go to Portugal. There's a way across the Pyrenees, have you heard about it?'

'Yes, I've heard about it, but it's too rough, and much too dangerous for a girl like you.'

'I'll be all right once I'm in a neutral country.'

It was exactly as Madame Belinska had said : she was talking him into it, as she had talked his mother into driving her away from the sanatorium. In less than five minutes, she had got him as far as Perpignan, handing her over to the smugglers who knew the paths across the mountains ! 'Stop a bit,' he said, 'it's a long way to Portugal. Let's begin at the beginning. A personal question – how old are you?'

'I was twenty last March.'

'Were you really?' She looked about eighteen to him, but Polly took an American passport out of a handbag lying on the bed, and there it was – Pauline Mary Preston, born in Paris, France, March 7th, 1922. So she was a Parisian by birth ! Her French was not Parisian. She spoke with a slight Italian accent – not that that would matter much in Nice.

'This passport's out of date,' he said.

'I couldn't get it renewed after the consulate was closed.'

'Have you any other papers?'

She silently handed him an Italian identity card, with a photograph more recent than the one on the passport, and a work permit attested to by the matron of a children's hospital in Naples.

'Now tell me this,' said Jacques, 'what made you decide to get away from Naples? Weren't you happy there, after your mother's Italian marriage?'

'Quite happy, until the war began. And now – Italy's at war with my own country.'

'And has been, for nearly a year.'

'The doctors told me Count Pradelli, my stepfather, hadn't long to live. I thought I ought to stay with him till it was all over, and I did. But I'm not going back again – ever.'

She had begun to shiver, whether from cold or emotion Jacques couldn't tell. From cold, most likely, because a faint warmth beneath his thighs told him that the shelf he sat on was the cover of a radiator, in which the central heating once a feature of the Alexandra Hotel had been reduced to the lowest level. The blazing log fire in Madame Belinska's salon had kept him from noticing the chill until now.

'May I see the travel warrant they gave you at the sanatorium?'

'Certainly.'

Jacques examined the paper. 'Valid only for the fifth of November, and two days out of date. It shouldn't be too difficult to turn that five into an eight.'

'And then?'

'Then you should walk into Menton tomorrow morning – it's barely two kilometres, not nearly as far as walking across the Pyrenees – and ask someone to direct you to the railway station. Present your warrant and get on the ten o'clock train to Genoa. Go back to Naples, where you have relatives in law if not in fact, influential people who've obviously been able to keep you out of an Italian internment camp, and carry on your work with the sick children until the war is over. Isn't that the advice your American kinfolk would give you?'

'I don't know,' she said. 'I haven't heard from any of them since my mother died.'

'But I thought you were so anxious to get back to Baltimore!'

'My grandfather and my uncle live in Baltimore. And my godfather, Mr. Calvert, lives in Washington. Only he's a diplomat, he was Minister to one of the Baltic states before the war. He may be anywhere, even in Russia by this time. He always wanted to go back to Russia again.'

'All right. Now let's suppose that by some fantastic turn

of events you could go back to the United States. What d'you mean to do when you get there?'

'Join one of the women's Services. Or work in an aircraft factory. Or make munitions – anything.'

'Ah!' said Jacques. 'Now you're being practical. Try to be more practical still. Ask yourself if what one girl can do for the war effort in America is worth putting the lives of twenty men at risk to get her out of Europe.'

It was his courtroom voice, the voice he used to browbeat a difficult witness into confusion, and Jacques could hardly believe his ears when Polly retorted, 'I don't want to put *one* man's life at risk for my sake. I *do* want to be on the right side of the war!'

'I appreciate that, but—'

'Are you really serious in advising me to go back to the Casa Pradelli?'

'That would be my judgment as a lawyer.'

'If the Allies step up the bombing raids on Naples, you might be sending me back to my death. So what would be your judgment as a man?'

'Oh God,' said Jacques, 'don't say such things!' It was an appeal to Alison, impossible to resist – an appeal to the girl who, loving and happy, had gone innocently to her death on a sunny English morning more than two years before. He closed his eyes for a moment to blot out the image. 'All right,' he said, 'you win. I'll take you on to Nice tonight – on one condition.'

'Which is?'

'That you do exactly as I say at the border, and trust me to do what's best for both of us.'

'But I trust you absolutely,' she said, radiant, and Jacques smiled.

'Then the first thing is, don't burden us with a lot of luggage.'

'I thought of that already. I was trying to put my big suitcase away when you came in. I'd planned to put a few things in the rucksack, and buy some more when I get to Nice.' She indicated her belongings on the bed.

'Were you as sure of me as that?'

'Oh yes,' said Polly. 'After your mother told me how good you were about helping people, I was quite sure you'd be willing to help me too.'

'Helping people!' said Jacques. 'What exactly did my mother say?'

Polly shifted her position on the bed. 'Lots of things.' She studied his troubled face. 'She told me you had a great many friends, and one of them was a man called Captain Jack, who might, if *you* asked him, put me on the way through Spain to Portugal . . . You do know him, don't you?'

'Yes, I know him.' Jacques stood up, and lifted the forgotten suitcase from the floor. 'First I must go and have a word with the baroness. Where do you want this put? Up here?' He slung the case to the top of the highboy. It was old and scratched, with no initials; nobody could tell it from the rest of the baggage in the boxroom. He looked up at the feeble light dangling on a worn flex from the ceiling, and at the high barred window. The room where the baroness had hidden her uninvited guest looked like a prison cell. 'Don't be long,' he said.

'I'll wash my hands, and get my coat, and then I'm ready. But first – please—'

'Yes?'

'Please let me thank you, Monsieur Brunel.'

He nodded, and touched her cheek. Outside, in the dim lobby, he wondered at himself.

Madame Belinska, seated at her writing table, turned as quickly as her bulk would allow when he came back to the salon. 'Well, Monsieur Jacques?' she said. 'What did you think of her?'

'Very charming, madame, and very obstinate. She's quite determined not to return to Italy.'

The old woman's face fell. 'I hope you told her—'

'I told her I would take her back to Nice tonight.'

'Oh! Oh well, that changes everything! I do appreciate your thoughtfulness, *mon cher*. I see you understand the difficulty of my position—'

'Perfectly, madame,' said her *cher*, so styled by Madame Belinska for the first time in his life. How badly she wants to get rid of that kid, he thought. He was on Polly's side now; that damned boxroom with the barred window had been enough for him, and he asked, sharply indeed, to see the letter she had written to Madame Moreau. It had not been easy to compose, as several sheets of crumpled paper testified, but the end product was a masterpiece of suavity, an appeal for 'any little attention' to the anonymous daughter of 'a dear late friend, who as Marie Hendrikova was such a comfort and support to me in the unhappy days of 1918'. There was a tender enquiry for the health of dear Chantal and the baby, and the pious wish that, 'a poor soli-tary old woman' might soon be reunited with her friends Doctor and Madame Moreau. Jacques nodded approval, and as she put the letter in its envelope he said, 'I'll deliver it myself next week.'

'Why not tonight? It isn't late!' she said in swift alarm. 'You won't take an hour to drive to Nice.'

'It takes longer to get up to Cimiez, and apart from that Miss Preston's papers are not in order. You saw that for yourself,' said Jacques, 'and nothing can be done about it until Monday. I'll take her to friends of my own for the weekend.'

'You're being very kind to the naughty child.' Madame Belinska asked no questions, and Jacques thought that in her haste to be rid of them both she would have given the same perfunctory approval if he had told her he meant to take Polly Preston to his own apartment and his own bed in the Palais Lascaris. He had been worrying at this problem while he was talking to the girl : the Lecampions, he knew, would gladly give her shelter if he introduced her as a young friend of his mother, but Madame Lecampion was only too likely to spread the story of her visitor over the whole of Cap

Martin. It looked as if Fabienne Leroux was the answer, and as he had told Charles Maxwell the Hotel Mimosa was reasonably safe.

'Well, so there you are, my dear, all ready to set out on your travels!' said the baroness with false heartiness, as Polly came into the room. In the bright light from the chandelier Jacques could see that she was really pretty, though still very pale. Her head was bare, and she carried her rucksack in one hand. She was wearing a plain black coat over her suit, and he was glad to see that her shoes looked strong and had flat heels. She went up to Madame Belinska's chair and dropped a schoolgirl curtsey.

'Thank you for letting me stay with you, Aunt Natasha,' she said. 'I'm sorry if I've been a nuisance.' The old lady muttered something about 'not a nuisance . . . difficult times . . . you must come again after the war,' and Polly looked nervously at Jacques.

'There's nothing complicated about what we're going to do,' he said easily. 'We've only got to cross a road and a wall, and then we'll be all right.' He banished from his mind the image of the black Citroën with the Paris number plates, parked conveniently near to the truck barrier, as he described the route they had to take. 'When we're back on the road in Carnolès we'll be quite close to the Russian church, and my car's parked not very far away. It doesn't sound too bad, does it?' She had talked so boldly about crossing the Pyrenees, but he saw that Polly's eyes were dilated, and hoped to God she wasn't going to panic now. 'It – sounds g-great,' she said.

Madame Belinska caught the nervous stammer, and with unexpected emotion took the girl in her arms. 'Oh, my poor child, you're so like your dear mother,' she said. 'To see you in that black coat – it might be Marie all over again, and she was brave, and wilful, just like you.' To Jacques's astonishment she began to cry.

'Don't, Aunt Natasha, you'll see everything will be all right—'

'We've got to go. Goodbye, madame,' said Jacques firmly, and hurried his charge out of the flat, through the silent halls, and on to the terrace, where he slung Polly's rucksack over his own shoulders and signed to her to stand still until her eyes were accustomed to the dark. The stars were bright, and he wished for the heavy cloud ceiling of two nights earlier, but her dark clothing was a help, and as he turned up the collar of his jacket to hide his shirt Polly imitated him by turning her own coat collar over the printed silk scarf at her throat. He pointed at what the starlight showed in outline, the dome of the Russian church with the Orthodox cross above it, and Polly nodded to show she understood how short a way they had to go. His sense of smell, outraged by the mingled odours of old age, old dog, *guimauve* and maraschino, told him that she had washed her face and hands with something fresh and clean, like lemon soap.

Jacques led her along the terrace to the steep, muddy service path, and she came down behind him quietly, slithering a bit at the end, to stand motionless, checked by his hand, while he looked and listened for the patrol. The truck was still in position, but there was no movement round it, and he could see the tiny points of lighted cigarettes further down on the Menton side, as if the Italians had moved away to smoke near the main gates of the hotel. At last he nodded, ran across the road and waited in the lane until Polly ran after him, thin and quick and only a degree darker than the shadows of the night. In silence, he pointed out the footholds on the wall and the place where the barbed wire was rolled back. He went up in two steps, balanced on the stonework and pulled Polly up after him before he jumped down on the grass verge along the fencing of the orange grove.

But the ground fell away on that side, and Jacques saw Polly hesitate as she swung her legs over and felt with her heels for a new foothold. He held out his arms to her and she jumped unhesitatingly, but the hem of her heavy coat caught on the stone and dislodged a shower of pebbles.

Jacques set her on her feet and whispered 'Run!' a second after the Alsatian watchdog set up a frantic barking.

Polly ran at his heels down the maze of lanes and alleys. Jacques strained his ears for the rush of heavy boots. There was no time, now, to cross the great empty garden and get to the car. There was perhaps a minute to get through the back door into the nursing home, where the matron was a friend of Dr. Lecampion and might give them shelter, but as they came near the buildings he knew that even that minute's grace would be denied them, for the brute of a dog could be heard over the whole neighbourhood, and there were shouts of 'Halte-là!' from the intersection where the truck was parked. He heard an engine starting up.

'The church!' he said between his teeth, and pulled Polly Preston through the little iron gate with a miniature Orthodox cross in wrought iron on the top, through the narrow path between tall cypresses, and into the sanctuary of her mother's faith.

The vesper service was still going on. They stood in a long empty corridor with pictures on the walls, and chairs on either side of a wide low cupboard with one of its doors ajar. Polly flung it open. 'My rucksack!' she whispered, and Jacques tore the thing from his shoulders, pushing it out of sight on one of the shelves. In this setting he was prepared to follow Polly's lead, as she had been prepared to follow him.

She walked ahead into the little church, as the noise of singing grew louder. Nobody turned to stare at them, though the whole congregation was standing : a congregation of barely twenty people, devoutly facing the closed doors of the ikonostasis. They were all elderly and poorly dressed, their lips hardly moving, and Jacques realised that the baritone chanting came from the record on a gramophone which an old man was winding on a table beyond the open vestry door. He saw that Polly had somehow managed to take the scarf out of the collar of her coat and tie it round her head.

'Kiss the ikon!' She meant the ornate ikon displayed on a kind of lectern in the middle aisle, and Jacques bent over it respectfully, stepping back to stand beside her in front of their wooden chairs as the gramophone music stopped. There was a dramatic pause. Then a living voice was raised in invocation, and the doors of the ikonostasis were opened to represent the rending of the temple veil. Through those doors in the little Russian church of Carnolès only two men had the right to pass : the pope and the Czar on the day of his coronation, and the pope came now, carrying the Holy Book, while behind him on the altar the candles burned in honour of the supreme moment of the rite. In the same instant the door of the church burst open and three men in the uniform of the *Milice* came in.

Polly Preston caught one glimpse of the black uniforms, the black Basque berets and the white gaiters before she pulled the scarf lower on her brow. The man in front had his hand on his pistol holster. The pope continued with the celebration. He laid the Book between the candles on the altar, and in his smoke-blue cope began the round of the congregation, swinging his silver censer. He bowed, as he bowed to each one of his flock, to the three militiamen by the door. As the incense rose about them they had the grace to look abashed, and one furtively crossed himself. There was a shuffle of heavy boots and the sound of a door closing.

The pope waited until they had gone before he again took his place at the altar, the sight of which represented the revelation of heaven to the faithful, and the gates of the ikonostasis shut behind him. The consecration was over, and as the gramophone music began again the people started to move about the little church, some to kneel before the crucifix, others to light candles before the ikons on their stands. Polly heard Jacques sigh beside her, and guessed that he had been holding his breath. She looked about her thankfully. Among the ikons on the wall she recognised the Virgin, Comforter of the Afflicted, who was the patron saint of a church which in its simplicity, with its ugly stained-glass windows of blue and yellow, might have belonged to one of the noncomformist congregations. It now appeared more beautiful to her than the cathedral of St. Alexander Nevsky in Paris, where her mother had taken her to hear the liturgy as a child.

They remained standing until the service ended. Before the pope's magnificent baritone chanted a final blessing, Jacques thought he heard an automobile being driven away, but that was no assurance that the militiamen were inside. They could be waiting at the gate, checking over the worshippers as they came out one by one, asking to see their papers, exercising their right to 'detain for further questioning' a girl with an expired American passport. He took Polly's hand as they followed the congregation into the passage, where the pope was waiting to say goodnight. It was the Russian himself, still impressive in his cope and long dark beard, who motioned them to wait until the rest had gone. He said something to Polly which made her smile, smiling himself at her stammered answer, and then turned courteously to Jacques.

'*Monsieur est français*? I was telling your wife how pleasant it is to see two new friends in my church. Do you live in Carnolès?'

'In Nice, *mon père*.'

'You intend to return to Nice tonight?'

'I left my car outside. Pauline—!' She was rummaging in the cupboard, pulling out the rucksack, and she said something to the priest which made him smile again. 'I agree it would have made you too conspicuous,' he said in French. 'Come, let me see you safely to your car.'

He walked between them, a protecting presence, and the black Citroën was nowhere to be seen. The ambulance had gone too, and the whole street was quiet. When they were ready to leave the pope gave Polly his blessing and offered Jacques his hand. 'I saw the militiamen drive up as I went into church,' he said quietly. 'My son, you must be more careful in the future.'

It was a great temptation to be reckless in the present, to smash the accelerator down to the floorboard, to cut all the

corners as the car swung on to the national highway and up
the hill. Neither Jacques nor Polly spoke. He knew that she
was watching all the side roads, just as he was moving his
eyes from the road ahead to the rear mirror, but no black
Citroën moved out to intercept or follow them. When he
was sure they'd got away with it, Jacques pulled the Peugeot
into the gateway of a roadside inn, closed for the duration,
and cut the lights. He put his arm around Polly's shoulders.

'You did well,' he said. 'That was quick thinking, back in
the church.'

'I made too much noise getting over the wall,' she said
miserably.

'It was too big a drop for you, and your coat caught in the
brickwork.'

'Those men who followed us into the church, were they
policemen? When I saw the black uniforms, I thought they
were *Fascisti*.'

'They *are* Fascists, the home-grown variety. They're the
French jackals of the Gestapo, and they get twice the pay of
the police, plus head money for every suspect on the wanted
list they manage to bring in.'

'Are you on the wanted list?'

'Not so far as I know. Don't worry about the *Milice*, we
were a bit too quick for them after that damned dog started
barking. They can't have seen us on the road, though they
probably heard us. If they'd been sure, they'd have stopped
the service at gunpoint and made an arrest.'

Jacques felt Polly shiver in the shelter of his arm. They
were parked at the top of a hill, from which he could see
the old semaphore on Cap Martin, erected at the time of
Bonaparte's wars, and the distant outline of the Trophée
des Alpes, celebrating a Roman victory over the Ligurians
of the Mediterranean shore. Always and everywhere in
France, those silent memorials to old campaigns! He
said, 'I'm going to take you to a hotel in Monaco now.
It's better we don't go to see Madame Belinska's friends
tonight.'

'Oh, I'm so glad. After Aunt Natasha's hospitality, I don't feel up to facing Madame Moreau right away.'

'She isn't really your aunt, is she?'

'That's what my mother used to call her. Monsieur Brunel—'

'After what's happened, I think you might call me Jacques.'

'Jack,' said Polly Preston, with a hint of laughter in her voice. 'I'll be glad to go to a hotel and pay for my room. Is it far?'

'Only a few kilometres.'

'Will there be something to eat at the hotel?'

'Are you hungry, Pauline?'

'I'm famished.'

'Good God!' Jacques turned the ignition key. By the dashboard light he could see that her pale face was sharp with hunger, while the luminous dial of the watch on his wrist told him that the modest evening meal of the Hotel Mimosa, always meagre on a Saturday night, when most of the regulars had gone home, was probably over already. He realised that several hours had passed since he ate boiled eggs for luncheon. They would have to go to the big brasserie on the corner, next door to the Hotel Mimosa, after he had made sure of a room for Polly. Or else—

'Let's go,' he said, switching on the headlights. 'I don't often eat in a black-market restaurant, but we've got something to celebrate tonight. We'll stop in Monte Carlo and treat ourselves to the best steaks money can buy!'

'I don't believe it,' Polly said. 'Real steak?'

'Tournedos or filet mignon, whichever you prefer.'

'With *pommes frites*?'

'Or *pommes duchesse*.'

'And vegetables?'

'Spinach? Or courgettes?'

'Oh hurry, please,' she begged, and Jacques laughed as the Peugeot ran through Cabbé, through St. Roman, the only car on the road, and into the Principality.

He parked outside a discreet restaurant in a side street behind the Hotel Metropole, so popular with British visitors in the days of peace, and ushered her into a small, well-warmed room with a few candlelit tables where the customers seemed anxious not to be recognised. The proprietor came forward beaming with the menu in his hand.

'I must tidy up,' said Polly. 'You choose for me, please. I'd like it to be a surprise.'

He wasn't sure about the surprise, for the proprietor's suggestions seemed very similar to the menu they had invented in the car, but Jacques ordered quickly, and by the time he had got rid of the grime of climbing over walls and through undergrowth Polly was back at the table. He made her drink a cup of strong beef consommé first, and then a glass of chambertin, admirably chosen to accompany the classic tournedos Rossini which followed. Polly ate and drank in a reverent silence, relishing every mouthful. Jacques watched her with amusement. She had been badly scared, but this was not the nervous hunger which he had known as the consequence of fright and shock. Here was a healthy young appetite which had been deprived, and Jacques wondered what 'little extras' the selfish old baroness could possibly have purchased for a girl excluded from the main meal of the day. Food and wine and warmth brought colour to Polly's pale face. It was all she needed to be very pretty indeed, with those clear hazel eyes and that brown hair just touched with bronze. He hadn't been sure about the loose, shoulder-length hair at first. French girls, who were wearing their hair in high, stiff pompadours, despised what they called *le style flou*, but it was somehow right for Polly Preston.

'That was absolutely marvellous!' she said when the steak was finished. 'I haven't had a meal like this for years.'

'How was the food at the sanatorium?'

'Institutional.'

'And in the city where you were before that?'

'I was getting very tired of polenta.'

'Supplies running low, are they?'

'My stepfather was very strict about rationing.'

'Then I gather he wasn't one of the favoured few – one of Mussolini's entourage?'

'Far from it! *His* father was one of Garibaldi's Thousand, and Garibaldi was one of his own heroes, not that – that *brute* who came later ... I couldn't possibly eat dessert!'

'Oh yes you could. Have a chocolate éclair, or a tangerine sorbet.'

She chose the sorbet, and paused before picking up the flat silver spoon to listen to the music from Radio Paris coming very softly from the wireless set half hidden by a bowl of flowers. There had been a conventional dinner music programme, kept too low to interfere with conversation, but someone must have turned up the volume when a familiar voice began to sing 'France Smells so Good!'

'Isn't that Maurice Chevalier?' said Polly. 'Himself or a record?'

'A record, probably. He's been in Germany, singing to the French prisoners of war.'

'I used to love his songs. Remember "Louise" and "A New Kind of Love"? But I've never heard *"Ca sent si bon, la France"*. Not that I've heard much lately but *"Giovinezza"*. How I hated it!'

Jacques nodded. To hate the Fascist anthem was one thing, but how was a Frenchman to feel about the song Radio Paris was broadcasting now:

> *Paris sera toujours Paris,*
> *La plus belle ville du monde,*
> *Ainsi qu'au loin le canon gronde,*
> *Son éclat ne peut être assombri*

It was what they had been singing on his last Paris leave before the embarkation for Norway, in the euphoric spring of 1940, and he decided savagely that some little man at Radio Paris must have a black sense of humour to play it in an Occupied capital where the cannon had ceased to rumble long ago. He said urgently to Polly :

'How long did you live in Paris? Did you like living there?'

Polly strugged. 'I'm not sentimental about Paris. I'd just started school in Baltimore before mother took me back to France, and I had to adjust to the French kids, and their fantastic load of homework. Mother was overworked too, but she wanted to be independent, and she liked her job.'

'Which was?'

'Multilingual translations for commercial houses. My mother was brilliant at languages, as most Russians used to be. I mean the Russians she knew in St. Petersburg.'

'And she taught you Russian too. You could follow the service in church tonight, and talk to the priest.'

Polly laughed. 'I think my Russian made him smile. I forgot most of it after we went to live in Italy.' She saw that Jacques Brunel was ready to draw her out on her life in Italy, but Polly refused to be drawn. As a young girl among the intelligentsia of St. Petersburg her mother had been taught one old-fashioned rule : never talk about yourself when a man is present, always talk about *him*, and she had passed on the maxim to her daughter. So from the brief mention of her own mother Polly moved with ease to complimenting Jacques on his, and was rewarded by seeing his thin serious face light up when she told him how much everybody at the sanatorium liked Madame Brunel, and admired the ingenious toys and games she made for the sick children. The waiter brought coffee and held a match for their cigarettes, and as the friendly talk went on Jacques fell more and more into a mood of peace. Chatting with a vivacious girl and eating a notable dinner were pleasures which had not come his way for a long time. He hardly realised that they were the only customers left in the restaurant, and that the radio had been switched off long ago.

'I suppose we must be on our way,' he said at last. 'They don't keep late hours at the Hotel Mimosa.'

'Is that the name of the place? You said it wasn't far away.'

'It's just beyond the Condamine, at the Monaco station. But they don't cater for railway travellers really; it's a small hotel with its own group of regulars among the salesmen and agents who work along the coast.'

'How did you find out about it, then?'

'I've known the girl who runs it for a long time. She was the fiancée' (Jacques drew the line at saying 'the mistress') 'of a friend of mine called Pierre Lavisse, who's a prisoner of war in Germany.'

'How sad. Is she a girl about my own age?'

'Oh no, she's older. Twenty-eight or twenty-nine. Her name's Fabienne Leroux.' Jacques looked round; there was no sign of the proprietor or either of the waiters. 'About *your* name : would you very much mind *not* being Miss Preston for the next few days?'

'No, not a bit, why?'

'I'd like something more French. Your mother's maiden name was Hendrikova, wasn't it?'

'Marie Alexandrovna Hendrikova – it's too much of a mouthful for me !'

'How would Henri do?' Polly nodded enthusiastically, and Jacques spoke more quietly still. 'One reason why I'm taking you to the Mimosa is that Fabienne isn't too fussy about her guests filling in the police *fiches*. But if you stay in France for any length of time you'll have to have a French identity card. Will you let me take that ID you got in Naples?'

'Of course I will, but what use will it be here?'

'It's got a photograph which can be copied. No, don't go rummaging in your rucksack now, give it to me in the

122

car ... You haven't got your money in that thing, I hope?'

'I'm wearing a money belt.'

'Very professional,' he said with a smile, and produced his own note case as the proprietor appeared with the bill on a plate.

The party was over. The door of the black-market restaurant was double-locked behind them, and Jacques and Polly were in the chilly street once more. Beyond the gardens of the Metropole and the parterres of Les Boulingrins subdued lights indicated that the world-famous casino of Monte Carlo was still in business.

'You told me one reason for staying at the Mimosa,' said Polly as she settled herself in the car. 'What's the other?'

'The other is, that you need a day or two to think things over. You were very positive about not going back to Naples – before we broke the law. Now you know what it feels like to be on the run. Has it made any difference to you?'

'The only difference is that I'll be smart enough to wear slacks next time.'

'More practical for crossing walls,' said Jacques dryly. 'I'll call you at the hotel on Monday, after the court rises. Until then, I'm not going near Madame Moreau.'

'And if I tell you that I've changed my mind?'

'I'll get another travel warrant cut in Nice.'

'Another one,' said Polly. 'And you were all set to turn a five into an eight on the first one. Also to have my ID photograph copied for a French identity card. You seem to know a lot about the wrong side of the law, Maître Brunel!'

'You have to be adaptable in times like these.' The barrister said no more as they drove through the Condamine and up the Rue Grimaldi to the station. He had to park behind another car outside the Mimosa, an old Delahaye which looked vaguely familiar, and the front door of the little hotel was already locked. But as soon as Jacques rang the night bell, he heard footsteps, and the voice of the porter asking who was there.

'*Bieuvenu, Maître Brunel. Entrez donc. Entrez, mademoi-selle.*'

There was no light behind the glass door of the little office, and Jacques, not entirely disappointed, asked if Madame Fabienne had retired for the night.

'Not she, sitting up till all hours as usual. Come this way, please,' grumbled the porter as he led them to the lounge. Jules was a sour, disgruntled old man, who found Fabienne Leroux a more exacting employer than her father, and was not unwilling to make a little mischief. He knew that 'Madame Fabienne' had fancied Monsieur Brunel and been turned down; he knew she had another, wilder bird in hand, and he wanted to see them face to face. After all, the lounge was a public place, wasn't it?

It was, but at that hour its only occupants were Fabienne and a man, sitting side by side on a sofa with a bottle of champagne and two glasses on the table before them, and Jacques swore inwardly as he identified, too late, the owner of the old Delahaye. Fabienne was entertaining Roger Malvy, husband of the absent Chantal and son-in-law of the couple to whom Madame Belinska had recommended Polly. It was a complication he could have done without, but it had to be accepted : Fabienne was already on her feet and coming forward with both hands extended in the ges-ture Jacques knew so well. She was as usual dressed in black, but with a florist's spray of red carnations on her shoulder. Her hair, brushed high above the black fringe, was in dis-order; her mouth, without lipstick, was swollen and vividly red.

'Jacques!' cried Fabienne Leroux. 'Roger and I were talking about you only five minutes ago. What on earth brings you here at this time of night?'

'A guest for you,' said Jacques, and drew Polly forward. 'A friend of my mother's, in Monaco for the first time. Mademoiselle Henri, this is Mademoiselle Fabienne Leroux.'

'How do you do, mademoiselle,' said Fabienne, shaking

hands, and estimating at a glance, as Jacques had not done, the value of Polly's expensive scarf, her rucksack of fine leather, and her well-cut if scratched Italian shoes. 'I'm so pleased you've come to the Hotel Mimosa. Have you travelled a long way today?'

'Only from Carnolès,' said Polly without blinking.

'In that case you've probably had dinner?'

'We dined in Monte Carlo,' said Jacques, and Fabienne raised her eyebrows. 'I think Mademoiselle Henri might like to see her room.'

'Nonsense,' said Roger Malvy, rising from the sofa, 'the evening's just beginning. Introduce me too, please, *mon vieux*, and let's send Jules – what are you standing staring at, you Jules? – for another bottle of champagne. I want you both to help us celebrate!'

'What's the celebration?' said Jacques. He saw that Malvy was more than a little drunk, that Fabienne was annoyed, and that Polly was taking off her overcoat and suit jacket like someone preparing to make a night of it. The only satisfaction he had was in deciding that the pattern of her blouse was dark red and not dark brown.

There wasn't, by his standards, a great deal to celebrate. The young architect had just signed a contract, at a time when new contracts were very hard to get, which was good. But his job was to reconstruct a villa at Cap d'Ail for a Marseille gangster who had used the fall of France to make a fortune out of prostitution and the black market. The villa had once belonged to a Russian Grand Duke and had extensive grounds; as Roger led them through it room by room, sip by sip of champagne, it was clear that he meant to transform a charming Italianate residence into something ultra-modern, a bad copy of le Corbusier's style. He had been having dinner with his new patron at the Hotel de Paris, where the gangster occupied a suite, and when the contract was signed and witnessed by two men who both happened to be carrying guns, one of the signatories had gone off to gamble at the casino and the other had driven up the hill to celebrate with his dear friend Fabienne.

Fabienne smouldered, Polly smiled, and Jacques Brunel came very near sulking as the tide of words flowed on. It was one thing to be adaptable, but Pauline Preston was almost too adaptable. It annoyed him to see her as attentive to that poseur Malvy as she had been to him, and apparently as fresh as if her day was just beginning. She had wisely refused more than one glass of champagne, and drank it slowly; it only made her more lively and alert, and Jacques remembered that his mother, when she asked him to take pity on the orphan girl from Naples, had referred to her as *cette pauvre petite*. He had never known any girl in his life, not even Alison Grant, who was less of a poor little thing than Polly Preston.

After half an hour, Jacques left them to drive back to Nice : whether Roger Malvy meant to drive to Nice that night he neither knew nor cared. It was late indeed when he opened Henri's garage with his own key, and put the Peugeot inside, and walked home up the Rue Droite. It was long before he could sleep, even after two broken nights, beneath the plunging horses and the chariots of his painted ceiling. New feelings, or feelings he had thought dead, had been aroused in him. Their names, he thought, were tenderness and jealousy, and between them they might breed desire.

When sleep came at last Jacques Brunel slept soundly; so soundly that he missed the news which every radio station in the world was broadcasting that Sunday morning, the eighth of November 1942 : that a great American invasion force had descended on French North Africa soon after midnight, and that a new phase of the Second World War had begun.

8

All over Britain that Sunday morning the church bells were ringing, not to announce an enemy invasion but to celebrate the first great pounce of the American ally. Coming so soon after the great British victory over Rommel at El Alamein, the three-fold American landings in Morocco and Algeria seemed to promise that the whole of North Africa would soon be in Allied hands.

To attack the Germans through French North Africa instead of metropolitan France was the decision at which the American Chiefs had reluctantly arrived in London during the last week of July. It had taken over four months to get Operation Torch off the planning tables and into action; there were diplomatic issues involved as well as military, for above all it was hoped that the invasion would be bloodless and that the French Army of Africa, never committed to combat in 1940 and owing allegiance to Vichy, would welcome the Americans as liberators. To make their path all the smoother the British were to play a subordinate part in Torch, for the French professionals had not forgotten the British attack on Admiral Gensoul's squadron at Mers-el-Kebir in 1940, or their support of de Gaulle in his abortive attempt to take Dakar. There were British ships and British troops in the landings, but the great British contribution was the Rock of Gibraltar, the command post and airfield from which the whole operation was to be led. One hundred and thirteen thousand American troops were committed to the action, transported in six hundred and fifty ships, some sailing from the Clyde and others directly from the United

States to Casablanca, and all by a miracle escaping any German attack by air or sea.

The news of this great argosy made for a happy Sunday morning in Britain. But when the bells stopped ringing and the news bulletins were broadcast one after another, the dusk brought a creeping suspicion that Operation Torch had not gone as well as had been hoped and planned. There had been unexpected resistance, there had been arrests of men in high places, soldiers and civilians, Frenchmen and Americans; there were denials of these arrests and then belated confirmations. The names of certain French generals, ignored in Britain since 1940, were back in the news again: Béthouart, Juin, Mast, Noguès, Giraud. And, most prominent of all and least expected, the name of Admiral Darlan.

The American generals, of course, had been given a briefing on the political complexities of French North Africa. They knew that the geographical term was a blanket name for three countries of quite different status, since Morocco on the west and Tunisia on the east were French protectorates, each with a native ruler, while Algeria, between them, was a French possession, taken by the right of conquest as long ago as 1830. *Algérie française* – it was a slogan of the future already valid in 1942 : whoever invaded Algeria was invading France.

The generals also knew that the political aspects of the landings had been studied and influenced by an unobtrusive network of American civilians, slipped into place under the cover of the American embassy to the Chief of State at Vichy. There was a flurry of movement in the network on the eighth of November, when the Vichy government at last broke off diplomatic relations with the United States, and Mr. Robert Murphy, President Roosevelt's political representative in North Africa, was incontinently placed under arrest with one of his ablest assistants. The generals had to proceed along the empirical lines which suited their character and training, and take their allies wherever they could find them; they had, after all, one positive order from their Commander-in-Chief, the President: they were to give no information, aid or comfort to General Charles de Gaulle.

The year 1942 had not been a successful one for the Leader of All Free Frenchmen. He had survived the fiasco of Dakar which, he later confessed, 'had been like an earthquake – like being in a house with all the tiles falling down' – and through 1941 had developed his propaganda and secret services on the lines laid down by Hitler in *Mein Kampf*. But the entry of the United States into the war had muddled his judgment, and the folly of his seizure of St. Pierre and Miquelon could perhaps be traced to his astonishing prophecy to his henchman André Dewavrin, alias Passy, that the world war would now move into two phases, first the rescue of Germany by the Allies and then a great war between Russia and the United States, which Russia would win. This theory dictated his approach, in June, to the Soviet Ambassador, to London, Mr. Bogomolov. He reported to the Kremlin that de Gaulle told him the Americans wanted to seize Dakar and the British to seize the Niger, of course without consulting himself, and if they did so he would break with Britain and ask the Soviet government to welcome himself and all his forces. Nothing came of this secret initiative, and after his outburst to Bogomolov it was possible that de Gaulle realised that when it came to subsidising his ambitions the Russians might not be such a soft touch as the British.

His state of mind that summer, after the appeal to the Russians and the snub from the American chiefs, would have interested a psychiatrist. He displayed, along with delusions of grandeur and feelings of persecution, the 'double orientation' in which the sufferer, while living in the normal world, identifies with great figures of the past (in de Gaulle's case Napoleon, Julius Caesar and Joan of Arc) and feels himself to be directed by a higher fate. Some of the Resistance, who like Alain Renaudon had come from France at great risk to join de Gaulle, found that he could voice his resentment of Britain and the United States 'every day for a month' while hardly ever mentioning the German enemy.

But no psychiatrist's report on Charles de Gaulle was called for, and the British public who were footing his bills continued to believe in him. They were as bored by his polemics against Vichy and his claim to be the legitimate head of a Free French State as the Foreign Office was bored by the arguments about Vichy's illegality presented tirelessly by his Jewish jurist René Cassin. But they had been told by all the media that Charles de Gaulle was the One and Only, the chap fighting on their side, the big fellow on the same level as Roosevelt and Churchill – who were of course his devoted friends. The man in the street was not aware, for it was not in the public interest for him to be told, that Roosevelt called de Gaulle 'unreliable, uncooperative and disloyal to both the governments', and that Churchill, when the general broke his promise to hold elections in Syria and the Lebanon, raged out at him, 'You say you are France! You are not France! I do not recognise you as France!' This was scarcely the comradeship in arms which the great British public had been taught to admire and respect.

But rows like these were kept secret for years to come, and the resilient Winston Churchill, in private as in public, still gave some support to his embarrassing protégé. Indeed he could hardly do otherwise. Churchill survived, by a handsome majority, a vote of censure proposed in the House of Commons at midsummer, when his direction of the war was called in question; he dared not risk a second vote of censure if he admitted that his impulsive acceptance of Charles de Gaulle had been a mistake of the first magnitude, likely to bring worse consequences for Britain than the fiasco of Dakar. He could only bow meekly to President Roosevelt's secret directives to keep the Free French from becoming the

Fighting French in Operation Torch. 'I agree with you that de Gaulle will be an irritant and his movement must be kept out,' Churchill had written in September, when D-day in North Africa had already been delayed for three weeks. Even so, even on November 5th, when all was ready at Gibraltar, he told Roosevelt that he would have to 'explain "Torch" ' to de Gaulle some time during D-day minus 1; even then he was ruthlessly told by the President that de Gaulle must know nothing until a successful landing had taken place.

The Leader of All Free Frenchmen was not entirely unaware that something serious was going on. He had agents in Gibraltar and Tangier, as in Vichy itself, who had passed on some information about the Allied plans for North Africa. But he was not prepared for the *fait accompli*, announced in the most correct manner by General Ismay, Chief of Staff to the British Minister of Defence, to his own Chief of Staff, General Billotte, in the early hours of that fated Sunday morning. 'The Americans have landed in North Africa,' he was told, and in a fury of humiliation he blurted out : 'Then I hope those Vichy fellows throw them into the sea. They can't enter France like burglars !'

'I wonder how Big Charlie's feeling this fine morning,' Bob Kemp remarked cheerfully to some of his O.S.S. colleagues, in the room they had set up as a communications centre at Number Twenty, Grosvenor Square. Kemp was no admirer of Big Charlie, and had kept in close touch, through his contacts in Hollywood, with the progress of *The de Gaulle Story*. William Faulkner was doggedly producing twenty-five new pages every week for a salary of three hundred dollars, all unaware of the excellent material coming to hand that day in London, where de Gaulle was denouncing his American allies as burglars, housebreakers and thieves in the night. Nor did Bob Kemp trouble to find out what Big Charlie might be feeling; he was concentrating, like every other man at General Eisenhower's London headquarters, on the news from North Africa, where those Vichy fellows were making an unexpectedly spirited attempt at throwing the burglars into the Mediterranean.

The stoutest French opposition was naturally at Oran, three miles from the military port of Mers-el-Kebir, where British action had been responsible for the deaths of twelve hundred French naval officers and ratings in the summer of 1940. The appearance of two small warships under British command, originally American cutters transferred under the Lend-Lease agreement, was the signal for withering fire from the French shore batteries. Nearly all aboard the two cutters were killed. They were American technicians, ordered to seize the port installations, but as the French destroyers put to sea in strength and engaged the invaders in the Bay of Oran these installations seemed likely to remain in Vichy hands. In Morocco, General Noguès disregarded President Roosevelt's call to aid the Allies, and three days of violent fighting followed between his troops and the Americans commanded by General Patton. It was the prelude to the events in Morocco which was being described when Jacques Brunel at last switched on the news.

As a rule he drank his first cup of coffee before the bread arrived. It was the custom, on Sunday mornings, for the concierge's son to bring Maître Brunel a *demi-baguette* about nine o'clock, and then he drank his second cup with a slice of fresh bread and a scraping of jam. Nico was an alert boy of twelve, willing to run a delivery service from the bakery across the street for anyone in the Palais Lascaris prepared to give him a few sous for his trouble, and Jacques was subconsciously waiting for his knock on the door as he went yawning into the kitchen, wearing a pullover and an old pair of slacks, to start the coffee in his great-aunt's earthenware coffee pot. He was hardly aware that he had begun to whistle as the pleasant aroma spread through the flat, until he realised that the tune was *'Paris sera toujours*

Paris'. In his cheerful morning mood he was almost prepared to believe that it was true.

'Bonjour, madame!' He was surprised to see Nico's mother, clutching the unwrapped bread to her blouse, instead of the boy himself. 'Nothing the matter with Nico, is there?' No, no, said the concierge, the boy was fine, she had come up herself – and while she paused to get her breath back Jacques was aware that the old 'palace' was buzzing with sound, while three unbrushed heads had appeared in the crack of the apartment door opposite his own – come up to find out what monsieur thought about the news.

'What news, madame?' He felt like a fool when the woman stared at him, and he heard giggles from the doors across the landing. Monsieur was really sleeping soundly, said the concierge, with a broad grin and a wink of complicity to indicate that her tenant's Saturday night must have been exhausting; she told him that the radio had been going on for hours already about the American paratroopers landing in Algiers, and the government's orders to resist them at all costs. 'Say then, monsieur,' she went on excitedly, 'do you think they'll come across and land at Nice? Will we be expected to fight 'em, or will the Boches come over the Line and fight 'em instead?'

It was his instinct to 'temporise', to say he had to find out more about it before giving his opinion, but Jacques Brunel flung out, 'I hope we welcome the Americans with open arms!' and with a word of thanks for the bread went back inside the flat. The coffee was ready. There was no time to boil the milk or cut the bread; he splashed coffee and cold milk into a bowl, drained it in one long draught and hurried into the bedroom to switch on the wireless.

'General Béthouart, the French Divisional Commander at Casablanca,' said the announcer, 'is now under arrest pending a court-martial. This officer with a small band of accomplices attempted to take over army headquarters in Rabat at

two o'clock this morning and invited the Resident-General
to accept General Giraud as Supreme French Commander.
General Noguès, indignantly refusing, ordered a general
alert throughout Morocco and the arrest of the subversive
officers. At seven o'clock General Noguès refused a United
States ultimatum and fierce fighting broke out between
the troops under his command and the American invaders
at Port Lyautey. Our next news bulletin will be broadcast
at ten a.m.'

The staccato voice faded out, and the martial strains of
'Sambre et Meuse' faded in from a gramophone record as
Jacques sat staring at the radio. The concierge had said
American paratroopers were landing in Algiers, but this
newscast was concerned only with a landing, presumably sea-
borne, in Morocco. Were there two invasion forces, then, or
even more? And how dare any general officer of the Army
of Africa, which never fired a shot in anger during the
disaster of 1940, put under arrest the victor of Narvik, Emile
Béthouart, one of the two French generals to win a clear
victory over the Germans in that calamitous year? And
Giraud – where did General Giraud, until recently a prisoner of war in Germany, come into it? Then the paratroopers – was General Juin resisting them in Algiers? Jacques swore, and began to twist the knobs of what was an
exceptionally powerful wireless set. He had no hope of rais-
ing the B.B.C. in such a crisis : it would be jammed all day
by the German radio engineers in Paris, but it might be possible to get Geneva. He had great faith in the impartiality
of the Swiss national radio, and in particular the newscasts
of René Payot, the editor of the *Journal de Genève*. He wondered if General de Gaulle had been haled to the B.B.C. to
endorse the Allied action, as he had been made to do after
Mers-el-Kebir. As Geneva came on the air he had time to
spare a thought for the kid at the Hotel Mimosa. She had
chosen the wrong night for her escapade.

The kid herself had breakfast rather later than Jacques

Brunel. Polly had been awake for only a few minutes, taking in her new surroundings in the plain but immaculate bedroom to which she had been shown soon after Jacques left for Nice, when an elderly woman brought her a breakfast tray with small jugs of coffee and milk, bread and a tiny pat of butter. She set the tray down on the bedside table and asked if mademoiselle had slept well. Madame Fabienne had said the young lady in Room Ten wasn't to be aroused too early, as she had been travelling.

'I only just woke up, thank you. How nice to have some coffee!'

'Madame Fabienne would like you to be her guest at lunch today.'

'Her guest! That's very kind of her, but don't you serve luncheons in the dining room?' She had seen the dining room, next to the lounge.

'Not on Sundays we don't, we can't manage with the rationing. Anybody who's here at the weekend eats in the brasserie next door.'

'I could do that, of course, but since Mademoiselle Leroux invites me, please tell her I gladly accept. What's your name?'

'Marie, mademoiselle.' The cook was delighted to go on chatting; she was very interested in the young lady in Room Ten. Marie had on several occasions carried up coffee to young men who arrived late at night, and who spoke French, if they spoke at all, in accents far stronger than this girl's faintly Niçois inflections. Such visitors never left their room by day and took their departure, as they had come, in the night hours. Their names did not appear in the hotel register, and neither did the new young lady's : under pretext of tidying the office, which was not part of the cook's duties, Marie had looked in the register to see. But this night visitor didn't mean to shut herself up in her room, for as Marie was crossing the hall half an hour later, there she was, dressed in a black coat and a little red knitted cap which hardly covered the back of her head. She smiled and said, '*A bien-tôt, Marie!*' swinging out of the door and off past the corner brasserie as if she had lived in Monaco all her life.

It was not a difficult town to find the way about in, for there was only one street to follow at the corner, and that led to the Place d'Armes, where the Sunday morning market was in full swing. Straight ahead lay the Rock, with the palace walls in view, and Polly, in the enjoyment of her freedom, went on up the long ramp which led into the Place du Palais and the narrow alleys of the ancient fortress town. The palace looked shabby and untenanted although the old sovereign prince and his grandson Prince Rainier were in residence, and the two bored carabiniers on sentry duty were sorely in need of new uniforms. They looked as unwarlike as the row of cannon, a present from King Louis XIV of France to an earlier Grimaldi, which stood under the trees of a little promenade above the sea. Polly settled herself on the wall, in full sunshine, and looked out at the dazzling view. From the Dog's Head in the foreground, across the peninsula of Cap Ferrat to the distant headland of Nice, the Côte d'Azur lay before her in all its peaceful splendour.

Polly Preston was very happy. She felt she had managed the whole thing rather well. On the one and only afternoon when the helpers at the children's sanatorium were driven into Menton for a brief outing she had posted a letter to Signora Pradelli, her stepfather's widowed sister-in-law, saying she had been asked to remain with the little Italians at the sanatorium for an indefinite time. She was sure the old lady wouldn't bother to write and check with the matron. Aunt Vittoria, as Polly called her, would be glad to see the last of the American girl who had offended her mightily by refusing to marry her son Pietro – a flight lieutenant who had distinguished himself by bombing helpless tribesmen during the Ethiopian war.

On that same holiday afternoon Polly had gone to one of the banks in the Rue St. Michel and changed her Italian currency, all she had been able to scrape together before leaving Naples, into a sum in French francs which the banker told her was worth about three thousand dollars. It made her money belt rather uncomfortable to wear, but she thought it would be enough to buy her an exit from France by one route or another. It had not occurred to Polly, until she met Jacques Brunel, that an escape might cost not only money but the lives of men, and the thought gnawed at her satisfaction as she sat basking in the Riviera sunshine. She hadn't made up her mind about Jacques Brunel. He was grave and uncompromising, utterly unlike the young Italians she had been permitted to know, like Pietro Pradelli and his Fascist friends, who were show-offs to the last man. Her stepfather had despised them for their bombast, and so did she, but Polly felt that the old gentleman, who in the Other War had fought for France in the legion raised by Garibaldi's son, would have approved of the passion beneath Jacques Brunel's reserve.

Roger Malvy, now, would have got on well with Pietro's set, if he had known them before Italy stabbed France in the back. His glossy good looks, half southern and half nineteen-twenties American movie star, would have melted easily into the Neapolitan scene, but they made no impression on the American girl. Her life at the Casa Pradelli had been limited by a hundred conventional restrictions, but she was not stupid, and she had a fairly accurate idea of the relationship between Roger and Fabienne Leroux. He wore a wedding ring and Fabienne wore no token from the 'fiancé' in the German prison camp : Polly felt that in their case the presence or the absence of the rings had ceased to matter.

Presently she slipped down from the sunny wall and began to explore the Rock, prowling round the ramparts and in and out of the narrow streets round the precincts of the cathedral. The great doors were open, for Mass had just ended, and some of the worshippers strolled away towards the broad Avenue St. Martin which ran along the heights above the sea to the great Oceanographical Museum. Polly walked slowly in the same direction. Where the avenue turned left above the harbour there was a small café where a few of the churchgoers were collecting for a pre-luncheon apéritif, and Polly, hoping that no ration ticket would be asked for, sat down at one of the tables on the pavement and ordered a cup of coffee. It was hot and good, better than the brew of the Hotel Mimosa, and the last thing needed to complete her pleasure in the day.

Presently she became aware that she was alone. One by one, the painted tables had been deserted, but nobody had paid and gone away. They were all inside the dark café, all looking in the same direction; twisting round in her chair Polly could see the cashier, moustached and bistre-skinned in her Sunday satin blouse, leaning an enormous bosom on the till, and the waiter who had brought her coffee twisting his table napkin in his hands. The people were as quiet as they had been at the elevation of the Host half an hour earlier, and an old, old voice, amplified by the radio, was saying tremulously :

'We are attacked. We shall defend ourselves. That is the order I am giving.'

The next words were inaudible drowned by the sobs of a woman at the back of the café. A man exclaimed, '*Ah, le pauvre maréchal! Pauvre vieux!*' and then Polly heard the opening notes of the *Marseillaise*.

The waiter came out to the pavement when Polly beckoned, and she asked him bluntly, 'Was that Marshal Pétain on the radio?'

'Yes, mademoiselle, a special broadcast about the invasion. One could tell that he was deeply moved—'

'What invasion? Where?'

'The Americans landed in North Africa soon after midnight. The French are resisting, and there's heavy fighting at Oran, they say.' The man was quite nonchalant about it; he was a native Monégasque and so by definition neutral.

He counted out the change for the money Polly gave him and slipped the tip into the pocket of his long white apron. 'Mademoiselle has a friend in the Army of Africa, maybe?' he insinuated.

'No, nobody.' Nobody but everybody, when it came to the American troops whom Pétain's men were fighting. Her own countrymen, in action in this theatre of war for the first time, and – not against the Germans! Against the French, and not in Europe but in Africa! What would the retaliation be, and where? Polly Preston went down the long ramp faster than she walked up, for the brightness had gone out of the day for her, and a wintry wind was blowing off the sea. The big brasserie on the corner was doing a roaring trade, and the noise of argument floated out to the girl as she walked up to the Hotel Mimosa. There Jules, wearing a green baize apron, was carrying out the bags of two middle-aged men, who seemed to be making for the station. One of them politely held the door open for Polly.

'Now I tell you, miss, there's to be no more of it! I know the chances you've been taking, just to please that fellow Malvy and his pals! You'll get us all arrested, you will, before you're done! Just remember that you're French, that we're all French here, and mind—'

The angry voice stopped as Polly in amazement halted at the door to Fabienne's little office. She saw a stout red-faced man, whose features, coarsened by good living, still resembled Fabienne's and who as soon as he saw her said 'Madame!' and made her a little servile bow. Fabienne turned round quickly.

'Mademoiselle Henri, I was quite worried when I heard you'd gone out—'

'But I'm not late, am I? It can't be lunchtime already!'

'Oh no, not for an hour yet, but—'

'Perhaps you'll spare me a few minutes, when you're free.' Polly looked coldly at the smirking man. 'I'll be in the lounge.' As she went through the lobby she heard the man say, in the same rough tone as before, 'Who's the little duchess? Don't tell me she's another of *them*!'

The lounge was chilly, for opened windows had got rid of last night's cigarette smoke, and posies of fresh flowers had been placed with clean ashtrays on the tables. There was nobody to read the new magazines and trade papers laid on a sideboard, and Polly, looking in vain for a newspaper, stood turning them over until Fabienne came. She was still wearing Roger Malvy's red carnations, pinned at the neck of a dark grey jersey dress, and her colour was high with exasperation.

'You seem to be having a busy morning,' Polly observed.

'Busier than our usual Sundays. Two of our guests decided to go home today instead of tomorrow, and be with their families. You've heard the news?'

'Yes.'

'I knew you had, as soon as I saw your face.'

'But what does it mean?' cried Polly. 'That's what I wanted to ask you, Madame Fabienne! I didn't mean to take you away from that – gentleman in the office—'

'That was my father,' Fabienne said. 'He doesn't live here, he lives at Beausoleil.' She made a pretty little excusing gesture. 'Retirement doesn't agree with him, poor dear. He's rather too fond of coming over on Sunday mornings and having a few drinks with his old friends, and perhaps a game of pétanque. He usually has time to look in here and find fault with everything I've been doing, and today especially . . . What did you hear in the town?'

'I heard the voice of Marshal Pétain, saying France had been attacked and would defend herself, and that's about all I know.'

'You heard *him* broadcast? I heard him too,' said Fabienne. 'And I remembered what he said when France surrendered. "With broken heart I tell you we must cease the fight." And now he wants to fight again – the old hypocrite!' She looked at Polly's unhappy face. 'There's fighting in Morocco and at two points in Algeria, and possibly in Tunisia too; that's all we know as yet ... Mademoiselle Pauline, I don't want to pry into your affairs, but – will this make any difference to your plans?'

'How can I tell till I know what's going to happen?'

'Would you like to telephone to Jacques Brunel? My father's on his way back to Beausoleil, you'll be completely private if you call Jacques from the office.'

'He said he'd call me tomorrow. I'd rather wait until he does.'

'As you please.' Fabienne went to the open window and shut it decisively. She knelt by the radiator in the empty fireplace and switched on two bars. 'It's not as cosy as last night, is it? Never mind, let's be comfortable while we can. The next news bulletin's at one o'clock; I'll get Marie to serve our luncheon in the office and we can listen to it together.' She slipped her arm round Polly's waist. 'And then you and I must have a long talk, my dear.'

That was how it went for most people in Unoccupied France as the long hours of the eighth of November dragged their way to darkness. They lived from news bulletin to news bulletin, interpreting, arguing, quarrelling in the intervals, staying off the streets, staying in their own homes some dreading what Monday might bring and others longing for the sameness of being back at work. Many men absent from their homes on business like the two guests at the Hotel Mimosa, took long journeys in slow trains to get back to their wives and families. The Jewish refugees on the Côte d'Azur thought of other trains which might soon be sent to take them, like the eight thousand Paris deportees of August, into the German concentration camps. Everybody knew that whether or not the Americans followed up their raid on North Africa by landings in the South of France, the Germans would make the North African invasion an excuse to occupy the whole country.

Jacques Brunel had been invited to luncheon at the home of a solicitor who often sent briefs in his direction, and who lived with his wife and sister in one of the apartment buildings on the Promenade des Anglais. He went there quite often on a Sunday, when after *un bon déjeuner* they played bridge all afternoon, but on this Sunday the green baize table was not unfolded, and they sat round the wireless set waiting for news and discussing it in a mounting tension which reminded Jacques of the French wards at Dykefaulds Hospital in the dreadful June of 1940. In those days it had been 'Captain Jack', as the young nurses called him, who had to translate the B.B.C. newscasts for his wounded countrymen – all of them ill, helpless and far from home. Now he was well and home again, the blue Mediterranean wavelets were breaking softly on the pebbles far below the balcony of his friends' flat, but he and they were still as helpless to control events as they had all been two years before. The one authentic piece of news released before he went back to the Rue Droite was that the Vichy government had accepted the German offer of air support to repel the American invaders, and that squadrons of the Luftwaffe had immediately flown from Sicily and Sardinia to occupy the key airfields of Tunisia. There seemed little likelihood that Admiral Esteva, the French Resident-General, would go over to the Americans while the Germans were arriving in strength.

Charles Maxwell listened to the radio too, in the shabby apartment of his new host in the Vieux Port of Marseille. The host, a docker named Marius and employed at the Quai de la Joliette, became steadily more emotional during the afternoon, more determined to pack the whole thing in and take the road to freedom. Charles became quieter and more reflective. He realised that the flap at Gibraltar on the fifth of November, which he had mentioned casually in the hut at Cap Martin, was not merely a naval flap, but the tremendous prelude to invasion; that while he, in his cell-like transit billet inside the fortress was concerned only with his passage to France, the generals and admirals had been directing the movement of a fleet, an army, an air arm to Africa. He was not aware that strange things had happened on those two days, the fifth and sixth of November, which had not been anticipated for Operation Torch.

The first happening was the arrival of General Giraud. This had been planned with care, and though much hampered by the bad weather it took place on time. What was unexpected was the general's attitude.

General Henri Giraud was a brave man, a soldier to his fingertips, and without the faintest idea of the intricacies of the game of politics. He had been taken prisoner in the Other War, and had escaped. Taken prisoner again in 1940, he had escaped – it was said with American connivance – from the strong place of Königstein, and after a brief appearance at Vichy had retired to a villa on the Riviera where he had been living quietly for the past six months. So quietly, that few people had any idea that he was being groomed by the Americans as the commander they wished to instal in place of Charles de Gaulle.

This idea had greatly appealed to General Giraud. He was eleven years old than de Gaulle, and outranked him; while commanding the Metz garrison between the wars he had had de Gaulle as one of his officers, and disliked him. After his escape from prison he had never even considered joining the ranks of Fighting France, but – without the capital letters – he was eager to command fighting soldiers, and with American arms to lead the Army of Africa to new victories.

The American Chiefs had not supposed that Giraud would be willingly accepted as their leader by generals like Noguès and Juin, and they were prepared for arguments in that quarter. What they had not expected was Giraud's bland intention, expressed as soon as he landed at Gibraltar, of assuming the supreme command of all the allied forces as soon as they touched the 'French soil' of Algeria, and then of deploying the United States Air Force to attack the Germans in Sardinia and occupy all the airfields in the South of France.

It took two days of persuasion and argument to talk General Giraud out of the misconception that because he was a French officer he outranked all others as soon as French soil became a theatre of war. This was exactly the line de Gaulle had taken with the British officers involved with him in the abortive attack on Dakar, and it was not a promising beginning for the man who was to supersede de Gaulle in the councils of the Allies. General Eisenhower, already recognised as the supreme conciliator on the Allied side, tried sweet reason on the stubborn Frenchman, while agitated messages passed between Gibraltar and Washington. But it was the British, who for all their wish to keep in the background of Operation Torch had had a far longer experience of this sort of thing than the Americans, who finally succeeded in making Giraud see matters in their true perspective and depart under American command for Algiers.

Which was where the great problem lay. Giraud, at least, had been encouraged, sent for, awaited but the man nobody expected or wanted to see had arrived in Algiers from Vichy on that same Guy Fawkes' Day as the big flap was on at Gibraltar.

Admiral Jean Darlan embodied in his own person all the professional jealousy of the Royal Navy which Frenchmen in the naval service had felt since the Battle of Trafalgar. His strong anti-British feelings had taken him to Vichy, and it was arguable that by refusing to order the ships under his command to accept internment or join the British he was ultimately responsible for the tragedy of Mers-el-Kebir. The same feelings had taken him to Berchtesgaden, where he had promised Hitler to let a certain number of Luftwaffe planes pass through Syria to Iraq – the pretext for the attack on the Vichy French in the Levant. As Vice-Premier at Vichy he had made his name execrated in London and to a lesser extent in Washington; as Minister of Defence he had concluded an inspection tour in North Africa while the Allied invasion forces were assembling at Gibraltar.

Darlan was therefore supposed to be safely out of the way in Vichy. But then one of the imponderables of history took over : the admiral received news that his son was in hospital in Algiers, stricken with infantile paralysis. He flew back to Algiers on the fifth. He was still there in the early hours of the eighth, when the American landings began. He telegraphed for orders to Vichy, he parleyed with the American civilian agents, he telegraphed again to Vichy asking for liberty of action, which was refused. At one time he was under house arrest, at another time the Americans were under house arrest as the orders of imprisonment fluttered from one headquarers to another like November leaves. But while this sorry harlequinade was danced in the streets (the 'French soil' streets) of *Alger-la-Blanche*, the American invaders pressed home the attack by sea and air. The airfield was captured, the commander of Fort l'Empereur gave up his sword, and at five p.m. Darlan authorised General Juin to negotiate the surrender of the city. He had gone over to the Allies, and by midnight on Sunday the stunned world knew that General de Gaulle was out of the picture, and Admiral Darlan was in.

PART TWO

*I am fed up with de Gaulle ... I am absolutely convinced
that he has been and now is injuring our war effort and that
he is a very dangerous threat to us. I agree with you [Chur-
chill] that he likes neither the British nor the Americans and
that he would double-cross both of us at the first opportunity.*

Franklin D. Roosevelt
Washington D.C. 1943

9

Daniel Profetti junior, known to an admiring teenage gang
as Dany the Terror, was anything but terrifying when he
appeared in court on Monday morning. He was in terror of
what might happen to himself. Dany had not been brought
from prison in the police 'salad basket', because his father
had gone bail for him, but after his arrest he had spent one
night in a police cell, and had no wish to prolong the experience behind prison bars. His father swore that Maître
Brunel would get him off, but Dany did not share his faith
in the quiet barrister who occasionally dropped in at the Bar
des Sports and drank a glass of wine in the private office. To
the eighteen-year-old, Maître Brunel – who had the irritating
habit of addressing him as '*jeune homme*' – was merely one
of the mugs who had lost the war for France, and Dany, as
the day of his trial drew nearer, pictured his counsel sur-
rendering to the police witnesses as easily as Pétain had

surrendered to Hitler. Young Dany was man enough to be opposed to Vichy, and on the Sunday of the landings, when the Profetti household rang with the counter-cries of 'What's to be done about Dany?' and 'What's to be done about Darlan?' he had indulged in a fantasy of escaping to Algiers and joining the Americans. This was a form of defence against his mother, whom her son's arrest had turned from a spiritless drudge into an alarming woman, as ready to box his ears as she had once been to set dainties before him. She had actually shouted his father down on Sunday evening, shrieking that if by good luck Dany escaped a felon's cell he must be sent far away from the rotten mob that had corrupted him. A bit of decent manual labour might knock the devil out of Dany.

At least she didn't follow her husband and son to the Palais de Justice, yelling and screaming, but had sent them off with freshly laundered shirts and handkerchiefs in their breast pockets. Dany's last year's blue serge suit, revealing the bony wrists and ankles of a still-growing boy, met with his counsel's approval, and Maître Brunel himself in robe and toque was a more impressive figure than Dany had expected. The boy was too young to understand that the occasion was tailormade for Brunel's peculiar ability to equate his client's circumstances with the unhappy state of France. The youth defrauded of his heritage as a Frenchman, growing up in the knowledge of defeat, seeing no hope in the future and releasing his energy in an outburst of what, *messieurs*, was no worse than folly – that youth seemed to a sympathetic courtroom to be an unsung hero of the times. The array of character witnesses was not really necessary, for the shopkeeper threatened and robbed by Dany (of the grand sum of 523 francs 63 centimes) was detested by his neighbours as a skinflint and a police informer.

Jacques knew better than his clients how totally irrelevant the minor delinquencies of Profetti junior appeared to the Fifth Chambre Correctionnelle on that day of strain and suspicion, with half the Chambre committed to Vichy and the other half to God knew whom. Darlan, Giraud, de Gaulle, Governor Boisson of Dakar, even Admiral Esteva, embattled in Tunisia, each had some supporters in the hierarchy of the Palais de Justice. The support had wavered and rallied through that anxious Monday morning, when a heavy censorship was obviously being imposed on the news from North Africa. Almost absent-mindedly, young Profetti was given a suspended sentence of nine months. He was warned that he would be 'kept in view' by the police, and on the slightest infraction of the law would serve out his sentence in the prison of Les Baumettes. The boy was nearly weeping with relief when he left the courtroom with his father's arm round his shoulders.

Counsel for the defence supposed them to be hurrying home to eat and drink their way through a copious celebration lunch, but when he put away his robe and stole they were waiting for him in the corridor, all smiles.

'Thank Maître Brunel, boy!' commanded the father, and the son said 'Thanks a lot, monsieur!' in a jauntier tone than he had used in court. 'Did I do all right?'

'Yes, you were very convincing. Just keep out of trouble in the future, *jeune homme*, we don't want to see you here again.'

'That's what we want to ask your advice about, *Maître*.'

'More advice?'

'About Dany's future.'

Jacques looked from one to the other with a faint smile. 'Can we settle that in what's left of the morning?'

'No, not right away, you're busy,' said Profetti ingratiatingly. 'Could we come to your *étude* this afternoon?'

'Certainly, come at five.' He wanted to get rid of them. He had to see his Resistance man in the Préfecture de Police before its doors closed for the sacred midday meal. 'Congratulations, Dany,' he said, turning away. 'Don't hang about now. Your mother'll be glad to hear the good news.'

Jacques lunched off bread and cheese and a glass of wine at home rather than face the babble of argument at 'Le Faisan', and tried to make sense out of the double-talk from Radio Vichy. Before switching on the wireless he telephoned to the Hotel Mimosa, and was slightly annoyed to hear from surly Jules that Mademoiselle Henri was out shopping with Madame Fabienne. Taken the station taxi, they had, and gone over to Monte Carlo. 'Aux Dames de France', down in the Condamine, wasn't grand enough, he supposed, for the young lady from Paris—

Jacques cut him short. 'Tell Mademoiselle Henri I'll call her again around six o'clock.'

'If she's back by then,' said Jules, getting in the last word.

Punctually at five the old law clerk, Bosio, announced Monsieur Profetti, who entered the barister's room alone,

'Where's Dany?'

'I left him in the waiting-room. I wanted a word with you first, *chef*. And to give you your fee.' It was not an orthodox proceeding, but Jacques, as he flicked a finger through the wad of notes, knew that the sight of actual money, bank notes lying on the desk, was intended to impress him as much as it would have impressed the regular clientèle of the Bar des Sports.

'Very punctual of you, Dan, I appreciate it,' he said, locking his fee inside a desk drawer. 'Just let me write you a receipt.'

'I thought some ready cash might come in handy,' said Profetti, watching the swiftly moving fountain pen, 'in case you might be thinking of taking a little trip.'

'Across the water, do you mean?'

'Just that.' He kept his eyes on Jacques' impassive face. 'I suppose you're wondering how it'll work out with Darlan, now he's broken with the Marshal?'

'If the Americans are smart they'll ship him over to the States as soon as they've got all they can out of him. His life's not worth a day's purchase in Algiers.'

'You think one of the Vichy mob'll try to rub him out, eh?'

'Somebody will, unless the Americans put a bodyguard on him right round the clock.'

'Dany wants to join the Americans.'

'*Dany* does? My God, how does he expect to reach them?'

'By way of Marseille, I suppose. *Chef*, I haven't said anything to the kid, of course, but I thought if you were planning to cross yourself you might take Dany with you. The same way you got Chabrol out last year.'

'Long before the landings, and Chabrol was a very different proposition from young Dany. And what about you, Dan? Wasn't the boy supposed to be helping out at the Bar des Sports?'

'I want to keep him out of the Rue Paradis for a while. It's the old girl's idea really. *She* wants him sent to her father, old Jurac, in the hills above Sospel.'

'Sospel!' said Jacques, struck. 'That makes a lot more sense. But don't you think I'd better have him in? He won't like to think we're discussing him behind his back.' He rang his bell, and Monsieur Bosio, who had been standing guard over Dany in case of an outbreak of threats or pilfering, brought the boy in under unarmed escort.

'Sit down, Dany, and have a cigarette,' said Jacques, more cordially than Dany had ever heard him speak. Maître Brunel looked tired and even untidy: a lock of black hair had fallen over his forehead and the hand offering the Gauloises was not quite steady. Dany had noticed before that the fingers were very slightly deformed, the effects of frostbite at Namsos, he had heard his father say. But there was nothing weary or unsteady about Jacques' voice when he began to speak.

He paused for a moment, not to collect his thoughts, but to think how easy it would be to solve the problem of Dany Profetti. He only had to tell the boy to take the night train to Marseille, go to a certain newsagent's in the Rue la Caisserie and say, 'I've a message for Marius from Captain Jack,' and he would be launched on the life of adventure he seemed to crave. The docker at the Quai de la Joliette could get him across to Algiers if any man could, perhaps as a steward on one of the passenger steamers, unless all passenger traffic was suspended – that was how Marius had got Marc Chabrol out, who had been in love with Roger Malvy's wife. Across to Algiers, or across the Pyrenees, there was more than one road open : what was the sense in wanting to keep Dany on the Côte d'Azur ?

Because he was needed there. Because in a country where one hundred army divisions had been mobilised in 1940, every single man counted in 1942. Because when the Americans landed in Provence as they had landed in North Africa there should be Frenchmen waiting, armed and ready, to fight beside them and drive the enemy from the soil of France. This was the one hope for their salvation, *the only hope* – Jacques emphasised the words with a passion which astonished Dany – which had kept him going ever since he came back from London. Let Dany forget his fantasy of joining the Americans in North Africa, where they would be unlikely to enlist French boys, and get over to Sospel while travel was still possible in the Unoccupied Zone.

'But the Italians are in Sospel, monsieur,' the boy objected.

'The Italians may be in Nice tomorrow, and the Germans too,' said Jacques. 'First thing you know, you'll be picked up by the forced-labour gang and carted off to work in Germany. You'll be a damned sight better off on your grandfather's farm. Where exactly is it? Up in the hills, your father says?'

It was in the fruit country, said Dany sulkily, not far from the Col de Castillon, about four kilometres above Sospel. Grandfather raised cherries and took them down to the local depot for sale in Nice.

'So there won't be too much to do until the spring,' said his father.

'Grand'père Jurac works the whole year round. If it's not the cherries it's the goats and if it's not the goats it's the olives.

Last time I was there in winter he made me break stones to repair the terracing round the lemon trees—'

'Do you good,' said Jacques. 'You're a bit overweight, do you realise that? And don't think for a moment that you'll be out of the firing line on a mountain farm. When the Germans cross the Line they'll hold the railway from Nice to Italy, and Sospel will be the key to all the mountain valleys, La Roya, La Bevera, and the strong points like Tende and Brigue. A bunch of boys like you could do a lot to harass the enemy and destroy that branch of his communications system.'

'A *bunch* of boys? Kids from Sospel?'

'I was rather thinking of kids from Nice.'

Dany grinned, sure of his ground at last. 'What you're really saying, monsieur, is that you want me to take to the maquis.'

Darsi alla macchia – it was an old Italian phrase, literally translated as to go into the undergrowth, the bushes whose scent perfumed the shores of Corsica as well as the Côte d'Azur. The maquis was caruba and wild olive, myrtle, lentisk and smilax, but in the cover of those sweet-smelling shrubs there was protection, for to take to the maquis meant to go outside the law. As a lawyer Jacques Brunel drew back from the implication. As a resistant he was more sure than ever that his first impression of Dany Profetti was the right one. The boy was a natural maquisard. Under questioning, he gave Jacques a complete description of the Jurac farm, its exact location, extent in hectares, outbuildings and in-dwellers, including the distance from the Col de Castillon and the village of Castillon which lay beyond. It was not easy for a boy to travel from Nice to Sospel, but Dany promised to be there next morning. He was now as fascinated by the idea of resistance in the mountains as he had been by the fantasy of running away to the Americans.

It was nearer seven than six when Jacques returned to the Palais Lascaris, and sat down to telephone to the Hotel

Mimosa without taking off his overcoat. On the previous day, engrossed in the news from North Africa, he had hardly thought of Polly Preston. Now, with a German invasion imminent, he blamed himself for not calling her first thing in the morning. Somehow he had pictured her still sitting in the hotel lounge and waiting for him to telephone. Who would have thought the little monkey would choose North Africa's D-day plus one to go out shopping for new clothes?

It was a relief to hear Fabienne's voice, cool and impersonal, and he guessed she was manning the switchboard herself while old Jules ate his supper. She greeted him pleasantly, and of course knew better than to mention the political situation other than by asking him if he'd had a busy day. 'I'm sorry we were out when you called earlier,' she said. 'I'd no intention of going to Monte Carlo this forenoon, but somehow I was talked into it.'

'I can imagine,' said Jacques with feeling. 'Mademoiselle Henri can be very persuasive.'

'She can certainly chatter away without telling you anything about herself.'

'That's a good quality these days.'

'Jacques, where on earth did you pick her up?'

'I told you, she's a friend of mother's.'

'She doesn't seem to be short of money, she bought a lot of expensive things in Monte Carlo. Were all her worldly goods in that funny rucksack?'

'Don't worry at it, Fabienne! If Pauline doesn't want to tell you her own story, that's her affair.'

'She talked a lot about living in Paris, but I don't believe she's been there for at least five or six years. My guess is that she's running away from some man or other, am I right?'

'Must there be a man involved?'

'Isn't there always?' It was the harsh, brittle tone Jacques knew so well. 'I'd like to talk to her, Fabienne. In your office, if I may.'

'I'll fetch her down myself.' The Mimosa didn't run to

telephones in the bedrooms. Jacques sat drumming with the fingers of his free hand on the desk top while he pictured Fabienne going upstairs to find the girl – so young, so apparently sincere in her desire for freedom – whom some man, some posturing Italian, might already have made unhappy. He felt again the prick of tenderness and jealousy. It made his voice sharper than he intended when he heard her tentative '*Ici Pauline.*'

'*Bonsoir, Pauline.* How was the shopping expedition?'

'Very successful, and Fabienne's been so kind. And you, how are you? When are you coming to get me?'

'You're still determined to come on to Nice, in spite of the latest news?'

'More than ever determined.'

'You understand that after what's happened you may have to stay here for a while?'

'Yes, I do.'

'How do you propose to live?'

'I'll have to get a job, but unfortunately I'm not trained for anything, except to look after sick children.'

'If Madame Moreau could get you that sort of a job, not with sick kids but with young children, would that do? A job in a day nursery?'

'I'd love it.'

'I'll be with you tomorrow then, some time after five.'

'I'll be ready. Good night, and thank you, Jacques.'

'Good night, Pauline.'

Jacques laid down the handset. She could be laconic enough on the telephone! Her voice was exciting, with the Italian inflections magnified by electronics, and it was even more exciting to picture her lips moving and her small hand putting back that loose fall of hair. Tomorrow, some time after five, he would bring young Polly Preston to Nice, as he had sent young Dany Profetti to Sospel, and God alone knew what might become of them both because of his manipulations. He wanted a drink, and there was cognac in the

kitchen cupboard, but Jacques turned resolutely to the telephone directory. There were at least two more calls to be
made before he could relax with a glass of brandy and tap
water.

The uneasy hours of darkness wheeled through the skies
of France. Many people in the Unoccupied Zone slept well
enough. Others awaited the morning and the death-knell of
total occupation. At Vichy the Marshal-Chief of State fell
more than once into the light sleep of extreme old age under
the lights burning above his council table. Darlan had deserted him and Pierre Laval was at Berchtesgaden, where
Hitler gave him a Note demanding French consent to joint
Axis landings in Tunisia. At Toulon the admirals commanding what was still a splendid French fleet cursed Darlan, who
had let the Navy down. In Algiers, Admiral Darlan ordered
all land, sea and air forces to cease firing against American
and British troops, and return immediately to their bases.
General Mark Clark, who had carried out the negotiations
with Darlan, had good reason to be delighted with a bargain
which saved thousands of American lives. As D-day plus
one turned into D-day plus two everything in Algiers seemed
to be going according to the American plan.

Some of the American civilians who had arrived in North
Africa to administer projects loosely described as 'medical
care' and 'food supplies' to the native populations, had accepted without question the *bona fides* of any Frenchmen
they recruited under the cover of their charities to help pave
the way for an American landing. In their inexperience these
undercover agents imagined that every loyal Frenchman's
aim was the defeat of Germany. They were not aware that
some had already sworn to procure the triumph of Charles
de Gaulle.

And if the lights burned late at Vichy they were burning
late in more than one comfortable villa and apartment in
Algiers, where conspirators who had fawned on the Americans at noon damned their souls at midnight for the deal with

Darlan and the presence of Giraud, and the public humiliation administered to 'the only leader, General de Gaulle'.

'What an absolutely fascinating place!'
That was Polly Preston's first reaction to Jacques Brunel's
apartment when she saw it at six o'clock on a November
evening. She had been fascinated as soon as they entered the
Palais Lascaris, first by the faded coat of arms in the ceiling
of the vestibule and the motto *Nec Me Fulgura*. 'Even
thunder can't kill me!' she translated it at once. Next she
exclaimed over the baroque sculptures in the staircase niches.
But the greater enthusiasm was evoked by Jacques' own
living-room, where the light from the green-shaded table
lamps cast strange shadows on the horses plunging across the
painted ceiling
'What marvellous furniture! Imagine owning things like
these!'
'People think it's First Empire, but my great-aunt said it
was Restoration and Louis Philippe. She inherited it all from
her father.'
'It must be very valuable.' It was also very neglected, crying out for beeswax and elbow grease, and there was verdi-
gris on the brass handles wrought with a design of Venus
rising from the waves. 'Don't bother to switch the fire on,
Jacques, it isn't cold.' Polly looked warm and glowing in one
of the Lyon silk blouses bought the day before, tied in a big
primrose yellow bow at her neck. 'Why do they call this the
Palais Lascaris?' she went on. 'I'm sure I've heard that name
in Naples.'
'The Lascaris princes used to own half the Mediterranean
coast,' said Jacques. 'This was their town house in Nice, and
they had a villa at Cap Martin as well. I can just remember
the last of the line, the Principessa Clara; she lived here when
I was a little boy.'
'Here in this apartment?'
'No, this was Grand'tante Marthe's long before I was born.

The old princess lived on the floor below, the *piano nobile*. It's all chopped up into little flats now.' He switched on the electric fire in spite of her. 'Do sit down, Pauline, and let me get you a Cinzano. We've really got to have a serious talk about your plans.'

Polly grimaced at his departing back. A long talk with Fabienne, a serious talk with Jacques – everyone wanted to talk portentously, when she was too excited to sit still! They had talked about the American landing in the car, and that was serious enough, but now Polly had recovered from the alarm of Sunday, and was buoyantly confident in an American success. She followed Jacques out to the tiny kitchen. 'Do you know the one thing this place really needs?' she demanded.

'What?'

'Masses of flowers.'

Flowers, *bon Dieu*! Jacques Brunel had sent flowers by messenger to his dinner-party hostesses before the war, and sometimes to girls who had caught his fancy, but the idea that a man might buy carnations in the flower market and carry them home for his own pleasure was novel and vaguely distasteful. 'I'll have flowers for you next time you come,' he promised. 'Meantime let's have a drink.'

Polly moved her black box-calf handbag, also new from Monte Carlo, to make way for the tray on top of the table, accepted the glass of white vermouth and murmured '*Santé!*' But she was like quicksilver, she wouldn't sit down, and Jacques perforce remained standing too, although he was tired after hours of climbing among the crags and steep hill paths between the villages of Roquebrune and Gorbio. He had gone down to his hut above the shore at Cap Martin first, to make sure there was no tiniest piece of evidence to show any invader that the place was anything more than a dump for old sports gear and disused picnic equipment. The bottle of dark rum, still a quarter full, he had brought away in his raincoat pocket.

Tomorrow, he told Polly, he planned to take her up to the Moreau villa at Cimiez. He had telephoned about her, the young friend of his mother and Madame Belinska, and Madame Moreau was delighted to hear that the under-staffed day nursery of which she was the patroness would soon have an experienced part time *monitrice.*

'That's what I'm called on my new identity card,' said Polly with a laugh.

'Yes, we thought that was better than *infirmière,* because, as I told you, those kids aren't handicapped in any way, ex-cept for being undernourished. Their fathers are prisoners of war and their mothers are out at work all day, so what they need is to be fed and played with and given some kinder-garten lessons—'

'And loved,' said Polly.

'And loved.' It was a while since Jacques had conjugated the verb *aimer.*

'French kids, not Italians, I'll like that,' said Polly. 'But,' she added rather wistfully, 'how long for?'

'How long? I warned you it might be for a while.'

'Yes, I know.'

'It's a paid job, of course. Not well paid, but I gather you're not short of cash.'

'Not short exactly, but if I stay in Nice I'll have to earn my keep.'

'I know that's how you feel, and I knew you didn't want to turn up like Cinderella on Madame Moreau's doorstep—'

'Not after what happened at the Maison Russe.'

'So I got you a room in a decent little pension run by a Madame Froment, the sister-in-law of a friend of mine. I think you'll be quite comfortable there.'

'Just so I can pay my way as I did at the Mimosa.' Polly had the receipted hotel bill, made out in Fabienne's beauti-ful clear writing, in the handbag which held the French identity card and ration books provided by the Resistance man at the Prefecture.

Jacques hesitated. Money was a delicate topic, but if she was carrying a large sum it could be dangerous, and she ought to think of renting a safe deposit box. He asked bluntly how much she had in her possession, and when Polly told him he whistled.

'That's an awful lot to be carrying around, even in a money belt,' he said.

'It's so uncomfortable, too.' Polly sighed, and leaned back against the writing desk like a stretching cat. Jacques stared at her. He had never before brought a girl to the Palais Lascaris, his short and brutal sex encounters having taken place in the anonymity of hotel rooms, and he was seduced by the grace and colour which this girl brought to his familiar surroundings. He had a sudden, erotic vision of the naked body beneath the yellow silk blouse, tautened by her breasts, and the narrow black skirt. He pictured the money belt of webbing like a *ceinture de chasteté* round her slender waist, and the red marks it would leave on her flesh when he unfastened it. Uncontrollably, Jacques took Polly in his arms and bent his dark head to kiss her.

'Pauline, you're very sweet!'

She turned her head away, so that his lips only met the soft cheek he had touched with his fingers in the first hour they met. He heard Polly's chilling whisper:

'Fabienne told me about your great loss ... and I'm so sorry ... but don't kiss me, please.'

'Fabienne told you *what*?'

'About your fiancée who was killed in the London blitz.'

Jacques' arms fell to his sides. He was completely at a loss. To say, 'She wasn't my fiancée!' was a quibble. To say, 'But that was then and this is now!' an infidelity to a fading dream.

'Hadn't you better answer that?' said Polly. The telephone was ringing.

'Who the devil can it be?' said Jacques furiously. '*Allô, j'écoute!*'

'Jacques? Alfred Lecampion,' said a voice. 'Calling from a café in the Place Rossetti.'

'On your way to that conference in Cannes?'

'Yes, but I've got a patient with me, a friend of yours. Could I bring him up for an hour's rest in your apartment?'

Jacques glanced at Polly. She was looking at his books and sipping her apéritif with her back towards him. 'An emergency, is it?' he said into the telephone.

'More or less. *Not* a hospital case, you understand?'

'Perfectly. Is there anything I can do before you get here?'

'Could you look out a couple of blankets and a pillow?'

'Right.' He heard the phone click and thought, what appalling luck. There went the evening, and his plan to take Polly to dinner at one of the good restaurants near the harbour, and to cap it all there wasn't even time to get her to Madame Froment's before the doctor arrived with some impetuous resistant who had put himself in the way of a *milicien*'s bullet. Hell! There was nothing to do but bluff it out.

'Polly,' he said, 'that was a doctor friend of mine from Cap Martin. There's been some sort of accident, and he wants to bring the – victim here for rest and quiet—'

'A road accident?'

'I really don't know. I'm terribly sorry—'

'You'd like me to go,' she said. 'Don't worry. I can find my own way to your pension, if you tell me the address.'

'You can't go off alone, lugging that suitcase.'

'Then let me stay and help.'

He didn't know what she might have to see, what mess of blood and bandage, but there was no time for more. 'They're coming from the Place Rossetti, where we left the car,' he said. 'They'll be here in five minutes. I've got to get some blankets out.'

Jacques fetched two heavy winter blankets from the armoire, with a big square pillow from his own bed, and Polly arranged them on the sofa in the corner by the fire. Then the doorbell rang, and Jacques opened the door to find Dr. Lecampion supporting a young man in a fisherman's jersey, heavy trousers and boots, with one of the doctor's overcoats bundled over all. A tweed hat was pulled low on the bandage round his forehead. His face was heavily bruised but quite recognisable. He was one of Jacques' Resistance group from Menton.

'François, for God's sake, what have you been up to?' said Jacques, as he took the man's weight on his own shoulder, and Polly came into the lobby to pull her new suitcase out of their way.

'Madame, I beg your pardon ... I had no idea ...' began Alfred Lecampion, and Jacques, easing the injured man into the nest of blankets, realised that the doctor thought he had interrupted an assignation. The pretty girl, the warm lamp-lit room, the tray with the glasses, were the conventional ingredients in Madame Lecampion's magazines for a night of sex and sin.

'Doctor, this is Mademoiselle Henri, a friend of my mother.' He had said it often enough to convince himself that Marguerite Verbier and Polly Preston had been at school together, but Polly barely acknowledged the formality: she was gently adjusting the pillow under the patient's head. They removed the borrowed gear and wrapped the blankets round him before he seemed to be aware of his surroundings.

'*Mon capitaine*, I'm very sorry to be a nuisance!'

'It's all right, François. Don't try to talk just yet.'

'What can I do for him, doctor?' asked Polly, and Dr. Lecampion asked her to bring a glass of water. She closed the kitchen door firmly and let the single tap run long and hard to give the men a chance to talk.

'What happened?' Jacques said instantly. 'Is he wounded, Fred?'

'Not his fault if he isn't! Damned fool tried to run for it in broad daylight, and an Italian patrol boat put a shot across him as soon as he was outside the fishing limits. They forced him ashore off the point of Cap Martin, but he got away from them across the rocks at the expense of a bad fall. All that bruising looks worse than it is, but he put his shoulder out when he fell, and he was in pretty poor shape after climbing up through the Grand Hotel gardens to my surgery. He asked me to give him a lift to Cannes, but he passed out in the car, and then I thought of bringing him to you. He *is* one of your lot, isn't he?'

'Yes, but how about taking him to the Hôpital St. Roch?'

'Not if we can avoid it. The Italians will have his description out by now, or at least the registration of his boat.'

'I wanted to go to Marseille, *mon capitaine*,' said François, as Polly came back with the water. '*Merci, madame*.' He raised his head to drink, and tried to smile.

'You're feeling better, aren't you?' she said.

'He'll be in fine shape by tomorrow,' said the doctor. 'All he needs is some medication and a few hours' sleep.'

'We'll make the sofa a bit more comfortable for you, François,' said Jacques. 'You're not going any further to-night. Dr. Lecampion can take care of you while I drive Mademoiselle Henri home. She's starting a new job at the *maternelle* tomorrow, Fred,' he added in explanation. 'They'll be expecting her for supper at her boarding house.'

The good-byes took longer than the greetings, because the first alarm was over, and François looking up quite brightly from the pillow expected to have his bandaged hand touched, if not shaken, as well as the doctor's. But the trip down the Rue Rossetti to the Peugeot, with Jacques carrying Polly's leather suitcase, was quick and silent until the girl said as the car moved off :

'What really happened?'

'He dislocated his shoulder in a fall on the rocks and passed out in the doctor's car.'

'Concussion?'

'I wouldn't know.'

'What was a fisherman doing, clambering about on the rocks?'

'Looking for sea urchins, probably.'

'On the way to Marseille?'

'Ah, you heard that, did you? Everybody and his brother wants to go to Marseille these days.'

Polly said no more until Jacques stopped the car in the Place Magenta, a space of quiet between two busy streets not far from the umbered walls of the great Masséna square.

'Here you are then. Come up and meet Madame Froment. I think you'll like her, and you won't have to see much of the rest of them." He was about to open the car door when Polly put her hand on his sleeve. He felt her warmth at his side, and the whisper of silk as she leaned towards him.

'Jacques, I want to go up alone to Madame Moreau's in the morning.'

'Why?'

'I think it might be wiser, that's all. And you'll be very busy with your own work, and getting François away safely.'

'François—'

'He's on the run, isn't he? He's one of the Resistance?'

'Yes, Polly.'

'And you're Captain Jack yourself, aren't you?'

'Yes.'

With that one word Jacques laid down the burden of secrecy and suspicion which had warped his nature for so long, and gave his trust into Polly Preston's keeping.

10

The eleventh of November was the day when everything happened at once. It was the anniversary of the armistice which ended the First World War, called in France *la Fête de la Victoire*, and in Germany remembered as a day of humiliation. On November 11th, 1942, in retaliation for the American landings, the Germans crossed the Line of Demarcation into the Unoccupied Zone, so that the whole of France was now in Hitler's power. There was a touch of mordant humour in the name given to this military operation. The Germans, thanks to an indiscretion of Kaiser Wilhelm II, had once been nicknamed the 'Huns'. The name of Attila, the chieftain of the Huns, had never been forgotten. The new advance of the German barbarians into Southern France was given the code name of Operation Attila.

Mussolini's men came strutting along in their rear, as usual. The Bersaglieri had their cocks' feathers curled and stiffened for the occasion, and the young levies which had been spared defeat in the desert stepped out behind the trumpets and drums as the Italians crossed the demilitarised area beyond Menton for the formal occupation of Nice. It had been an old ambition for the Fascists. Now it was a token only, for the actual occupation of the Riviera was effected by the Germans. Not, in the first few days or weeks, by the full strength of the Wehrmacht, but by the Gestapo, the Abwehr and the Sicherheitsdienst which, under Vichy, had already infiltrated the coast from Menton to Marseille.

On this same eleventh of November when Operation Attila was launched, one Frenchman, and one alone, dared to challenge the German invaders. He was one of the two

French generals who had actually won a victory in 1940. The other was General Béthouart, who was under arrest at Rabat.

The fighting general, the victor of Rethel, was Jean de Lattre de Tassigny, commanding the XVI Military Division at Montpellier. When the Germans crossed the Line on November 11th de Lattre attacked, and successfully occupied the heights of Les Corbières. Then collaboration triumphed, and the Secretary of War at Vichy (for Vichy kept the titles if not the status of a belligerent) ordered the general to surrender. He was arrested and imprisoned at Toulouse pending his trial for treason.

In Algiers, Admiral Darlan declared that the Germans by crossing the Line had violated the armistice agreement, which restored to himself and others their liberty of action, and he sent a message to the commander of the French Mediterranean Fleet 'inviting' him to bring his warships to French North Africa. Admiral de Laborde, as violently anti-British as Darlan used to be, sent a message that if he took his ships to sea it would be to attack the Allied convoys. Darlan gloomily repeated to his new friends what he had said to the disbelieving British in 1940, that the French Navy would scuttle its ships rather than let them fall into German hands.

In London, far from the firing line, the Leader of All Free Frenchmen could only share in the action by holding a rally in the Albert Hall. Ostensibly it was to celebrate the armistice of 1918 and the victory of France, with which he had come to identify himself.

Charles de Gaulle had suffered three days of intense mortification since his exclusion from the American landings. He writhed under the double wound of knowing that Darlan, Marshal Pétain's 'Dauphin', now held the civil power in Algeria and that General Giraud commanded the military. His rage was not assuaged by Mr. Churchill's promise that in the very near future the Fighting French should have an invasion all to themselves and 'swoop' on French East Africa.

Djibouti, a long way from Algiers, was a miserable consolation prize. The entourage at Carlton Gardens, so quarrelsome among themselves, united in denouncing the perfidy of '*les Anglo-Saxonnes*' (for Hitler's name for the Allies had been included in the Gaullist vocabulary) and the general himself lashed out to Roosevelt's envoy, Admiral Stark, 'So the United States buys the treachery of traitors!' The American chiefs were mildly surprised and quite unmoved by the storm which their deal with Darlan had roused in their own and the British press. None of them liked the Little Fellow, as General Clark called him, but the Darlan deal fulfilled one of the basic requirements of American involvement in the war : it worked.

To add to the seething background of de Gaulle's unlucky week, Warner Brothers had given up the idea of filming *The de Gaulle Story*. William Faulkner, on his way to glory and the Nobel Prize for literature, had achieved one hundred and fifty-three mimeographed pages of the screenplay by the middle of November, at which point President Roosevelt's opposition to the project caused it to be shelved once and for all. 'No movie for Big Charlie,' commented Bob Kemp to Joe Calvert, as they waited in the Albert Hall for the rally to start. 'I'm beginning to wonder if he needed it. He's got the other media in his pocket already.'

Joe Calvert sighed. He had been depressed ever since his visit to Moscow in August, and not only because he knew now that Averell Harriman and not himself would be appointed ambassador to Russia. Personally he got on well with Harriman, and welcomed an assignment to assist him in the co-ordination of Lend-Lease Supplies. It was because his trip to Moscow had taught him that Stalin's Russia had not changed, except for the worse, from the Russia of 1918, where as a young vice-consul he had seen one hundred million U.S. dollars squandered and pocketed by the men at the top. He was pretty sure the same thing was going to happen again.

'He's got a big turn-out tonight,' he said, and it was true. If a political rally counted as part of the publicity media, General de Gaulle had come a long way since his first appearance at the Y.M.C.A. in the Tottenham Court Road. The four tiers of the Albert Hall were packed with his troops quartered in England and padded with his supporters from *Les Français de Grande Bretagne*, and if some less indulgent observers were scattered through the rows, the audience was big enough to raise a satisfactory cheer when the Leader strode on to the vast stage. Behind him hung an enormous Tricolore, with spotlights in a V playing on the superimposed Cross of Lorraine, which played the same part as the swastika did at similar rallies in Berlin. Inspired by the strains of the *Marseillaise*, de Gaulle gave his followers exactly the message they needed to hear.

'From the Fighting French alone,' the Leader intoned, 'will liberation come. We suffer no one to come and divide out country's war effort by these so-called parallel enterprises!'

'He's sure fond of the ten-dollar words,' grunted Bob Kemp under cover of the cheering. ' "So-called parallel enterprises" – why the hell can't he come right out and say he wants to hang Jean Darlan to a sour-apple tree?'

'He really laid it on the line tonight,' conceded Joe Calvert as they drove back to Grosvenor Square. 'More trouble ahead, Bob! I hope Giraud can get his new French Army together fast and shove ahead into Tunisia. The British are a long way from Tripoli, and if we're in for another winter stalemate it'll play right into de Gaulle's hands.'

While de Gaulle speechified in London, the citizens of Unoccupied France waited in fear and resentment for the arrival of the Germans, Radio Vichy had confirmed what was in store for them, and by the time Polly Preston left the Pension Froment the people of Nice had assumed the mask worn for more than two years by the people of Paris. The blank eyes, the deaf ears, were ready to ignore the occupants whenever they arrived.

Polly stood for a quarter of an hour in a long line of silent Niçois waiting for the bus to the suburb of Cimiez. Madame Moreau, spoken to by telephone, had given the directions in a manner as pleasant as vague. The Moreaus lived beyond the Roman arenas, far up the hill, and one had to allow at least half an hour by public transport. The house was called the Villa Les Floralies. Polly grew impatient as the minutes passed. She had been trained to be punctual, and hated to seem impolite to Madame Moreau. At last the bus came lumbering along and took her up the Boulevard de Cimiez into the high suburb which the Romans had colonised thirteen hundred years before. Roman Cemenelum, Polly saw as she clung to a strap in the overcrowded bus, had become a British enclave, with street names like Georges V, Prince de Galles and Edith Cavell, and it was easy to guess that Queen Victoria, who enjoyed her winter visits to Cimiez, had inspired the name of the Hotel Regina.

Polly got off at the Regina, because the driver was shouting '*Les Arènes!*', and lost her way at once. She saw more hotels, some divided into apartments rented by the better-off refugees, backing on to the broken walls and ruined arches which had once enclosed a Roman place of pleasure. She hurried up the Impasse des Arènes, passing unaware the handsome villa belonging to Pierre Orenga, alias Couteau, the head of the 'Knife' circuit, and found it ended in front of an ancient church and monastery. A man working under the olive trees beside the ruins said she had turned off the boulevard too soon. The Villa Les Floralies stood behind the Impasse, in its own grounds, with flowers ! He kissed the tips of expressive fingers.

It was obvious that Dr. Moreau employed a full-time gardener, for the short gravel drive was raked, the lawns on each side watered and clipped, and the flower beds filled with late-blooming roses. The winter mimosas which formed a hedge on each side of the entrance gate gave out a delicious perfume. The same perfection reigned indoors. A smart house-parlourmaid showed Polly through a hall gleaming with polished furniture into a salon decorated in reseda green and honeysuckle pink, with a variety of gilt and brocade chairs and sofas, and Lalique vases holding camelias from the doctor's conservatory.

'Mademoiselle Henri, how very nice to meet you!' A little lady with snow-white hair brushed up in a pompadour, and a pretty face as rosy as a sugar almond, came into the room with outstretched hand.

'It's very kind of you to let me come, madame,' said Polly. 'I do apologise for being so terribly late.'

'I was afraid the buses might have gone on strike. The news this morning was so – alarming.'

'Everything seems to be normal so far. I was stupid enough to lose my way at the Roman ruins.'

'Cimiez is confusing to a stranger, and it was rather naughty of me to ask you to come all the way out here, because the *maternelle* is really no distance from the Place Magenta. But I did want to have you all to myself for a little while, and hear about the dear baroness! I must pick up the doctor at the Children's Hospital at half past twelve, but we have plenty of time. Do take your coat off and sit down.' She gave a glance of approval at Polly's black skirt and fresh white blouse, and touched the bell.

'Juliette' – to the smart maid, who came in quickly enough to have been listening at the door – 'tell Marie we'd like some chocolate, please. Or would you prefer coffee, Mademoiselle Henri?'

'Chocolate would be wonderful.'

'Ah, you've a sweet tooth, like my daughter Chantal. *I hear you met my son-in-law the other night!*'

'In Monaco, yes I did, madame.'

'He told us he went to supper at a friend's villa, after signing that magnificent contract – he told you about it of course – and met you there with Jacques Brunel. *How well do you know our clever Jacques?*'

'Not nearly as well as I know his mother.' Sugar Almond came up fast with the questions, calculated to throw a stupid girl off balance, but Polly was used to the prying of Neapolitan dowagers, and Jacques had warned her about the Moreau-Malvy connection while he was driving her in to Nice. She was interested to find that the astute Monsieur Malvy had got his story in first.

'Have you good news of Madame Malvy?' she asked. 'I understand she's been taking the cure at the Mont Dore.'

'Poor darling!' said Madame Moreau. 'She's had a wretched time since her little boy was born. An asthma sufferer, alas! The doctor positively forbade her to spend the summer in Nice. That apartment on the Promenade des Anglais – so noisy, so hot and dusty in July and August! We're hoping to get her back any day now ... and here comes Juliette with our chocolate.'

It was served with cream, hot and frothing, in Sèvres cups so thin as to be almost transparent, and Sugar Almond, dispensing it with ringed hands, reminded Polly of her own mother serving tea from a Russian samovar, a relic of their Paris days. She belatedly produced the Baroness Belinska's letter, somewhat the worse for being carried in Jacques Brunel's wallet since Saturday evening. Her hostess read it with little whimpers of sympathy. The Russian Revolution ... what an ordeal ... escaped together down the Volga, did they, poor dears? What stories Polly's maman must have had to tell of her adventures!

'As a matter of fact she hated to talk about it. She always said her real life began when she reached Paris, where she met my father.'

'Monsieur Henri. Was he – a professional man?'

'He was in the diplomatic service.' *Il était de la carrière* – it was always impressive, and Polly omitted to say in what country the career began. In the same way Madame Moreau made no comment on the odd similarity between the name 'Henri' and the 'Marie Hendrikova' of Madame Belinska's letter. She had lived long enough among white lies and evasions to know when not to press the truth too far.

So they chatted very comfortably, as if the war was far away, about the old baroness and her colourful past, and the days when Chantal Moreau and Jacques Brunel won the mixed doubles tournament at the Grand Hotel du Cap Martin against Chantal's cousin Marc Chabrol and his partner. They looked at a studio portrait of Chantal as a bride and another with her infant on his christening day. Patrick was the baby's name. 'Not a family name,' said Madame Moreau, 'but very fashionable this year.'

'How old is Patrick now, madame?'

'He'll be a year old in January. Chantal writes that he's trying to take his first steps already.'

Polly studied the baby face under the christening cap. 'He'll look quite different when you see him again, won't he?'

The Louis XV clock in its glass case chimed eleven before Madame Moreau replied. 'Yes, he will,' she said. 'The doctor and I haven't seen him since the end of May. And now I think I hear Gustave bringing the car round, he's always prompt. You must come back on Sunday and have luncheon with us. I haven't asked you yet if you play bridge?'

'Yes, I do, madame.'

'Then I'll invite your friend Jacques to come too.'

Polly's friend Jacques telephoned to her late in the afternoon, when she was in her clean little room at the Pension Froment, arranging newly-bought smocks for the nursery school work in her chest of drawers. The telephone stood on the hall table, hardly a private place, and she was very guarded in her replies.

'Pauline, are you all right? No trouble of any sort today?'

'None at all.'

'How did you get on with Madame Moreau?'

'She was sweet.'

'And what about the job?'

'I'm starting tomorrow.'

'Good. Have you noticed the English Tearoom in the Place Magenta?'

'Of course, it's on the ground floor of this building. I almost went there for a cup of tea.'

'Can you wait fifteen minutes, and have some tea with me?'

'Right there? Of course I can.'

'Then *à bientôt*.'

Most of the cafés in Nice were deserted when Jacques walked along from the Place du Palais, but there was a flurry of activity in the English Tearoom, where a group of English residents, too old to fear the internment camps, had resolved to stick to the habits of a lifetime on occupation day. They had come by twos and threes to drink tea and eat what passed for seed-cake, waited on by a wheezing waitress and surveyed by an equally ancient cashier. Jacques smiled as Polly's red cap with her piquant face beneath it appeared in the doorway.

'This place is as lively as the morgue,' was his greeting, 'but it's right where you live, and I didn't want to suggest dinner until we know what the curfew hours are going to be.'

'Everything seems quiet enough so far.'

'You missed the triumphal entry of the Italians,' said Jacques, breaking off to order tea and toast. Polly changed the subject by asking for François.

'Better, but not well enough to travel yet. He'll be staying with me until tomorrow night, or Friday morning.'

'I thought that doctor was a bit too optimistic.'

'He went on to Cannes. Now tell me about *your* day.' He sat back with a smile while Polly poured the tea ('real tea, no tea bags here!') and chattered about the day nursery, the women who ran it on a shoestring, and the little French kids, so cute. 'I start at eight tomorrow morning,' she said importantly. 'Eight to two one day, and midday to six the next. It'll be fun, having different times of the day free, and Sundays off all day.'

'And you got on well with Madame Moreau? How did you like her house?'

'The house was lovely. Oh Jacques, you were so smart! I'd have died if I'd turned up in a place like that on Saturday night, with a torn hem to my coat, and the rucksack! Madame Morcau gave me a thorough vetting, I can tell you. Once she was sure I wouldn't eat peas with my knife she asked me to luncheon and bridge next Sunday, and she's going to ask you too.'

'That's too bad, because I'm off to Aix on Sunday morning."

'Aix-en-Provence? But why?' She looked at the English ladies, oblivious of all but tea, and lowered her voice. 'You mean on a *job*?'

'There's nothing cloak-and-dagger about the job, Polly. If the trains are running at the weekend, and Justice still exists in France, which of course is open to doubt, the law will take its course at the Aix Assizes on Monday morning, and I have to be there.'

'How long?'

'All week, probably.'

'Then if you can't go to Les Floralies on Sunday, I do think you might give me a briefing on the Malvys. I nearly put my foot in it today when Madame Moreau mentioned Roger's friends in their villa at Monaco, and I didn't know what was coming next. What's the mystery about Chantal Malvy? Why's she still at the Mont Dore long after the season must be over? Is it because her husband's having an affair with Fabienne Leroux?'

'Fabienne came after, not before, the Malvy split,' said Jacques. 'I don't know much about it really. I do know that Chantal was very much in love with her cousin, Marc Chabrol, and the doctor was dead against first cousins marrying. He rather pushed her at Roger Malvy. Who on his side was chiefly interested in the money.'

'The Moreaus obviously have a lot of money. That huge place, the gardener who drives the car, and two maids—'

'Plus the butler-valet who's been with Dr. Moreau for the past twenty years. Yes, the money's there all right, but it's new money, and the Malvy's have an old name and a lot of prestige. All the parents thought it was a fair exchange.'

'And Marc Chabrol, did he marry too?'

'Chabrol got out of the country last year and went to Algiers.'

'Poor Chantal.'

Jacques laid his hand over hers. 'Polly,' he said, 'I asked you to meet me here for a special reason. First, what we talked about last night, sitting in the car. That must be a secret between you and me.'

'I know it. I was hoping you'd let me help, if you think I can.'

'There *is* one thing you could do while I'm away. Of course it may be nothing at all, but I was interested when you told me the Moreaus had been seeing Roger Malvy. I thought he never went near Les Floralies these days. If he shows up on Sunday, pay attention to what he has to say.'

'Say about what?'

'Any new contracts he may have made. I hear he's throwing his money about, gambling on the Bourse as well as at the casino, and it can't all be coming from his earnings.'

'What about an advance on the job at Cap d'Ail?'

'It wouldn't be on that scale. I think he might be getting money from some other source, and I want to know what. You may be able to get a line on it. I watched you sizing him up the other night.'

'I can try. But' – with a touch of spite – 'wouldn't Fabienne do it better than me?'

'*Fabienne!*' said Jacques with an exasperated sigh. 'That's the other thing I wanted to say to you, Pauline. I don't know why Fabienne felt she had to tell you about Alison—'

'Alison?'

'Alison Grant, the girl who was killed in England, in an air raid. You said you were sorry for my loss—'

'Yes.'

'It *was* a great loss once, and I was half crazy with anger at the waste of her life when I came back to France. I told Fabienne about Alison, when I couldn't talk about her to anybody else – one night when we were both down on our luck, and she was miserable about Pierre Lavisse. I told her Pierre was at least alive to come back to her, while my girl was dead.'

'Fabienne said your heart was broken.'

'Listen, Pauline.' She was listening intently, with her eyes on the man's dark eyes, and his serious face now taut with feeling. 'Alison was an enchanting girl. I met her first in May, when I was in hospital in Scotland, and then again at the end of July, when we were both in London. We had just six weeks together before she was killed, and we fell in love. Love was all people had in England that summer, when the sun was always shining and every day might be your last. I was never Alison's lover – never even had the chance to ask her to marry me – but for those six weeks, we were happy together.'

'It's not a long time to be happy in.'

'Is it wrong to wish to be happy again?'

'No, it isn't wrong.' Polly sighed. 'How old was she?'

'About the same age as you are now. About twenty-one.'

'Do I remind you of her?'

'Do *you* remind me of her? No, of course you don't, whatever put that in your head?'

'Fabienne said I probably did.'

'I wish Fabienne Leroux would learn to hold her tongue. She never knew Alison, so how could she . . . Polly, you and Alison are – were – two quite different people. Oh, you've got two things in common, courage and gaiety, because Alison was brave too, and fun to be with, just like you. But she wasn't a girl on her own, except for having a job, and even that was in the Ministry where her brother had a post. She lived with her brother and his wife, she had parents in Scotland. I don't think she could ever have done what you did, starting out from Naples, all on your own, and landing up here in a funny little pension and a funny job with those poor little kids, when you had such dreams of going to America and joining one of the Services—'

'At least I'm on the right side of the war,' she said, and Jacques thought he saw tears in her eyes. His fingers tightened on hers. 'You're good, Polly,' he said. 'I admire you very much.'

'Thank you.'

When the waitress laid the bill on the table it startled them both. The tearoom was empty and the lights were being put out.

'I hate to be the last to leave,' said Polly. 'Do let's go!'

Everything was quiet in the Place Magenta, and though it was hardly the usual closing time the iron shutters were being run down on the shops in the busy streets on either side. 'People aren't waiting for the curfew,' said Polly, 'they want to get home early tonight. And here I am, right at my own front door.'

There was a faint light behind the glass and iron grille of the door to the apartment building where Madame Froment, in a large second floor flat, ran her little pension. Jacques drew Polly into the shelter of the doorway.

'If I don't come back to Nice as soon as the Assizes are over, you mustn't worry, Polly. I'm sure you're going to be all right, and people you don't know yet will be looking out for you.'

'You mean you're going – far away?'

'Not very far. But if you want me for any reason, ask Madame Froment to put you in touch with her brother

Henri. He runs a garage behind the Cours Saleya, and he's the one who'll know where to find me. And he knows about you.'

'You're not planning to go to – Africa?'

'No, not yet. Don't fret about it, Polly! When the time comes that I have to leave France, I mean to take you with me.'

'Is that a promise?'

'On my heart.' Jacques took Polly in his arms and kissed her chilly hands. But this time Polly Preston gave him her mouth to kiss.

Jacques had done well – thought Polly, before she slept that night – to tell her so speedily and so fully about his lost love. She wasn't yet in love with him herself, the man who had taken her across the border, but she was woman enough to know what Jacques did not, why Fabienne had betrayed his confidence and made a romance out of his 'broken heart'. It was the old story of the dog in the manger. Fabienne Leroux might be having an affair with another man now, but if Jacques had lifted a finger he could have had her when he came back from the war, thought Polly : he probably told her about poor Alison in self-defence. Last Sunday she had a real try at putting me off him, and she might have done if he hadn't made a pass at me in his own apartment and I blurted out the whole thing ... And Polly fell asleep smiling, on the first night Nice was an occupied city.

She woke to reality next morning, like everybody else. In succeeding days the crushing weight of Germany was felt everywhere inside and outside the town. Knocks fell on certain doors in the small hours, and Jews were hustled into trains that led to prison. The *Service du Travail Obligatoire* came into full force as soon as Pierre Laval was named by the Marshal-Chief of State as his successor instead of Admiral Darlan, who had defected to the Allies. This was on November 17th, and thenceforward unemployed men from eighteen to sixty-five, were liable to be rounded up like the Jews and sent, not to the death camps, but to labour in the factories and fields of Germany.

Three of Dany Profetti's mates left Nice to dodge the *Service* and went to join him at the Jurac farm. Before Christmas they were followed by two more. Old Jurac swore at having six hungry boys to feed instead of one, but people from Castillon, which was in the free zone, sent food to the maquisards, and the would-be toughs from the back streets of Nice grew hard and strong as they learned to hunt for wild game and follow the secret tracks which led behind the Col de Castillon into the great forest of Menton. The Sospel railway station was in German hands now, and sometimes Dany and his friends took turns in watching the *Kontrol's* behaviour patterns through Grand'père Jurac's old field glasses from the bushes above the valley of the Bevera.

Dany Profetti was glad he'd taken Maître Brunel's advice. He grew to love life on the mountains, which was as wild as any he could have wished for, and he knew that the greater mountains to the west had become practically impassable. Marseille came swiftly under the German ban. The Vieux Port, that centuries-old haven for pimps, thieves, cardsharps, drug peddlers, abortionists and *mafiosi*, was declared a menace to the innocent German soldiery and scheduled for immediate demolition. Forty thousand inhabitants were to be evacuated from the old rookeries where, among so many fugitives from justice, the men and women of the Resistance had found sanctuary. Charles Maxwell, running a school for saboteurs from an attic in the Rue la Caisserie, moved out a day ahead of the German inspectors, while Marius, the docker, carried out his intention of escaping over the Pyrenees. That was the end of Marius, who was shot dead when he ran into a detachment of the mountain division, ten thousand strong, which the Germans deployed along the French side of the Spanish border.

Only one part of the coast remained unoccupied territory, and that was the enclave round the French naval base at

Toulon. Admiral de Laborde, who had replied insultingly to Darlan's appeals to bring the Mediterranean Fleet to Africa, came to an agreement with the Germans to 'respect' this area, which was to be garrisoned by French troops.

On the other hand, the neutrality of the Principality of Monaco was abruptly violated. A Panzer division arrived under General Kohlermann, who with his staff was lodged in the Metropole Hotel. The Gestapo occupied the Hotel de Paris. Soup kitchens for the Monégasques were opened in both these hotels, and sometimes the old prince, Louis, who had fought with the French in the Other War, went down from the palace on the Rock to line up for a bowl of soup with his people. There was no soup kitchen at the Hotel Mimosa, but its discreet lounge was soon thronged with German officers from the railway *Kontrol*, ordering wine and beer lavishly, and paying equally lavish compliments to *die schöne Fraülein Fabienne*.

Jacques Brunel, at Aix, was in a curious state of mind. He was having a considerable success at the Assizes, enough to make one or two of the older men, too near retirement to be jealous, say that he was wasted in the Midi and ought to set his sights on Paris. Such encouragement would have come at exactly the right moment if the world had been at peace. He was thirty-one, highly qualified, unmarried, with a comfortable family background – in peacetime it would have been the year to try his luck as a junior counsel in Paris, where his father had the proper contacts, and the money, to enable his only son to make a start. But France was defeated and the world was at war, so young Maître Brunel was condemned to Nice and the eviction orders, with a routine appearance at the Aix Assizes to give him a taste of the higher criminality.

But the talk of Paris had given him the germ of an idea. Like Polly, he was glad of Fabienne's silly chatter – it had cleared the air right at the beginning of his relationship with the American girl and had done much to purge himself of the old pain. He had no qualms about leaving Polly alone in Nice for a week or ten days, because he had given her every protection which the law allowed, and besides that she had proved herself to be equal to any emergency. She could talk well, and reveal nothing, and she could, when she wished, be inconspicuous. He was charmed by Polly Preston, but Jacques didn't mean to keep her beside him in Nice for longer that he could help. With his reputation at the Bar it might be possible for him to get an *Ausweis* from the Germans to go to Paris on business, taking Polly with him as his secretary or *chère amie* or however they liked to think of her, and once in Paris handing her over to whatever Ministry was the Protecting Power for the belligerent United States – he thought it was the indispensable Swiss. They could put her in touch with her godfather in the American Foreign Service, Mr. Minister Calvert, or get her via Switzerland to London, while he, Jacques, would return to the Côte d'Azur and his Resistance groups. And when peace came they would meet again.

He already regretted having asked her to gather what information she could about Roger Malvy. It seemed quite probable that the money Malvy was throwing about, or losing at the casino, was part of the large sum of £3,000, so recently brought by Charles Maxwell from London, which had stuck to the fingers of the 'Knife' circuit's second-in-command. It was less probable but still possible that Malvy was getting a subsidy from Carlton Gardens for backing up Renaudon in his campaign to unify the Resistance for de Gaulle. Either way, it was the sort of thing that sounded simple enough for a clever girl who now had opportunities to meet Roger Malvy often, but things that seemed simple often boomeranged, and Jacques knew that if he drew Polly Preston into the Resistance and brought her to destruction he would never recover. Alison's death in an air raid had been a hazard of war, and it was by an accident having nothing to do with Jacques Brunel that she had met her death in a certain place and at a certain time. But for Polly, who trusted him, he had made himself completely responsible. To love again and to lose again would be more than he could bear.

His other anxiety was that he was not doing enough to keep the members of his groups together. The defection of François from the Menton group had worried him, because it showed that the group was beginning to disintegrate. The young fisherman had planned his ill-judged attempt to escape from an occupied town without consulting any of the other five members : he had simply tired of inactivity and left. The peasant farmers in the Roquebrune and Gorbio areas, whom Jacques visited two days after the American landings, would never leave their olive groves and terraced vineyards, but he knew they were very discouraged by the Darlan deal. 'What's the good of fighting if *they're* going to sell us down the river?' was what the suntanned stocky peasants said, as they looked acros the blue Mediterranean and shook their heads. *Vendu*, sold, gypped, done, was a word Jacques had heard only too often when the news of the armistice reached the French wards at Dykefaulds Hospital.

Sometimes he thought he should chuck the whole thing and release his thirty men to join up, if they wished, with the huge 'Knife' circuit, which at least was run from London by the S.O.E., and not by André Dewarvrin alias Colonel Passy. Then he could go off himself and fight under General Béthouart, for the hero of Narvik had been released on November 17th, after General Noguès, who arrested him, had reluctantly come to terms with Darlan. There would soon be a solid French contribution to the Allied drive into Tunisia. But Jacques Brunel clung to his vision of fighting the Germans on the soil of France – even if it meant taking to the maquis himself.

Since Dr. Lecampion left for Cannes, one day late for his medical conference, Jacques had heard nothing from him, nor did he expect to, now that telephoning had become a calculated risk. He didn't know if the doctor had met the sage Nestor and sought his opinion on Renaudon's reliability, and Jacques toyed with the idea of going to Cannes when the Assizes ended and seeing Nestor for himself. But the Sunday trains were cancelled on the twenty-second, and he was getting anxious about the state of affairs in Nice – which was only two hundred kilometres away but difficult of access over the complicated railway system, now jammed with German troop trains. Jacques sent a telegram to his office on Monday morning, announcing his arrival for five that afternoon. He wondered how soon after that he could see Polly Preston.

Polly had the morning turn at the day nursery, and set off enthusiastically to begin her second week as a *monitrice*. She had adapted herself as easily as ever to life at the Pension Froment, where the only other boarders were three women teachers from the girls' high school, a senior clerk from the central post office and a fussy man from the railway offices called Louis Ratazzi, who marked the level of his personal bottle of wine with an indelible pencil and argued about his ration tickets at dinner, which was the one meal the boarders took together. It was only a short walk from the Place Magenta to the Place Wilson, where the *maternelle* occupied two ground-floor rooms in one of the tall buildings.

Of kindergarten equipment they had almost none, nor any place for games, and Polly had made history already by taking some of the bigger children to romp in the gardens of the square. This had resulted in complaints about the noise they made, and an amused remonstrance from Madame Moreau, who visited the place regularly, though without seeming to be very fond of the children. Polly had been to lunch twice at Les Floralies, and had met Dr. Moreau, the leading pediatrician of Nice, whose skill had bought all the beautiful things by which his wife was surrounded, but hadn't bought his daughter happiness. Not that Roger Malvy, respectfully present on both Sundays, was anything but a model son-in-law, speaking hopefully of his wife's return, completely cured, 'any day now'. They were only four at luncheon and the bridge table on the first Sunday, all four as

183

competently masked as the citizens of Nice, looking through the German soldiers in the town below : the doctor's mask bluff and genial, Sugar Almond without a crack in the icing, Malvy waiting to be discovered by a Hollywood talent scout, and Polly with her schoolgirl face arranged for the occasion. Next time there was a larger party and four bridge tables, for Dr. Moreau liked to entertain on Sundays and holidays, and was noted for his hospitality. Chocolate and petits fours were handed round at four o'clock by Juliette the parlourmaid and the butler-valet, a black-clad, secretive Italian called Carlo. Crystallised fruits were offered too, and the whole *goûter* would have made a Christmas treat for the children at the *maternelle*.

Polly was thinking about it as she walked home on Monday afternoon. The children had been put down for their naps before she left. They were thriving on the regulated rest and the filling midday meal of cereals and vegetables, and would be rosy and gay when their pale exasperated mothers came to take them home. They were adorable asleep, with their black eyes closed and dark curls moist on their temples, exactly the same physical types as the little Italians of Naples and the sanatorium. The enemy children, separated from each other by a few hundred miles of the same Mediterranean shore.

Madame Froment followed Polly upstairs, looking anxious.

'My brother left a message for you, mademoiselle,' she said. 'My brother Henri, who keeps the garage on the Rue Barillerie.'

'I don't know the Rue Barillerie,' said Polly.

'It's behind the flower market, and the garage is on the corner of the Rue de la Poissonerie. Henri would like you to go and see him as quickly as you can. It's something to do with Maître Brunel, I think.'

'I'll go right away.'

As soon as she saw Henri Froment's square honest face

Polly knew that he was one of the unknown friends who, Jacques had promised, were looking after her; she thought she had passed him once or twice on her daily walks. Henri's hands were black and greasy as usual. He touched the back of Polly's hand with the back of his in greeting, and led her past Jacques' Peugeot and one or two other vehicles into a large untidy back room where a man with greying blond hair, wearing a mechanic's overalls, stood up to greet her with a pleasant smile.

'*Bonjour, Mademoiselle Henri,*' he said, 'how very good of you to come.'

'Who are you, please?'

'You can call me César, I'm a friend of Captain Jack's. There's no need to be afraid of me, or of Monsieur Froment.'

She had looked round once, in a scared way, as she realised that Henri had closed the door of the garage behind her and she was alone with two strangers. But Polly spoke up bravely : 'Has anything happened to – to Jack?'

'Nothing yet, and he's on his way home now. But a man in Nice did something silly yesterday, something that may affect us all, and we want Jack to know about it before he goes to his office, or back to the Rue Droite. His train's due at five o'clock,' he added, seeing Polly's bewilderment. 'We telephoned his office to find out. What we'd like you to do is go to the station and meet him. The *miliciens* or the cops may be on the look-out for us, but nobody at all knows you. All you have to do is go up to Jack and say, "Sabre lost his brief-case, please come to the garage," and we'll tell him the rest.'

'On the look-out for Jack and you? Monsieur Froment too? Is it that bad?'

'Pretty bad.'

'Does mademoiselle know where the station *is*?' asked Henri.

'At the top of the Avenue de la Victoire, isn't it? How long will it take me to get there?'

185

'You can't count on getting a bus. It would be better to start now. Mademoiselle,' said the man in the mechanic's overalls, 'we do thank you very much.'

Polly had been nervous in the crumbling street, the run-down garage, but the nervousness became a mounting excitement as she hurried up the long avenue to the station. It increased during the twenty minutes' wait for the five o'clock train, it became a physical thing of faster heartbeats and cold hands as the bright eyes of danger shone from the red lamps which marked the buffers where Jacques' train would come to a stop. There were policemen about, and once she saw the hated Basque beret of a militiaman, but nobody paid any attention to a girl in black, who went up to a tall traveller with open arms, like a young wife who had come to meet her husband.

'*Chérie!*' Jacques exclaimed. 'How sweet of you to meet me! Did you bring the car?'

'No petrol,' said Polly, pouting. 'And your train was late!'

'Poor sweetie, did you have a long time to wait?' They were outside the station now, and clear of the people; Jacques bent down as if to kiss her again. 'What's the matter?' he whispered, and she whispered back, 'Sabre lost his briefcase, please come to the garage.'

'Who sent you?' said Jacques between his teeth.

'César.'

'Let's see if we can find a taxi.'

Unbelievably, a taxi was there, the driver having deposited his passengers at the station was about to go in the opposite direction. He demanded a substantial sum for taking them to the Opéra, Jacques breezily explaining to Polly that he wanted to buy tickets for tomorrow night's performance. They talked about his trip to Aix until they reached the theatre, and then Jacques led the way across the deserted flower market, making Polly tell about her visit to Henri's garage. He asked if anybody knew where she had gone. When she said, 'Yes, Madame Froment,' he seemed to breathe more easily, and hurried her along the Rue Barillerie.

After the briefest of greetings to César and Henri : 'Tell me about Sabre,' he said.

'Sabre took a bunch of essays home in his briefcase on Saturday afternoon,' said César in his easy way. 'He left it in the trolley bus. He didn't realise he'd done so until after lunch on Sunday, when he got down to work, and then he thought he might have left it at the *lycée*. He wasted some time going back there and tipping the janitor to let him search his classroom, and by that time, of course, the bus company's lost property office was closed. They told him this morning to report his loss at the nearest *commissariat de police.*'

'Which is where you come into the picture?'

'Precisely.'

'I take it there was more in the briefcase than his pupils' essays?'

'There was a complete list of the top echelons of the "Knife" circuit, twenty names in all, with aliases and addresses. And a note of all those present at the meeting in "Le Faisan", including your name and mine.'

'I see,' said Jacques, and Polly gasped. He looked at her with a smile. 'You did splendidly, Pauline. Now, Henri, will you get my car out and drive mademoiselle back to your sister's place? Better put your "*Fermé*" sign on the door unless you can trust your new garage hand to change a tyre ... I'll see you later, *chérie.*'

Jacques pulled a chair up and sat down. 'Sabre seems to have done a thorough job,' he said, lighting a cigarette. 'Blown the whole "Knife" circuit. Does Couteau know?'

'I went to see him at the Orengo warehouse as soon as my man at the police station reported the loss to me.'

'You've got a Gaullist agent in the station?'

'We've got a Gaullist agent in every *commissariat* in Nice, *mon vieux.*'

'Very interesting. And the arrival of a teacher from the *lycée*, giving his own name, announcing a piece of carelessness that any boy in the *sixième* could have avoided, was considered important enough to be reported to de Gaulle's personal representative on the Riviera?'

'We've been keeping our eyes on Sabre for some time,' said César. 'That outburst of his at the "Faisan" meeting was very revealing.'

'What outburst? Oh, about the sacrifice of Menton, and the Armée des Alpes, I remember. Never mind the outburst. I always thought Sabre was a menace, now I see I was right, but let's concentrate on the briefcase. What reason have we to think whoever found it will bother to read the "Knife" lists and then go hurrying to the Gestapo?'

'Every reason.'

'We have to consider the possibility, of course. But suppose that person sees nothing but a batch of essays entitled *A Comparison between Mignet and Thiers*, what's he going to do? Take the whole thing apart page by page? He chucks it into the nearest dustbin; the dustmen will have picked it up and destroyed it hours ago. Meanwhile Sabre's precious briefcase has been cut up to sole a pair of shoes.'

'For a man as security conscious as you are, Jack, you're taking it very lightly.'

Jacques knew that what Renaudon said was true. He was making light of Sabre's near-fatal carelessness because of his own antagonism to de Gaulle's representative. If Alain Renaudon, alias César, took the line that the loss of a briefcase had put a score of men at risk, Jacques Brunel would automatically take the other side.

'It's Couteau's problem, not mine,' he said. 'What's Couteau going to do about it?'

'He's got Sabre on the carpet at this minute.'

'Much good that'll do. Now another thing – whose bright idea was it to use Pauline? Yours or Froment's?'

'I knew she existed, thanks to your fisherman friend, François. Froment knew where to find her.'

'You've turned François round, have you?'

'Look, Jack, you're not the counsel for the prosecution here. You should thank me for warning you not to go back to the Palais Lascaris and get yourself picked up by the Gestapo or the *Milice*—'

'That's exactly where I'm going,' said Jacques coolly. 'Home. What else do you want me to do? Take a room in some flop-house where the cops come to do a spot check on papers as a matter of routine? Or get the hell out of town, leaving a clear field for yourself and the gospel according to de Gaulle?'

'I could have you flown out to England from our own landing field at Tournus, two nights from now. That would give you time to travel, while I get a signal through to London.'

'To the Special Operations Executive, or Colonel Passy and his boys?' asked Jacques. 'Thanks, I'll take a chance on the Gestapo.'

'Then I hope you never fall into their hands.'

11

If it was possible for a Gaullist agent like Renaudon to find or to place Gaullist sympathisers among the police force of the city of Nice, it was a small feat compared with the infiltration of Algiers by the supporters of the Leader of All Free Frenchmen. Some of them had been there long before the American landings. Others, flown in with British approval, made their appearance after a formal agreement was signed by Admiral Darlan and General Mark Clark, U.S.A.

General Clark frankly admitted that he 'didn't understand the psychology of the men with whom he had to deal'. So much strife among the French themselves had baffled him, and he was glad to sign a document setting up a provisional arrangement for the administration of the whole of North Africa, with Darlan holding the key to power. General Clark wanted to get on with the fighting. So did General Giraud, so did the British General Anderson, who was leading the Allied expeditionary force in Tunisia. So, more than anyone, did the fire-eating General Patton, who was champing at the bit in Morocco. All of them underestimated the power of public opinion in London and Washington, and the pressure of Gaullist propaganda in Algiers.

The Clark–Darlan Agreements were signed on the Sunday when Polly was playing cards at Cimiez and Sabre was searching for his briefcase at the *lycée*. The signature was followed, on the day after Jacques Brunel returned to Nice, when he and the leaders of the 'Knife' circuit were braced for the fatal knock on their doors, by one of Darlan's great successes. When the admiral became High Commissioner, the Governor of Dakar brought over that great naval base, and with it the whole of French West Africa, to the Allied side.

Thus was accomplished without a shot fired, what de Gaulle had failed to do in the three disastrous days of September 1940, when with massive British support he had failed to effect a landing at Dakar. 'France has entrusted me with Dakar, I will defend Dakar to the death,' had been the sturdy old governor's defiance to the rebel general, but now he was prepared to return his mandate to what he chose to regard as a properly constituted French authority. It was a fresh humiliation for Charles de Gaulle, since the fiasco at Dakar was the only feat of arms in which he had engaged, or ever was to engage, from his flight to London until the end of the war. His invective grew shrill. Over the B.B.C. he broadcast to France his repudiation of all that had to do with Giraud and Darlan in North Africa. His propaganda newspapers redoubled their attacks on *les Anglo-Saxonnes*. A few months earlier he had been given an allocation of newsprint and some more British money to start a paper called *La Marseillaise*, edited from Carlton Gardens as the reflection of his own opinions. The editor, by name Quilici, declared that the American invasion struck a blow at French honour, and was worse than the German occupation of France.

These strictures did not circulate in Nice, and it was doubtful if many people listened to de Gaulle on the B.B.C., because with the arrival of the Germans their D/F vans prowled the streets, picking up the sound of wireless sets tuned in to London. It was not worth risking arrest and deportation to listen to *Les Français parlent aux Français* (from a studio in Portland Place) or even the imperturbable chimes of Big Ben, which brought comfort to so many in Hitler's 'Fortress Europe'. Radio Vichy, of course, raged as wildly as de Gaulle against the treason in Algiers, and from Radio Vichy Jacques culled a morsel of news which was funny enough to take the edge off the anxiety he had felt since Monday night.

Three days had passed since Polly's warning at the station. He had been afraid to go near her all that time, in case Sabre's criminal carelessness should lead to his arrest while he was in her company, but they had a guarded conversation on the telephone every day, and on Thursday met in the late afternoon in a little café not far from the *maternelle*. It seemed to be frequented by the racing set, studying the track results in the evening paper.

'What d'you think of the latest from Algiers?' asked Jacques. 'I heard it on the radio this morning.'

'Monsieur Ratazzi and the man from the post office listen to the radio at breakfast time, but I always have coffee in my room.'

'Quite right. Well, what d'you say to a movement to restore the Bourbons to the throne of France?'

'You're joking.'

'Somebody's joking, and it isn't me. You knew we had a royalist pretender to the crown?'

'Yes, of course, the Comte de Paris. I thought he lived in Tangier.'

'He did, but apparently a group in Algiers want to bring him over the border from Spanish Morocco and set him up as king in opposition to Darlan.'

'So poor General Clark has a royalist party to contend with now.'

'It would be funny if it weren't so damned silly,' said Jacques. 'The Comte de Paris, of all inoffensive human beings! I remember when his first child was born. I was at the Sorbonne then, and there was a big laugh when cheap paper leaflets were distributed in all students' lodgings, saying *"Peuple de Paris, un dauphin est né!"* The news didn't cause a royalist uprising, I can tell you that.'

'It seems rather odd to start one now,' said Polly slowly.

'Why not? Algiers is nothing but a free-for-all.'

'Yes, but who's behind the Comte de Paris? Do you know?'

'Vichy's accusing Henri d'Astier de la Vigerie, a big shot in the *Chantiers de la Jeunesse* out there. He has two brothers, both with de Gaulle in London.'

'Then, could the Comte de Paris be a front man for de Gaulle?'

'That's hardly likely, dear.' Jacques smiled at the far-fetched idea. Polly was getting to be as distrustful as he was himself. She was right, of course, although Jacques was beginning to think the heat was off in the Sabre affair. If the fool's briefcase had fallen into the wrong hands a score of people, himself included, would be under arrest by now. Give it a week, and the 'flap', as Alison used to call it, would be over. He walked back to the pension with Polly, saying he would see her on Sunday next at the Moreaus', where they now had a standing invitation for lunch and bridge. He wondered if he could ask her to come back to the Rue Droite for supper when the bridge was over. He was beginning to be tantalised by their short unsatisfactory meeting in stuffy tea-rooms and cheap cafés. His nerves had never settled since that encounter at the station, when their bodies had been shaken by their embrace under the whipping stimulus of danger. 'Love was all people had that summer,' he had said of England in 1940. Was life so very different in France in 1942?

He hardly knew what to plan for Sunday, a declaration or a grand seduction scene. But Friday brought the news from Toulon, the worst news since the armistice, enough to chill any man's passion : the news of the scuttling of the Mediterranean Fleet.

The Germans had broken their promise to Admiral de Laborde to maintain a free zone round the harbour, garrisoned by French troops. It was on the strength of this promise that the Admiral had refused to sail his ships to Algiers, or any port controlled by the Allies, precisely as Darlan himself had refused to sail his ships to British ports in 1940. When it was clear that the Germans intended to seize the capital ships and submarines at Toulon, Admiral de Laborde, coming over to the right side too late, gave orders to scuttle the whole fleet under his command. Seventy-three vessels, the backbone of what remained of the French Navy, were scuttled on the twenty-seventh of November. This time there was no conflict, no loss of French lives as at Mers-el-Kebir. There was only a huge material loss, and another shattering blow to the pride of a defeated nation.

This blow, following on the arrival of the Wehrmacht, crushed the usually lively citizens of Nice for the time being, but had the opposite effect on Jacques Brunel. He felt that as France had fallen so low there was nowhere to go but up, and after a depressing Saturday he appeared at Madame Moreau's dining table on Sunday at noon, as debonair as any of the party. The Toulon disaster was hardly referred to at Les Floralies, except with pursed lips and shakes of the head, and along with the red ribbon of the Legion of Honour the doctor was now wearing the Frankish battle-axe, a Vichy decoration. Polly, who seemed to be very much at home, played an excellent game of bridge, and Roger Malvy, obviously not feeling the petrol shortage, drove them both back to the city and left Polly at the door of the Pension Froment.

'Where to now?' he asked Jacques.

'The Place Rossetti will be fine, I usually walk up from there. Would you like to come back to my place for a nightcap?'

'Thanks, it's getting too near curfew time.' Roger stopped the Delahaye in front of the Cathédrale de Ste. Réparate. 'Isn't Chantal's mother something?' he said. 'What do you bet that next week she'll have an *Obersturmbannführer* at her Sunday bridge?'

'They do seem to be more *collabo* than they were before.'

'Papa-in-law says a doctor is the servant of humanity and above politics.'

'What, with the *francisque* in his button-hole?'

'Sometimes he reminds me of Fabienne's old man. Very Vichyste.'

'Have you seen Fabienne since the landings?'

'Only once. Her father's back in charge these days, always willing to drink with the Boches when they'll buy him a *pastis.*'

'They surely haven't got Germans billeted on them?'

'Not yet.' Roger took off his pigskin driving glove and scratched the tip of his nose. 'The Sabre thing seems to have blown over.'

'Thank God for that.'

'Your theory must have been the right one, after all.'

'My theory?'

'That somebody pinched the briefcase and threw away the papers. Isn't that what you told Renaudon?'

'Yes, it was. You've seen Renaudon, have you? Is he still around?'

'He comes and goes. He's not very happy about the Algiers set-up.'

'I imagine not,' said Jacques, getting out of the car. 'Thanks for the lift, Roger. See you soon.'

Jacques walked up to the Rue Droite, where the sound of his own footsteps alone broke the unnatural stillness, half-convinced that there was no harm in Roger Malvy. He was unstable, that was all, and Jacques thought it a pity that Dr. Moreau, with his interest in eugenics, should have mated two such unstable characters as his daughter Chantal and Roger Malvy.

As for Jacques and Polly, after living for three weeks on the knife-edge of expectation, they entered on a short period of calm in which they made no demands upon one another, neither his to possess her nor hers to be taken further on her journey to a freer world. Jacques was able to see her nearly every day, for work at the Law Courts had fallen off in the uncertain climate of the times, when the swastikas hung black over the words *Liberté Egalité Fraternité* above the great doors of the Palais de Justice. Very soon the courts of Grande and Petite Instances would close for the long hiatus in the legal calendar which gave the litigants of the Maritime Alps such a convincing illustration of the law's delays, and there were very few briefs for the spring session on the desk of Maître Brunel. With Polly he walked beside the Baie des Anges, where the winter waves broke on the pebbles in sunsets of cinnabar and gold, and took her to the Russian Church built in memory of a dead Czarevich, with its five-fold domes so much grander than the little church at Carnolès which had sheltered them from the *Milice*. Once, with a new ration of petrol, he took her to Cap Martin, and after a private talk with Jean Dupont left his car outside the grocery and joined the enraptured Polly beside the carnation fields. They walked down the road skirting the rows of flowers, passed the little hut half hidden in the ivy, and came out on the plateau of grass where Jacques had met the British agent from the sea. It was a mild December afternoon, and they sat among the rocks listening to the gentle surge of the waves, talking about the Grand Hotel just out of sight, where Jacques had played tennis in the summers before the war. He told Polly that a beautiful house called the Casa Lumone had once stood on the site. It had belonged to the last of the long line of Lascaris princes, killed in battle against the Austrians before Jacques' Grand'tante Marthe was born, and sold years later by his sister the Principessa Clara, who lived to a great age in the old house on the Rue Droite.

'The neighbours said she had the evil eye,' said Jacques. 'When I was a little kid I thought she was a witch. She lived with a maid about as old as herself : two tiny bent creatures who liked to mutter and gibber and point their sticks at children.'

Polly loved to hear him tell about being dressed up in a white sailor suit and taken to pay his respects to Grand'tante Marthe, always afraid of meeting the old princess on the stairs. Her own stories were more cheerful, and she made Jacques rock with laughter at her imitations of the pompous Signora Pradelli and her Fascist son Pietro in an imaginary meeting with Mussolini, for Polly turned out to have a talent for mimicry. Down by the shore at Cap Martin she mimicked nobody. She was content to sit there with his coat over her shoulders and his arms around her, and between long kisses to whisper, 'If only it could always be like this !'

These peaceful weeks coincided with a silence on the North African front. The British Eighth Army had advanced twelve hundred miles westwards across the desert since the battle of El Alamein, and was preparing to fight Rommel again, but General Anderson's force had bogged down in the rain and mud of Tunisia, bombarded by the Luftwaffe and attacked by the Germans flown in by troop-carrier planes. Hitler landed 50,000 men in Tunisia, and intended to send in as many again to prevent the British and the Americans from meeting in Africa.

Chantal Malvy came home a few days before Christmas. Only the children had an appetite for festivity, and Polly helped to make coloured paper chains to hang from the ceilings and arrange the *santons de Provence* at the day nursery. At Les Floralies, by special invitation, she was putting the finishing touches to a marvellous Christmas tree made of white feather plumes and trimmed with gold and silver baubles when the Moreau motorcade came up the gravelled drive, Gustave driving Dr. and Madame Moreau in their own car, with a nurse girl holding the baby in her arms, and Roger driving the Delahaye, with his wife beside him. They all came into the house laughing and pleased, the butler and the two maids coming forward to greet 'Madame Chantal', who handed Carlo her fur coat and cap and sank down on a sofa.

'You must be Pauline, I've heard so much about you,' she said, holding out a languid hand. Roger bent over her, whispering that she must be tired, Juliette brought tea and dainties, Madame Moreau bounced her grandson until he wept with fright and was carried away by his nanny to an extemporised nursery. Chantal took all this commotion as the tribute to her return, and Polly got the impression of a perfectly helpless person, who had learned to exploit her invalidism for all it was worth. She was an attractive young woman, falling short of actual beauty by a heavy lower lip and hands too powerful for her slender wrists, but with strong and supple arms and legs. Polly could well believe that a few years earlier she had been a local tennis champion.

Polly had been driven back to Nice by Gustave, using the inexhaustible petrol of the Moreaus, before the husband and wife were together in the spare bedroom on the ground floor which they were to occupy over the Christmas holidays, until Chantal became accustomed to the change of air. Even then they were not alone, for Madame Moreau insisted on taking them to see the nursery where Patrick was napping with his nanny knitting by his side. She was a stout farm girl from the Auvergne, who had been looking after Patrick since his mother first took him to the Mont Dore.

Madame Moreau brushed her hand lovingly over her grandson's mop of blond hair. 'Exactly like my own when I was a little girl,' she said. Roger Malvy, who had never known his mother-in-law before her hair was white, agreed at once. 'He's fond of sleeping, this little fellow,' he said. 'When I saw him at the Mont Dore in September, he was always being put down for a nap, Chantal.'

'He'll have plenty to say to his papa when he wakes up,' said Chantal. 'Mother, I'm going to start unpacking.'

'Juliette will do that for you, darling.' But Roger drew his wife away, into the pretty guest room where a log fire was burning, and took her hungrily into his arms. 'My God, how I've missed you, Chantal,' he whispered. 'Are you happy to be back?'

'Of course I am.'

'A little bit sorry not to be in our own apartment, away from all of them?'

'But it's lovely to be here for the holidays,' she said like a child. 'Maman says it'll be dreadfully difficult, keeping house down in the city, with all the shortages, and only a *bonne à tout faire* to do all the work.'

'We'll get by,' said the man. 'We're going to make a new start, aren't we, darling? Forget the past and all the silly arguments, and be happy together, you and me and Patrick?'

'If *you're* good,' she said pettishly. 'You promised, Roger. You were naughty too, you know.'

'I promise, Chantal.' Roger Malvy's weak, handsome face was touching in its sincerity. He held her close, and kissed her passionately, and in their own apartment would have taken his wife to bed then and there. But she slipped away from him, with Look at the time, and What will maman think, and They'll be waiting for us, with the evasiveness which had chilled him when she was a bride, and they were both too determinedly cheerful when they joined her parents for a glass of sherry. Patrick was brought in and crawled about on the carpet. He was not shy with strangers, and pulled himself up from one friendly knee to another with chuckles of delight. A common possession in a white romper, not quite one year old, with blond hair and rosy cheeks, was so delightful to the younger couple that the grandparents withdrew a little from the group round the fire. 'They're all right now,' whispered Madame Moreau, and the doctor nodded without words.

The white feather tree was bending its glittering branches over a pile of presents in scarlet and tinsel wrappings, the salon was decorated with holly and poinsettia plants by the early afternoon of Christmas Eve, and the two ladies at the Villa Les Floralies retired, like little Patrick, for a siesta under their satin quilts. Madame Moreau had planned a big *reveillon* party to usher in Christmas Day – 'Nothing really,' she said when her husband shook his head, 'just a glass of champagne and a slice of turkey and foie gras for a few of Chantal and Roger's friends, to celebrate her return. Surely nobody could object to that?' Of course the party had increased in numbers and importance. It was an occasion to be prepared for with face cream and hair curlers, and the drawing room was empty, with a Christmas log on the firedogs ready to be set alight, when four shots rang out at the entrance to the Summer Palace in Algiers, and Admiral Darlan fell dead, shot through the face and chest.

Some days before, one of General de Gaulle's right-hand men, one of the *chers compagnons* who had been with him since the start of his quest for power, had arrived in Algiers as de Gaulle's liaison officer with the French in North Africa. His name was François d'Astier de la Vigerie, and he was a brother of Henri d'Astier, said to be the champion of the Bourbon-Orleans pretender, the Comte de Paris.

So little welcome was François d'Astier that Darlan threatened to put him under arrest, and only the conciliatory powers of General Eisenhower brought about a meeting between the two men. But when the meeting was over even Eisenhower refused to let François d'Astier remain in Algiers. He was put on an aircraft and was back in London before a young assassin, hysterical but resolute, fired his four shots outside the Summer Palace.

Who killed Admiral Darlan? General Mark Clark, faced with yet another complication in his dealings with the French, put his troops on the alert and cabled to General Marshall for instructions. Mr. Churchill cabled urgently, saying he hoped the blame would be placed on the Germans and their agents, and the first announcements of the murder, made over Radio Morocco and Radio Alger, duly stated that 'it was not yet known whether the assassination was of German or Italian inspiration'. But this was for public consumption abroad; it was soon known in Algiers that the boy who had been seized outside the Summer palace was a Frenchman, the son of a law reporter on the *Dépêche Algérienne*, and, while studying in Paris, one of the first group of students to demonstrate in favour of de Gaulle. The Americans and General Giraud, who became High Commissioner for North Africa in Darlan's stead, believed the boy who shot the admiral was the front man for a Gaullist plot.

His name was Fernand Bonnier de la Chapelle, and never since the French Revolution had any citizen been so quickly condemned to death. It was clear that he was not to be allowed to talk. Bonnier was tried by a French court for murder, and found guilty on the morning of Christmas Day. He was sent back to prison to await instant execution. He did not believe in the sentence, boasting that he had 'powerful friends in London' who would set him free. The two army officers who guarded him in the death cell spent a wretched night as the boy's agony of disbelief increased, and he asked them again and again where the messenger was, who would bring him the pardon he had been promised. All he had done was to rid France of a man who had committed treason, who had collaborated with the enemy. He had been told that his act would make him a hero, for ever to be honoured . . . Then he fell to weeping, and that was easier for the guards to hear than the boasting which came next, that if – if the pardon was delayed, and he were taken to the prison yard and blind-folded, it would only be a mock execution as in the opera *La Tosca*, the squad would fire blanks, and his powerful friends would spirit him away. But fantasy turned to reality at a quarter to eight next morning, when Bonnier was taken from his cell, bound to the stake, and shot.

Madame Morcau might lament her ruined party, but her *reveillon* was not the only one which fell to pieces in Nice that night. Nobody could even pretend to be gay after Radio Vichy repeated the official statement from Algiers. It was not that Admiral Darlan was mourned, except by his family. The Vichy government, which held him guilty of treason, shed no tears for him. The Gaullists for years after laid flowers on the grave of Bonnier de la Chapelle. General Mark Clark had been trying to get Darlan out of Algiers and into the United States with the bribe of treatment for his son at Warm Springs, and this bribe was offered only the day before the murder of the Little Fellow. Even General Clark could only say that his murder 'solved a very difficult problem of what to do with him in the future'. It was the manner of his death which added another burden to the conscience of France, and the manner of his killer's death was a stain on the due process of the law.

So it was felt to be by Jacques Brunel. He like thousands of others knew none of the details of Bonnier's attack, for these were not revealed for years – the tie-up between de Gaulle's envoy, François d'Astier, and his brother Henri, the so-called royalist whom young Bonnier had served with hysterical enthusiasm in the Youth Workshops. But like thousands of others Jacques thought France had reached rock-bottom when politics led to murder and civil strife walked in the streets, and he despised the kangaroo court which granted no stay of execution, listened to no appeal. Bonnier had been tried by what was nothing but a drum-head court-martial and shot out of hand, and the shadow of the double cross was beginning to fall over the land.

From this dark mood even Polly could not charm him, and wisely, she didn't try. It was left to Charles Maxwell to rouse Jacques to his own danger, when late one night at the very end of the year the telephone rang in the flat in the Palais Lascaris, and a voice with a strong Marseille accent said, 'You see I memorised your number, just as you told me to.'

'Glad you did,' said Jacques. 'Are you far away?'

'At the railway station. All right if I come along to see you?'

'I can give you a bed for the night, if you like. It's getting too near curfew time to start hunting for a hotel room.'

'Thanks a lot. Be with you in half an hour.'

Charles must have caught the last bus, for he was at the Rue Droite in fifteen minutes, demonstratively glad to see Jacques, and much less diffident than on the day of his arrival in France.

'Have you had anything to eat?' asked Jacques as he poured brandy for them both.

'Sure, I had some food before the train left Cannes.'

'You've come from Cannes? I thought you were in Marseille.'

'So I was, moving from one room to another, until the twenty-sixth. I've had a "pianist" with me for the last two weeks, and we've been getting through to London nearly every day. That's how I got my orders to go back to Cannes. I'm sorry, Jack, but *Nestor's* blown.'

'*Nestor's* blown?'

'Blown and on the run. We got him off to Toulouse yesterday with new papers and a railway pass, and he's going to hole up at Madame de Mongélard's for a day or two before he moves on to Limoges. The reason why I'm here is that he gave me a message for you.'

'Nestor on the run! I can't believe it! And going to Paris – will he be any safer there?'

'They may take him to a safe-house in the country, until the next moon period begins.'

'Nestor's nearer seventy than sixty; it's not a good age for being on the lam. Go on,' said Jacques impatiently. 'Tell me what happened. Who gave what away? We've had a scare here, thanks to Sabre and his lost briefcase; it wasn't anything to do with that?'

'I don't think so. Nestor was very reserved, but as far as I can make out the whole thing began with a visit from César.'

'Alain Renaudon!' said Jacques on a deep breath. 'How does he come into it?'

'Remember that César told us at "Le Faisan" about de Gaulle's plans to organise a secret army inside France? With himself as the sole leader of the Resistance, giving the order to rise and strike when the right time comes? You asked César if that meant de Gaulle would actually fight at the head of the secret army—'

'I remember.'

'César arrived in Cannes a few days ago carrying a new directive from Carlton Gardens. It announced that on the eleventh of November, just after the American landings in North Africa, de Gaulle gave the command of the secret army to General Delestraint.'

'Never heard of him.'

'Neither have I. But Renaudon means to call a meeting either in Nice or Cannes early in the New Year, to tell the circuits and groups about this development, and get them to take an oath of allegiance to de Gaulle.'

'That has a familiar ring.'

'De Valbonne – I mean Nestor – wasn't too keen on the

idea. He saw it as a move to break the hold of Special Operations Executive over the Resistance movements in south-eastern France. He told César it would need a lot of thinking over. Two days later one of our men in the Cannes Préfecture de Police discovered that an order of arrest was being made out for Baron de Valbonne. He tipped the locals off, and they had him out of the Villa Rivabella and into a safe-house just in time.'

'Does Nestor think *Renaudon* denounced him?'

'He didn't accuse Renaudon. But his message to you is, whenever that meeting is called, you're to attend, and speak up as he would have done against the way the Resistance is to be used to further de Gaulle's own ends.'

'It'll be a pleasure,' said Jacques grimly.

'It might be also be the end of Captain Jack.'

'How so?'

'You might be blown as high as Nestor, as soon as the meeting's over.' He finished his drink at a gulp. 'That's the other message I've got to give you. It's from London. Baker Street thinks you ought to start planning a trip to England.'

'What the devil for?'

'Your own safety. They think you've had too many narrow shaves, and they don't want you to be blown like Nestor before they've talked to you again.'

'But my life's in Nice!'

'So might your death be. Come on, Jack, you can turn over your *reseau* to somebody else, and let things cool off for a bit. They'd like you to go over in the New Year.'

'Over the Pyrenees in January?'

'No, by the Paris route, the way Nestor's going. Have you any contacts of your own in Paris?'

'I never even crossed the Line, when the Line existed.'

'But you *know* Paris?'

'I was a student there.'

'We've got a good safe-house off the Rue du Faubourg St.

Honoré, an apartment in the Cité du Retiro. An actors' agent called Bertrand lives there, his wife sings in cabaret. They're your best bet when it comes to a getaway by air.'

'Can you let Bertrand know when I'm coming in?'

'We can send a message via London.'

'And where can I contact you?' They discussed telephone numbers and codes phrases and the Darlan murder before Jacques made up a bed on the sofa for his guest. He went to bed himself, arguing in his mind the pros and cons of a trip to London, and whether he could ask Baker Street to try to trace the present whereabouts of an American diplomat called Joseph Calvert. He knew that Charles's 'pianist' would be sending messages at the risk of his life, and the lives of those who were sheltering him, and wondered if he dared ask, even for Polly's sake, for the transmission of a private message to London. But in the morning Charles was gone, leaving only the neatly folded bedding on the sofa, and a printed message which said *Merci*.

Polly, during the week between Christmas and the New Year, spent a good deal of time at the Villa Les Floralies. Chantal Malvy, in her languid way, had taken a fancy to Madamoiselle Henri, into whose antecedents she enquired no more closely than her mother had done, and as the *maternelle* was closed for the holidays Polly was glad to keep the older girl company. A crowd of friends had been invited for the cancelled *reveillon*, but not one of them came near the villa in the next few days, and Roger Malvy's business kept him down in Nice from breakfast until dinner time. With no word spoken, Polly realised that Chantal was nervous and apprehensive. She seemed to like getting outside Les Floralies with Polly and little Patrick, the nurse from Auvergne pushing the pram up and down the avenues of the Parc des Arènes while the two girls sat chatting idly on one of the benches beneath the olive trees. When the pram was turned at the stairs leading up to the Franciscan cloister where a temple to Diana had once stood, Patrick began waving as soon as he could see his mother and her friend. 'Maman! Lollee!' he shouted joyfully. They were two of the few words he could say clearly.

After the fiasco of Christmas Eve, Madame Moreau declined to plan a midnight *reveillon* for New Year's Eve. Some tea or a glass of *porto* at five o'clock, when the day's work was done for most people, then two tables of bridge followed by an early dinner would be in better taste than sitting up yawning and waiting for the clock to usher in a year whose ending no man could foretell. Nobody in France had great hopes of deliverance in 1943. But the Moreau house was as warm and welcoming as ever when Chantal Malvy sat before her dressing-table, making Polly test the contents of several scent bottles and sprays.

'*Arpège* or *Tabac Blond* for you, I think.'

'You've splashed so much on, I can't tell which is which,' said Polly, waving her hands to make the scents evaporate. 'Be careful now, you're going to spill it on my dress.'

'It's a lovely dress,' said Chantal enviously, touching the coral silk. 'Is it Jacques' favourite?'

'He's never seen it before. I bought it last month in Monte Carlo, and I'd been saving it for Christmas Eve.'

'Pauline, is Jacques Brunel in love with you?'

'A little bit, maybe.'

'More than a little bit, I think! Oh, Pauline, I've never seen him *look* at a girl the way he looks at you!'

'Madame Chantal,' said Juliette, entering after a hasty knock, 'madame says to tell you Doctor and Madame Brisson are here.'

'Oh bother the Brissons.' But Chantal went dutifully into the salon, followed by Polly, to greet her father's colleague and his elderly wife, and to begin pouring tea from the big silver teapot.

Roger Malvy had time for one quick word with Jacques Brunel before the Brissons came, and that was to tell him 'the secret army meeting' would be held at Couteau's villa on Tuesday afternoon, at four.

'Up here at Cimiez?'

'Couteau thinks it'll be safer.'

'The safest thing will be to keep Sabre out of it ... Madame Brisson, *quel plaisir* ...'

'I think maman must have gone to get Patrick,' smiled Chantal, offering a plate of little sandwiches to the guests. 'I know she's longing to show him off to you.'

'We're longing to see him, Chantal dear. So nice for your parents to have you all here together.'

Polly glanced at Roger Malvy. He had been silent and moody since she arrived at Les Floralies, and now he was lounging against the white marble chimney piece, smoking, with a glass of port in one hand. He didn't respond to his wife's smile.

'Here they come. Oh, look at *bébé*, all dressed up!' cried Chantal, clapping her hands.

Madame Moreau had bought her grandson his first little-boy suit. He wore tiny black velvet shorts with a plain white silk shirt, white socks and black strap slippers, and he was laughing as she carried him proudly into the salon. The men said '*Bravo!*' the women cooed, and Patrick struggled to get out of his grandmother's arms.

'Is he walking yet?' asked Madame Brisson, after the hugs and kisses were over.

'Show them, Patrick,' said his mother.

The child took three steps towards the white feather tree, snatched one of the golden balls, and turned to face them with a triumphant laugh. He gave his fair head a little shake, and squeezed the bauble in his two fat hands. He was a baby no longer, but a tough little boy in a shirt and trousers. The shirt was spattered with gilt particles as the golden ball disintegrated.

'*Now* look what you've done!'

'Naughty Patrick!'

'Nanny, take him back to the nursery !'

Patrick's balance failed him and he sat down unsteadily on the carpet. 'Loll-ee !' The little boy had vanished, it was a baby's appeal for help. Polly picked him up and kissed him. 'All right, Patrick,' she said. 'You go along with nanny now.' And turned towards the fireplace, laughing with the others, to look appalled into the naked hate in Roger Malvy's eyes.

It was gone in a moment, the social mask came down, and Polly thought she had dreamed that glare of hatred and anger when Roger said in his natural voice : *'Eh bien,* if the children's hour is over, shall we cut for partners?'

The Auvergne nurse girl, as she afterwards told the police, took off the little boy's finery and washed his face and hands before putting him to bed, and Juliette, the house-parlour-maid, tiptoed in to admire him. The two young women returned to the kitchen, where the staff ate an early supper before the cook started the dinner preparations. The eight people in the drawing-room played cards for an hour. During that time, it was easy to prove, only four of them left the room, separately, each when holding the dummy hand. Chantal was the first to go, and came back saying Patrick was sound asleep. The doctor, summoned by Carlo, took a telephone call in his study. Roger went out to the cloakroom in the hall. Finally, when the servants' supper was over, the mistress of the house went to the kitchen to have a word with the cook.

That was just ten minutes before the nanny heard screaming in Patrick's nursery.

The screams were so appalling that all the members of the family hurried out of the drawing-room, leaving Polly, Jacques, and the Brissons staring at each other across the green baize tables. A moment, and they heard the thin opening wail of Chantal's hysteria, followed by a rush of feet from the kitchen premises. Two minutes more, and Dr. Moreau, his ruddy face haggard, was back in the drawing-room.

'Dr. Brisson, will you come with me, please?' he said. 'And

you, Jacques. The ladies will please ... please ... stay—' He sketched a wavering gesture, and the two men followed him to the nursery.

'Take nurse to the kitchen,' Dr. Moreau said. 'Juliette, look after madame.' He had seen a child's death so often, in the labour rooms, in the hospital wards, in homes rich and poor, that his iron calm was not unnatural. But this time the dead child was his own grandson, hideously transformed from the rosy boy who had clutched the golden ball, lifeless on his little bed with a white frilled pillow lying on the floor. A Mickey Mouse nightlight had fallen from the white table by the bed.

'Take Chantal to your room, Roger,' said Dr. Moreau, still with that terrible calm. She had been lying on the rug, prostrate, and with her flushed face and wild black hair she looked like an animal when her husband raised her to her feet. She clung to him, sobbing, as he helped her through the bathroom which divided the bedroom from the nursery, and they could hear her retching while she hung blindly over the bathroom basin. Dr. Brisson, after a horrified exclamation, went forward to the bed and bent over Patrick's body.

'The child was suffocated,' he said, after a brief examination. 'There is no possible hope of resuscitation. My poor friend, what can I say or do?'

'Maître Brunel?'

Jacques, no less horrified than Dr. Brisson, had given a swift considering look all round the room. The french windows leading to a brick terrace outside the improvised nursery were slightly ajar; that, with the baby pillow on the floor and the overturned nightlight, was the only sign of disorder.

'First, you must telephone the police,' he said gently, 'and leave everything in this room exactly as you found it. No, don't touch the terrace door whatever you do! Where's Madame Moreau?'

'With Chantal, probably. I told Juliette to look after her.'

'Then, if you'll telephone to the *commissariat*, Dr. Brisson and I will stay here beside Patrick.'

The police cars came up the suburban boulevard with sirens shrieking and revolving lights flashing, so that the edges of blinds were raised and shutters eased ajar in many homes to see if another *razzia* was in progress. The sergeant and his men went through the house, heard the story, telephoned for the *commissaire* himself, telephoned to the Prefecture for reinforcements. There were twelve people involved: four servants, the nurse, four guests, the dead child's father and his grandparents. For the present, they said, it would not be necessary to interrogate the unhappy mother. They intended to arrest Carlo, the butler-valet, on suspicion: he was the only foreigner in the house.

It was at this point that Jacques advised Dr. Moreau to send for his solicitor.

It was the first time in his life that he had been in at the beginning of a criminal investigation. He always came in at the end of the story, after the *procès-verbaux*, after the examining magistrate, after the due process of law, when arrayed in toque and stole he would defend the innocent or accuse the guilty. Now he was being taken down in writing – and what writing! The brocaded chairs of Madame Moreau's salon were covered with pages of depositions for the examining magistrate : the opening of the first dossier on the murder of Patrick Roger Malvy, aged eleven months and two weeks. Outside, police with flashlights were examining the brickwork of the terrace and the garden paths beyond, while others tested the knob of the french doors for fingerprints, with no success. The police surgeon came, and the men to photograph the tiny corpse, and in their wake came the professional ambulance chasers, the reporters from the *Eclaireur de Nice*.

It went on for hours. A possible theory, apart from the guilt of the Italian, was that some vagrant or gipsy had come in from the woods or country roads which led still further up the heights of Cimiez, though what motive a vagrant or gipsy could have had for child murder without robbery was not apparent. Then politics was advanced as a motive. Dr. Moreau's political sympathies were not to everybody's taste, suggested the *commissaire*, with a glance at the *francisque* in the doctor's buttonhole. Could the poor child's death represent some dreadful vengeance by a political antagonist? And the shorthand writers took it all down, question and answer, until the family solicitor arrived from his own New Year's Eve party, sorry and yet irritated at the need which brought him out.

Among the servants Juliette kept her head the best. She made Marie prepare coffee for everyone, and cut sandwiches less dainty than Madame Moreau would have approved for the policemen and anybody else who had an appetite : Polly saw the Brissons taking furtive bites. She herself drank a cup of coffee and went, at Roger's request, to sit by Chantal and stroke her head until the sleeping tablets took effect. She watched, fascinated, the twitching of Chantal's powerful hands, and listened to the wheezing, asthmatic breathing. Shivering, she heard the sounds in the nursery, where strange men took Patrick from his cot and laid him on a canvas stretcher. The police ambulance pulled softly away from the house.

After nearly an hour Dr. Moreau came to fetch her. 'Thank you, my dear,' he said, 'she's sound asleep now. And Jacques is waiting to drive you back to Nice.'

'Can we really go?'

'Oh yes.'

'You four are in the clear,' the police commissioner had said to Jacques. 'You and Mademoiselle Henri and the Brissons. None of you left the salon between the times the child was seen alive and found dead. As for the servants and the family—' He shook his head.

'How are you going to file it, *commissaire*?'

'Tonight? Accusation against X,' said the *commissaire* briskly. 'We may have a different picture in the morning. Sooner or later somebody will break.'

The police chief thought it was an inside job. That was clear to Jacques as he drove down the long avenues with one eye on the petrol gauge, where the red needle was swinging dangerously close to Empty, and all his thoughts on Polly, sitting stiff and silent by his side. She didn't cry until the car stopped in the Place Magenta, and then she burst into noisy sobs, snuffling like a child and burrowing her face into his shoulder. Jacques let her have her cry out. 'He was such a darling ... laughing ... with all that gilt stuff on his little hands' – he heard the broken words between the sobs. He waited until she was calm again, and had dried her eyes, before he took Polly's chin in his hands and studied her face by the light of the one street lamp.

'You ought to go straight to bed, *chérie*,' he said. 'Have you any gardenal tablets, or some other sleeping stuff?'

'I never took a sleeping tablet in my life.'

'Then get Madame Froment to heat some red wine for you, with a lump of sugar in it, and you'll sleep the New Year in.' He kissed her. 'Remember this is going to be *our* year – yours and mine.'

She couldn't have been listening to him, for Polly said, 'Do the police really think Carlo did it? Wasn't he in the kitchen the whole time?'

'He called Dr. Moreau to the telephone.'

'That's true.' Polly laid her cheek against Jacques' cheek, and whispered, 'I wish I hadn't seen Roger Malvy's face!'

'When? Polly, *when*?' Jacques found that he was whispering too.

'When Patrick pulled that bauble off the tree. Roger looked at him like a *fiend* – it was horrible.'

'I didn't see it, darling. You mustn't start imagining things.'

He hadn't seen the look of fury Roger turned on Chantal's

son, because he had been looking at the child himself. What Jacques saw, as the baby suddenly became a little boy, was a toss of the blond hair, a set of the mouth, a way of standing, which he had seen a thousand times in Chantal's cousin, Marc Chabrol.

'My God,' he said, more to himself than to Polly Preston, 'I think this country's going mad.'

12

Fabienne Leroux, too, was beginning to doubt the sanity of her country as she read the story of the murder at the Villa Les Floralies in the *Eclaireur de Nice*.

For a whole week the lead story in the local paper had been the murder of Admiral Darlan. Guilt had been laid to this door or that, according as the wind of opinion shifted at Vichy : sometimes de Gaulle and his minions were held responsible, sometimes the unlucky Comte de Paris, who decidedly ought to have remained in Tangier. General Giraud, who had 'usurped' the post of High Commissioner, came in for his share of the blame, which diminished when it was announced that the High Commissioner intended to arrest Henri d'Astier and his housemate the Jesuit *abbé* Cordier. Plots, arrests, accusations and counter-accusations in Algiers gave little hope of opening a second front to aid the Russians, who had at last counter-attacked north-east of Stalingrad, and were winning new successes every day.

Darlan had to move off the front page of the *Eclaireur* to make way for Dr. Moreau's grandson. *'Plainte contre X'* had all the appeal of a thriller, and the paper went to town on it, giving biographies, with all the names and facts wrong, of every member of the doctor's household. Carlo the butler, was still in prison. Madame Roger Malvy the baby's mother, had attempted suicide on the day after the New Year. 'She was transported urgently to the St. Roch Hospital, where her days are not in danger' – it was a phrase kept permanently in type at the newspaper, being much required for use in traffic accidents.

Actually Chantal was still at Les Floralies, suffering from an attack of asthma, but Fabienne was not to know this when she read the story on January 3rd. She felt completely cut off from all her so-called friends since the Germans moved in to the Riviera. Roger she had seen once, Jacques not at all, and of Pierre Lavisse, now a prisoner of war in Germany she had heard nothing for many months. Her sense of isolation was only deepened by the popularity of the Hotel Mimosa with the Germans. It was too small to be requisitioned, but the comfortable lounge was just the right size to make an appealing wine bar for the officers. They started calling it the *Stübli*, and crowded it out in the winter evenings. Fabienne's father came out of retirement to run the *Stübli*, for the patriotic Frenchman who objected to his daughter giving a bed for the night to a British flyer or a French resister on the run saw nothing wrong in catering to the enemy. 'If we don't, others will,' he said, and putting on the long white apron he had hung up a year before, he stood behind the sideboard where the magazines had been, cutting slices of Italian sausage and liverwurst and French bread to serve (at a price) along with the wine and beer. He looked out some old chamois and antelope horns and nailed them to the walls, and the piano kept in the dining room for wedding parties was tuned and wheeled into the lounge. The Germans were a musical people. They enjoyed it.

The Mimosa prospered as never before, and Fabienne engaged two pretty Monégasque girls to serve the tables, dressed in the Monaco costume of red and white striped skirts and black velvet bodices. They had a great success with the younger officers. But they were no competition for Fabienne herself, who walked regally through the lounge once or twice every evening, smiling her professional smile and enquiring if *ces messieurs* found everything to their liking. She would never accept a glass of wine, or even sit down for a few minutes at any table : that would be to consort with the enemy, a different thing from taking all the money he cared to spend. It was enough to hear the whispers, '*Ach, wie schöne!*' as she made her rounds.

But Fabienne at her dressing table knew that, almost imperceptibly, the bloom was off her beauty. The black hair was burnished, the lips as naturally red as ever, but there was a faint line here, a hollow there, where none had been before. 'I ought to be in Paris,' she told herself. 'I'm wasted here!' She began to feel resentfully that she had been used by the Resistance and cast aside. At the time of the great break-out from Fort de la Revère, when some of the R.A.F. men were hidden in the hotel for days on end, she had, so she told herself, risked her life for France. Now she was nobody and her resentment began to brim over into a desire for vengeance.

Patrick Malvy was murdered on New Year's Eve, which in 1942 fell on a Thursday. Most people who could afford it 'made the bridge' until the following Monday morning, January 4th, and it was not until that morning, just before noon, that a man whom he had never seen before approached Jacques Brunel in the street and said M. Orengo hoped to see him tomorrow afternoon, at the villa, at five. The meeting was to take place an hour later than had been planned. He nodded, and the man made off, leaving Jacques with the feeling that there was not a great deal of time left for all he had to do.

Late on Monday, after the curfew, Fabienne Leroux walked through the ground floor of the Hotel Mimosa switching off the lights, and went on to the kitchen premises to check the locks on the wine cellar and pantries. The

Germans always left well before the curfew to return to their billets, because they prided themselves on being exceedingly *korrekt*, and Monsieur Leroux was safely back in Beausoleil. The hotel was quiet, so quiet that even in the kitchen Fabienne heard the faint scratching at the door on the stairs which led down to the Rue de la Turbie.

'Who's there?'

'Roger. Let me in.'

'Roger!' She unbolted the door, turned the key, and Roger Malvy stumbled across the threshold and took her in his arms. His cheek, when he pressed it against Fabienne's, was burning hot.

'Oh, my poor darling, I'm so sorry for you!' she said.

'I had to come. I had to get away from all of them—'

'Your jacket's wet.'

It was a dark leather *canadienne* like Jacques Brunel's, and the rain was dripping off the fur collar and off Roger's hair.

'I'm soaking.'

'But how did you get here? Didn't you drive?'

'The car's parked in the Place d'Armes. But I've been hanging around waiting to see your lights go out.'

'You poor dear, you've had an awful time. Let me get you a glass of brandy.'

'Oh God *no*!' Fabienne began to realise that he was drunk.

'Then come upstairs and get your wet clothes off. We've got half a dozen empty rooms tonight, and you can't go out until the curfew's lifted tomorrow morning.'

Roger braced his muscles against her and shook his head. 'I can't stay here – I can't get you into trouble – what I really came for was the key.'

'What key?'

'The key to the hut at Cap Martin – where you and Pierre Lavisse used to make love in the afternoons before the war.'

'Did Pierre tell you about that?'

'Sure he did. And if I can get into the hut, I'll lie up there for a few hours and try and cross the border before daylight.'

'The Italian border? But why darling, *why*?' She thought of the Resistance and asked fearfully, 'Are you blown?'

He laughed loudly and repeated, 'Blown? Not tonight, but I will be tomorrow if I stay.'

'S-sh, Roger! Marie or Jules will hear and come poking down, you don't want that, do you? Come up to the room at the head of the stairs and rest. I'll wake you in good time to go home before daylight. Your – Chantal will be distracted if she finds you've gone.'

'Chantal's doped to the eyes. She has her parents to look after her. They don't need me, they never did, except last January. I came in handy then.'

More and more perplexed, Fabienne piloted him through the dark lobby and up to a single bedroom where she helped him off with the *canadienne*, and saw him sink limply down on the narrow bed.

'I think I'd like that brandy now, *chérie*.'

She kept a small bottle in her bedroom in case any guests were taken ill in the night, and having brought it Fabienne poured him one finger, no more, which Roger drank at a gulp.

'They won't give up the body.'

'*Who* won't? The police? Oh my poor Roger, why?'

'Old Moreau and the police surgeon got together and postponed the application to inter until the murderer is found.'

'Dr. Moreau did? But surely he had no right to inter-fere! I mean *you* were the baby's father.'

'Like hell I was.'

Fabienne dropped to her knees beside the bed. 'You don't know what you're saying!'

The man reached out and pulled her closer to him.

217

Fabienne's black hair shook free from its pins and fell round her pale face as Roger leaned forward to kiss her.

'I suspected it, you know,' he said with drunken solemnity. 'I suspected it a long time ago. When they took her away to the Mont Dore, *and kept her there*, so long. When she wouldn't come back with me to our own home in Nice ... She promised to come back after the holidays. Then on New Year's Eve she told me she wasn't coming back at all, she and the kid were going to stay with papa and maman for ever and ever amen. That's when I should've walked out of the house, Fabienne, out of temptation's way. Because whatever I suspected, I wasn't *sure* till that night. When I saw him standing there laughing at me—'

'Who laughed at you? Oh Roger, Roger, who are you talking about?'

'The kid, of course. Chantal's kid. Marc Chabrol's kid, whose else? Lie down beside me.'

Fabienne pulled herself up to the edge of the bed and lay down, stiff, her body barely touching the man's and goose-fleshed with the oncoming horror. He too lay prone, not embracing her except by laying one arm across her breast.

'So that's why I need the key to the hut Fabienne. Where have you put it?'

She thought it best to give him an honest answer. 'I never had the key, darling. Pierre kept one, and Jacques Brunel had the other.'

'Were you with Brunel too, in the hut at Cap Martin?'

She fought the desire to strike him and said No.

'I'm glad of that. He's a callous devil, Jacques Brunel. He was there on New Year's Eve. And he saw what I saw, I'm sure of it. Saw that bastard Chabrol in little Patrick's face.'

'Roger – what did you do?'

'Do? I want to sleep, that's what I want to do. I haven't slept for three nights ...' His voice was trailing away, and the drink was catching up with him at last. Fabienne moved slightly, and took his head on her shoulder.

'You can sleep for hours, darling, if you'll only tell me first. What did you do to Patrick?'

'I went into the nursery to look at him sleeping. To see if the look was still there when he was asleep. He wasn't sleeping. He looked up at me and laughed at me the way Chabrol used to do, after Chantal and I were married, and that bastard laughed as if he knew more than I did ... You bet he knew! He knew my wife, every inch of her. I took the pillow and put it over Chabrol's face and held it there.'

Fabienne moved her head back on the clean pillow – the pillow! and stared into the slack-lipped face so near her own. Roger yawned. His eyelids closed. She lay there in a trance of horror until his breathing changed, and his arm across her breast became limp and heavy. Very gently she slid from beneath it and switched out the bedside light. In her stockings, with her high-heeled shoes in one hand, she crept across the dark room to the door.

In her own bedroom she poured herself a steadying measure of brandy before going down to the private office. There, with her head in her hands, she sat at her desk and thought.

In the bedroom at the top of the stairs there was a child-murderer. No amount of special pleading could mitigate that fact. Whatever wrong had been done to Roger Malvy it could not be avenged by the horrible crime of infanticide. The fact that he had been for a few months her own lover should not influence her judgment at all.

Chantal Malvy. So the gossips had been right who said that soon after her marriage she had begun to see her cousin Marc again. And in January a year ago, Roger had been of some use – as the husband, of course, to give his name to the child conceived in April, before Marc Chabrol managed to get out of France. Poor devils thought Fabienne with a flash of sympathy, it might have happened at their last rendezvous.

Far stronger than sympathy was her absolute horror of

Roger's crime. And beneath the horror, anger; she was being used again, used as a sanctuary, used for the outpouring of Roger Malvy's contempt. 'Were you with Brunel too, in the hut at Cap Martin?' What right had Roger to insult her? What right had Pierre Lavisse, her first and best love, to tell another man about the secret hut, and the long drowsy peacetime afternoons? Once again she felt the impulse to be revenged on all of them, the compulsion to betrayal. With a glance at the card of special telephone numbers on her desk, Fabienne lifted the handset, and dialled a call to the central police station at Nice.

Dr. Moreau's fame extended so far beyond the Riviera that the murder of his infant grandson had been an item on Radio Vichy on New Year's morning. On January 5th it was still good for a couple of lines about a new lead the police were following in the hills above Cimiez, and this was elaborated into a two column spread, with pictures inset, on the back page of the *Eclaireur de Nice*.

Jacques Brunel heard the broadcast and read the news story with professional interest. Both had obviously been inspired, but the 'new lead in the hills' angle had been given convincing coverage : there were pictures of the motor cycle brigade interrogating gipsies in a caravan encampment, and a good interview with one fierce looking old peasant woman, bent double with age and infirmity, who had heard 'running footsteps' passing her door on the night of the crime. But there was no news of an arrest, and *'Plainte contre X'* still stood on the books.

Neither Jacques nor Polly had heard anything from the stricken family since the fatal New Year's Eve. Jacques had sent flowers to Madame Malvy and her mother, and Polly had telephoned, to be told by a strange female voice that Madame Malvy was in the throes of an asthma attack and Madame Moreau had a migraine headache. Of course Les Floralies had been overrun by Moreaus and Malvys and in-laws of all ages and degrees as soon as the tragedy was known.

If everything went well at the meeting at Couteau's, Jacques thought he might drive on to Les Floralies and at least leave cards of sympathy. He didn't know if Roger Malvy would attend the meeting at the Villa des Oliviers or not. He had heard in the corridors of the Palais de Justice that permission to give up the child's body to the relatives had been withheld, and in the extremely grave circumstances it was doubtful if the father would care to appear at a Resistance meeting. If he did there would be seven from the 'Knife' circuit, as at the meeting at 'Le Faisan', and four from a smaller circuit called 'Fire', attending under the aliases of Bois, Charbon, Ligot and Margotin. With himself as an independent, and Renaudon to spread the news about de Gaulle's secret army, the members present would reach the unlucky number of thirteen. Perhaps it would be as well if Malvy stayed away.

Malvy, or Canif, was second-in-command of the 'Knife' circuit, and would take over if anything happened to Couteau. Jacques had been thinking about who should take over from him, if he had to get out of France in a hurry. He thought Froment in the city would make as good a team with Jean Dupont at Cap Martin as his small network needed for leadership, as good a team as they had been in Norway. He wasn't worried about that at all.

Jacques had looked up General Delestraint in the Army List. He was a retired general officer of about sixty, living at Bourg-en-Brest, who had once commanded an armoured division in which Jacques knew that Charles de Gaulle had served. Maxwell had said that General Delestraint was originally chosen to lead the secret army by members of the Resistance, and de Gaulle had merely endorsed him, which made Jacques wonder what qualities – or the lack of them – in the senior general had commended themselves to the Leader at Carlton Gardens. Renaudon would have to make a big sales pitch to put over the idea of a secret army organised on regular lines, with a chain of command, instead of companies of guerilla fighters.

Before he went to get his car he opened the wall safe in his apartment. It was an old-fashioned one, but secure; Grand'tante Marthe had had it installed to hold the jewels which item by item she had given away to Jacques' mother. It now contained little but ready cash for an emergency, a set of false papers, and a revolver, loaded with a box of ammunition. He had no such thing as a shoulder holster – that was for the gangster movies – but Jacques slipped the gun into the pocket of his sports jacket before he moved *Nana* and *A Rebours* back into place. Grand'tante Marthe who was not without a sense of humour had caused the safe to be installed behind the false back of the bookcase, protected by her collection of mild pornography.

He clipped his sheath knife to his belt, closed the shutters in both rooms, and took his raincoat from the armoire as he left the flat. The Peugeot was in the Place Rossetti, where he often parked, and he drove off feeling that only Nestor, even when absent, could have persuaded him to attend a meeting where so many of the Resistance were gathered under one roof. It was the rendezvous at 'Le Faisan' all over again only worse, and he felt the unworthy suspicion that Renaudon had called them all together for some dark purpose of his own. He started the upward drive to Cimiez in an uncertain mood.

There was hardly any traffic on the suburban boulevard. Although it was barely five o'clock, any person having business in Nice who was free to go home at that hour had already left the city, and only two or three private cars, ahead of the Peugeot, turned off the avenues into the streets with the English names. A trolley bus came downhill empty, and Jacques overtook one which was full, with passengers jammed between the seats and on the outside step. It was twilight already, but after Jacques passed the office blocks

nearest the city he saw few lamps lit in the apartment buildings. One, very conspicuous, which stood up like a cliff at
the intersection of the avenues, was brightly lighted from
attics to cellar : it was Queen Victoria's Hotel Regina, now
the headquarters of the Gestapo.

Something moved in the dusk, on the pavement in front
of the Regina. A woman's figure – a girl's – in black, and
inconspicuous, but when the Peugeot was almost abreast of
her, on the other side of the road, this girl snatched off the
red knitted cap she wore, and waved it twice, in long sweeping movements, as the car went past. Polly ! Polly, who
should have been playing with the toddlers at the day nursery, in the darkness and alone at Cimiez ! He flashed his
headlights to show he recognised her, made a U-turn and
stopped, throwing his raincoat into the back seat to make
room for Polly on the passenger seat beside him.

'Pauline ! What's happened?'

'Roger Malvy's been arrested for Patrick's murder.'

'How do you know?'

'Juliette told me – the maid at Les Floralies. Fabienne
turned him in last night, just before midnight.'

'*Fabienne!*' Jacques put the car in gear again, and pulled
away from that sinister pavement, now reserved for the
Gestapo, and drove downhill until he could enter one of the
quiet suburban streets, where big gardens hid his car from
the houses.

'Tell me what *you're* doing here,' was the first thing he
said. 'I thought it was your afternoon at the *maternelle*.'

'Three of the babies are down with whooping-cough, and
Mademoiselle's afraid of an epidemic. She hired a little van
and we drove round Nice at lunchtime, delivering all the
others to their homes. Then I thought I'd get some flowers
and try to see Chantal.'

He could see the glimmer of a bunch of the earliest
freesias in Polly's lap.

'Chantal's got a trained nurse with her now,' Polly went

on. 'She isn't seeing anybody, and after what Juliette whispered in the hall I wouldn't have known what to say to her. I even forgot to leave the freesias. But Juliette left me alone when she went to find out what the nurse would say, and I heard the doctor shouting at Madame Moreau. I didn't hear all of it, but I did hear him say something like 'He thought he could save his miserable skin by talking, but I'll make sure he gets his punishment!' That was when I knew I had to warn you, and I thought – up there – was the place where you could see me best.'

'So Roger talked,' said Jacques. He had subconsciously been waiting for this catastrophe since he looked into the little face that was so like Marc Chabrol's. 'I wonder how long for?'

'I thought of that. I asked Juliette when the doctor came home, and she said he'd been in the house about half an hour. He'd been at the *Commissariat* since ten o'clock this morning.'

Malvy talking. Malvy betrayed by Fabienne, and desperate, listening to the police offer to do a deal with him, allow him to plead the unwritten law, or *crime passionnel*, or whatever sounded most dramatic in his ears. Then Malvy spilling it all out, names, addresses, dates, the meeting this afternoon—

'Pauline,' he said, 'can you drive a car?'

'Sure I can.'

'Right. Then we're going back to the Impasse des Arènes.' But he paused before switching on the engine; he could get to the Villa des Oliviers and warn the resisters of imminent danger but what about Polly? Did she know the streets of Nice well enough to take the car back to Froment's garage? And without a car, how was he to get away? He thought of telling her to go back to Les Floralies, but that wouldn't do. The police would still be keeping the Moreau house under surveillance. In desperation he asked her if she knew the Parc des Arènes.

'I know the main paths pretty well.' She knew the central path best of all, where Patrick had sat up waving and laughing in his pram.

'You know there's a gate on the lower level, by the ruins of the thermal springs?'

'I know where it is.'

'Then here's what we do. I'll drive up to the Villa des Oliviers, you drive back to the lower gate and wait for me. I'll try not to be too long. If anyone asks you what you're doing there, say you're waiting for a friend. Don't act scared, just sit still and wait – Polly, I don't know how much time we've got!'

He turned the car and raced back up the boulevard, past the upper gate to the old Roman arena, a gate which was nothing but a broken archway, with flowers and grasses growing between the stones. He hadn't been there since he was a boy, but Jacques remembered how small the arena was compared with the Roman amphitheatre at Arles, how vast, by contrast, the park with the olive trees and the ruins on the lower level, where the outline of the baths and thermal springs could still be traced beneath tall cypress trees. In summer overgrown with harebells and wild lavender, the pillars and broken columns of old Cemenelum were hardly visible in the dark of the winter moon.

The Orengo villa was halfway between the arena and the Franciscan church. 'This is it,' said Jacques, stopping the car. 'Thank God I told you I was going to a meeting. If they get away with their lives, I'll tell them someday it was all due to you.'

'You didn't tell me this was the place,' she said, bewildered. 'If I'd known, I would've waited for you here.'

'Never mind. Now *drive*, my darling!' She slid over into the driver's seat as Jacques got out. He waited one minute to see her start, and then ran up the garden path to the Villa des Oliviers. He could see light under the blind in the front window and hoped the meeting was in the room behind, the nearest to the front door. He kept his finger on the electric bell until the door was opened by Pierre Orengo himself.

'Don't talk,' he said roughly, 'are any of your family here? Your servants? No? You had that much sense at least. You've heard about Malvy?'

'Canif?'

'Oh damn your silly aliases,' said Jacques, 'he'll stand his trial under his own name, and so will you, but on another charge. Where are they?'

'In – in the dining room. What's happened Jack?'

They were round a polished dining table with the leaves in, all seated except Orengo-Couteau and César, who jumped to his feet. Even Sabre was there, whose fault of carelessness had been nothing to this, and who looked as if he had been interrupted in the middle of a fiery speech. César, or Renaudon, was the only one who seemed to guess at what Jacques had come to tell them.

'Malvy's been arrested on a charge of murder,' Jacques flung out, 'he's been in custody and singing his head off since the small hours of this morning. Get out of this house, the lot of you, and out of Nice if you can until the heat's off, if it ever is. Who's got transportation? I saw two cars outside. Fleuret, you and Epée? Good. Get as many as you can aboard and make for the back roads—'

They let him get so far without interruption. But then the moment of shock was over, and the voices burst out in the usual disagreement, some asking Jacques for evidence of what he had come to say, some objecting to his implication that Canif would betray them, each and every one with a separate solution of the problem. To leave Nice was impossible. The wife, the children, the office, the shop, the contracts, all were adduced as reasons for refusing to take flight.

'So stay and get yourselves put on the trains to Dachau,' said Jacques, 'but make sure you destroy your papers first. Couteau, have you an incinerator?' The master of the house nodded dumbly. Of them all, he seemed to be the most dazed by the thought of danger. Jacques snatched up a wastepaper basket. 'Everything incriminating goes in here,' he said. 'Your pocket diaries – everything.' The four men from the 'Fire' circuit had each brought notebooks with a memorandum of the meeting and its purpose : to discuss the appointment of General Delestraint as the commander of the secret army. Jacques groaned.

'Couteau, put this lot in the incinerator,' he said. 'Fleuret, go with him and take care nothing's left. The rest of you get into the cars, and make sure you've got all your belongings with you when you leave the house.'

'I told you we needed you on our side, Jack,' said Renaudon. 'Are you sure you won't change your mind and join the secret army? You'd be promoted colonel in no time.'

'Thanks, I don't care for the high command,' said Jacques. And slightly lowering his voice, he added, 'I've got my own car, not too far away. You'd better come with me, and I'll do my best to get you out of here alive.'

'I appreciate this, *mon vieux*. I'd no idea—' He stopped short as Poignard ran in from the street, shouting, 'It's too late! The police are coming!' They could hear the wail of sirens rising from the boulevard.

'The cars—' Jacques began, and stopped. If the motors belonging to Epée and Fleuret had been nearer the entry to the arena, and if there had been time, it might have been possible to place them across the road and make a barricade. But it was too late for that now. They were caught in a trap, with a church at one end and the Gestapo headquarters at the other, unable to move either left or right. Orengo and Fleuret, the latter carrying the empty paper basket, burst in from the incinerator and shouted something about the back garden.

'Where does that lead to?' asked Renaudon. His blue eyes were blazing, his grey-blond hair falling over his forehead; he looked very much as an admiring new boy had seen him on his last sports day at the Ecole des Roches.

'You come out opposite Les Floralies,' said Orengo. 'Dr. Moreau will surely give us shelter!' —

'I wouldn't bank on it,' said Jacques. 'The only way out now is through the park. Good luck all!' He ran down the garden path, with Sabre and Renaudon at his heels, as the leading police car turned into the Impasse des Arènes.

Sabre was small and light, he jumped for the park wall as nimbly as Jacques, and they both balanced themselves on the top to see what became of their friends. The police were piling out of their cars and running towards the Villa des Oliviers, where Orengo was standing helpless at the door like the host at a party. The worst sight was a truckload of militiamen in black, who were taking possession of the re-sisters' cars.

'*Alain!*' Jacques shouted. For Renaudon was no longer by his side. He was running, with something of his boy-hood's turn of speed, in the direction of the Franciscan church.

'Alain, watch out! It's a cul-de-sac!' It was all he had time to say, as *milicien*'s bullet sang past his head. Jacques dropped down into the park, where Sabre was already run-ning like a hare among the olive trees. Jacques, confused by the darkness and the unfamiliar scene, remained crouching at the foot of the wall.

He was a young *milicien*, with a powerful electric torch in one hand and a revolver in the other, emerging from the Roman arena to shine a searchlight beam on the figure of Sabre. And the schoolmaster was limping now, that burst of speed had been a nervous effort, he must have fallen awk-wardly and done some damage to his foot. Jacques felt for his own gun, took aim at the moving target, and shot the torch out of the *milicien*'s hand.

It was too late to save Sabre. The enemy's bullet caught him in the back, and he fell forward with a long bubbling scream, as firing broke out in the street above, and, as far as Jacques could judge, from the direction of the church. His

only plan, now, was to stop this young thug who was pump-
ing shots into Sabre's body, and who might bring another
half dozen men into the gardens, ranging far and wide until
they came on Polly at the lower gate, waiting in the car. He
fired again and missed, broke away, and ran past some
blacked-out buildings to the stairs leading to the thermal
springs. He could hear the booted feet in hot pursuit.

The Roman world opened and engulfed them both. The
cypresses were black against the leaden sky, and even in
January the wild lavender, bruised beneath their feet, gave
out a hint of fragrance. In the grassy track which had been
streets, where the Romans had walked to bath house and
fountain, or bought coral ornaments and sponges from the
Mediterranean deeps, two Frenchmen stalked one another
in a struggle to the end. Moving recklessly between the
broken columns, stumbling over walls only forty centimetres
high, they played their deadly game of hide and seek, while
from the Impasse des Arènes the noise of police whistles
grew louder, and Jacques could hear the deeper siren of an
ambulance. He could see his man, crouching, moving in; he
did not risk another shot. Let the two of them be forgotten
in their private arena while the arrests were made and the
wounded tended in the suburban street above. They had no
umpire and no audience, for the lights in the flats and houses
overlooking the Parc des Arènes had been extinguished as
soon as the shooting started. Nobody wanted to get involved.

He changed the gun to his left hand, and threw a heavy
stone with his right to indicate his whereabouts, and then
his sheath knife sprang into that same hand and was ready
for the leap of the grunting, heavy body dressed in black.
Jacques hadn't been prepared for so much weight, though
he was ready for the fellow's knife : it was at his throat for
an instant when he was knocked backwards in the *milicien*'s
first rush. He felt the point in his arm as he rolled over, he
had the suppleness and strength where the other man had
blubber, and he brought his own knife up in a stroke that

went through the uniform, through the envelope of flesh, piercing the lung, while a life ended in spasms of bloody froth upon the grass.

Jacques Brunel got to his feet. The thing on the ground was too heavy to drag into any sort of hiding place. It would have to lie there among the broken columns until the search was on which might be when the militiamen went back to barracks after the great *razzia* in the Impasse des Arènes, or possibly not until their next roll call. He stooped, and wiped the knife clean of blood on the grass, used grass to wipe his hands, put the knife back in its sheath and transferred the gun to his right hand pocket. Then he made his painful way through the ancient stones to the lower gate, tore his clothes on the barbed wire nailed along the top, and walked quietly towards his car – and Polly.

She was sitting there, just as he had told her to sit, but now in the passenger's seat, waiting for him to come to her. He said her name, and she got out of the car at once, not speaking, not questioning him only pressing herself against him and shivering, making him think of the night they had dodged the *Milice* at Carnolès. His first words were utterly prosaic.

'Let me get at my raincoat, *chérie*.'

He had no idea what his face looked like, but his suit he knew must be torn and dusty; the raincoat would hide the worst of it. He pulled it out of the car, and a bunch of fading flowers came with it, the petals scented and ghostly as they touched his hands. They were the freesias which Polly had forgotten.

He threw the stalks away from him with a kind of horror, and told her to get back into the car. They were far down the boulevard, coming into the populated streets of Nice, before Polly spoke again.

'I heard the police sirens, and then firing on the hill. Jacques, did it all go wrong?'

'Yes, it did. I know one of our men was killed, and maybe

others. I don't know if anybody else got clean away but me. And I may only have a few hours' start on the law.'

'But you're – all right?' By the light from the street lamps he could see dark bruises on the back of his hands on the wheel, and knew that she could see them too. The blood was oozing out of the abraded skin.

'I'm all right.' Some of the shops were still open as he drove past the Place Wilson, but the *maternelle* was closed, he could see the first words of a new notice, 'Shut because of' – the whooping-cough, he supposed. A policeman waved him on at the crossing of the Avenue Jean Jaurès.

'I'm going to drive straight up the Rue Droite, Pauline, and put you down outside my door. Keep your fingers crossed that we don't meet another car.' It was hardly likely, very few motors came up that narrow lane, except an occasional delivery van.

'What are you going to do?' said the scared voice by his side.

'Take the car back to Froment and put him in the picture. A lot of people have to be told what happened at Cimiez tonight.' Of what had happened at Cimiez on New Year's Eve, it wasn't yet the time to speak. Malvy's crime and Fabienne's betrayal were two deeds to be set in their proper context; the first thing was to save what could be saved in the destruction of the Resistance.

'I'll give you the key off my ring, and you let yourself into the flat. You'll be all right alone for half an hour, and then I'll be back.' Jacques got out of the car at the Palais Lascaris, and made sure the big front door was open. Polly was alone beneath the shield with the Maltese cross, the double-headed eagle and the motto *Nec Me Fulgara.*

At six in the evening – and it was no later – the old house was humming like a hive of bees. Behind each heavy door too many people had gathered for the evening meal, the evening's fruitless discussion, and the lamps were lit in the windows on the far side of the inner patio. By their light

Polly found the *minuterie*, the push button which illumina-
ed each stair for so few minutes that she arrived on every
landing in darkness, but she groped her way past the
mouldering busts in their baroque niches, under the faded
terra-cotta ceilings, to the third floor.

It was only the second time she had been in Jacques'
apartment. She lit the table lamps in the living room, hung
up her overcoat on a hook in the little hall, and went into
the bathroom to wash her hands and face in cold water. She
had powder and lipstick in her handbag, but all the cosmetics in Nice would not have covered the shock beneath
her pallor, and all Polly did was to pull her comb through
her disordered hair until the bronze lights sparkled. She remembered, after an instant of panic, that she had put the
red knitted cap into her coat pocket.

It was hard to know what to do to fill in time till Jacques
came back. She was certain he was physically hurt, because
all his movements were so stiff and slow, but in her inexperience she pinned her faith to the first-aid box in the bathroom, and perhaps to the brandy bottle in the kitchen cupboard. She hesitated about putting the bottle and glasses on
a tray. It looked too like playing housewife, moving in! The
kitchen's inadequacy struck her more than when she had
been in there getting a glass of water for François. It had one
high window in the wall, operating like a skylight on the
outside landing, and a stone sink with a cold water tap. Two
gas burners were set in a table installation above shelves
holding chipped pots and pans, but a corner cupboard contained Sèvres china and a few valuable pieces of Limoges.
It was a queer mixture. She glanced in at the bedroom door,
which was standing ajar, and saw the mixture there too, the
radio set and the Restoration furniture with the classical
figures among the painted clouds and chariots.

'Jacques?' She had put the chain on the door when she
came in, and had to ease it back, after she heard his voice,
to let him inside his own apartment, but that at least made

Jacques laugh and even tease her for her prudence, as he took his raincoat off and hung it up beside her coat. Then she saw the ruin of his jacket and trousers, felt the weight of the gun as she helped him take the jacket off, and gasped.

'You'll have to help me with my shirt, Polly. Froment put iodine on my hands, but I think something's the matter with my left arm.'

The matter was a long cut, angry but shallow, with the drying blood oozing again when the shirt was gently peeled away. 'I can dress it for you,' Polly said. 'I don't think it needs stitches.'

'Neither do I.'

He sat down in his undershirt and torn trousers on the wide sofa where François had lain, and joked, when she brought a bowl of warm water and the first-aid box, that she always had to act nurse when she came to the Palais Làscaris. But Polly, deftly binding up his arm, had no smile to give him. She only said, 'You had to fight, hadn't you?'

He took the basin from her hands and drew her down beside him. 'Yes, I had to fight,' he said. 'I saw one of our men killed, and I had to fight *to the death*, do you understand me, Polly?'

She looked from his jacket flung on the table, with the gun in one pocket; she saw the knife still in its sheath hung at his belt, and shuddered. 'Yes, I understand,' she said. 'But *you're* alive!'

It was the affirmation of life he needed to hear. Jacques seized Polly and began to kiss her; between kisses he heard her whisper:

'Was it a German?'

'No, darling. It was one of the scum who make me ashamed to be a Frenchman. A *milicien*.'

'Then I'm glad.'

'Polly, you were wonderful!'

These were the last coherent things that either of them said. There were words, sometimes tender and sometimes crude, there were kisses and blind strugglings, there was a slow, stumbling, halting, embracing walk from the sofa to the wide bed in the shadow of the brocade curtains. Jacques, sleepless in that bed, had sometimes thought how it would be when he was Polly's lover, the first to possess this virgin of furious gold. He meant to be gentle, forbearing, patient, loving : he had not reckoned that after the lust to kill would come the lust to deflower. He took her like a madman, and Polly's passion woke to match his madness, as if the swan above their bed had stretched out its neck and was flying to the sun.

13

On the Friday after the events at Cimiez, Joe Calvert was in his office at the American Embassy in London, re-reading with perplexity a very long cable received direct from Baltimore. He was bound to take it seriously, but it was interruption to his morning, for Joe was one of the men setting up a new project devised by the President of the United States.

Since the end of November, when the American landings in North Africa had encountered such resistance in Tunisia, Mr. Roosevelt had felt the need, as he put it, 'to sit down at the table with the Russians'. The second front was still a long way from being opened, and his military advisers had been obliged to report that there was no hope of invading continental Europe in 1943. True, the great concentration of American troops in Britain since the previous July, used in North Africa, had been replaced by others, and still the huge build-up of man power went on. The U.S. Air Force had joined the R.A.F. in bombing enemy targets in Germany and Italy, and to some extent in France. But the great assault on Fortress Europe would have to be postponed until 1944.

The President's original idea was for a conference of military experts from the United States, Britain and Russia, either in Cairo or in Moscow, early in 1943. Developed by Mr. Churchill, the plan was enlarged to include the national leaders at the head of the military delegations, and Mr. Roosevelt breezily hoped that 'Uncle Joe', as he called Stalin, would agree to that. Calvert had access to some of the classified correspondence, and every time he came across the name of 'Uncle Joe' he winced; he thought it was as silly to give a schoolboy nickname to the Russian tyrant as to call Admiral Darlan 'the Little Fellow'. But these were the prejudices of a veteran diplomat, and some of his colleagues told him the language of diplomacy was out of date.

One of these was a young man called Randall, cheeky but capable, who was Bob Kemp's deputy in the French section of the Office of Strategic Services. Mr. Kemp had departed for Casablanca, observing that that was where the action was, for the idea of a military conversation in Moscow had been shelved in favour of a top-level conference in Morocco, 'Uncle Joe' declining to be present at a Moscow meeting with his dear allies. When Calvert digested his cable he rang Jim Randall at Twenty, Grosvenor Square, and they agreed to meet for lunch in the embassy canteen.

The prime topic of that day, the eighth of January, was Stalingrad, where Field-Marshal Paulus and his Sixth German Army had been caught by the Russian pincers and were suffering a siege in great privation. On this Friday Paulus rejected a Russian ultimatum to surrender. It was a hopeless gesture; every man in the embassy canteen knew that the end was not far off, and Joe discussed the implications thoroughly with Randall. When coffee was served he took out the cable from Baltimore and asked the O.S.S. man to have a look at it.

'I'd better explain who these people are,' he said. 'George Preston is a friend of mine, though I knew his brother Paul better; we were on the same team at the Paris Peace Conference in 1920. Paul's dead, a good many years ago, and this message has to do with his daughter, young Pauline. I'm her godfather, and incidentally one of her trustees.'

Randall was reading rapidly. 'Who's Vittoria Pradelli?' he enquired. 'She got a message out of Naples through the Red Cross.'

'Beats me, but I suppose she's related to Pauline's stepfather.'

The gist of George Preston's cable, mutilated in transmission, was that Signora Vittoria Pradelli had informed him that his niece Pauline Mary Preston had left a sanatorium near Menton in Italian-occupied territory and was believed to have crossed the border into France. She had deceived Signora Pradelli as to her intentions of remaining at the sanatorium, and Mr. Preston must now assume full responsibility for his niece during her minority.

'Which has only two months to run,' interposed Joe at this point of the reading. 'She'll be twenty-one in March.'

'And you're her trustee, Joe? Is she coming into a fortune then?'

'I'm her trustee, along with her uncle George, under her grandfather's Will, and she can't touch the principal of the trust until she's twenty-five. Even so she won't be what we used to call a dollar princess, but she'll come into a comfortable sum of money – I wonder if she knows anything about it!'

'And now you don't know where she is, right?'

'Right.'

'She flew the coop from a sanatorium. What's the matter with her – t.b.?'

'God knows,' said Joe. 'She was a perfectly healthy kid of twelve when I saw her last. That was in Paris, just before her mother married Count Pradelli. She may be sick, she may be crazy (*must* be crazy to cross into Occupied France), she may be involved with a man, but you can read for yourself that

George Preston expects me to produce her like a rabbit out of a hat – *one* girl roaming about in occupied territory! Just like her poor mother, wandering all the way from Petrograd to Paris with a bunch of feckless refugees—'

'Oh, the mother's Russian!'

'*Was* Russian,' said Joe. 'She died a while back; she was never very strong after the 1918 winter. I remember advising her to go to the Crimea while the going was good, but she held on too long in Petrograd, like they all did.'

'You knew the mother too, did you?'

'She was at the very first Russian party I ever attended in St. Petersburg,' said Joe, and his anxious face softened into a smile. 'Marie Alexandrovna – she must have been about sixteen then, younger than Pauline is now. She was the cousin of a girl called Dolly Hendrikova, whom I thought the world of in those days. But that's ancient history, Jim! Tell me if there's anything I can do to find Pauline.'

'She's probably in the internment camp at Vittel by this time,' said Randall dryly. 'If she's not, where do you think she's likely to head for?'

'Paris.'

Randall whistled. 'And I suppose you think some of our agents ought to keep a look-out for her – a girl you last saw nine years ago, who may have changed her name, or married, since she left this sanatorium—'

'I've been thinking she might turn up with her American passport at the embassy of the Protecting Power, and ask for help.'

'A long shot, Joe, but it might just work. Tell you what: you give me the particulars, and a rough idea of what Miss Preston may look like now, and I'll brief our agents at the camps and in Paris. That way, you'll be able to tell her uncle that you're leaving no stone unturned. And anyway there's nothing more we can do unless your girl decides to surface by herself.'

With that Joe Calvert had to be content. He would have

been amazed if he could have seen Polly Preston, alias Pauline Henri, who at that moment was sitting in the corner of a first-class carriage in a train bound from Nice to Paris via Marseille, in the company of three German officers, one French black marketeer, and Jacques Brunel.

Polly had lived through a year's experience in the three days since she went to Cimiez to ask for Chantal Malvy. Fathoms deep in love with her first lover, she had to school herself into accepting the rarity of their hours together when she longed for days and nights alone. She had to observe how her lover's more complex and far more disciplined personality reacted to the stress of their situation. On their first night Jacques kept her beside him until morning. They had a picnic supper about midnight, and loved and slept again, in a trance of happiness unbroken by the slightest fear of a knock on the door and a shout of *'Ouvrez, ouvrez! Police allemande!'* But the next day it was different. Jacques made her go back to the pension, where Madame Froment, warned by her brother, had no comment to make on Mademoiselle Henri's overnight absence. He told her the first thing she could do to help him was to say to Monsieur Ratazzi, as the railway clerk fussed out of the dining-room after breakfast, 'Captain Jack wants two seats to Paris at noon on Friday.'

'Monsieur Ratazzi! That funny little cross old thing! Do you mean he's one of *us*?'

'They come in all sorts and sizes, Polly.'

She said 'us' now, and there was no reason to contradict her. Polly Preston was the girl who had warned the Resistance, under the very noses of the Gestapo, she was the girl who had driven the getaway car, and was perfectly willing, if need arose, to carry a gun for her lover. She was part of the French Resistance, and far more reliable than Jacques had ever dreamed a girl could be.

From Jacques Brunel, in the next two days, Polly Preston got a lesson in patience and public self-control. She began to realise how hard it was for Maître Brunel to go about his business quietly while the arrest of Roger Malvy was only equalled in the *Eclaireur* headlines by the 'Gun Battle at Cimiez' and the 'Capture of a Band of Terrorists'. The haul had been a big one. Pierre Orengo, alias Couteau, had surrendered on his own doorstep, while Epée and Fleuret had been captured inside their cars, along with all four members of the 'Fire' circuit. Poignard and Coupoir had escaped through the back garden to the Villa Les Floralies, where at gunpoint they had made the not unwilling Gustave drive them into the warren of the Old Town at the wheel of his master's car. The whole of Nice was in a turmoil at the news, but Jacques knew the full story of Thursday night was still untold.

From his sources at the Préfecture and the gossip in the corridors of the Palais de Justice, he learned that when the police from Nice arrived in Monaco and roused Roger Malvy from a heavy sleep, he was just sober enough to realise that Fabienne had betrayed him. He roundly accused her of lying. He denied that he had confessed to little Patrick's murder. It was not until hours later, when he was about to go before the examining magistrate, that his father's solicitors told him a plea of *crime passionnel* would be accepted if Roger were to help the police in certain other and unrelated investigations. He then informed them that 'a notorious Gaullist agent' would be at Monsieur Orengo's villa at Cimiez at five that afternoon. So far as was known he had only named César and Pierre Orengo. The other names would no doubt come later, before what promised to be a *cause célèbre* was heard in court.

It was impossible to conceal the death of Sabre. The little man might be called a terrorist, but by his real name of Yvon Méry he had been much respected, and his colleagues and pupils at the *lycée* were determined to make a public occasion of his funeral. It would be a day of flags and anthems which might well end in a clash with the police. Nothing had been revealed about the dead *milicien*. Either his body had not yet been found, or if found had been connected in some way with Sabre's; or, more likely, the Germans had not considered his death to be worth reprisals. If it had been one of their own it would have been a different story, and Jacques, remembering the death of the fifty hostages at Nantes, and of other hostages in other towns who paid with their lives for the killing of a single German soldier, felt a cold sweat on his brow as he thought what his act might have brought upon his fellow townsmen.

Renaudon was in the hands of the Germans. The police had captured him at the very door of the Franciscan church, tripped and sprawling on the steps with his hands on the lintel, like some medieval victim seeking sanctuary. He was the one they were after, the one Roger Malvy had 'given' at the end of the long hours of his interrogation, César the archterrorist, too big a capture for the Nice police to handle, or even the Italians who were setting up an efficient house of torture at the Villa Lynwood. They had turned Alain Renaudon over to the Gestapo.

'They took him off to Marseille by road next morning,' said Daniel Profetti in a low voice. He was sitting with Jacques Brunel in his office in the Bar des Sports, and there was nobody within twenty metres of them; the lowered tones were a mark of respect rather than a necessity. 'They didn't risk any of us taking a chance at springing him. He's in the prison of St. Pierre now, marked top security and highly dangerous, and if César sings there's not a Resistance network between here and the English Channel that won't be in danger.'

'I don't think he'll sing,' said Jacques.

'I hope you're right, *chief*. But you've got to get the hell out, before you're taken too.'

'That's what I've come about.' He needed the forger to prepare an *Ausweis*, or pass, for a journey to Paris, one for himself and one for Pauline Marie Henri, *célibataire*, etc., an *Ausweis* for a return journey with the date left blank. It was more difficult than obtaining a false identity card for Polly. Edouard at the Préfecture had only to steal one of the actual cards from the reserve and fill it in with the names, dates and photograph; for an *Ausweis* Profetti had to work from cardboard, using copies of the special stamps and inks. It was risky, but not so risky as for Jacques to put his head in the lion's mouth by going in person to the German authorities.

'Don't tell me when you're going and don't tell me why,' said Maître Pastorelli, the elderly barrister with whom Jacques shared the services of Monsieur Bosio. 'I don't want to know. Business in Paris, that's quite enough for me, and so it ought to be for *them*. Things have come to a pretty pass when an *avocat* can't move freely about the country on his lawful occasions! But don't stay away too long, *mon cher maître*. You may miss big money if you do. Monsieur Henri Malvy may want to brief you for the defence of his hopeful son Roger at the next Assizes.'

'The Malvy family'll brief Maître Isorni, or some other hot shot from Paris, when that case comes to trial,' said Jacques. 'I'd rather defend poor Fabienne.'

'Mademoiselle Leroux? But she's a star witness for the prosecution!'

'I wasn't thinking of the case in court.' Jacques knew that Fabienne, jealous and introverted, would accuse herself to the end of her days for her betrayal of the man whom in her fashion she had loved. 'Isorni should plead diminished responsibility for both of them,' he said as he took his leave.

Everybody said he ought to go, but not stay too long away – they all insisted upon that. Profetti said he would gladly take his orders from Froment, who would drive to Cap Martin and tell Dupont, who would be in touch with Dr. Lecampion: as long as Jacques' circuit was complete it would function well enough without him. Dany Profetti and his nucleus of a maquis were safe enough up at the Jurac farm.

Madame Froment promised to go in person to the *maternelle* when it reopened after the whooping-cough, and tell *mademoiselle la directrice* that Mademoiselle Henri had been called away to nurse a sick relative — 'tell her my Aunt Vittoria,' said Polly maliciously. 'Better say "Tante Victoire".' Jacques saw that Polly herself was as gaily prepared to leave the day nursery as she had been to leave the sanatorium behind her, or to say good-bye to Madame Belinska the night they crossed the border. The ever-moving-on Polly! He was mad about her, but he was far from sure of her, a girl ten years his junior, much more American in her ways than Russian, so headstrong and so brave! Would she be true to him? She was his present joy and brightness, would she tire of a nature so unlike her own? She lived, and vividly, for the moment, while he looked to the past nostalgically and to the future with foreboding. Would she teach him her keen enjoyment of the fleeting hour? He took her to bed, and then he was sure of her. She was his and he meant to keep her, come hell or high water; and all the time he was listening for the knock of the Gestapo on the door.

In the train, that Friday morning, she read the collaborationist papers *Gringoire* and *Aujourd'hui* with every appearance of enjoyment. She declined the fresh peaches, hothouse-grown, out of season, offered her by the black marketeer, but she did so with a pleasant smile and a warning glance towards Jacques, as if she couldn't accept the fruit from a stranger without his permission. He was busy with a sheaf of legal papers dealing with a complaint about the municipal sewage system, while the Germans, whose language he understood well enough to know that they were engineer officers, talked about the problems of demolishing the Vieux Port. Jacques thought they might be leaving the train at Marseille, but to his relief they remained in their seats; at least Polly would not have to cope with a new intake of enemy strangers in his absence. He made rather a fuss about going to get something to eat and drink for the next part of the journey : the restaurant cars were not dependable and very dear, and so on, until the Germans looked up with smiles at the French bourgeois fretting about his food, and Polly said in a bored and wifely tone, 'Anything will do, darling!'

That set him free to go to the railway buffet, where sandwiches were sold in paper bags and wine in quarter bottles, and where, in the adjacent and very busy restaurant, Lieutenant Charles Maxwell was sitting in a corner reading an early edition of the evening paper.

It was a huge relief to know that the telegram he had sent to the newsagent's shop, ordering fifty copies of the most collaborationist of all the literary reviews, had had the desired result in Charles's presence. For once, an agreed code had worked; but Jacques was so impatient of all the codes and elaborate recognition signals dear to the Resistance that in the present extremity he merely said, 'Hallo, how are you?' held out his hand, and took the chair from which Charles removed a heavy bag of tools.

'Any news?' he said quietly. The noises of the Gare St. Charles, and the buzz of conversation round about them, were cover enough for all they had to say.

'César's in maximum security, and it won't be easy.'

'Anybody trying? Any Gaullist contacts?'

'They're talking about a break through the house and garden next the prison, but that takes time, and time is what we haven't got. He's under torture.'

Jacques groaned. 'Are you sure?'

'I've bought one of the medical orderlies. He saw César after the last interrogation. They got nothing out of him.'

'Do you want me to stay?'

A stout woman, pushing two crying children, began slowly moving out of the row of chairs beside their table, and under cover of the small commotion Charles handed Jacques the folded newspaper. One glance at the headlines was enough.

'The Terrorists of Cimiez', Jacques read. 'New Developments Revealed. Was there a Third Man in the Parc des Arènes?' The story, of the now-it-can-be-told variety, described the brutal murder of a *milicien* from Grenoble, aged twenty, previously unemployed, whose patriotism was praised in terms which would have been excessive if used to describe the legendary Roland or the Chevalier Bayard.

'*Vous désirez, monsieur?*' That was the waiter, at his elbow. He cast a glance at Charles's half-empty glass, and asked for the same thing – a beer.

'I'd better be on my way,' he said after two swallows, and the British agent nodded. The train was due to leave in fifteen minutes.

'It doesn't look too good, Jack. That orderly thinks the only hope for a break is if they take him into hospital, and if they do that, what shape will he be in? You know that brute's reputation better than I do.' In fact the reputation of the Gestapo officer commanding the military prison of St. Pierre was well known throughout the Resistance in the south. He was a sadist and a torturer of the worst type, who would rather see a man die than earn a reprieve in hospital.

'Keep in touch,' was all Jacques could say as he stood up. They shook hands again, casually, and Charles returned to his study of the racing pages. Jacques bought sandwiches, apples, some wine and mineral water at the buffet trolley and returned with a heavy heart to the train. It was scheduled to leave in a few minutes, but nearly an hour elapsed before it left Marseille, and after a longer wait at Lyon-Gare Perrache, the train from the Riviera arrived in Paris four hours late.

'It doesn't really matter,' said Polly in her cheerful way, 'if we'd got in at midnight we'd still have had to wait in the station till the end of the curfew at half past five. This way we won't have so long to sit in the waiting room.' As it turned out they had to sit on their suitcases on the arrival platform, while the freezing fog of a Paris January filled the concourse of the Gare de Lyon, because all the waiting-rooms were reserved exclusively for Germans. They waited until six o'clock struck, when the station restaurant ran up its iron shutters, and a yawning waiter in a grimy apron brought them coffee made from acorns and liquid saccharine in a clouded bottle.

'We can't ring up the Bertrands at half past six, or even seven,' said Jacques. 'I'm going to take a room in the Terminus Hotel, and call them when we've had some sleep.'

'What about the police *fiches*?'

'Damn the *fiches*, we're travelling in our own names, aren't we?'

'Yes, but—' Polly was thinking of the Nice police, and their possible desire to renew investigations into the Malvy murder. Jacques had said they would both be called as witnesses, but not until the next Assizes, by which time they would be far away. They had to take a chance, for they were both exhausted : they slept until lunchtime in a brass bed with a white honeycomb spread and a red satin quilt which kept slipping down to the carpet as the little hotel shook with the passage of the trains.

It was not until afternoon that they took the subway to the Place de la Concorde. There were no taxis outside the Gare de Lyon, and they both loathed the idea of being drawn by men in the wooden trailers mounted behind bicycles which were called velo-taxis. The metro was crowded and smelt of poverty. The Parisians were sullen and weary, some of them were Jews who wore the yellow star. It was a relief to come up to the surface and breathe the winter air. The fog had lifted and the true light of Paris, the light made from powdered gold, bathed the splendid square which had held the guillotine of the Terror and seen the Prussian conquerors of 1871 marching past in their victory parade. Now, in days no less terrible and no less humiliating, it was the core and heart of the German occupation.

Jacques could just remember, as a child on holiday, being

brought to the Place de la Concorde and shown the eight great female statues which represented the cities of France, with the statue of Strasbourg draped in black in mourning for the German seizure of Alsace and Lorraine. In his student days after the war the black draperies were gone, the lost provinces were French again; but now more than a statue was in mourning for the fate of France. On the north side of the square the Ministère de la Marine and the Hotel Crillon were hung with huge swastika banners. On the south, across the Seine, the Palais Bourbon – which had housed the French legislative body since the days of the Convention – was now tenanted by the secretariat of the Luftwaffe, and above the words '*Chambre des Députés*' was a huge V and the legend, on a flapping canvas stretching right across the building, '*Deutschland Siegt an Allen Fronten!*'

Germany victorious on all fronts ! The lettering was huge, and for young eyes easy to read even across the breadth of the Place de la Concorde and the bridge. For Jacques Brunel it was one of the worst moments he had ever known, the final affirmation of his country's defeat, and the negation of all his secret ambitions to sit some day in that historic Chamber as one of the Deputies for the Alpes Maritimes. Polly heard his indrawn breath. He was carrying both their suitcases, and she caught at one bare hand where the bruises of Tuesday night had begun to heal. 'Don't grieve, my darling,' she whispered. 'It isn't for long. It'll all come right some day – you'll see.'

'I wish I had your faith, Pauline.' But he braced himself to the weight of the two suitcases, and turned away to find the Cité du Retiro. 'I feel like a regular country cousin,' he said more cheerfuly, and told Polly he was not really familiar with the classic centre of Paris. While she was living with her mother in a tiny backwater of Passy, unchanged since the early nineteenth century, he had lodged as a student in the Latin Quarter, and had known the St. Honoré *faubourg* only as a child. His mother's favourite cousin, Rose Verbier, had lived there after her marriage and widowhood. He pointed out the house, not far from the Rue Royale; the Cité du Retiro was on the other side, entered by an L-shaped courtyard with a second gate on another street. The entrance was flanked by the fascinating shops which were as brilliant as in peacetime, but, by order of the German authorities, with price tags clearly stating the cost of every item in the windows. It was years since Polly Preston had seen such displays of lingerie, such laces, silks and crêpes de chine. She had never seen such hats, great towering erections of satin and velvet, nor the new nylon stockings, exquisitely transparent, and priced – she did a hasty sum – at the equivalent of twelve dollars a pair.

They were in the Paris where the racketeer was king, where the little corner dairies selling butter, eggs and cheese had brought affluence to their owners, where some women wore great square-cut jewels in heavy gold settings and others walked clumsily on wooden-soled shoes which thumped on the pavements, and queued endlessly for the bare necessities of life. This was the Paris of the eighth *arrondissement*, where the British Embassy stood locked and barred and the presidential palace, the Elysée, was empty; where parties like Roman triumphs were given every night by an ex-convict called Laffont and his partner Bony, a bent policeman broken out of the force after the great Stavisky scandals of 1934. Bony and Laffont were now accredited torturers to the Gestapo, although the guests at their lavish entertainments swore that the cries heard coming from the cellars of the house on the Rue Lauriston came in reality from the nursing home next door. It was a desperate Paris, cynical and fraudulent, but it was not crushed. It was not the capital of the country of total silence which Antoine de St. Exupéry, writing in America, had movingly imagined for the benefit of the *New York Times*. Where there was silence, it was enforced, and in the shadows of the Cité du Retiro there were voices and the hands of friends.

There was no concierge's *loge* at the Faubourg entrance, which was no bad thing, and Louis Bertrand's instructions, given when Jacques telephoned from the station hotel, were so explicit that they went confidently across the courtyard to one wing of the Cité complex which had a garage on the street level beneath a façade of white stucco, unwashed since the outbreak of war, and decorated by blue plaques in the Della Robbia style. Two open doors, one on each side of the courtyard, led to dark stone staircases with imitation marble walls, nearly as ancient and far less ornate than the stairs of the Palais Lascaris. On the top floor at the right, under the attics in the mansard roof where the servants' rooms had been, the door at the far end of a corridor had a visiting-card with the name 'Bertrand' under the electric bell. The door was opened at once by a man of about fifty, wearing a Sulka dressing-gown and ascot of crimson silk above black dress trousers, who said '*bonsoir*' and '*entrez, s'il vous plaît*' while the door was open, and shook Jacques' hand enthusiastically as soon as it was shut.

'My dear Monsieur Brunel, I'm delighted to see you!' he exclaimed. 'I've been looking forward so much to meeting you. And madame, what a charming surprise ... Not too tired after your long trip from the south? How *are* things in the south? Not too bad, I hope? Come this way. My wife is resting. She's singing this week at the Doge, you'll meet her later. Upstairs, please.'

'Why, it's a flat inside a flat!' said Polly, delighted. On the mansard level under the eaves, two little bedrooms with round windows were separated by a still smaller bathroom, equipped with an electric kettle, a hot plate, and a corner cupboard holding cups, saucers, and some provisions. 'It's a little house all by itself!'

Bertrand laughed. 'You'll be on your own up here,' he said. 'Not that it matters, because tomorrow's Sunday, and the daily woman doesn't come in. We might even be able to get you away tomorrow night.'

'How marvellous!'

'I'm glad you like the doll's house,' said Bertrand. 'Shall we leave Mademoiselle Henri to unpack and settle in, while you and I discuss our plans, monsieur?'

Jacques followed him down the attic stairs into a huge living-room, which had a north light from a big window in the roof, covered for the night with a black curtain, and was glacially cold. A half-open door revealed a smaller room with bookshelves and filing cabinets and a desk with a reading lamp, which Bertrand said was his office – 'closed from one o'clock on Saturday until Monday at nine' – and at the other side of the living-room he showed Jacques another small apartment, which he said had its own entrance on the other stair. 'This is where Monsieur de Valbonne lived, when he was our guest,' he said.

'He's gone, has he?' said Jacques. 'I was hoping we would meet here.'

'We got him safely out two nights ago,' said Bertrand. 'You'll see him in London.'

'You've got an ideal set-up for the job,' said Jacques. He tried to close the door of the little apartment, but it opened gently when he released the knob. 'They all do that,' said Bertrand quietly. 'Defective hinges, I suppose. But there's a legend in the Cité du Retiro that Robespierre lived here during the Terror, and when the doors open of their own accord people say it's Robespierre passing by ... Yes, it's a fine apartment, if only we had decent heating. Have a drink to keep the cold out.'

He poured two measures of rum from a well-stocked drinks trolley standing next to an open cabinet gramophone. Jacques, accepting his glass, looked at the record on the spindle, and the label '*Anne Marie Chante*'. It was scratched with much playing.

'The signal from London said nothing about the lady,' said Louis Bertrand, at his back. 'Does she expect to go to London with you?'

Jacques turned round sharply. 'I told you so on the telephone,' he said. 'Why? Are there any problems?'

'No problems as far as I'm concerned, but I'm only the passeur. I deliver you both to the group at Compiègne, and then they're in complete charge. They may get you out tomorrow or they may not. But if they've got someone of their own to send to London, somebody important from one of the Paris circuits, maybe, then it's possible they'll insist he takes priority and Mademoiselle Henri drops out. There's only room for two passengers in a Lysander.'

'Then I'll drop out too,' said Jacques, 'and wait for an aircraft that can take us both.'

'You may have to wait some time for that.'

'The moon period doesn't begin until the thirteenth, there's plenty of time. And I'm not leaving without Pauline. She's not a camp follower. She's been doing good work for the Resistance in the south, and she deserves a fair priority.'

In the doll's house flat above their heads Polly had switched out the lights and opened the round window. Like a sailor surveying the sea through an open port, she looked out across Paris and was thrilled. Paris was her native city, when all was said and done; American passport and Russian ancestry counted for little tonight compared with her very earliest memories of a flat not far away in the Rue de Rivoli, where the father she could hardly remember had played with her, and taken her out on Sundays to sail a toy boat in one of the ponds in the Tuileries. Once he bought her a big red balloon. That was Paris as it was, and would be again : the Paris of summer and flowering chestnut trees, and even on this bitter January night its mood was perfectly expressed by the poor woman who appeared in the courtyard far below and began to sing :

> Paris . . . est un-e blond-e,
> Paris . . . rein-e du mond-e

Someone threw open a window on the other side of the Cité, and Pauline had a glimpse of a lamplit interior as the coin was thrown down to the cobbles. The woman picked up the money and began again, drearily, *Paris est un-e blond-e,* they seemed to be the only words she knew. But someone coming up the narrow staircase to the doll's house was singing, magnificently, the rest of the refrain, and Polly switched the light on hastily as a knock fell on the door and the singer swept into the room. 'All alone in the dark?' she said. 'Im Anne Marie Bertrand.'

'I'm Pauline Henri; *bonsoir, madame.*'

Anne Marie was as tall as Jacques Brunel. She must tower, thought Pauline, over her little husband, and not so very long ago she must have been a magnificent show-girl. She was still on the right side of thirty, just a bit too old to top the bill in cabaret, and as she candidly and immediately explained to Pauline, she wasn't topping the bill at the Doge. She opened the show, before the curfew at eleven sent the more conservative clients home, and sang as many times as they wanted for the regulars who made a night of it, drinking and dancing until the curfew was lifted at half past five. The Bertrands were going to take their guests to the Doge that evening, so Jacques and Pauline would be able to catch her first *tour de chant.* Yes, she'd been talking to Jacques downstairs (they had got to first names already) and he was all set to go. It would be something for him to tell those people in London, how Paris was *gai Paris* still, in spite of everything. Anne Marie lolled on the bed, smoking, with her splendid limbs revealed by a white satin robe trimmed with ostrich feathers. With her tawny mane she looked like a big friendly lioness, sure that she was giving pleasure, sure that Jacques Brunel and Polly Preston could have no other aim in their visit to Paris than to hear Anne Marie sing.

'I think it'll be lovely. I've never been in a night club in my life.'

'Fantastic!' said Anne Marie. 'Now let's see. What are you going to wear?'

Jacques Brunel had often been in Paris night clubs, but never one like the Doge. The *boîtes* of his student days had presented their shows in the dungeons of the Ile St. Louis and the cellar bars of St. Germain des Prés, with candles stuck in bottles to give the right Bohemian atmosphere, and out of work male dancers dressed up in cloth caps and red neckerchiefs pretending to be apaches. Now the apaches were not pretending. They sat in the satin and velvet box that was the Doge, dressed in the best money could buy, showing off their women and listening indulgently to a dance orchestra playing between the white rococo pillars. They were the B.O.F.s, the butter-eggs-and-cheese boys, the scrap iron merchants begotten on the piles of rags the beggars picked over at midnight in the *gai Paris* of forty years ago; the Rumanian Jews who were the V-men of the Gestapo; the cronies of Messieurs Bony and Laffont. Jacques looked them over contemptuously, and wondered what the hell he and Pauline were doing there.

For one thing they had come to eat, for Anne Marie said frankly that she hated cooking, had nothing for their supper in the larder, and while she was singing at the Doge could feed them 'on the house'. Besides, Bertrand chimed in, it would be a good idea for the concierge on the other gate of the Cité to see them all going out together, as friends with nothing to hide; she was apt to ask questions about the visitors who were never seen in the yard or going out to shop. It was only a short walk along the Boulevard des Capucines. They could return on foot before the curfew, and before the German prowl cars began to roam the streets. Of course, said Anne Marie – no fool when it came to summing up a man – Jacques mustn't mind too much if there were Germans present. They liked the Doge, and because of that the boss made her sing at least one German song in every *tour de chant*. Jacques said he understood.

He had just been getting accustomed to seeing Germans in the streets of Nice without wanting to hit them. But the men in Nice were on duty and obeying orders, while the patrons of the Doge were there for enjoyment. The beautiful French girls who were their companions of the night were coaxing them, the French wine waiters were fawning on them, the band leader was willing to play any tune they fancied. A fraction of the huge war indemnity which France was paying to Germany every day flowed out of their wallets and back into the coffers of the Doge. Jacques averted his gaze. It was far pleasanter to look at Polly, glowing in her coral dress. She had done something different to her face. He knew Anne Marie had brought her a box of theatrical cosmetics, for he heard the two of them giggling over it in the little bathroom, and now Polly's creamy pallor had become a smooth apricot, her painted mouth was a deeper coral than her dress, and green eye shadow had subtly altered the colour of her hazel eyes. She was excited and she excited him. Bertrand obviously admired her too. The theatrical agent, spruce in a dinner jacket and black tie, was in great form. Sitting between his guests, sipping the house champagne, he kept up a running commentary on the company. There was the lovely young actress who had been performing in Germany, having supper with the Central American playboy turned diplomat. At the next table the editor of the leading collaborationist newspaper was chatting with the man who had got the works of Rousseau and Descartes put on the list of banned books. And there, just coming in, was the girl they called the uncrowned queen of Paris – Jacques recognised her?

Jacques nodded. No magazine reader, he had never seen a picture of the young actress, but he had admired her just before the war in a movie called *Women's Prison*. It was Corinne Luchaire. Now she was living her own movie on the arm of her lover, the German ambassador Otto Abetz, at the height of her blonde beauty and her dubious fame, and without a thought of the prison gates which might some day close upon herself.

The drums rolled. The leader of the orchestra announced loudly :

'Anne Marie chante!'

There was only a splattering of applause when she came out, the tawny hair coiled and curled, the silver sheath dress sumptuously revealing. The diners were still enjoying their food, and Anne Marie's first two songs, in French, were not intended to do more than set the pace. But the waiters whisked the empty plates away before she sang again, while Anne Marie walked round the tables at the front of the room, greeting friends and making play with a huge red chiffon handkerchief. The haunting tune that brought her back to her place by the piano seemed to gather up the attention of the whole company. The lights were dimmed, a single spot was trained on the singer.

Vor der Kaserne, vor dem grossen Tor,
Stand eine Laterne steht sie noch davor

In London at the beginning of the blitz Jacques had heard people in the Tube shelters singing the songs of the Other War, 'Tipperary' and 'Keep the Home Fires Burning', just as he had heard the French singing 'Madelon'. Now he was hearing the great song of his own war, which had swept across the desert from the German soldiers to the British, and which even here in a Paris cabaret had power to move them all. Anne Marie not only sang it well, she acted it well; the statuesque show-girl became the waif waiting for the soldier outside the barracks gate, and there were tears in sentimental German eyes as she sang a reprise of the refrain. Her husband, who had heard her sing so many times, was concentrating on the audience rather than on Anne Marie. He touched Jacques's foot with his own when a party of five came in quietly, waved the waiters away and sat down to listen with rapt attention.

'That's the *capo* of the Mafia in Marseille,' he breathed. 'They say he's buying up half the hotels on the Riviera.'

'I've heard of him,' said Jacques. He had also heard of the man's young mistress, whom artists vied with each other to paint, and he saw that the German general who was with them was wearing the Iron Cross and the medal ribbons of the Other War. It was the third man, grey-haired like the general, who interested him.

'Isn't that de la Rochejacquerie?' he whispered. 'And could the other girl be his daughter Valérie?'

'That's who they are.'

Madame Alain Renaudon. It was hard for Jacques to contain himself as he looked at the beautiful young woman, with her burnished hair and carefully tended hands, as she smiled and leaned towards the general. He wondered if she knew what had happened to her husband, or if she loved him still. Could she be here tonight with this fat German – slobbering over one of her pretty hands now – if she knew that Renaudon was in the St. Pierre prison, holding through torture the lives of many people in his grasp? Could he, Jacques, if his turn came, play the man as well as Renaudon?

He looked at Polly, his hope for the future, and she smiled at him. Happy Polly, who knew nothing of the dark waters slowly engulfing France, and who was as confident as the words Anne Marie was singing to that haunting tune :

> *And so we both shall meet again,*
> *Beside the lamp post in the rain,*
> *As once, Lili Marlene,*
> *As once, Lili Marlene*

14

When the band began to play dance music the tiny floor of the Doge was packed immediately, and Louis Bertrand unobtrusively led his guests from the room. It was still fifteen minutes to the hour of the curfew, and no distance at all from the Rue Volney to the Cité du Retiro, taking the short-cut through a glass-covered shopping passage on the far side of the Place de la Madeleine, but the three of them walked fast and said very little as they hurried down the deserted boulevard, a link in the great chain which had once sparkled so brightly in the heart of the City of Light. Back in the flat, Polly bubbled over with admiration of Anne Marie's performance. She was marvellous!

'And imagine singing again and again tonight! She'll be exhausted by the morning! Will she have to walk home, too?'

'No, the management sends her home by velo-taxi,' said her husband comfortably, 'and then she'll sleep till lunch time. *I'm* the one who takes charge of the cooking on Sundays, and if you don't mind waiting for your coffee until about nine, that'll give me time to do some shopping in the Cité Berryer, at the street market—'

'Oh, let me come too!' cried Polly. 'I *adore* a street market! I could carry one of the baskets, and help you choose the vegetables. And I do want to see some more of Paris!'

'I don't see why not,' said Bertrand in answer to Jacques's look. 'It's only five minutes' walk away. But you'd better stay indoors in the daylight, Jacques; we won't be leaving for Compiègne until five o'clock.'

'Meantime I'm going to bed,' said Polly. 'I've had a

wonderful evening, Monsieur Bertrand, but I don't think I can keep my eyes open much longer.'

The men wished her goodnight, and watched the coral dress disappear up the narrow stair to the mansard rooms. Bertrand proposed a nightcap in the big studio.

After an abundance of champagne at the expense of the Doge's management, and a supper of lobster in a rich sauce, Jacques neither needed nor wanted a cognac, and his mouth was dry with smoking, but it seemed churlish to refuse. While Bertrand poured the drinks he repeated his earlier praises of Anne Marie's singing, which he had genuinely admired. Bertrand made a move towards the gramophone.

'I'd like you to hear her singing "Lili Marlene" again,' he said. 'But it's getting late, and the neighbours love to complain to the concierge about music after ten o'clock. There's no point in drawing attention to ourselves.'

'How long have you lived here?' Jacques was moving down the big room, looking at the pictures on the walls. The lights were too low for him to see clearly, but they seemed to be poor imitations of contemporary artists like Dali and Van Dongen.

'Since the beginning of the Occupation, when the owner skedaddled to Florida. He's a rich amateur who fancies himself as a painter, and also a fan of Anne Marie's; he rented us this place for a song, just to keep the squatters out. Or the Boches, if it comes to that. Well, I suppose it'll all come to an end some day.'

With that the theatrical agent launched into a boastful account of the money a smart operator could make in the Paris of 1943, where the theatres were crowded, the concert halls and cinemas packed out, and the night clubs, as Jacques had seen, doing a roaring trade.

'With the Germans,' said Jacques.

'Ah! I thought you didn't enjoy yourself at the Doge.'

'Did you expect me to? It made me ashamed to be a Frenchman.'

'Live and let live,' said Bertrand, unabashed. 'We can't all go into mourning for our misdeeds, as the Marshal-Chief of State would like – and the theatre world is as good a cover for the Resistance as any you can find.'

'I'm sorry, Louis,' said Jacques. 'Of course you're doing a great job. I don't know – I'm on edge tonight—'

'You ought to get some sleep.' But Bertrand continued what soon became a monologue : he was so completely a night person that twelve o'clock came and he was talking still. While Jacques, listening to what sounded like a long confession of self-regard and greed, reflected that the little man had put his life, and Anne Marie's, at risk again and again for resisters on the run, and would be on his way to Gestapo headquarters in the Avenue Foch within the hour if the police found him sheltering the 'third man' of the Parc des Arènes. It was true that, as he had told Polly at Nice, they came in all sorts and sizes in the Resistance.

'By this time tomorrow night you may be in London,' said Louis Bertrand, getting to his feet at last.

'I hope so, Louis. I hope there won't be any hitch at Compiègne.'

'They got de Valbonne out, only five hours after he left Paris. Well! See you in the morning, Jacques.'

'*A demain.*'

At the top of the stair Polly's bedroom door was ajar, and as Jacques stood still on the dark landing he could hear her even breathing. He wondered if she had left the door open deliberately, or if it had come ajar gently to admit what the house tradition called the passing of Robespierre. He left it that way; she needed her sleep even more than he did, and it was not a night to disturb her by an unusual sound, or even by his presence. In the bathroom he locked the door behind him, and in his own little bedroom shut the door very carefully, listening to the latch click home. As he undressed he watched, fascinated, as it opened again without a sound.

'*C'est Robespierre qui passe!*'

That was what Bertrand had said, and Jacques in his over-wrought state could almost imagine that he heard the foot-steps, the silent tread of France and vengeance, coming in-exorably after the rich and the powerful of that night. Lu-chaire and Abetz, the editor, the gangster, the Marquis de la Rochejacquerie; his daughter Valérie and her German lover; all, all in due time would reap what they had sown. But as Jacques tried to sleep he was thinking less of the vengeance which would overtake Valérie than of how the day might have gone for her husband in his prison at Marseille.

The day, in terms of Alain Renaudon's life, was very near its ending. In a France on German time it was two o'clock in the morning when the doctor made his last examination of the man lying on a pallet in a room which was neither a cell nor a surgery, but a literal ante-room of hell. Hell was the torture chamber of the military prison of St. Pierre, and there the lights burned bright on the meat hooks on the wall, on the guillotine with the burnished blade, and on other instruments whose sheen was dimmed with blood. The men in the ante-room, listening for Renaudon's breathing, could hear nothing but the swish of brooms in the chamber, where two men in rubber aprons were sweeping the gutters clear of blood, and the sound of a hose playing over all the floor.

'It's no use,' said the doctor, removing the ear pieces of his stethoscope, 'he won't regain consciousness. I warned you yesterday afternoon the heart would soon give out.'

'What right had he to have a heart condition?' said the prison commandant. 'He was still quite a young man.'

'He probably wasn't aware of it himself,' said the doctor. He was not in love with his job, nor was he sorry that the prisoner, who had suffered unspeakable things, had come to the moment of escape. He glanced at the men in the back-ground : at the Gestapo lieutenant, correct to the last detail of gloves and boots, impassive of face, standing two paces behind the commandant, and at the nervous medical orderly, bending over a trolley holding bandages and stimulants.

Neither of them dared to show emotion. The commandant was coldly furious. He was even more faultlessly groomed than the lieutenant, his fair hair smooth, his black boots shining, and his gold watch on its woven golden strap in perfect alignment on his gloved wrist. But the pulse beating visibly in his temple told the doctor that the man's sadistic fury was still not appeased by the brutalities he had been supervising for the last hour.

'Is he dead?'

'No.'

The other pulse, the pulse in Renaudon's broken wrist, was very faint, but it was there. He was almost unrecognisable. His temples were blue where his head had been gripped in a vice, and his mouth sagged open above the broken teeth and jaws. Every nail had been pulled from his toes and fingers, and on what could be seen of his naked torso there were burns. But it was only the human heart that was failing, not the courage; even the man who had ordered his suffering paid Renaudon the tribute of a brief 'Incredible!'

'Four days, and not a word out of him,' he added to the lieutenant. 'Obstinate devil!'

'*Herr Kommandant!*' exclaimed the doctor. 'Look!'

There had been the faintest movement of the bloodstained head. The bruised eyelids lifted, and the watchers, bending forward, saw that their victim's eyes were blue. He moved his lips in an attempt to speak. The doctor took a sponge from the bowl of cold water and wiped his mouth.

'Speak, man! Who is to be the commander of the secret army?' The commandant had his face close to the face on the pillow. He caught the one word which came with Alain Renaudon's last breath.

'*Vendu!*'

'What did he say, sir?' whispered the lieutenant.

'He said "*vendu*" – sold,' said the commandant. 'And I should think you *were* sold, my friend,' he added, as the doctor drew the sheet over the dead man's face. 'Sold right

down the river by your precious pals in the Resistance!
– Order a burial detail for five o'clock.'

'Sir,' said the lieutenant. The orderly whom Charles Maxwell had suborned prepared to wheel his trolley from the
room. But not before he heard the army doctor murmur,

'With respect, *Herr Kommandant*, you misunderstood his
meaning. The prisoner meant it was we who were "sold" –
not him.'

Renaudon's body was buried in quicklime within the precincts of the prison, and in darkness. It was not until some
hours later, when the sun was bright above the sea, that the
orderly came off duty and earned his wages by going to a
newsagent's shop in the Rue la Caisserie and whispering a
message destined for Charles Maxwell to the spectacled proprietor.

At that time the sun was hardly visible in Paris, although
the fog was lifting. The frost had been intense during the
night, and Jacques saw great whorls and stars of white rime
on the round window when he awoke. He had forgotten to
wind his watch, and got out of bed cursing; he supposed it
must be about half past eight. Polly's bedroom door was wide
open, her bed made, and there was evidence in the bathroom
that she had made herself a milkless cup of tea. They must
have gone to market early! Jacques shaved quickly and ran
downstairs. All was silent in Bertrand's flat, as strange in its
own way as the flat in the Palais Lascaris, and the studio just
as they had left it the night before. The only thing he could
think of to do by way of help was to roll back the black curtains from the great north light in the roof, a task requiring
careful manipulation of the cords. He had just finished when
he heard voices, and went into the passage to greet Bertrand
and Pauline.

'Was it fun?' he asked.

'Great fun! It's a wonderful street market,' she said gaily,
and gave the basket she was carrying to Louis Bertrand, who
was impatient to start the coffee. She was rosy-cheeked from

the cold, and had tied the printed silk scarf, worn in the Russian church at Carnolès, tightly round her head. But Jacques saw that under the pink cheeks and the gaiety Polly was nervous and disturbed.

'What's the matter, darling?'

For answer she handed him a newspaper, folded to the centre page. At one glance Jacques saw that it was an amplified, Sunday-edition rehash of the story he had read in Maxwell's evening paper on Friday, concluding with the statement that the Nice police were confident of making an early arrest of the 'third man' in the Parc des Arènes.

'It's all right,' he said quickly. 'I knew about this. I read it at Marseille on Friday afternoon.'

'You never told me!'

'I didn't want to upset you. Did *he* see this?' – with a jerk of his head towards the pasage down which Bertrand had disappeared.

'No, I was looking through the paper while I was waiting for him outside the wineshop.'

'And you didn't tell him?' Pauline shook her head. 'Good girl! What he doesn't know he can't give away. And he's got plenty on his plate without getting mixed up with the Arènes murderer.'

'Oh Jacques! Oh, I hope we can get away tonight!' She was trembling in his arms, longing for reassurance, and he kissed her and told her again and again that everything would be all right. And Polly made a brave pretence of believing him, going off to find Bertrand in the kitchen and put the coffee cups and saucers on a tray. They were dependent on their host for conversation at breakfast. He was worried, he said, about the weather. If the fog came down again over southern England and northern France their chances of getting clear away were bad. If the snow came on they might have to hole up at Ferme La Folie for several days.

'Ferme La Folie sounds rather nice,' said Polly.

'It's a nice place in summer. A bit too near the German

staging camp at Royallieu for my liking, but the farmer thinks right under the nose of the enemy is the smart place to be.'

'He's probably right,' said Jacques, and the talk fell flat again. The staging point for Jews en route to the concentration camps was not a pleasant topic, and all their topics seemed to end in the same flat silence. It was Anne Marie who saved the day when she appeared, much earlier than usual (as she told them) so as to see more of Jacques and Pauline before they left Paris. She set herself to entertain them, and she succeeded. Anne Marie's songs and spirited anecdotes of the show-business world took them quickly through the afternoon, and Anne Marie at the station, laughing and joking while her husband bought the tickets, made their departure by the omnibus train to Compiègne seem the most natural thing in the world.

They were not to go into the town, Bertrand had told them. The owner of La Folie farm would meet them at the station and take them to his home, which lay between Pierrefonds and Vieux-Moulin, on the edge of the great forest of Compiègne. Once they were in Bernard's care, Bernard being the man's real name and not a code name, he would take the last train back to Paris. He was not keen on spending a night in the vicinity of the camp at Royallieu, said Louis Bertrand, and besides, he wanted to catch Anne Marie's act all over again, when Sunday night brought the gay company back to the Doge. If a certain entrepreneur showed up with some of his German friends, Bertrand had hopes of booking his wife into the Alcazar.

On that characteristic note he took his leave of them and wished them luck, while a gruff farmer dressed in his Sunday suit threw their luggage into the back of an ancient carry-all. 'Is this your wife?' the farmer asked Jacques, and without waiting for an answer swung Polly off her feet and over the wheel into the vehicle, which he told them had been resurrected from a barn to beat the petrol shortage. The plough horse between the shafts moved off at a sober pace.

'Any chance of getting away tonight?' was Jacques's first question, when they had left the buildings of Compiègne behind.

'Not a hope in hell. We had a message about an hour ago; the fog's dense in England, and the pilot can't take off.'

'It's clearer here.' Jacques hesitated. 'You're in wireless contact, then?'

'There's a "pianist" working the area; couldn't tell you where even if I wanted to. He moves around a lot, but my oldest boy usually knows where to find him. Gee *up*!' he said to the plodding horse.

Jacques, who was sitting in front of the driver, turned round to look at Polly, who was in a rear corner of the jolting carry-all. 'Lady all right?' said the farmer, rattling an old whip in its socket. 'Just three more kilometres to go. I'm not taking you up to La Folie, too many kids and cackling girls at my place. I'm taking you to my old dad in what used to be our dairyman's cottage. He's as deaf as a post, but he won't bother you.'

In the country darkness they saw nothing but a background of bare trees when the carry-all stopped in front of a whitewashed cottage, but there was warmth and light indoors, and an appetising smell from a big iron pot suspended over a huge fire of logs. A little old man in a black suit stood up and pulled a beret from his bald head when they came in, muttering some words of welcome when Polly put her hand in his.

'You're Monsieur Bernard, I know, and he's Monsieur – who?' she said to the owner of Ferme La Folie.

'His name's Armand, but my kids call him Petit Père,' said the farmer with a grin. 'He likes company, but he's too deaf to talk with. He had the "pianist" with him for a week, and he was quite disappointed when the old gent who came here last just ate his supper and was off. There's supper for all of you in the pot, a rabbit stew my wife made special, and when dad's had his he'll go to bed. I'm going to put a match to the fire in the other room. Burn all the wood you want. The chimneys are back to back, so you don't have to worry about a Boche patrol seeing smoke in the morning. They don't bother us very much anyway.'

Even so, when he was alone in the 'other room' and Polly was stirring the rabbit stew, Jacques loaded his gun and slipped it beneath one of the pillows on the huge old feather bed. With a stone-deaf old man as their front line of defence, he wanted a weapon to his hand. The fire was burning up, and by its light he saw an old-fashioned room with a crimson paper and crimson rep curtains drawn across a little window, a round table and four chairs in the middle and a wooden chest of drawers with a scuttle bookcase on the top holding a nearly complete set of Zola. There was a red plush armchair on each side of the fire.

'Isn't it lovely?' said Polly from the door. 'Come and have your supper, darling. It's going to be a real feast – as good as our first one at Monte Carlo.'

She was back in her usual form, adaptable and easily pleased as always, and Jacques watched her lovingly as she dished up the rabbit cooked with herbs and onions and the mealy potatoes served with butter. There was more butter for the bread and cheese from La Folie's dairy, and a litre of strong red wine which the old man enjoyed. He told them, in his feeble voice, a long rambling story of his wife's last illness and death – la vieille he called her – pausing all too often in expectation of their replies. Jacques's deep voice got through to him; Polly he could hardly hear at all.

There was a sink in the kitchen, and hot water in the kettle to wash the dishes. Beyond the kitchen, on the far side from the red room, there was a place where the old gentleman slept, and some rough and ready sanitary arrangements, which had at least the merit of being indoors. The old man bade them goodnight and went off to bed with a candle in his hand, although the cottage was wired for electricity.

There must have been a power cut in the area, and Jacques remembered hearing that there were often such cuts when a new contingent of deportees arrived at Royallieu. It was psychological warfare, he supposed, and nerved himself for the things he had to say to Polly.

After seeing her distress at the 'third man' story, he felt the time had come to explain more fully the consequences of the Malvy murder. So far they had only talked about the people she knew : the Moreaus, Chantal, Fabienne and Roger himself, and a very little about Renaudon, whom Polly had never met. She hadn't seemed to grasp that as well as Malvy himself, on a charge of murder, there were seven other men in prison at Nice – accused, he supposed, of terrorism and intelligence with the enemy. Any one of the seven might talk under pressure, might give away the names of Jacques Brunel, who had raised the alarm at Cimiez, and after that it would be an easy matter to connect him with the killing of the *milicien*. 'You're on the right side of the war, Pauline, but I'm on the wrong side of the law!' was what he meant to say to her, jocularly if he could; in fact, after his years of legal training, it was not pleasant to be an outlaw.

He had to make it clear to her that as he had no intention of going back to Nice to stand trial for murder, the right thing for him to do was to get himself sent from London to North Africa, to join the new French Army under General Giraud. That army would have American arms and a definite objective, the link-up with the British, and whatever the Vichy French might do in Tunisia, it would be Germans whom Giraud's men would fight. Jacques made a good start by telling Polly that when he was a boy he had wanted to be a soldier. He had tried to persuade his father to send him to St. Cyr instead of the Sorbonne, but the solicitor, in those days easily the master of his son in argument, had pointed out the boredom of barracks life in time of peace and the rewards of the fine law practice he would inherit at Menton. But like all prepared speeches this one fell apart when the dialogue began, and Polly interrupted him to ask if he hadn't had enough of soldiering at Namsos.

'Namsos was a disaster and the whole Norwegian campaign was a shambles,' Jacques began, but then she rubbed her cheek against his and called him poor darling, with her lips tickling his ear. It was a mistake to have taken her in his arms when he meant to talk seriously. The plush armchair was big enough to hold them both, or had been at the start, but quite suddenly it appeared to be too small, and clothes a harness. They slipped together to the floor, and made love by the light of the fire of beechwood, while the red room swallowed them up like the open mouth of a great beast.

Whether it was the force of her lover's passion, or the country wine she had drunk at supper, Polly was dazed and trembling when they at last rose to their feet, and Jacques half carried her to the bed. At first it was cold, and they had never, either one of them, slept on feathers before. They seemed to sink down into a soft chilly mass which rose round them, as the two square pillows slipped sideways, and the goffered linen of the pillowcases felt like a thin film of ice. But then the warmth crept back, slowly, comfortingly, bringing an animal peace and acceptance, until desire rose again, and the frenzy which only sleep could cure. Far in the night Jacques woke. The room was chilly and stale with cigarette smoke. He built up the fire with a few splinters of kindling and logs before he drew the curtains back and opened the little window. There was not a breath stirring in the frozen forest.

'Is it morning yet?' He had no idea how long he had slept when Polly spoke.

'It must be,' Jacques said, listening. 'I can hear the old boy moving about.'

'But it's so dark!'

'I can't find the matches. Here! I'll light the candle. Good Lord, it's half past seven.' Jacques got out of bed, shivering, and went close to the window. Even on German time, there should be grey streaks in the sky by now. Outside was grey. 'Polly!' he said, 'it's snowing!'

'Perfect,' said Polly, curled up in his vacant place in bed.

'D'you want to be snowed up, you crazy girl!'

'Just you and me and Monsieur Père, snowed up in the forest for ever and ever, you crazy boy.'

That was how the second day began, with kisses and laughter, the day which brought the farmer of La Folie to the cottage before noon to tell them the fog was still heavy over southern England, but that a message had come promising a flight on the next night. They're going to fly two fellows in and they'll take you out,' he said. 'Nobody's expected to turn up from Paris, so you'll both go. You're not superstitious, are you, madame, about flying on the thirteenth?'

'Not a bit.'

'Then all you've got to worry about is the snow.'

'It hasn't come to much so far,' said Jacques. The cottage garden had hardly been whitened by the flurry of the morning.

'The forecast's pretty good. Now see here, I've brought you enough food for a couple of days, and I won't come back until ten o'clock tomorrow night. We'll have about a mile to walk then on the open road, and my brother and four of our farm hands'll meet us at the place where the Lysander lands. Hope you'll be all right here until then.'

'How about Monsieur Père?' asked Polly. 'Will *he* be all right? Not too lonely, alone with Jacques and me?'

'Oh bless you, madame, he's never lonely. My kids are always running in and out to see their Petit Père – when they're allowed to, that's to say. They'll be racing over here the day after tomorrow, as soon as you're safe away . . . Now don't stand about outside, you'll catch a chill. I bet it's a lot colder here nor where you've come from.'

The icy calm, the occasional flakes of snow, lasted all that day and the next. Jacques and Polly put the world behind them, imparadised in their red room where all time had stopped. In those hours they learned to love each other truly, learned that they were part of one another, and if Pauline Preston discovered new pleasures in her own body, Jacques Brunel had never imagined that such a fusion of flesh and spirit could exist. On that second day they began to say 'when we're married', and neither of them could remember which of them said it first. When we're married we'll come back again to La Folie. We'll swim, we'll play tennis, we'll listen to Anne Marie sing. We'll visit the Baroness Belinska—

'Hope she doesn't offer us her guest room,' said Jacques, and that fantasy dissolved in a gale of laughter. The day went by. They went into the kitchen to share the splendid meals with Monsieur Père, who watched over them like an amiable gnome, and who every time that Jacques and Polly entered got to his feet and took off his dusty black beret. They slept enlaced in the deep feather bed and woke to hear the patter of rain against the window. The frost had broken, and by midday the skies were clear.

Jacques retained enough sense to tell Polly, at the end of the last afternoon, about the Patriotic School and the interrogation they would undergo there when they landed in England.

'I think they've got their nerve!' she said indignantly.

It makes sense, darling. And I'm sure they won't bother you too much. Now here is what you do. You show your American passport and ask to be put in touch with your embassy in London. If Mr. Calvert's there, that's marvellous, but it's a pretty long shot, Pauline. If we're not allowed to leave this School place together, then we'll have to meet at an hotel.'

'Which hotel?'

Jacques could only think of Claridge's.

'But why shouldn't we be allowed to leave the Patriotic School together?'

'Because they'll be far stricter with a man from France

than a girl from America. The British have had their troubles with the men from France.'

'But surely they'll pass on a message! It isn't the Gestapo, after all!'

'I hope your message will say you're safe in Mr. and Mrs. Calvert's care.'

'There *is* no Mrs. Calvert – unless my godfather married in the past twelve months.'

'I don't know why I took it for granted that he was a married man.'

'Most people his age *are* married,' said Polly wisely. 'But mother used to tell me he was once in love with her cousin, Dolly Hendrikova. She married his best friend, a British officer, and escaped with him to England in the Revolution.'

'Are *they* in England now?' said Jacques, jumping at the thought of another place of shelter for Pauline.

'No, Captain Allen left the army after the war, and they went to farm in Kenya. We used to hear from them at Christmas.'

Kenya, too far away to be practical. Jacques stopped worrying about the hazard of the Patriotic School – after all, they would be on British soil, and therefore safe – and settled down with Polly in his arms to enjoy the twilight hour. The quarter moon rose over the forest, ushering in the January moon period, and across the Channel the pilot of a Lysander was being briefed on the operation for the night.

Bernard came for them at ten o'clock, and affected surprise when Jacques gave him a roll of notes, 'with many thanks from both of us'.

'We're well enough paid for what we do,' said the farmer, but he pocketed the roll without further protest, and the next person to be surprised and delighted was Petit Père, when Polly flung her arms round him and hugged him as she said good-bye.

'I hate to go!' she said to Jacques as they went through the cottage garden – Polly, who was always eager to go on! – but

Bernard motioned them to silence as they came out on the country road which divided the cottage from the house and barns of Ferme La Folie. Soon it led them down into the Route d'Eugénie, which Napoleon III had built for his empress to drive from their château of Compiègne to the church at Vieux-Moulin, and skirting the edge of the forest and a chain of ponds and water meadows, they entered the flat lands of the valley of the Oise.

A group of men stood in the lee of a hedge, beating their arms on their chests in an effort to keep warm.

'Got the flares ready?' asked Bernard, when the ritual handshakes had been exchanged.

'All ready, *patron*.'

'Then you'd better stay among the holly bushes, *ma petite dame*,' said Bernard to Pauline. 'The frost's setting in again, so keep out of the wind.' He set down her suitcase, which he had been carrying, and took Jacques's case from his hand. 'What d'you think of our landing ground?'

'It's amazing, in forest country,' said Jacques. It was a big square field, protected by low-lying hills, one of them rising higher than the others, at which Bernard pointed. 'That's the Mont St. Marc,' he said. 'The Englishman comes in that way.'

Jacques nodded. The sense of isolation was so strong that it was hard to realise the Germans were as close as their detention camp at Royallieu. 'How many passenger drops have you done in all?' he asked.

'Ten since the beginning of September.'

'That's quite a record, so near Paris.'

'It's gone like a charm so far.'

A fox was barking somewhere in the woods. Jacques thought of the men in the incoming plane. An Englishman with two Frenchmen aboard, and who were they? Two more of de Gaulle's men, possibly; one a special agent like Alain Renaudon, the other an officer for General Delestraint's secret army? Would they be friends or foes, and how would he and they greet each other in this winter landscape by the banks of the Oise?

'Here he comes!'

They all heard the low drone in the sky. The men on the ground moved forward with drilled precision, and set alight the small piles of kindling drenched in paraffin which they had placed at intervals down the middle of the field. The flares would not last long, but they burned up quickly as the Lysander came across the Mont St. Marc. The pilot circled the landing ground once and levelled out for his approach.

Jacques looked back at Polly. All he could see was the pale blur of her upturned face, but she was motionless. For Polly Preston was in the grip of the same powerful excitement as had seized her when she ran to warn Jacques of trouble at the Nice railway station, the love of danger for its own sake which was her natural response to the sexual stimulus of war. Once again, in the rough and ready flare path which would guide Jacques and herself to a land of freedom, she saw the bright eyes of danger.

15

The moon favourable to Jacques's and Polly's flight to England shone on the south bound flight of a far more illustrious traveller. In their Lysander they had nothing worse to put up with than a bumpy ride, whereas Mr. Churchill on his way to Casablanca was in some danger of being burned alive, and – when this danger was averted – of being frozen in the ice-cold plane. But the great man arrived safely, and was soon enjoying a stroll along the Moroccan beaches, where only two months earlier some of the fiercest fighting of the North African landings had taken place. At Fedala, the nearest point to the city, and at Port Lyautey and Safi, there had been strong resistance to the all-American landings. At sea the whole strength of the American invasion fleet was called into action against a French flotilla, the cruiser *Primaguet*, and the unfinished battleship *Jean Bart*, an action which ended in heavy French losses and a thousand casualties. Since then the kaleidoscope of war had been shaken into a new pattern, and Mr. Churchill, now that the guns were silenced, could enjoy the sight of waves fifteen feet high and enormous clouds of foam over the rocks.

The meeting at Casablanca had been built up into a conference of the highest importance. The suburb of Anfa was almost entirely requisitioned for the notabilities, who would include the fighting generals, the Joint Planners, and the Combined Chiefs of Staff. The President of the United States was expected to arrive soon after Mr. Churchill. General Alexander was there, confident that Tripoli would soon be in British hands. Louis Mountbatten was present, and General Eisenhower. General Giraud was eager to report progress on the new French Army. There were only two invited guests who declined to be present : Joseph Stalin, who was unable to leave Russia in the middle of the winter campaign, and Charles de Gaulle, who was in the middle of a majestic sulk.

President Roosevelt had insisted on absolute secrecy. The American people were not to know that he had left the country until he returned, for as he said, 'There will be a commotion here if it is discovered that I have flown across any old seas.' His immense journey took him to Natal in Brazil and then to Dakar in Africa, for since Governor Boisson had gone over to the Allies (a final turn of the screw to General de Gaulle's conceit) a landfall at Dakar was possible. And secrecy was kept all the way; neither press nor public knew the President's whereabouts, while the same secrecy shrouded Mr. Churchill's movements. A number of people, of course, were in the secret, among them Joe Calvert, who had helped to set the programme up, and whose elastic, not to say ambiguous job with Lend-Lease enabled him to act as a liaison officer with all kinds of planners. He was allowing himself a moment of relaxation, of relief at the news of the President's safe arrival in Morocco, when a telephone call came in from Jim Randall of the O.S.S.

'Hi, Joe!' the brash voice said. 'Your girl turned up!'

'What girl?'

'Your goddaughter. Pauline Preston.'

'The devil she did!' cried Joe. 'Where? How'd you know? Where is she?'

'The Brits. have got her at the Patriotic School. She flew across from France last night and landed at Tangmere, cool as you please. She asked for you, and the M.I.5 boys put in a call to the embassy.'

'I'll go out there right away. Oh hell no, I can't, I've got to see Harriman at six, and it's half past five now. I don't like to think about her hanging round that damned place alone, though. Jim, I don't suppose you're free and willing—'

'Sure I am, I'll be glad to drive out and collect her. What do I do about the guy?'

'What guy?'

'The guy she travelled with, a Frenchman called Brunel. She says he's working for S.O.E. Seems he got her across the Italian border into France—'

'Oh, she talked to you herself?'

'She sure did.'

'Just bring her to my flat alone, will you, Jim? I'll alert the housekeeper, and you'll be let in.'

'Okay.'

Joe Calvert sat for a moment lost in smiling thought. Then he put in two telephone calls : one to the housekeeper of the service flats where he had been living since his return from Moscow, asking her to have the guest room prepared in his apartment. The other was to a contact high in the echelons of S.O.E.'s 'F' section, asking for some information on a

French operative called Brunel. He learned some interesting details in ten minutes, and had ample time left over to be punctual for his meeting with Averell Harriman.

Polly, as Jacques had predicted, had an easy passage through the Patriotic School. The first flight of her life, in the Lysander, had been a rugged experience, and she was very queasy when they landed at Tangmere, quite unable to touch the big breakfast of eggs and bacon and cocoa which was set before the new arrivals. She had a cup of tea, a slice of toast, and then a long wait, had she known it the usual wait, while civilian transportation was laid on. They reached South London shortly after ten.

The Patriotic School, where refugees were vetted, was an object of particular resentment to de Gaulle's entourage. Knowing the place only by its abbreviated name, the leaders of his secret service usually referred to it as 'the *so-called* Patriotic School' as if patriotism was a piece of presumption on the part of *les Anglo-Saxonnes*. In fact the original name of the place – an ugly building all too reminiscent of a mid-Victorian workhouse – was The Royal Patriotic Asylum for the Orphan Daughters of Soldiers and Sailors killed in the Crimean War, and Queen Victoria herself had laid the foundation stone in 1857. The name 'asylum' was eventually changed to 'school', and the Patriotic School functioned as such until the outbreak of the Second World War, when the pupils were evacuated and the buildings requisitioned for another purpose. De Gaulle's men spoke of it as a second Dachau.

The retreat from Dunkirk, and the arrival in Britain of so many refugees, had imposed a strain on the slack British security of 1940. Too many enemy agents slipped through the traitors' gate, and slowly it dawned on those in authority that it was not enough to intern suspected aliens in the Isle of Man, or even to commit them to Holloway Gaol : the important thing was to prevent them from entering the country in the first place. Now all foreign arrivals, even those with credentials from their own Resistance movements and burning to serve in some fighting force, had to undergo a lengthy and searching interrogation at the Patriotic School. There were beds for those kept overnight, but there was no release until the interrogators were satisfied.

Jacques Brunel was kept overnight, because more men than usual were in the line-up for processing when he and Polly were brought in from the R.A.F. station at Tangmere. He waited his turn for a long time, sitting on a bench and reading frayed back numbers of *Picture Post*, and when he was called at last he was unlucky in his examiner, who feigned to disbelieve such details as Jacques thought it wise to give him.

The interrogations were done by the departments called M.I.5 and M.I.19, working together. M.I.5 was responsible for clearing the new arrivals for security, and M.I.19, the refugee section, cross-questioned them on their journey to Britain and the conditions of daily life in the country from which they had escaped, or left. The examining technique was an adroit mixture of patience and surprise, at which when it was Polly's turn she thought Madame Moreau would have excelled : the long, easy chat on innocuous topics and then the loaded question, suddenly snapped out. Jacques's man from M.I.5 was a Major Dempster, whose name seemed vaguely familiar. He was slow and on the stupid side, but Jacques was as patient as he was; after a long experience of incoherent litigants he let the man do the talking, and sometimes answered only by a sympathetic nod. Presently he was accused of being unco-operative, and Major Dempster was sufficiently riled to refuse to put through a call to the Special Operations Executive's 'F' Section to establish Jacques's bona fides. The trouble was that he had been recruited in London so long ago, when S.O.E. was only a branch of the Ministry of Economic Warfare, that he knew none of the new names or reputations of the men at the top. Set free in London he would have known where to go but not whom to ask for, and freedom, Major Dempster said ominously, would depend on what his colleagues in M.I.19 had to say after Jacques appeared before them in the morning.

Hours had gone by in this profitless conversation, and a bell was ringing for supper. Jacques was steeling himself for another repast of coca, this time with dried milk, and powdered eggs, when an orderly slipped a half-sheet of paper into his hand. It held the pencilled note of a street and telephone number, and the words, 'Miss Preston is with Mr. Calvert at the above address.' The dispirited refugees at his table saw the Frenchman's thin face light up, as if the message had been written in letters of gold. Pauline free and with a trusted friend – it was all Jacques had asked for; that, and to know he had kept his word to the letter, and brought her from France to a place of safety.

Joe Calvert's service flat was in Hill Street, in the very heart of Mayfair, and only a short walk from the American Embassy in Grosvenor Square. But the traffic from South London across the Thames must have been light that evening, for when he reached his apartment building – still bearing the marks of the blitz – the porter saluted and said confidentially:

'The young lady 'as arrived, sir. Mr. Randall said to tell you 'e was sorry 'e couldn't wait, and the housekeeper took the lady straight up to your flat.'

'Perfectly fine, thanks.' The lift had been temperamental since the last bomb fell on Hill Street: it clanked and wheezed ominously as Calvert mounted slowly to the fourth floor. He felt an excitement from the long past as he turned his key in the lock. He remembered the schoolgirl in Paris, he remembered her pretty mother, and the Dolly Hendrikova of twentyfive years ago; he expected to see someone who looked like all three. Instead a perfect stranger rose from the ugly blue tweed sofa, and waited shyly for his kiss.

'Polly!' said Joe. 'Polly, it's so good to see you!'

'I'm so thankful you were here.'

Joe Calvert was not an emotional man, but he felt something like a lump in his throat as he gave her a quick hug. One little girl, saved out of the madness of Europe – a worse madness, even, than the one he and her mother had known in their young days, when Marie Alexandrovna set out on the long trek from Petrograd to safety! 'You're staying here, of course,' he said. 'Now that we've found you, after looking for you all over, we're not going to let you slip through our fingers again.'

'Mr. Randall told me you'd been looking for me, but he wouldn't tell me how you knew I was in France.'

'Ah, he left that up to me. But look here, Polly, let me get my coat off, let me get you a drink before we talk. Are you hungry? Would you like to have dinner early? Did they treat you all right at the Patriotic School?'

'They were very nice. They wanted to know all about the conditions of life in Naples, people's morale, and the rationing, and that. No, I'm not a bit hungry, thank you!' She helped him off with his coat, and asked where his briefcase ought to go, while Joe opened the rickety drinks cabinet and took out a sherry decanter and two glasses. It all helped to bridge the slight embarrassment, the gulf of the years since Polly was a child.

'Please what am I to call you?' she said when they sat down.

'What would you like to call me?'

'When I was a kid I used to call you Uncle Joe.'

Calvert shuddered. 'Not that, Polly, please. That's what they're calling Stalin now.'

She laughed. ' "Godfather"?'

'I never heard anybody called "Godfather" to his face. I think you're old enough to call me Joe.' As Polly smiled and nodded, he went on : 'I want to tell you that before I left the embassy tonight I sent off a cable to your Uncle George in Baltimore. He's been worrying about you too.'

'My uncle has?'

'Yes. He'll be glad to know you're safe and well ... Polly, did you know your grandfather was dead? We never had an answer to our cables. We lost touch with you completely, all last year in Naples.'

'We got one cable. It arrived just before my mother died, and – I can hardly remember my Grandfather Preston, Joe!'

'But he remembered you, my dear. He left you a very handsome legacy, and named your Uncle George and me as trustees in his Will.'

'He left me money?' she said, bewildered. 'But I thought the Prestons weren't rich.'

'Your grandfather was richer than anybody knew. He left your Uncle George and his family very comfortably off, and to you he left one hundred thousand dollars, to be held in trust until you're twenty-five. Then it'll be absolutely yours.'

'But not for four years!' she said. 'I think I'm glad of that.'

'Why, my dear?'

'Because the war will *have* to be over in four years, won't it?' she said swiftly. 'How kind – how wonderful of my grandfather. I only wish I could remember him. So this, the legacy I mean, is why my Uncle George was trying to get in touch with me?'

'Especially after he was stirred up by a rather angry lady called Vittoria Pradelli.'

Pauline sat upright on the sofa. 'Aunt Vittoria!' she said. 'What did she do?'

'She didn't believe in a letter you wrote her, and checked up with the people at the sanatorium,' said Joe dryly. 'Come now, Polly, you didn't expect a lady in her position to let a girl under age decamp in the way you did?'

'A lady in her position, I like that! What she wanted to do was marry me off to her horrible son Pietro—'

'Did she though?' said Joe, and wondered if a rumour of old Preston's wealth and intentions had crossed the Atlantic before Polly's mother died. He liked to see his godchild in a tantrum. She had been rather pale and forlorn when he first came in, sitting there in the plain black wool dress with the gold belt which his conventional mind thought of as mourning, but now the sparks were flying, and Joe laughed.

'You're your own woman, Polly,' he said, and crossed the room to refill her glass. 'I can see a little of my old friend Paul Preston in you, when you set your jaw like that, but nothing of your mother. Except of course the colour of your eyes.'

'Russian hazel. You've always like that colour best, haven't you?'

'I suppose so.'

'Have you been able to go back to Russia yet?'

'I went there in Mr. Churchill's party, about six months ago.'

He hardly realised that he, a veteran diplomat, was being manipulated by a girl not twenty-one, as she put the questions which eased Joe Calvert gently into his favourite subject. Russia's present and future, above all Russia's past – before he knew it he was back a quarter century in time and in a way of life that had vanished for ever. He knew already that Marie Preston had never liked to talk about her girlhood in Russia. In Paris, where he had often been the guest of the young Prestons at their flat in the Rue de Rivoli, Joe was made aware that a curtain had fallen across Marie's mind where Russia was concerned, a deliberate defence against intolerable memories; she had accepted the destruction of her family with the same fatalism as her daughter accepted the deaths of those closest to herself. But she had taught the child some Russian, and Polly, speaking haltingly in that language, encouraged Joe to talk about his first Russian lessons from Madame Hendrikova, in whose flat on the Fourth Line of St. Petersburg he had met Marie Alexandrovna as a schoolgirl of sixteen. He told her about Marie's cousins, Dolly (but from her little smile he saw that Pauline knew about Dolly) and Simon, a soldier who had survived the war to end wars only to fall to a Bolshevik bullet in the autumn of 1918. 'He was killed fighting with the White Army, Polly, just six weeks after I saw him for the last time at Ekaterinburg' – and on that evocative word Joe Calvert stopped. It stood for depths of suffering and years of experience which he could never convey to this child of another war, whose experiences were so immediate and so positive. 'I'm being self-indulgent,' he confessed. 'Now I want to hear about your journey from the south to London. You haven't told me about Monsieur Brunel.'

It was something like the Patriotic School technique, the loaded, unexpected question, and Polly stammered as she tried to frame a reply. 'Did Mr. Randall tell you about Jacques?' she achieved, and Joe said all he knew was that she had travelled from France with a friend.

'It's rather a long story.'

'We've got the whole evening. Would you like to go out to dinner, or shall I have them send up something from the kitchen?'

'Oh, please, I'd rather stay in. I'm not a bit hungry – and Jacques may telephone.'

'Does he know the number?'

'I left a message for him, after Mr. Randall gave me this address.'

She was probably listening for the phone to ring, all the time I was maundering on about St. Petersburg, Joe Calvert thought. He took up the phone himself and ordered the meal, with no choice of dishes, which the kitchen of the service flats produced as a favour to the tenants, and strictly in conformity with the five-shilling price limit established by government order. It arrived on a trolley and was soon disposed of with the assistance of a glass of wine from the war-damaged cabinet. Then Polly, more relaxed now, curled up in a corner of the sofa, told Joe the part Jacques' mother had played in her departure from the sanatorium, and the work she had found to do in Nice until Jacques arranged for her to travel to England with him. Joe Calvert was fully aware of the many gaps in her story. He let her understand that he knew Maître Brunel was a barrister, working as an undercover man for the Special Operations Executive; but Polly had learned discretion from her lover, and was not to be drawn into any talk of the Resistance. One thing she revealed without words, that she was in love with Jacques Brunel : it was in Polly's lips and eyes whenever she spoke his name.

When it was nearer ten o'clock than nine she sighed, and looking ruefully at the silent telephone said they must be keeping Jacques in that dismal place all night.

'If he doesn't show up before I leave for the embassy I'll get the S.O.E. people on the job,' Joe promised. 'There's nothing to worry about. Your Jacques is probably the victim of some interdepartmental rivalry – there's a lot of it around.'

In fact it was getting the S.O.E. on the job which delayed Jacques' release until the following afternoon. M.I.19 was not to be dictated to by Baker Street, and the interrogation of a refugee described by Major Dempster as unco-operative was conducted with especial zeal. Jacques did not improve matters by saying, when asked about Paris, that everybody he saw there seemed to be having a high old time. But it was finally admitted that he was not an enemy infiltrator; he was given a certificate which he thought of as a *pièce justificative* and tucked unconcernedly in his wallet, and told that a conducting officer from the S.O.E. had come to fetch him.

'My name's Morton,' said the officer, shaking hands with Jacques. He was in battledress, and looked too old to be wearing the insignia of a lieutenant. 'Sorry we took so long to winkle you out of this bottleneck, but there's been a bit of a flap on today—'

'It's all right,' said Jacques. 'Just let me pick up my suitcase, and I'm ready . . . What happens now?' he asked a few minutes later, returning with the battered case.

'Strictly speaking I should take you right to Baker Street,' said Morton, 'but my orders are to take you to your billet first, and then to an address in Hill Street. You certainly seem to have some top-level contacts at the U.S. Embassy!'

Jacques smiled for the first time that day. 'Wonderful!' he said. 'Can I put in a telephone call first?'

'There's a public phone box in the lobby.'

'Oh hell,' said Jacques as they came up to it. 'I haven't any English money.'

'I can give you threepence, that's all the coppers I've got on me. You phone, and I'll see if anybody here will do a fiver's worth of francs for you.'

Lieutenant Morton came back to the lobby in time to see Jacques emerging from the call box, smiling still, and he saw the Frenchman's face change and harden as two strangers, whom Morton had noticed hanging about the entrance, came quickly up and accosted him.

'*Vous êtes français, monsieur?*' said one of the two. They were both in French uniform and wore enamel Crosses of Lorraine on their breast pockets.

'Yes, I'm French,' said Jacques. 'Who are you?'

'*Service d'Action Politique, monsieur.* Be good enough to accompany us to our central depot for your welcome and de-briefing.'

'Sorry,' said Jacques, 'nothing doing. Now let me pass, please; I'm in a hurry.'

'Our orders are to take you to the depot,' said the second man, laying his hand on Jacques' arm. Jacques shook it off with fury as Lieutenant Morton came to the rescue.

'You heard the man,' he said. 'He doesn't want to go along with you. Now buzz off, or I'll report you to the police for loitering. My car's parked down the road,' he said to Jacques. 'Let's get going.'

'What the devil's the *Service d'Action Politique*?' said Jacques, as Morton led the way to an ancient Riley, parked at the kerb. 'It's a new one on me.'

'It's loosely attached to Passy's organisation, the B.C.R.A. Very loosely, I would say; they're oftener at loggerheads than not. Very quarrelsome people, the Fighting French.'

'Is Colonel Passy the actual head of the S.A.P.?'

'No, it's André Diethelm, de Gaulle's Commissioner of the Interior.'

'Interior of what?'

'France, I suppose.'

'My God!' said Jacques, and was silent as the Riley entered the main stream of the diminished wartime traffic. He had never been in South London before, and he was shocked to see how much the district had suffered in the blitz. Whole streets were down, roofless warehouses stood open to the sky, and where the rubble had been swept behind temporary hoardings these were liberally covered with the legend 'Open Second Front Now!' They drove across the Thames. The bridges were undamaged, the familiar bulk of the Houses of Parliament and Westminster Abbey appeared, then the Horse Guards and the Admiralty. All was unchanged, but the people waiting in long queues at the bus stops looked different from the Londoners Jacques remembered. They were thin and gaunt, very shabby, and above all dispirited, as if more than two years of defeats, of the blitz and the petty frictions of the daily struggle for existence had left them drained of everything but courage.

'Those S.A.P. fellows really are the limit,' said Lieutenant Morton, who had been following his own train of thought. 'I warned off a couple of them last week – not the same two as today – when they tried to intercept an older man I was sent out to meet. He reacted just the same way you did—'

'An older man!' Jacques interrupted. 'Was it Nestor?'

'Oh, of course, you knew him. Yes, it was Nestor. He seemed to feel that after the Patriotic School the S.A.P. was the last straw.'

'Apart from that, how is he?'

'Pretty tired. He went off down to the country, but you'll certainly see him on Monday, if not tomorrow.'

Tomorrow would be Friday, and Resistance, espionage

and counter-espionage would have to take a break at the weekend. Jacques looked out at Piccadilly. There was St. James's church, an early victim of the blitz, but the broken glass had been repaired in the shop windows, and here the worst damage had been in the side streets. Clarges Street, with its double row of eighteenth-century houses, looked much the same as Jacques remembered, when the car stopped outside the Park Hotel.

'Here's your billet,' Morton said. 'You'll want to leave your bag before you go on to Hill Street.'

'*And* have a bath and a shave,' said Jacques. 'Well, thanks very much for your safe conduct. What time do they want me at Baker Street tomorrow?'

'I'll pick you up at half past nine. But look here!' said Morton, joining Jacques on the pavement, 'I'm afraid you're stuck with me for a bit longer. I'll take you round to Hill Street when you're ready.'

'Why, it's not ten minutes' walk away, and I know this part of London like the back of my hand—'

'This is the way we've got to do it, I'm afraid. You see, you came in without a visa or an entry permit, and if there was a police enquiry it could be awkward ... They'll straighten it all out for you at Baker Street tomorrow.'

'Of course,' said Jacques. 'Do you want to come up to my room with me, or will you trust me to unpack alone?'

'I'll wait in the lounge – and don't worry about signing the register, I'll see to all that. Oh, and,' said Morton, as an elderly porter took Jacques' luggage and rang for the lift, 'I forgot to give you back your money. 'Fraid I couldn't persuade them to change it at the School. They're very sticky about Exchange Control these days.'

Sticky about money, sticky about visas, suspicious of everyone and everything – yes, Jacques had come back to a very different London. But the Park Hotel seemed to be efficient: the porter produced an old valet, who pressed the blue suit last worn in a Paris night club while Jacques bathed and shaved, and was optimistic about getting the tweed suit professionally cleaned next morning.

'Friday's not a good day, but I know a place where they'll do it, over in Shepherd Market,' he confided. 'Making their fortune round the Market, they are, since the Yanks came to town. Great ones for dry-cleaning, the Yanks are! Laundries, too, that's booming, and as for the pubs! You just back in town, sir? You'll see the Yanks when you go out. Staying with us long?'

It was maddening not to have as much as half a crown to tip this cheerful Cockney. But the blue suit and the fresh white shirt looked very presentable, and Morton, who had seen so many unkempt arrivals from France, was impressed when the latest of them came into the hotel lounge with his well-brushed dark overcoat on his arm. The lounge was filling up with American officers, for the Park Hotel was conveniently central for men on leave, and round the corner on Curzon Street the Washington Hotel had become the Washington American Red Cross Club, with a crowd of G.I.s on the pavement. The American Red Cross was busy in Charles Street too, running a club for officers of the American women's services, and it was still light enough to see the flags of other Allied nations all along the same street. But everywhere in Mayfair the Americans were in the majority, and that was the biggest of all the changes in London since Jacques went away. He stood on the Hill Street pavement, looking up Chesterfield Street to the short cut through the public garden which he had taken so often in the summer of 1940. He wondered who was living in his rented flat on Mount Street now.

The porter at the door of Joe Calvert's building told them Mr. Calvert had asked to be called on the house telephone when the gentlemen arrived. Joe came down to the lobby promptly: he had left the embassy earlier than usual, he said, to be in good time for them, and he shook Jacques's hand warmly as he welcomed him to London.

'You're the first person to say that to me, monsieur,' said Jacques, and Lieutenant Morton slyly reminded him that he had turned down one French welcome already.

'Why don't you go on up to my apartment?' suggested Joe. 'It's number D on the fourth floor, and the door's ajar. I'd like to have a word with your conducting officer.'

What they could have to say to one another Jacques didn't know; he guessed it was the American's thoughtfulness which was making it possible for him to have a few minutes alone with Polly. The lift was slow, the corridor seemed a mile long, the last few steps to the door marked D longer than their whole journey from Nice, but then she was in his arms again, clinging to him, half-crying and kissing him wildly. She had been so cool and cheerful when he called her from the Patriotic School that Jacques had not expected such an outburst as his physical presence had released. He strained her to him, trembling, until he heard the lift gate closing and guessed that Joe Calvert was returning to his flat.

'Well, my dear, are you happy now?' said Joe as he entered, and found his guests had got no further than the hall. 'Come in, Jack. Polly tells me that's what you're some-times called, and it comes easier to my tongue than a French name.' He was talking nonsense, merely to give Polly time to compose herself and use her powder compact; he pressed Jacques into service at the drinks tray, which on this occasion was ready and waiting. 'I've squared your conducting officer,' he said. 'I gave him my word I'd walk you back to Clarges Street tonight and he accepted it. One could say he paroled you to me for the evening.'

'All that red tape!' said Polly happily, and Jacques re-marked that it was odd for a man to be conducted who had done so much conducting himself. He was sure that Mr. Calvert's intervention with the S.O.E., pulling all the rank of a former Minister, had enabled him to discover at least the outline of Jacques Brunel's career as an operative, and on that frank assumption their talk from the beginning was open and relaxed. Even the house dinner was better than on the night before, for Joe had visited the American P.X. at noon and bought some extra provender – 'not as good as what you had in the forest of Compiègne,' he said. By this time the two of them, talking in turn, had given him a fuller account of Polly's escape to freedom.

During the meal Joe watched them both closely, and if he had been sure, last night, that Polly was in love, he felt as soon as he saw them together that they were already lovers. There was nothing in Jacques' manner to betray it: he was more formal than any young American would have been towards a girl who pleased him, but the possession was there, implicit in every glance, every time he turned to Polly for confirmation of this or that incident on their journey, and in the softness of her acquiescence, her pride in him. She's got a right to be proud, thought Joe, this is quite a guy. I couldn't wish anybody better for Paul and Marie's daughter – if it wasn't for this damned war. What sort of a future will he have, now he's out of France? A commission in Giraud's army? President Roosevelt aimed at arming and equipping five hundred thousand men, from North Africa and anywhere, to fight on from Tunisia through Italy to the ultimate liberation of France. And if Jack decides to leave for North Africa, what's Miss Polly going to say to that?

It was almost a relief when Jacques, taking Polly's hand in his, said, 'Sir, Pauline and I would like you to know that we are hoping to be married soon.' That seemed to Joe to simplify everything. He got out the champagne, quite cool enough for drinking in the unheated kitchen of the service flat, he claimed the right to kiss the future bride, he congratulated her lover over and over again. But there was still something on Joe's mind, and as he walked back to the Park Hotel with Jacques he told him what it was.

'I don't know how Polly feels tonight, now you've told me your marriage plans,' he said. 'But last night she asked me to be the one to tell you about her legacy. Her grandfather's left her a substantial sum of money, in trust until she's twenty-five. Four years from now. She's very pleased about the four years, though heaven knows why; but now you know she won't be coming to you empty-handed.'

Jacques walked on in silence. His words, when he spoke at last, were not what Joe Calvert had expected.

'I'm very glad,' he said. 'Now she'll *have* to go back to America; there will be business of all sorts to attend to, even if her legacy is in trust. She told me on the night we met that she wanted to go home, and I promised to help her. Now I'll know she's safe there – out of this hell.'

The waxing moon, which had shone on the cottage in the forest, shone now on a scene as desolate as a lunar landscape, from the huge bomb crater on Hill Street to the ragged spaces where houses had stood by the side of Shepherd Market. Pinpoints of light from the blue-coated lamps of feeble electric torches marked the progress along their beats of the ladies of the town.

'Do you think she still wants to go back to America?' said Joe dryly, as they turned into Curzon Street. 'From all I heard tonight it looks like she's planning to spend the rest of her life with you.'

The Special Operations Executive had come a long way since the days when Mr. Churchill gave it the mandate to set Europe ablaze, and Jacques Brunel was recruited by three anonymous men, one of them a general officer, in a make-shift office in St. Ermin's Hotel. The Western European Directorate had six sections devoted to France alone – the latest, A.M.F., was about to be set up in Algiers – of which 'F' and 'R.F.' were the most important. There was liaison with the governments-in-exile; there was liaison of a sort with the Free, or Fighting French. The French B.C.R.A. had proliferated too, and five sections had developed from the old *Deuxième Bureau*, which de Gaulle had entrusted to Captain Dewavrin's charge at their first meeting, before the young officer turned into Colonel Passy. A stranger, walking from Dorset Square to Manchester Square via Baker Street, with a foray down certain side streets and with the omniscience to know what was going on behind those impersonal façades, might have been forgiven for thinking that the real war was being waged by the espionage experts, and that the armed struggle was nothing but a waste of time.

Jacques Brunel, when Morton delivered him punctually at Orchard Court, took stock of an impressive office set-up of clerks and typewriters and filing baskets, the base of the pyramid, he supposed, from which men like Charles Maxwell were despatched all over Europe to fight behind the lines. He was becoming aware that some of the typists were taking stock of him, when a young woman in uniform came from an inner office and said, 'Major Aylmer will see you now.'

'Sorry about this,' said Major Aylmer, who had greying hair and a limp, as he shook hands. 'I know you were expecting to see the chief. He sent his apologies. He was detained at one of our country establishments last night, but he looks forward to seeing you on Monday. We must find something amusing for you to do over the weekend, eh?'

'Thank you, I've got friends in London.'

'Jolly good! Of course, you were here in '40, weren't you?'

Major Aylmer was amusing enough to be going on with, at least in a Frenchman's eyes. He was the very type of English staff officer with which war novelists had already familiarised their French readers : the Guards type, with a monocle, a drawl, and a pseudo-amateur approach to soldiering. Jacques was too intelligent to take the type at its face value. He waited for the major to begin his interrogation.

But John Aylmer took up a pencil, and doodled on the desk pad before he spoke.

'I've some bad news for you,' he said. 'Your friend César is dead.'

Jacques swallowed. He had expected the news ever since

he saw Charles in the railway restaurant at Marseille, but still it came as a shock. He said, 'When did you hear?'

'The day before yesterday. There was a bit of a delay in getting through, but Charles was able to give us absolute confirmation – he had a contact inside the prison.'

'Yes, I know.'

'This man said Renaudon was under torture for four days and never spoke a word.'

'While everybody else was shouting their heads off,' said Jacques bitterly. 'What news have you had from Nice?'

'We've been waiting for you to give us the news from Nice.'

It took a long time, broken by questions and interjections from Aylmer, for Jacques to give – for the first time – an absolutely complete account of the fate of the 'Knife' and 'Fire' circuits, linking them to the Malvy murder and his own killing of the militiaman in the Parc des Arènes. John Aylmer's face grew longer as he listened, and the pad was filled with doodles as he heard Jacques describe the newspaper speculation on the identity of the 'third man' in the Cimiez story.

'That's rather awkward,' he said, with massive British understatement. 'Very unfortunate! That's going to upset all the plans the chief was readying for you. I'll have to try to get him on the scrambler this afternoon.'

'Do you know what sort of plans they were?'

'Roughly. When we got the news that Orengo was taken, and the others with him, our first thought was how to resuscitate the "Knife" circuit. Orengo – Couteau – claimed to have five hundred men in "Knife", it was one of the biggest of our ninety circuits in France.'

'And one of the most expensive,' Jacques put in, and Aylmer gave him a sharp look.

'We rather thought you might be the man to take over from Couteau,' he said. 'You could have amalgamated the "Knife" lot with your own little network, couldn't you?'

Jacques shrugged. 'I've purposely kept my own *réseau* small.'

'Yes, well, we've always been interested in the smaller circuits. You say two of your men, Froment and Dupont, were quite able to take over from you?'

'Absolutely.'

'Then how about the two "Knife" men who got away from Cimiez – what were their code names?'

'Poignard and Coupoir.'

'Could they run the show, d'you think?'

Jacques didn't think they could run a skittle alley. He said, 'They were smart enough to get out of the Impasse des Arènes that night. They blackjacked Dr. Moreau's chauffeur into driving them down to Nice.'

'And they haven't been picked up yet, as far as we know. Not by the police, nor by our *passeurs* in Marseille or Toulouse.'

'They're probably still in the Old Town, within a kilometre of wherever they made Gustave set them down. A man on the run could live for a year inside that rabbit warren, and never even be seen by the law.'

As he spoke Jacques felt a sensation inside his head as if the tumblers of a lock had fallen open to a key.

'Well,' said Major Aylmer, throwing the doodled sheet into the wastebasket, 'this is going to take a bit of thinking over. In the meantime, d'you feel like having a spot of lunch with me? There's a pub at the corner of Portman Square where some of us foregather, if you care to join us about one.'

'Thanks, I'd like to.' Jacques stood up. It was barely twelve. He would have time to telephone to Polly and arrange a meeting for the late afternoon. 'Can you tell me how Nestor is?' he asked as they moved towards the door.

'Nestor's down in the country, but he's coming up again on Monday. He had a very busy time last week, seeing Colonel Passy *and* General de Gaulle—'

'*Nestor* went to see de Gaulle?'

'By special invitation. He got the V.I.P. treatment at Carlton Gardens, I believe.'

'But he was so antagonistic to Renaudon and the idea of the secret army!'

'He probably told the general exactly what he thought, and Passy too.'

Jacques shook his head. The whole thing was out of character where Nestor-de Valbone was concerned. But Aylmer, misinterpreting the gesture, put a hand on his shoulder. 'I'm sorry I had to be the one to tell you about Renaudon,' he said. 'Charles said you'd known him for a long time.'

'I knew him at school, but I never knew him well.'

'He was one of de Gaulle's protégés, not one of us, but he was a good man, Jack!'

'He was a brave man when it came to dying.'

Jacques was downstairs and in the courtyard before he remembered that he meant to ask about changing money. He had put all his French currency in the Park Hotel safe, less the equivalent of twenty pounds, which he needed to see him through the weekend : surely S.O.E., which sent thousands at a time to circuits like Couteau's, and 'wasn't particular to five hundred or so', as Charles had said, wouldn't object to taking his francs for a mere twenty? He had turned on his heel to go back inside the building when a young man who had been waiting outside the gates came running in with a great show of spontaneity and called after him in French :

'Maître Brunel! What a piece of luck! I was afraid I'd missed you. I came round in a hurry from our press office, with a message for you from Monsieur de Valbonne.'

Jacques surveyed him : candid face, French lieutenant's uniform, Cross of Lorraine. 'Your press office,' he said, 'where might that be?'

'Just round the corner, sir, in Wigmore Street.'

'I thought Monsieur de Valbonne was in the country.'

'He came up for the day and heard you were at Orchard Court. He hoped you wouldn't mind coming along to our office for a few minutes and giving him some professional advice. He's preparing a statement for a press release, and wants to know the legal angle.'

'What sort of statement?'

'About his recognition of General de Gaulle as the legitimate representative of the government of France.'

'I should think he does need legal advice, and medical advice as well,' said Jacques angrily. 'I'll come with you.'

He knew with one part of his mind that the thing was a plant, the boy's approach a piece of ham acting which in the Place du Palais de Justice at Nice he would have turned down with a jeer. But another part said, 'It could be true. You were wrong about Renaudon, who died a hero's death. You could equally well be wrong about the sage Nestor. Go and find out!' While yet another part, the dominant, said, 'What have you got to lose? What danger can there be in London, where there's no Gestapo, no *Milice*, only the matrix of freedom?' He walked alongside the young man down Wigmore Street.

Not very far. They turned a corner, and Jacques stopped. For the name on the wall sign was Duke Street, and the number above the unpretentious door was Ten.

'This is Colonel Passy's headquarters,' he said. 'Does he run a press office as well as the secret service?'

'Just to handle the Allied press, Maître Brunel. And to issue statements by new adherents like Nestor.'

Jacques allowed himself to be escorted through the door. It all seemed very normal: a girl receptionist in uniform seated at a small table, talking to a British officer with a face like a skull, and a blown-up photograph of General de Gaulle upon one wall.

'This is the gentleman for Monsieur de Valbonne, mademoiselle,' said the young man. 'Will you let them know?'

'Certainly, *mon lieutenant*. This way, please, monsieur.'

She showed Jacques into a waiting room, with comfortable chairs, and papers and magazines on the table. 'May I get you a cup of coffee, please?' she said.

'No thank you.'

'I'm sure they won't be long.'

Jacques turned over the publications. It was his first encounter with the Gaullist press, and he marvelled at the variety and number of the papers and newsletters. He counted ten in all, a remarkable contribution from a Britain desperately short of newsprint, and covering all interests from the pious to the merely vulgar. He was soon immersed in *La Marseillaise*, which contained one of Quilici's particularly vituperative attacks on the American ally, reading with such astonishment that he forgot the passage of time, and was startled to find that forty-five minutes had passed since he left Orchard Court. He ought to have telephoned Polly before leaving the S.O.E. offices, but surely these people would be civil enough to let him use one of their phones! He opened the door. The table where the girl had been sitting was empty, and there was no sign of the death's head British officer or of the young Frenchman. But two soldiers, one a corporal, had mounted guard outside the waiting-room door and almost as Jacques began 'Can I—' the corporal barked out:

'Get back inside, you! You're under arrest.'

16

It was a mistake to rush the front door. The door was locked, the soldiers armed and powerful. They soon had an unarmed man, his jacket torn at the armpit, back inside the room and locked in too, not physically damaged as yet but furious with himself for having walked into a trap.

Jacques had an idea that while he was struggling with the guards another door in the hall had opened and a tall fair man had looked out. It was only a momentary impression, and the man had not spoken, nor intervened in any way. He was clinically detached, like a doctor observing the onset of a malady, and like the patient under observation Jacques felt a fever of rage through his whole body. He could see no means of getting out of the room other than through the door, for the window was made of double panes of frosted glass, through which he couldn't even hear the traffic of Duke Street, if indeed the window was on the Duke Street side. He had no sort of weapon, not even a pen-knife or a fountain pen. There was nothing for it but to await a confrontation with his captors.

They kept him waiting for nearly another hour. It was meant to shake his nerve, he knew, and he resisted the impulse to hammer on the door or cry out. He could play the waiting game as well as they could, although it was monstrous that he should be having to play the game at all, here in London, and not in the prison of St. Pierre! He tried to read some more of the propaganda, but the words made no sense now : the hitting at America, the unctuous praises of the one and only Leader were of no importance compared with the predicament of Jacques Brunel.

Just before two o'clock the door was unlocked and a man he had never seen before came in and greeted him pleasantly. 'Sorry to have kept you waiting, monsieur. Sorry you felt you had to attack the men on duty. They were only posted to make sure you didn't leave the building before we were free to talk to you. Will you come this way, please?'

Jacques said nothing until they were in a small office, where another man was sitting behind a desk, under another copy of the official portrait of the Leader. He was alone with the two of them, short, thickset men, both dark, both about his own age and both armed. He was told to sit down.

'I came here to see Monsieur de Valbonne,' he said. 'Why was I told that I'm under arrest?'

'Yes, well, there's been a slight misunderstanding. Monsieur de Valbonne had to leave us, unfortunately, before your interesting conference with the British ended. As regards the "arrest", that's only a technical expression. We prefer to call it "protective custody".'

'What right have you to take me into custody?'

'Come, Monsieur Brunel, this slight inconvenience could have been avoided if you had had the courtesy to report at our welcome centre yesterday, instead of going off with your British bodyguard to that S.O.E. transit camp on Clarges Street. We only want to ask you a few questions, and then you'll be free to go.'

'Make them quick, then.'

The captain behind the desk took up a sheet of paper, and read in a toneless voice : 'One. We want to know the names of the British agent and his wireless operator working out of Marseille, and the codes you use to communicate with them. Two. The names of the new leaders of the "Knife" and "Fire" circuits. Three. The names of all the section chiefs of your own circuit. Four. The whereabouts of Poignard and Coupoir.'

'And that's all?'

'That's all.'

'If I were to tell you, would it do anything towards the defeat of Germany?'

'We're not concerned here with the defeat of Germany!' The man behind the desk raised his voice, his face suddenly suffused with red. 'Our job is to break the influence of the British in the South of France! You, and men like you, betrayed the best interests of our country when you sold yourselves for money to the S.O.E.—'

'I never took a sou from the S.O.E.,' said Jacques. 'General de Gaulle and his hangers-on have been living on British money for two and a half years.' He noticed that the Cross of Lorraine on the captain's blouse was askew.

The man standing behind his chair, the officer who brought him from the waiting room, took a step nearer to Jacques. 'Just answer the questions, Brunel, will you?'

'Like hell I'll answer your questions,' said Jacques. 'I've had enough of this. You haven't the shadow of a right to detain me here against my will.'

'We have every right, Brunel. You're a French citizen, of military age. You ought to be serving in the forces of Fighting France—'

'What fools you are,' said Jacques contemptuously. 'I was in the House of Commons when the Allied Forces bill was debated, over two years ago. De Gaulle has no longer the right of imprisonment, or even of coercion, and neither have his – servants, do I call you, or his slaves?'

'I'll give you one more chance,' said the man behind the desk. 'First, tell us the name of the British agent in Marseille. And the wireless operator. And—'

'Cut it out,' said Jacques. 'I'll tell you nothing.'

'Oh, but I think you will,' said the voice behind him. 'Miss Pauline Preston is a charming girl. You wouldn't want anything disagreeable to happen to her, would you?'

Jacques leaped up, knocking over the flimsy chair, and he got in one blow with all his weight behind it to the man's jaw, and then sprang for the door. But the other Gaullist was coming round the desk with a strap in his hand. Jacques felt a smashing weight crash against the lower part of his back, and fainted.

When he regained consciousness he was in a cellar. His jacket and waistcoat had been removed, and all his belongings. He was in his shirt and trousers, without shoes, and his face and the front of his shirt were wet; he thought a basin of water had recently been thrown over him.

The cellar was small, and so low that Jacques, when he

pulled himself unsteadily to his feet, could hardly stand erect. What little light and ventilation there was came in through a barred opening at the top of the heavy door. It was impossible to tell if it was day or night.

He was clear-headed enough to look at the watch on his interrogator's wrist when they took him back to the room with the picture of de Gaulle. It said half past nine, and as the lights were blazing in that room he supposed it was evening, nearly twelve hours since he entered Orchard Court. This time they refused to let Jacques sit down. He stood before them swaying, his hands tied, a bright light tilted to shine into his eyes, and he said 'No!' to all the questions. Not 'No comment,' or 'I don't know,' and he had no more breath to waste on sarcasms. Just *non, non* to everything. No

The man he had struck in the morning was no longer there, and when Jacques could no longer keep his balance he was held erect by two others whose faces were a blur to him. He looked only at his interrogator, smiling now; he looked hard at the leather-covered strap lying on the desk between them. When the Gaullist picked it up and moved towards him, Jacques braced himself for the blows, falling always and terribly on his back, and this time he was still conscious when they carried him back to the cellar.

That ended Jacques' first day in captivity. He was able to sleep for an hour or two, and while he slept someone placed a mug of water and a few slices of bread on the floor beside his pallet. He ate a little and drank all the water at some unknown hour of the night. His head was clearer, and he knew quite well where he was: in a cellar at Ten, Duke Street, Manchester Square. Somewhere in the offices above his head there would be the famous files, Colonel Passy's detailed dossiers of those who would and those who wouldn't join de Gaulle. He was sure that his own card bore the record of the kidney which he received at Namsos, for which he had been hospitalised at Dykefaulds after the Norwegian campaign. The two beatings had been directed at that part of his body and the pain was now very great. But still it was nothing compared to what Renaudon had suffered. They were only beating him, there were no mechanical tortures, no maiming of his limbs. Renaudon had suffered everything German sadism could devise, for four days and four nights, and had not betrayed his friends. If Renaudon held on, so can I, he thought. He slept again, and was taken back for another interrogation in the morning.

In the hours that followed, all through the long Saturday and the Sunday forenoon, he often thought of Polly, but in a queer impersonal way. The living girl was less vivid in his cellar than the dead Renaudon, whom he could sometimes hear saying 'I hope you never fall into the hands of the Gestapo,' as he had said on the day they heard the news of Sabre's folly. Polly's sweetness, Polly's loving, had no place in these vile surroundings. He was only thankful that she couldn't see her lover now.

Polly Preston began to worry on Friday evening. She was not much disturbed when Jacques failed to telephone before luncheon, because she understood that he might be too busy with the men he went to see, and in any case it was plans for the evening they had meant to make at noon. But when evening came and brought no Jacques, nor any message, she did worry: at nine o'clock, with Joe's approval, she telephoned the Park Hotel, and was told that Mr. Brunel had left with a British officer about nine thirty, and had not returned.

'They may have taken him down to one of their country depots,' suggested Joe. 'They've got every kind of training going on outside London – parachutage, wireless telegraphy, unarmed combat. Yes, I know, Polly, Jacques is not about to take a course in W/T, but if there was somebody they wanted him to meet, down in the country, and he had to go?'

'Without letting us know?' Joe was forced to admit it

didn't seem likely. But he refused to do anything more until the morning, when to calm Polly's rising alarm he telephoned to Baker Street, and was told that Jacques' pass to leave the building had been clocked at twelve-oh-three; nobody had seen him since. Major Aylmer unfortunately was not available, for he could have told Joe about waiting in the pub at the corner of Portman Square with some of his colleagues, and their mild irritation when the Frenchman failed to show up. Not that this would have added much to their knowledge of Jacques' movements; as far as was known he had disappeared off the face of the earth in Baker Street at a few minutes past twelve.

'Do you think he could have gone to see Monsieur de Valbonne?' Polly was clutching at a straw. 'Jacques admires him so much. Ever since we left Nice he's been hoping to catch up with him. Can't we find out where Monsieur de Valbonne has gone?'

But the duty officer at Orchard Court flatly refused to divulge the address of the Baron de Valbonne, formerly of Cannes. He was with friends in the country. 'Yes, Minister,' said the disembodied voice, 'I'll make sure he gets your message in the beginning of the week. He's expected here on Monday or Tuesday.'

By Saturday evening Polly was beside herself, and Joe had to soothe her through bursts of crying and self-reproach. By an entirely feminine process of reasoning she had convinced herself that Jacques had ceased to love her, and said – when Joe remonstrated – if he'd spoken of marriage in the Hill Street flat, it was only 'to be nice'. What she meant by that Joe Calvert had no idea. He went over and over the conversation he had with Jacques on the way back to Park Street, and Jacques' wish that she should go home to the absolute safety of the United States : this produced the heart-broken cry of 'You see? He's tired of me !'

'He adores you, Polly. I saw that for myself—'

'Then why doesn't he telephone?'

Joe, instead, telephoned to all the London hospitals; he was beginning to think that Jacques Brunel was just reckless enough to have got himself knocked down by a motor car. But no casualty answering his description had been brought in on Friday, or since; and Joe refused to believe that a grown man who knew the locality and spoke good English could have lost his way in the heart of London.

'Suppose he was kidnapped?' Polly sobbed next morning. 'Oh, Joe, don't you know *anybody* who could help us?'

'I wish Bob Kemp was here.' But the thought of the O.S.S. man put Jim Randall into Joe's head, and soon Randall, torn from coffee and the Sunday papers in his own flat, was at Hill Street, full of sympathy and interest.

'Miss Preston thinks her fiancé has been kidnapped,' said Joe apologetically. 'I've been telling her such things can't happen here in London.'

Jim Randall cocked an eye. 'I don't know,' he said. 'Baker Street's just round the corner from Duke Street, and we've had complaints already about Passy's mob. It may be a long shot, Joe, but I'd be inclined to pay a social call at Number Ten.'

'You wouldn't be let in.'

'I'd have to take a Brit. with me, of course. And a copper at that. We've got a very useful contact now at Scotland Yard.'

'Will he be there on Sunday morning?'

That was when the luck turned, for Detective-Sergeant Brownlow was there to lend the authority which caused the doors of 'Passy's mob' to open at the sight of his warrant card. Jim Randall and Joe went in behind him. The façade of Friday had been replaced, a smiling girl sat behind the desk, and much regretted to say that Colonel Passy was spending the weekend in the country. Captain Royer was the duty officer—

Captain Royer caved in at once at the sight of a Scotland Yard search warrant. Yes, there was a French national in the building, whose name might be Brunel. He had come to their offices voluntarily, but with a string of abuse and complaints, and when he attacked one man brutally enough to break his jaw, they were obliged to keep him in confinement for his own sake. He thought the plan was to release him in the afternoon—

'Release him now,' said the detective. They waited fifteen minutes before Jacques appeared, haggard and dirty and unsteady on his feet.

'Jacques, are you all right?' cried Joe.

'Apart from being beaten half a dozen times,' said Jacques, 'I'm fine.'

'Do you want to charge these people with assault?' said the detective. 'Is this the man who beat you up?'

'I never saw him before, nor the girl either,' said Jacques with an effort. 'Just – get me out of here. Joe – where's Pauline?'

'She's waiting at Hill Street, in a terrible state.'

'Don't let her see me like this.'

'Better take him along to the Middlesex Hospital,' said the detective. 'You'll need witnesses to his condition.'

'Can you walk, Jacques?'

'If I had my shoes.'

'You're wearing them.'

They had bundled him into his outer clothing and his shoes down in the cellar. The girl receptionist, alarmed and resentful, brought his overcoat and hat, watch and wallet, in which a rough check showed the money was intact.

'I'll have to see our law department about this,' said Jim to the detective. 'I'll be in touch after Brunel's seen a doctor.'

'He's going to be all right, Polly, there's nothing to worry about,' said Joe Calvert for the tenth time. 'The doctors want to keep him under observation tonight and maybe through tomorrow, just to make sure there was no permanent damage done, and then Jacques will be as good as new.'

'But why doesn't he want to see *me*?'

'I told you, because he's very much ashamed of the way he fell for some cock and bull story about this man Nestor, de Valbonne or whatever his name is, and he doesn't want you to see him in a hospital bed, covered in ointment and bandages.'

'As if that mattered!'

'His great consolation seems to be that he broke one Gaullist's jaw.'

'That sounds more like Jacques,' said Polly. 'Can't the men who hurt him be put in prison now?'

'That's another thing we have to thrash out on Monday. And besides, Jacques is determined to see this man de Valbonne before we get down to cases. Jim Randall's going to use some muscle with the top brass at S.O.E. to find out where de Valbonne is, so Jacques can find out if it was all a fake at Duke Street, or if de Valbonne has really gone over to de Gaulle.'

'Oh, damn General de Gaulle,' said poor Polly, and 'You can say that again,' said Joe with feeling.

General de Gaulle, of course, was loftily unaware of the proceedings at Duke Street. That was the weekend when the British public was rejoicing at the irresistible march of the First and Eighth Armies towards Tripoli, with all that a victory at Tripoli meant to the clearing of the Tunisian tip, and de Gaulle had to make one of the major decisions of his search for power. Since the conference opened at Casablanca a few days earlier, he had been more than once invited by Mr. Churchill to fly to Morocco; a R.A.F. plane was standing by to bring the general and the weight of his wisdom to the survey then proceeding of the whole field of the war. President Roosevelt, though in lukewarm terms, had added his own invitation.

Still furious at the slight inflicted on him in November, de Gaulle had steadfastly refused to leave London. Now he was forced to consider whether he had said *Non* (his favourite word) too often, and worn out even Mr. Churchill's patience. Another man than Churchill would indeed have given up at this point and plucked the thorn of de Gaulle out of his flesh once and for all. The history of France would have been altered for thirty years if Mr. Churchill had not decided to give his protégé a final chance. On Monday he sent a telegram to the Foreign Secretary, Mr. Eden – always inclined to be soft on de Gaulle – instructing him, for de Gaulle's own sake, 'to knock him about pretty hard', and tell him that if the general rejected this unique opportunity to meet the President at Casablanca he would never be invited to America. H.M. Government would have to review its attitude to the Free French movement as long as de Gaulle remained at its head, and then – wrote Mr. Churchill – 'we shall endeavour to get on as well as we can without you'.

The reluctant general came to heel at last.

By a quirk of fate, Jacques Brunel learned about the general's decision to submit earlier than most of the Allied diplomats in London. He learned it from his first visitor, the Baron de Valbonne, late on Monday afternoon, when having been allowed to get up and dress he had the further privilege of talking to his friends in a small vacant anteroom in the Middlesex Hospital.

'By dear Jacques, my poor dear fellow, what a horrible story!' said the man who had been Jacques' first mentor in the Resistance. 'I could hardly believe my ears when Mr. Randall reached me on the telephone, and told me the whole thing. Those wretched fellows had no right to use my name—'

'Occupational hazard, for both of us, monsieur,' said Jacques with a smile. 'Tell me how *you* are.' He thought the man from Cannes looked worse than he did, ten years older than his sixty-eight, though as always very well dressed and groomed. But de Valbonne was not to be put off. He questioned Jacques about everything that happened at Duke

Street, punctuating the story by sighs, and finally saying it was a great pity there were no witnesses for Jacques, and that he had begun the trouble by breaking that fellow's jaw.

'Assault and battery,' said Jacques, unconcerned. 'Yes, I know. In France I could have them cold for unlawful detention and grievous bodily harm, but I'm not sure how the law stands in England. The American lawyer Randall brought in doesn't seem to think I've got much of a case.'

'It might be wiser to let the whole thing drop,' said de Valbonne, and Jacques's eyes narrowed.

'Are you going soft on de Gaulle, monsieur?' he said. 'Were those thugs right when they told me you mean to come out for him at last?'

'No, no, certainly not,' protested de Valbonne. 'I'm beginning to think I'm too old to come out for anyone or anything. I'm not going back to France, Jacques. The British have given me a residence permit, and I shall go on living with my friends in Hampshire, at least until the war is over. But I'm not going to come out for de Gaulle, at least until we can tell what he's going to do after this new development—'

'You've been to see him, haven't you?'

'I saw him last week, and again for a short time today.'

'And what's the new development?'

'He's flying out to Morocco for talks with General Giraud. No, let me finish, Jacques' – as the younger man lifted his hand in protest – 'this is exactly what I, and other reasonable people, counselled him to do last week. A joint leadership of the two generals, de Gaulle and Giraud, unifying their ideals and their, er, military genius might be the best solution to all the troubles of our country.'

'If you can believe that you'll believe anything,' said Jacques wearily. As far as he was concerned their conversation was at an end, although de Valbonne stayed with him for half an hour. He listened courteously to what the older man had to say by way of extenuation and excuse, talked about the Bertrands in Paris and the farmer of La Folie, agreed they had both misjudged Renaudon, and dismissed him as soon as the tall elegant figure with the silver grey hair and the neatly rolled umbrella went through the door of the anteroom. If the Baron de Valbonne, once known as Nestor, wasn't going to jump on the Gaullist bandwagon he was going to do a fine job of sitting on the fence, and good luck to him. His service to the Resistance was at an end.

Joe Calvert, when he came to see Jacques two hours later, had also heard that de Gaulle was flying to meet Giraud. He was of course unable to reveal that the man would also meet President Roosevelt, and obviously Jacques hadn't even guessed it. He was not of de Valbonne's opinion that Jacques could let the matter of his imprisonment and beating drop, but he confessed himself unable to see how a successful law suit could be brought.

'You said you never heard any of those fellows' names,' he pointed out. 'But Randall thinks it wouldn't be too difficult to find out who they are.'

'And if we did find out, what then?' said Jacques. 'They're small beer. Even if I sued them *and* Colonel Passy, their commanding officer, it still wouldn't do much good. The one I want to get at is de Gaulle.'

'Who will disclaim all responsibility for the undue zeal of his patriotic followers.'

'Yes, I know; *son entourage est lamentable*, we've all heard that for years. But he's responsible for them before the law. Do you think the British are going to let the great French folk hero be sued like any common man? I'm sure they don't want to know about anything that goes on in Ten, Duke Street, Manchester Square! If they did, they could have closed the place up long ago.'

'I agree with you, Jacques.'

'And now that de Gaulle has graciously condescended to meet poor old Giraud, he'll be more of a hero than ever. Joe, there's no end to it! The two real fighters, de Lattre and Béthouart, were accused of treason. De Gaulle, the deserter, goes scot free.'

'Treason doth never prosper : what's the reason?
For if it prosper, none dare call it treason'

Joe quoted. 'If de Gaulle plays his cards right at Casablanca, he'll take a big step towards his own prosperity.'

'I've been thinking about that. Joe, you came in an embassy car, didn't you? Will you take me back to Pauline now?'

'You don't say "home to Pauline", do you, Jacques?'

'We haven't got a home. Not yet.'

Joe looked at him. Jacques's face had been very little bruised, and the discoloration was fading. The cruel welts on his back were invisible. There was a brand somewhere in his mind, that was obvious; Joe could only say, as he picked up his coat, 'She's been worried sick about you, Jack. Be gentle with her.'

It was a gentle evening at Hill Street, what there was of it, for Joe insisted that the embassy car should take Jacques back to the Park Hotel at nine o'clock. In Joe's flat, Jacques and Polly seemed content to sit hand in hand like two children while the saga of Ten, Duke Street, was told again, and when she kissed him goodnight Polly told her lover he must have another long restful day tomorrow, and let the car bring him back for dinner. She was going to have her hair done in the morning, and help out at the Red Cross Club in Charles Street in the afternoon.

'You'll soon find another *maternelle, chérie.*'

'Not as nice as the one in the Place Wilson.' She was happy about Jacques again, and the future seemed bright to Polly. She might have been less confident if she had known how he spent the restful day. True, he spent it in the Park Hotel, where the tweed suit cleaned in Shepherd Market was all ready to put on, and where nobody made any comment on his absence – there was too much coming and going among the men on leave for that. But he had visitors, with whom he talked long and unrestfully. Major Aylmer came first, shocked to hear the Duke Street story, but delighted when Jacques said what had happened made him think he should return to the men he could trust in France. Did he feel up to it, Jim Randall asked, when he visited the hotel in the afternoon. Randall was not concerned with the future of the 'Knife' circuit, as the S.O.E. man had been, but solely with the means of sending Jacques back to France. The felucca line was out now, and the Royal Navy was growing tired of lending submarines. Parachute training, in Jacques' present condition, was out of the question.

'There *is* another way to France, if you're determined to go back,' Jim said finally. 'The S.O.E. people run it, but our boys use it almost as much as they do. It's the Cornwall to Brittany run, if you're prepared to carry the can from there. They say it's not so bad once you get through the German maritime area. That's the way Renaudon went back, incidentally.'

'The *British* put Renaudon ashore in Brittany?'

'Yes, at St. Cast beach west of Dinard, where you'll land yourself if I can work it.'

So. Jacques' last suspicions of Renaudon as a German V-man, put into Brittany with German connivance, evaporated in an access of shame. More than ever, he was determined that the only solution for himself was a return to France. He allowed a day or two to pass, taking Polly out to lunch and walking in Hyde Park as his strength returned, but taking care not to be alone with her at the flat – for then, he knew, he wouldn't be able to trust himself not to make love to her. He loathed the thought of her seeing the marks of the beatings on his body. Finally he summoned up his courage to tell the girl he loved of his decision.

He began by reminding her, as they strolled by the Serpentine, that he had thought at first of going to North Africa to join Giraud's new army. But in the last few days he had realised that it wouldn't work out. Giraud might be superseded by de Gaulle, and he, Jacques, would be nothing but a pawn in the game of dirty politics which went on twenty-four hours a day in Algiers.

So he had made up his mind to go back to Nice. Not to live there, exactly, and certainly not to practise at the bar; no, most likely he would make his headquarters at a farm in the mountains near Sospel, where a few friends of his had got together already.

'You mean in the maquis?' It was the first thing she had said, and he was thankful for the control which had kept her from crying out at the mere name of Nice.

'You could call it a maquis, the beginning of one.'

'And you mean to make it bigger—'

'I hope so.'

'You've always dreamed of fighting in Provence, haven't you?'

'Alongside our liberators, yes.'

'And what about me?'

'You'll be in Baltimore with the Prestons, darling. Joe says he can get you priority on a Clipper, and you'll soon be safe at home. That was what you wanted, wasn't it, that night at the Maison Russe? And next year, when the war's over, I'll get to Baltimore too, and we'll be married there—'

'I see you've settled it between you, Joe and you.'

That was how it started, with anger and resentment on Polly's part, and pleading, laced with words of love, from Jacques. No, of course he didn't want to say goodbye to her. He adored her, he wanted nothing so much as marriage and a home with her, but – the eternal *but* – there was duty, there was his responsibility to the men who trusted him, above all there was France.

Polly's theme, in reply to all this, was simple. Take me back to Nice with you. I won't be in the way, you know I won't, you said I did well before. I never whined, did I, when we were on the run from Nice? I did warn you, didn't I, that night outside the Gestapo headquarters?

'I know you did, darling, you were wonderful, but this is going to be a different sort of life. You couldn't stand living rough in the maquis, no woman can for long '

'I could live at the Palais Lascaris and work at the *maternelle*, couldn't I?'

'While the Malvy case comes up for trial? Oh, Polly, do be sensible!'

It went on for days. In the parks and streets, at Joe's flat, in Jacques's room at the Park, without any of the sexuality which each had roused in the other, but with tears and remorseful kisses from Polly, they argued the rights and wrongs of a return to France. Joe Calvert, a compassionate bystander, wished the ordeal over for them both.

Meantime the eyes of the world were turned to Casablanca, where the presence of President Roosevelt and Mr. Churchill was at last revealed, along with their demand for the unconditional surrender of the Axis Powers before any peace settlement could be signed. The British took Tripoli, and were arranging a victory parade in Mr. Churchill's honour, with the pipes and drums of the Highland Division at its head. And Charles de Gaulle had met Franklin Roosevelt, who insisted that the two French generals, de Gaulle and Giraud, should be photographed for the world press in the act of shaking hands.

'We forced them to shake hands,' Winston Churchill was to write long after, 'in public' before all the reporters. The picture cannot be viewed, even in the setting of those tragic times, without a laugh.'

General de Gaulle did not permit himself to laugh. His aim now was to oust General Giraud from any participation in French affairs, and as a beginning he was, as usual, requiring his own followers to take a special oath of allegiance to himself, as follows:

'I swear to recognise General de Gaulle as the only legitimate leader of the French, and to exert myself in earning
him recognition by using, if necessary, the means and
methods employed against the Germans.'

That time bomb was still buried in the African sands on
the night when Jacques Brunel said goodbye to Polly
Preston. He had come to Joe's flat to tell her he was under
twenty-four hours' notice for departure, and this time she
listened to him quietly. She had given up fighting his stubborn determination, and said only one word of complaint.
'I hope you do go in the morning, Jacques; I couldn't go
through all this again.' She kissed him and wished him luck,
dry-eyed; it was Joe who got the force of the emotion and
the sobbing when they were alone together. Joe had been
through a good deal since his goddaughter came to London; now, as a last resort, he tried a new line of argument.

'I know I'm only an old bachelor,' he began apologetically, 'but I do remember what it was to be young and in
love. I think you know I was in love with Dolly Hendrikova? Yes, and she married Dick Allen instead of me. But
I think I might have made her love me right at the beginning, if I hadn't been so slow to speak. I thought she was so
young that I had time to plan our future my way, but she
thought I didn't care, and turned to Dick instead. Afterwards I believed I would find another girl, the right girl to
love, but I never did, and work took the place of home and
family for me. If you think Jacques Brunel is the right man
for you – and I believe he is – don't lose him. Hold on to
him. Fight for him, against France if you have to, with
France if you can. You'll see, it'll be worth it in the end.'

The telephone rang in Jacques' hotel room at seven next
morning, and he was asked to be ready to meet his conducting officer downstairs at eight. He was glad to find it was
Lieutenant Morton, who had met him at the Patriotic
School, and who was a quiet and untalkative companion for
an early morning start. It was not, after all, to be so very

312

early, for no sortie ever did get off on time, and Jacques found he was expected to have a final briefing from the men at Orchard Court. They went through the timetable together : the night was to be spent at Falmouth in Cornwall. He would go next day to the Helford River, the base of S.O.E.'s 'fishing fleet'. A motor gunboat would take Jacques and three other passengers across the channel towards Dinard, lie off-shore for two hours after sunset, and then use silencers on the way to the landing beach. There would be people on the shore to help, and then it was up to them. Jacques said he meant to make for Rennes, and there take the train to Paris.

They started after another delay for coffee and rolls. It was a mild January day, and Lieutenant Morton remarked that they had a long drive ahead, but a pleasant one when the sun was shining. He was driving himself, and pointed out the landmarks; with the road signs still down in case of an enemy invasion it was not easy for a foreigner to know his whereabouts. Jacques looked about him dutifully. Villages, towns, farms, country houses went past him in a kind of montage as slowly, unwillingly, painfully he became aware that he was in the process of making the greatest mistake of his life. He had put Polly in the second place, where she deserved the first. He had made her miserable, who had loved him and made him happy, all for an ideal which could let him down as easily as Chantal Malvy had betrayed her husband, as Fabienne Leroux had betrayed her lover as Malvy the Resistance, or – he had to face it – as Nestor had betrayed the ideas Jacques had so much admired.

When they stopped for lunch at an American army camp in Devonshire, and he got out of the car, Jacques could feel the effect of the Duke Street beatings, and was stiff enough to wonder how he was going to climb the cliff paths at St. Cast. He set his teeth, he wasn't going to go back to France a weakling. The Americans were hospitable but their luncheon was soon eaten, and Jacques was rather surprised when Morton was called to the telephone and was absent for some time.

'We won't get to Falmouth until after dark at this rate,' he observed, when they crossed the river into Cornwall.

'We're not going to Falmouth. I just heard, we've got to pick up another passenger at St. Mawes.'

'Oh really.' It was a matter of indifference to Jacques, but in spite of himself he was beginning to enjoy the drive, once they were through Truro and were catching glimpses of the sea. The Cornish bays, in the sunset light, were as blue as his own Mediterranean. A string of villages with enchanting names began, ending with St. Just-in-Roseland and an ancient church.

'Next stop St. Mawes,' said Morton, slowing down. 'Pretty place, isn't it?'

'Very pretty.'

Here were red tiled houses, lying above the sea, a small harbour with fishing boats at their moorings, and a row of hotels with lighted windows, pleasant and ordinary as in the days of peace.

'We're going to the "Ship and Castle". The next one, with the big picture window.'

'Are we staying here for the night, or going on to Falmouth?'

'I don't know. Why don't you cut along in and get a couple of beers for us while I find a filling station? It'll be blackout time in twenty minutes.'

'Okay.'

Jacques was still stiff, damnation, and limping a little as he went indoors. He saw some people talking round a wood fire, and made for what he supposed was the bar. He was stopped by someone who got up from the nearest settle, and held out his hand.

'Joe! What are you doing here? Is anything the matter?'

'Can't you guess?'

'It's Pauline, isn't it? Something's happened to Pauline?'

'She'll tell you that herself,' said Joe. 'Upstairs. First door on the left.'

It was the room with the big window which looked over the indigo sea. And she was standing in the window bay, wearing a black coat and skirt and a white blouse with a dark red pattern, just as Jacques had seen her first.

He went forward incredulously and took her in his arms.

'When – where did you come from?'

'We passed you when you stopped at the American camp.'

'And when Morton was on the telephone, that was you?'

'That was Joe.' Her eyes were wide in her pale face, and fixed on his.

It came to him then, that the day's long pain was over and all the conflicts were resolved.

'You!' he said. 'You're the extra passenger? You're coming back to France with me?'

She lifted her face for his kiss, and said,

'But I never meant to let you go alone!'

CATHERINE GAVIN

THE HOUSE OF WAR

A dramatic novel of the passion and power of Kemal
Ataturk, founder of the Turkish Republic, and the
self-sacrifice of Evelyn Barrett, who put his honour
before their love.

'History and romance locked in a fierce embrace'
Times Educational Supplement

'A marvellous portrait of Kemal'
Aberdeen Press and Journal

'A good fast plot'
Glasgow Herald

CORONET BOOKS

BRIAN CLEEVE

SARA

Never has there been such a spirited, indestructibly inviolate heroine as

SARA

half Spanish, half gypsy

SARA

penniless and alone, thrown to the mercy of Regency London, whose squalid underworld threatened to swallow her without trace ... and almost succeeded

SARA

a superb novel of a sensuous spitfire and the men who loved her to the edge of obsession and beyond

'vivid ... lusty'

Publishers Weekly

'What we've all been waiting for'

The Bookseller

CORONET BOOKS

BRIAN CLEEVE

KATE

The passionate saga of a beautiful young orphan determined to survive ...

KATE

the destitute daughter of a travelling actress, she escaped the perils of the French Revolution only to find her past had pursued her across the Channel to London ...

KATE

from the bloodstained crypt of a Breton church, the tawdry glitter of London's theatres, a smugglers' den in Kent and the stinking hell of Newgate Prison – this is an unforgettable story with a heroine whose courage is as unquenchable as her love.

CORONET BOOKS

ALSO AVAILABLE IN CORONET BOOKS

CATHERINE GAVIN

ELIZABETH GOUDGE

NIGEL TRANTER

All these books are available at your local bookshop or newsagent, or can be ordered direct from the publisher. Just tick the titles you want and fill in the form below.

Prices and availability subject to change without notice.

CORONET BOOKS, P.O. Box 11, Falmouth, Cornwall.

Please send cheque or postal order, and allow the following for postage and packing:

U.K. – One book 25p plus 10p per copy for each additional book ordered, up to a maximum of £1.05.

B.F.P.O. and EIRE – 25p for the first book plus 10p per copy for the next 8 books, thereafter 5p per book.

OTHER OVERSEAS CUSTOMERS – 40p for the first book and 12p per copy for each additional book.

Name ....

Address ....

....